JAMES CLAVELL

James Clavell is a half-Irish Englishman who was born in Australia and now lives mostly in Canada and the States. He was brought up in England and served as a Captain in the Royal Artillery during the war. In 1942 he was captured by the Japanese and sent to Changi. His first bestselling novel, KING RAT, is based upon his experiences there.

After the war James Clavell went into the film business and has written the screenplays of such highly successful films as *The Great Escape*. He has written, produced and directed four films, including *To Sir With Love* and *The Last Valley*. KING RAT was followed by TAI-PAN, an even greater bestseller which spent nearly a year on the American bestseller lists. Then came SHŌGUN, James Clavell's record breaking epic novel set in feudal Japan which has recently been filmed for Paramount. After NOBLE HOUSE, this magnificent story of Hong Kong, came THE CHILDREN'S STORY, a chilling tale, not just for children.

**Also by the same author,
and available in Coronet Books:**

Tai-Pan
Shōgun
Noble House
The Children's Story

King Rat

James Clavell

CORONET BOOKS
Hodder and Stoughton

For those who were there and are not. For those who were there and are. For him. But most, for her.

There was a war. Changi and Outram Road jails in Singapore do—or did— exist. Obviously the rest of the story is fiction and no similarity to anyone living or dead exists or is intended.

Changi was set like a pearl on the eastern tip of Singapore Island, iridescent under the bowl of tropical skies. It stood on a slight rise and around it was a belt of green, and farther off the green gave way to the blue-green seas and the seas to infinity of horizon.

Closer, Changi lost its beauty and became what it was—an obscene forbidding prison. Cell-blocks surrounded by sun-baked courtyards surrounded by towering walls.

Inside the walls, inside the cell-blocks, storey on storey, were cells for two thousand prisoners at capacity. Now, in the cells and in the passageways and in every nook and cranny lived some eight thousand men. English and Australian mostly—a few New Zealanders and Canadians—the remnants of the armed forces of the Far East Campaign.

These men too were criminals. Their crime was vast. They had lost a war. And they had lived.

The cell doors were open and the cell-block doors were open and the monstrous gate which slashed the walls was open and the men could move in and out—almost freely. But still there was a closeness, a claustrophobic smell.

Outside the gate was a skirting tarmac road. A hundred yards west this road was crossed by a tangle of barbed gates, and outside these gates was a guardhouse peopled with the armed offal of the conquering hordes. Past the barrier the road ran merrily onward, and in the course of time lost itself in the sprawling city of Singapore. But for the men, the road west ended a hundred yards from the main gate.

East, the road followed the wall, then turned south and again followed the wall. On either side of the road were banks of long 'go-downs' as the rough sheds were called. They were all the same— sixty paces long with walls made from plaited coconut fronds roughly nailed to posts, and thatch roofs also made from coconut fronds, layer on mildewed layer. Every year a new layer was added, or should have been added. For the sun and the rain and the insects tortured the thatch and broke it down. There were simple openings for windows and doors. The sheds had long thatch overhangs to keep out the sun and the rain, and they were set on concrete stilts to escape floods and the snakes and frogs and slugs and snails, the scorpions, centipedes, beetles, bugs—all manner of crawling things.

Officers lived in these sheds.

South and east of the road were four rows of concrete bungalows, twenty to a row, back to back. Senior officers—majors, lieutenant-colonels, and colonels—lived in these.

The road turned west, again following the wall, and met another bank of atap sheds. Here was quartered the overflow from the jail.

And in one of these, smaller than most, lived the American contingent of twenty-five enlisted men.

Where the road turned north once more, hugging the wall, was part of the vegetable gardens. The remainder—which supplied most of the camp food—lay farther to the north, across the road, opposite the prison gate. The road continued through the lesser garden for two hundred yards and ended in front of the guard-house.

Surrounding the whole sweating area, perhaps half a mile by half a mile, was a barbed fence. Easy to cut. Easy to get through. Scarcely guarded. No searchlights. No machine gun posts. But once outside, what then? Home was across the seas, beyond the horizon, beyond a limitless sea or hostile jungle. Outside was disaster, for those who went and for those who remained.

By now, 1945, the Japanese had learned to leave the control of the camp to the prisoners. The Japanese gave orders and the officers were responsible for enforcing them. If the camp gave no trouble, it got none. To ask for food was trouble. To ask for medicine was trouble. To ask for anything was trouble. That they were alive was trouble.

For the men, Changi was more than a prison. Changi was genesis, the place of beginning again.

BOOK ONE

I

'I'm going to get that bloody bastard if I die in the attempt.'
Lieutenant Grey was glad that at last he had spoken aloud what
had so long been twisting his guts into a knot. The venom in
Grey's voice snapped Sergeant Masters out of his reverie. He
had been thinking about a bottle of ice-cold Australian beer and
a steak with a fried egg on top and his home in Sydney and his
wife and the breasts and smell of her. He didn't bother to follow
the lieutenant's gaze out the window. He knew who it had to be
among the half-naked men walking the dirt path which skirted
the barbed fence. But he was surprised at Grey's outburst.
Usually the Provost Marshal of Changi was as tight-lipped and
unapproachable as any Englishman.

'Save your strength, Lieutenant,' Masters said wearily, 'the
Japs'll fix him soon enough.'

'Bugger the Japs,' Grey said. 'I want to catch him. I want him
in this jail. And when I've done with him—I want him in
Outram Road Jail.'

Masters looked up aghast. 'Outram Road?'

'Certainly.'

'My oath, I can understand you wanting to get him,' Masters
said, 'but, well, I wouldn't wish that on anyone.'

'That's where he belongs. And that's where I'm going to put
him. Because he's a thief, a liar, a cheat and a bloodsucker. A
bloody vampire who feeds on the rest of us.'

Grey got up and went closer to the window of the sweltering
MP hut. He waved at the flies which swarmed from the plank
floors and squinted his eyes against the refracted glare of the

11

high noon light beating the packed earth. 'By God,' he said, 'I'll have vengeance for all of us.'

Good luck, mate, Masters thought. You can get the King if anyone can. You've got the right amount of hate in you. Masters did not like officers and did not like Military Police. He particularly despised Grey, for Grey had been promoted from the ranks and tried to hide this fact from others.

But Grey was not alone in his hatred. The whole of Changi hated the King. They hated him for his muscular body, the clear glow in his blue eyes. In this twilight world of the half alive there were no fat or well-built or round or smooth or fair-built or thick-built men. There were only faces dominated by eyes and set on bodies that were skin over sinews over bones. No difference between them but age and face and height. And in all this world, only the King ate like a man, smoked like a man, slept like a man, dreamed like a man and looked like a man.

'You,' Grey barked. 'Corporal! Come over here!'

The King had been aware of Grey ever since he had turned the corner of the jail, not because he could see into the blackness of the MP hut but because he knew that Grey was a person of habit and when you have an enemy it is wise to know his ways. The King knew as much about Grey as any man could know about another.

He stepped off the path and walked towards the lone hut, set like a pimple among scores of other huts.

'You wanted me, sir?' the King said, saluting. His smile was bland. His sun glasses veiled the contempt of his eyes.

From his window, Grey stared down at the King. His taut features hid the hate that was part of him. 'Where are you going?'

'Back to my hut, Sir,' the King said patiently, and all the time his mind was figuring angles—had there been a slip, had someone informed, what was with Grey?

'Where did you get that shirt?'

The King had bought the shirt the day before from a major who had kept it neat for two years against the day he would need to sell it for money to buy food. The King liked to be tidy and well-dressed when everyone else was not, and he was pleased that today his shirt was clean and new and his long pants were creased and his socks clean and his shoes freshly polished and his hat stainless. It amused him that Grey was naked but for pathetically patched short pants and wooden clogs, and a Tank Corps beret that was green and solid with tropic mould.

'I bought it,' the King said. 'Long time ago. There's no law against buying anything—here, anywheres else. Sir.'

Grey felt the impertinence in the 'Sir'. 'All right, Corporal, inside!'

'Why?'

'I just want a little chat,' Grey said sarcastically.

The King held his temper and walked up the steps and through the doorway and stood near the table. 'Now what? Sir.'

'Turn out your pockets.'

'Why?'

'Do as you're told. You know I've the right to search you at any time.' Grey let some of his contempt show. 'Even your commanding officer agreed.'

'Only because you insisted on it.'

'With good reason. Turn out your pockets!'

Wearily the King complied. After all, he had nothing to hide. Handkerchief, comb, wallet, one pack of tailor-made cigarettes, his tobacco box full of raw Java tobacco, rice cigarette papers, matches. Grey made sure all the pockets were empty, then opened the wallet. There were fifteen American dollars and nearly four hundred Japanese Singapore dollars.

'Where did you get this money?' Grey snapped, the ever-present sweat dripping from him.

'Gambling. Sir.'

Grey laughed mirthlessly. 'You've a lucky streak. It's been good for nearly three years. Hasn't it?'

'You through with me now? Sir.'

'No. Let me look at your watch.'

'It's on the list—'

'I said let me look at your watch!'

Grimly the King pulled the stainless steel expanding band off his wrist and handed it to Grey.

In spite of his hatred of the King, Grey felt a shaft of envy. The watch was waterproof, shockproof, self-winding. An Oyster Royal. The most priceless possession of Changi—other than gold. He turned the watch over and looked at the figures etched

13

into the steel, then went over to the atap wall and took down the list of the King's possessions and automatically wiped the ants off it, and meticulously checked the number of the watch against the number of the Oyster Royal watch on the list.

'It checks,' the King said. 'Don't worry. Sir.'

'I'm not worried,' Grey said. 'It's you who are to be worried.' He handed the watch back, the watch that could bring nearly six months of food.

The King put the watch back on his wrist and began to pick up his wallet and other things.

'Oh yes. Your ring!' Grey said. 'Let's check that.'

But the ring checked with the list too. It was itemed as *A gold ring, signet of the Clan Gordon*. Alongside the description was an example of the seal.

'How is it an American has a Gordon ring?' Grey had asked the same question many times.

'I won it. Poker,' the King said.

'Remarkable memory you've got, Corporal,' Grey said and handed it back. He had known all along that the ring and the watch would check. He had only used the search as an excuse. He felt compelled almost masochistically, to be near his prey for just a while. He knew, too, that the King did not scare easily. Many had tried to catch him, and failed, for he was smart and careful and very cunning.

'Why is it,' Grey asked harshly, suddenly boiling with envy of the watch and ring and cigarettes and matches and money, 'that you have so much and the rest of us nothing?'

'Don't know. Sir. Guess I'm just lucky.'

'Where did you get this money?'

'Gambling. Sir.' The King was always polite. He always said 'Sir' to officers and saluted officers, English and Aussie officers. But he knew they were aware of the vastness of his contempt for 'Sir' and saluting. It wasn't the American way. A man's a man, regardless of background or family or rank. If you respect him, you call him 'Sir.' If you don't, you don't, and it's only the sons of bitches that object. To hell with them!

The King put the ring back on his finger, buttoned down his pockets and flicked some dust off his shirt. 'Will that be all? Sir.' He saw the anger flash in Grey's eyes.

Then Grey looked across at Masters, who had been watching

nervously. 'Sergeant, would you get me some water, please?'

Wearily Masters went over to the water bottle that hung on the wall. 'Here you are, sir.'

'That's yesterday's,' Grey said, knowing it was not. 'Fill it with clean water.'

'I could've swore I filled it first thing,' Masters said. Then, shaking his head, he walked out.

Grey let the silence hang and the King stood easily waiting. A breath of wind rustled the coconut trees that soared above the jungle just outside the fence, bringing the promise of rain. Already there were black clouds rimming the eastern sky, soon to cover the sky. Soon they would turn dust into bog and make humid air breathable.

'You like a cigarette? Sir,' the King said, offering the pack.

The last time Grey had had a tailor-made cigarette was two years before, on his birthday. His twenty-second birthday. He stared at the pack and wanted one, wanted them all. 'No,' he said grimly. 'I don't want one of your cigarettes.'

'You don't mind if I smoke? Sir.'

'Yes I do!'

The King kept his eyes fixed on Grey's and calmly slipped out a cigarette. He lit it and inhaled deeply.

'Take that out of your mouth!' Grey ordered.

'Sure. Sir.' The King took a long slow drag before obeying. Then he hardened. 'I'm not under your orders and there's no law that says I can't smoke when I want to. I'm an American and I'm not subject to any goddam flag-waving Union Jack! That's been pointed out to you too. Get off my back! Sir.'

'I'm after you now, Corporal,' Grey erupted. 'Soon you're going to make a slip, and when you do I'll be waiting and then you'll be in there.' His finger was shaking as he pointed at the crude bamboo cage which served as a cell. 'That's where you belong.'

'I'm breaking no laws—'

'Then where do you get your money?'

'Gambling.' The King moved closer to Grey. His anger was controlled, but he was more dangerous than usual. 'Nobody gives me nothing. What I have is mine and I made it. How I made it is my own business.'

'Not while I'm Provost Marshal.' Grey's fists tightened. 'Lot

15

of drugs have been stolen over the months. Maybe you know something about them.'

'Why you— Listen,' the King said furiously, 'I've never stolen a thing in my life. I've never sold drugs in my life and don't you forget it! Goddammit, if you weren't an officer I'd—'

'But I am and I'd like you to try. By God I would! You think you're so bloody tough. Well, I know you're not.'

'I'll tell you one thing. When we get through this shit of Changi, you come looking for me and I'll hand you your head.'

'I won't forget!' Grey tried to slow his pumping heart. 'But remember, until that time I'm watching and waiting. I've never heard of a run of luck that didn't sometime run out. And yours will!'

'Oh no it won't! Sir.' But the King knew that there was a great truth in that. His luck had been good. Very good. But luck is hard work and planning and a little something besides, and not gambling. At least not unless it was a calculated gamble. Like today and the diamond. Four whole carats. At last he knew how to get his hands on it. When he was ready. And if he could make this one deal, it would be the last, and there would be no more need to gamble—not here in Changi.

'Your luck'll run out,' Grey said malevolently. 'You know why? Because you're like all criminals. You're full of greed—'

'I don't have to take this crap from you,' the King said, and his rage snapped. 'I'm no more a criminal than—'

'Oh but you are. You break the law all the time.'

'The hell I do. Jap law may say—'

'To hell with Jap law. I'm talking about camp law. Camp law says no trading. That's what you do!'

'Prove it!'

'I will in time. You'll make one slip. And then we'll see how you survive along with the rest of us. In my cage. And after my cage, I'll personally see that you're sent to Outram Road!'

The King felt a horror-chill rush into his heart and into his testicles. 'Jesus,' he said tightly. 'You're just the sort of bastard who'd do that!'

'In your case,' Grey said, and there was foam on his lips, 'it'd be a pleasure. The Japs are *your* friends!'

'Why, you son of a bitch!' The King bunched a hamlike fist and moved towards Grey.

'What's going on here, eh?' Colonel Brant said as he stomped up the steps and entered the hut. He was a small man, barely five feet, and his beard rolled Sikh style under his chin. He carried a swagger cane. His peaked army cap was peakless and all patched with sack-cloth; in the centre of it, the emblem of a regiment shone like gold, smooth with years of burnishing.

'Nothing—nothing, sir.' Grey waved at the fly-swarm, trying to control his breathing. 'I was just—searching Corporal—'

'Come now, Grey,' Colonel Brant interrupted testily. 'I heard what you said about Outram Road and the Japs. It's perfectly in order to search him and question him, everyone knows that, but there's no reason to threaten or abuse him.' He turned to the King, his forehead beaded with sweat. 'You, Corporal. You should thank your lucky stars I don't report you to Captain Brough for discipline. You should know better than to go around dressed like that. Enough to drive any man out of his mind. Just asking for trouble.'

'Yes, sir,' the King said, outwardly calm but cursing himself inside for losing his temper—just what Grey was trying to make him do.

'Look at my clothes,' Colonel Brant was saying. 'How the hell do you think I feel?'

The King made no reply. He thought, That's your problem Mac—you look after you, I'm looking after me. The colonel wore only a loincloth, made from half a sarong, knotted around his waist—kiltlike—and under the kilt there was nothing. The King was the only man in Changi who wore underpants. He had six pairs.

'You think I don't envy you your shoes?' Colonel Brant asked irritably. 'When all I've got to wear are those confounded things?' He was wearing regulation slippers—a piece of wood and a canvas band for the instep.

'I don't know, sir,' said the King, with veiled humility, so dear to officer-ear.

'Quite right. Quite right.' Colonel Brant turned to Grey. 'I think you owe him an apology. It's quite wrong to threaten him. We must be fair, eh, Grey?' He wiped more sweat from his face.

It took Grey an enormous effort to stop the curse that quivered his lips. 'I apologize.' The words were low and edged and

17

the King was hard put to keep the smile from his face.

'Very good.' Colonel Brant nodded, then looked at the King. 'All right,' he said, 'you can go. But dressed like that you're asking for trouble! You've only yourself to blame!'

The King saluted smartly. 'Thank you, sir.' He walked out, and once more in the sunshine he breathed easily, and cursed himself again. Jesus, that'd been close. He had nearly hit Grey and that would have been the act of a maniac. To gather himself, he stopped beside the path and lit another cigarette and the many men who passed by saw the cigarette and smelled the aroma.

'Blasted chap,' the colonel said at length, still looking after him and wiping his forehead. Then he turned back to Grey. 'Really, Grey, you just must be out of your mind to provoke him like that.'

'I'm sorry. I—I suppose he—'

'Whatever he is, it certainly isn't like an officer and a gentleman to lose your temper. Bad, very bad, don't you think, eh?'

'Yes, sir.' There was nothing more for Grey to say.

Colonel Brant grunted, then pursed his lips. 'Quite right. Lucky I was passing. Can't have an officer brawling with a common soldier.' He glanced out of the door again, hating the King, wanting his cigarette. 'Blasted man,' he said without looking back at Grey, 'undisciplined. Like the rest of the Americans. Bad lot. Why, they call their officers by their first name!' His eyebrows soared. 'And the officers play cards with the men! Bless my soul! Worse than the Australians—and they're a shower if there ever was one. Miserable! Not like the Indian Army, what?'

'No. Sir,' Grey said thinly.

Colonel Brant turned quickly. 'I didn't mean—well, Grey, just because—' He stopped and suddenly his eyes were filled with tears. 'Why, why would they do that?' he said brokenly. 'Why, Grey? I—we all loved them.'

Grey shrugged. But for the apology he would have been compassionate.

The colonel hesitated, then turned and walked out of the hut. His head was bent and silent tears streamed his cheeks.

When Singapore fell in '42, his soldiers had gone over to the enemy, the Japanese, almost to a man, and they had turned on their English officers. These soldiers were among the first prison guards over the prisoners of war and some of them were savage. The officers of the regiment knew no peace. For it was only theirs *en masse*, and a few from other Indian regiments. The Gurkhas were loyal to a man, under torture and indignity. So Colonel Brant wept for his men, and the men he would have died for, the men he still died for.

Grey watched him go, then saw the King smoking by the path, 'I'm glad I said that now it's you or me,' he whispered to himself.

He sat back on the bench and a shaft of pain swept through his bowels reminding him that dysentery had not passed him by this week. 'To hell with it,' he said weakly, cursing Colonel Brant and the apology.

Masters came back with the full water bottle and gave it to him. He took a sip and thanked him and then began to plan how he would get the King. But the hunger for lunch was on him and he let his mind drift.

A faint moan cut the air. Grey glanced abruptly at Masters, who sat unconscious that he had made a sound, watching the constant movement of the house lizards in the rafters as they darted after insects or fornicated.

'You have dysentery, Masters?'

Masters bleakly waved away the flies that mosaiced his face. 'No sir. At least I haven't for nearly five weeks.'

'Enteric?'

'No, thank God. My bloody word. Just amoebic. An' I haven't had malaria for nearly three months, I'm very lucky, an' very fit, considering.'

'Yes,' Grey said. Then as an afterthought, 'You look fit.' But he knew he would have to get a replacement soon. He looked back at the King, watching him smoke, nauseated with cigarette hunger.

Masters moaned again.

'What the hell's the matter with you?' Grey said irately.

'Nothing, sir. Nothing. I must have . . .'

But the effort to speak was too much and Masters let his words slip off and blend with the drone of flies. Flies dominated the day, mosquitoes the night. No silence. Ever. What is it like to live without flies and mosquitoes and people? Masters tried to remember, but the effort was too great. So he just sat still, quiet, hardly breathing, a shell of a man. And his soul twisted uneasily.

'All right, Masters, you can go now,' Grey said. 'I'll wait for your relief. Who is he?'

Masters forced his brain to work and after a moment said, 'Bluey—Bluey White.'

'For God's sake, get hold of yourself,' Grey snapped. 'Corporal White died three weeks ago.'

'Oh, sorry, sir,' Masters said weakly. 'Sorry, I must have . . . It's . . . er, I think it's Peterson. The Pommy, I mean Englishman. Infantryman, I think.'

'All right. You can go and get your dinner now. But don't dawdle coming back.'

'Yes, sir.'

Masters put on his rattan coolie hat and saluted and shambled out of the doorless door, hitching the rags of his pants around his hips. God, Grey thought, you can smell him from fifty paces. They've just got to issue more soap.

But he knew that it wasn't just Masters. It was all of them. If you didn't bath six times a day, the sweat hunt like a shroud about you. And thinking of shrouds, he thought again about Masters—and the mark that he had on him. Perhaps Masters knew it too, so what was the point of washing?

Grey had seen many men die. The bitterness began to well as he thought about the regiment and the war. Damn your eyes, he almost shouted, twenty-four and still a lieutenant! And the war going on all around—all over the world. Promotions every day of the year. Opportunities. And here I am in this stinking POW camp, and still a lieutenant. Oh Christ! If only we hadn't been transhipped to Singapore in '42. If only we'd gone where we were supposed to go—to the Caucasus. If only . . .

'Stop it,' he said aloud. 'You're as bad as Masters, you bloody fool.'

It was normal in the camp to talk aloud to yourself sometimes. Better to speak out, the doctors had always said, than to keep it all choked inside—that way led to insanity. Most days were not so bad. You could stop thinking about your other life, about the guts of it—food, women, home, food, food, women, food. But the nights were the danger time. At night you dreamed. Dreamed about food and women. Your woman. And soon you would enjoy the dreaming more than the waking, and if you were careless you would dream while awake, and the days would run into nights and the night into day. Then there was only death. Smooth. Gentle. It was easy to die. Agony to live. Except for the King. He had no agony.

Grey was still watching him, trying to hear what he was saying to the man beside him, but he was too far away. Grey tried to place the other man but he could not. He could see from the man's arm-band that he was a major. By Japanese order all officers had to wear armbands with rank insignia on their left arms. At all times. Even naked.

The black rain clouds were building fast now. Sheet lightning flecked the east, but still the sun thrust down. A fetid breeze broomed the dust momentarily, then let it settle.

Automatically Grey used the bamboo fly-swat. A deft, half unconscious twist of the wrist and another fly fell to the ground, maimed. To kill a fly was careless. Cripple it, then the bastard would suffer and repay in tiny measure your own suffering. Cripple it and it would soundlessly scream until ants and other flies came to fight over its living flesh.

But Grey did not take the usual pleasure in watching the torment of the tormentor. He was too intent on the King.

II

'By George,' the major was saying to the King with forced joviality, 'and then there was the time I was in New York. In '33. Marvellous time. Such a wonderful country, the States. Did I ever tell you about the trip I made to Albany? I was a subaltern at the time . . .'

'Yes, sir,' the King said tiredly. 'You've told me.' He felt he had been polite long enough and he could still feel Grey's eyes on him. Though he was quite safe and not afraid, he wanted to get out of the sun and out of the range of the eyes. He had a lot to do. And if the major wouldn't come to the point, what the hell! 'Well, if you'll excuse me, sir. It was nice to talk to you.'

'Oh, just a minute,' Major Barry said quickly and looked around nervously, conscious of the curious eyes of the men that passed, conscious of their unspoken question—What's he talking to the King for? 'I—er, could I see you privately?'

The King gauged him thoughtfully. 'We're private here. If you keep your voice down.'

Major Barry was wet with embarrassment. But he had been trying to bump into the King for days now. And it was too good an opportunity to miss. 'But the Provost Marshal's hut is—'

'What have the cops to do with talking privately? I don't understand, sir.' The King was bland.

'There's no need—er—well, Colonel Sellers said that you might be able to help me.' Major Barry had only the stump of a right arm and he kept scratching the stump, touching it, moulding it. 'Would you—handle something for us, I mean me.' He waited until there was no one within hearing distance. 'It's a

22

lighter,' he whispered. 'A Ronson lighter. Perfect condition.'
Now that he had come to the point, the major felt a little easier.
But at the same time he felt naked, saying these words to the
American, out in the sun, on the public path.

The King thought a moment. 'Who's the owner?'

'I am.' The major looked up, startled. 'My God, you don't
think I stole it, do you? Good Lord, I'd never do that. I've kept it
safe all this time, but now, well, now we've got to sell it. The
unit's all agreed.' He licked his dry lips and fondled the stump.
'Please. Would you? You can get the best price.'

'Trading's against the law.'

'Yes, but please, you—would you please? You can trust me.'

The King turned so that his back was towards Grey and his
face towards the fence—just in case Grey could lip read. 'I'll
send someone after chow,' he said quietly. 'Password is
"Lieutenant Albany said for me to see you." Got it?'

'Yes.' Major Barry hesitated, his heart pumping. 'When did
you say?'

'After chow. Lunch!'

'Oh, all right.'

'Just give it to him. And when I've looked it over, I'll get in
touch with you. Same password.' The King flipped the burning
top off his cigarette and dropped the butt onto the ground. He
was just about to step on it when he saw the major's face. 'Oh!
You want the butt?'

Major Barry bent down happily and picked it up. 'Thanks.
Thanks very much.' He opened his little tobacco tin and carefully tore the paper off the butt and put the half inch of tobacco
into the dried tea leaves and mixed them together. 'Nothing like
a little sweetening,' he said, smiling. 'Thank you very much.
It'll make at least three good cigarettes.'

'I'll see you, sir,' said the King saluting.

'Oh, um, well—' Major Barry did not know quite how to put
it 'Don't you think,' he said nervously, keeping his voice low,
'that well—to give it to a stranger, just like that, how do I know
that—well, everything will be all right?'

The King said coldly, 'The password for one thing. Another
thing, I've got a reputation. Another thing, I'm trusting you
that it's not stolen. Maybe we'd better forget it.'

'Oh no, please don't misunderstand me,' the major said

23

quickly, 'I was just asking. It's, well, it's all I have left.' He tried to smile. 'Thanks. After lunch. Oh, how long do you think it'll take to, er, to dispose of it?'

'Soon as I can. Usual terms. I get ten per cent, of the sale price,' the King said crisply.

'Of course. Thank you, and thanks again for the tobacco.' Now that everything had been said, Major Barry felt an enormous weight off his mind. With luck, he thought as he hurried down the hill, we will get six or seven hundred dollars. Enough to buy food for months, with care. He did not think once of the man who had owned the lighter, who had given it into his keeping when the man had gone to the hospital, months ago, never to return. That was in the past. Today *he* owned the lighter. It was his. His to sell.

The King knew that Grey had been watching him all the time. The excitement of making a deal in front of the MP hut added to his well-being. Pleased with himself, he walked up the slight rise, responding automatically to the greetings of the men— officers and enlisted men, English and Australian—that he knew. The important ones got special treatment, the others a friendly nod. The King was conscious of their malevolent envy and it bothered him not at all. He was used to it; it amused him and added to his stature. And he was pleased that the men called him the King. He was proud of what he had done as a man—as an American. Through cunning he had created a world. He surveyed his world now and was well satisfied.

He stopped outside Hut Twenty-four, one of the Australian huts, and poked his head through a window.

'Hey, Tinker,' he called out. 'I want me a shave and a manicure.'

Tinker Bell was small and wiry. His skin was pigment-brown and his eyes were small and very brown and his nose was peeling. He was a sheep shearer by trade but he was the best barber in Changi.

'Wot's this, your ruddy birthday? I gave you a manicure the day before yesterday.'

'So I get another today.'

Tinker shrugged and jumped out the window. The King sat back in the chair under the lee of the hut's overhang, relaxing contentedly as Tinker put the sheet around his neck and settled him just right. 'Look at this, mate,' he said, and held a little cake of soap under the King's nose. 'Smell it.'

'Hey,' said the King, grinning. 'That's the real McCoy.'

'Don't know about that, mate! But it's Yardley's ruddy violets. A cobber o' mine swiped it on a work party. Right from under the nose of a bloody Nip. Cost me thirty dollars,' he said with a wink, doubling the price. 'I'll keep it just for you, special, if you likes.'

'Tell you what. I'll make it five bucks a time, instead of three, as long as it lasts,' the King said.

Tinker calculated quickly. The cake of soap would last perhaps eight shaves, maybe ten. 'Strike a light, mate. I 'ardly makes me money back.'

The King grunted. 'You got taken, Tink. I can buy that by the pound for fifteen a cake.'

'My bloody oath,' Tinker burst out, feigning anger. 'A cobber taking me for a sucker! Now that ain't right!' Furiously he mixed hot water and the sweet-smelling soap into a lather. Then he laughed. 'You're the King all right, mate.'

'Yeah,' the King said contentedly. He and Tinker were old friends.

'Ready, mate?' Tinker asked as he held up the lathered brush.

'Sure.' Then the King saw Tex walking down the path. 'Wait a minute. Hey, Tex!' he called out.

Tex looked across at the hut and saw the King and ambled over to him. 'Yeah?' He was a gangling youth with big ears and a bent nose and contented eyes, and he was tall, very tall.

Without being asked, Tinker moved out of earshot as the King beckoned Tex closer. 'Do something for me?' he asked quietly.

'Sure.'

The King took out his wallet and peeled off a ten-dollar note. 'Go find Colonel Brant. The little guy with the beard rolled under his chin. Give him this.'

'You know where he'd be?'

'Down by the corner of the jail. It's his day for keeping an eye on Grey.'

Tex grinned. 'Hear you had a set-to.'

'The son of a bitch searched me again.'

'Tough,' said Tex dryly, scratching his blond crewcut.

'Yes.' The King laughed. 'And tell Brant not to be so goddam late next time. But you should have been there, Tex. Man, that Brant's a great actor. He even made Grey apologize.' He grinned, then added another five. 'Tell him this is for the apology.'

'Okay. That all?'

'No.' He gave him the password and told him where to find Major Barry, then Tex went his way and the King settled back. Altogether, today had been very profitable.

Grey hurried across the dirt path and up the steps to Hut Sixteen. It was almost lunchtime and he was painfully hungry.

Men were already forming an impatient line for food. Quickly Grey went to his bed and got his two mess cans and mug and spoon and fork and joined the line.

'Why isn't it here already?' he wearily asked the man ahead of him.

'How the hell do I know?' Dave Daven said curtly. His accent was public school—Eton, Harrow or Charterhouse—and he was tall like bamboo.

'I was just asking,' Grey said irritably, despising Daven for his accent and his birthright.

After they had waited an hour, the food arrived. A man carried two containers to the head of the line and set them down. The containers had formerly held five gallons of high-octane gasoline. Now one was half full of rice—dry, pellucid. The other was full of soup.

Today it was shark soup—at least, one shark had been divided ounce by ounce into soup for ten thousand men. It was warm and tasted slightly of fish, and in it there were pieces of eggplant and cabbage, a hundred pounds for ten thousand. The bulk of the soup was made from leaves, red and green, bitter and yet nutritious, grown with so much care in the garden of the camp. Salt and curry powder and chilli pepper spiced it.

Silently each man moved forward in turn, watching the serving of the man in front and the man behind, measuring their portions against the one he was given. But now, after three years, the measures were all the same.

A cup per man of soup.

The rice was steaming as it was served. Today it was Java rice, each grain separate, the best in the world. A cupful per man.

26

A mug of tea.

Each man took his food away and ate silently, quickly, with exquisite agony. The weevils in the rice were added nourishment, and the worm or insect in the soup was removed without anger if it was seen. But most men did not look at the soup after the first quick glance to find out if there was a piece of fish in it.

Today there was a little left over from the servings and the list was checked and the three men who headed it got the extra and thanked today. Then the food was gone and lunch was over and dinner was at sundown.

But though there was only soup and rice, here and there throughout the camp a man might have a piece of coconut or half a banana or piece of sardine or thread of bully or even an egg to mix with his rice. One whole egg was rare. Once a week, if the camp hens laid according to plan, an egg was given to each man. That was a great day. A few men were given one egg every day, but no man wanted to be one of the special few.

'Hey, listen, you chaps!' Captain Spence stood in the centre of the hut, but his voice could be heard outside. He was officer of the week, the hut adjutant, a small dark man with twisted features. He waited till they had all moved inside. 'We've got to supply ten more bods for the wood detail tomorrow.' He checked his list and called out the names, and then looked up 'Marlow?' There was no reply. 'Anyone know where Marlow is?'

'I think he's down with his unit,' Ewart called out.

'Tell him he's on the airfield work party tomorrow, will you?'

'All right.'

Spence started coughing. His asthma was bad today, and when the spasm had passed he continued: 'The Camp Commandant had another interview with the Jap General this morning. He asked for increased rations and medical supplies.' He cleared his throat in the momentary hush. Then he went on and his voice was flat. 'He got the usual turndown. The rice ration stays at four ounces of grain per man per day.' Spence looked out of the doors and checked that both lookouts were in position. Then he dropped his voice and all the men listened expectantly.

'The Allies are about sixty miles from Mandalay, still going strong. They've got the Japs on the run. The Allies are still going

27

in Belgium but the weather's very bad. Snowstorms. On the Eastern front, the same thing, but the Russians are going like bats out of hell and expect to take Krakow in the next few days. The Yanks are going well in Manila. They're near'—he hesitated, trying to remember the name—'I think it's the Agno River, in Luzon. That's all. But it's good.'

Spence was glad that this part was over. He learned the news by heart daily at the hut adjutants' meeting, and every time he stood up to repeat it publicly, his sweat chilled and his stomach felt empty. One day an informer might point a finger at him and tell the enemy that he was one of the men who delivered the news, and Spence knew that he was not strong enough to stay silent. Or one day a Japanese might hear him tell the others, and then, then . . .

'That's all, chaps.' Spence went over to his bunk, filled with nausea. He took off his pants and walked out of the hut with a towel over his arm.

The sun beat down. Two hours yet until the rain. Spence crossed the asphalt street and stood in line for a shower. He always had to have a shower after he gave the news, for the sweat-stench was acrid on him.

'All right, mate?' Tinker asked.

The King looked at his nails. They were well manicured. His face felt tight from the hot and cold towels, and tangy with the lotion. 'Great,' he said as he paid him. 'Thanks, Tink.' He moved out of the chair, put on his hat and nodded to Tinker and to the colonel who had been waiting patiently for a haircut.

Both men stared after him.

The King walked briskly up the path once more, past clustering huts, heading for home. He was pleasantly hungry.

The American hut was set apart from the others, near enough to the walls to share the afternoon shade, and near enough to the encircling path which was the life stream of the camp and near enough to the fence. It was just right. Captain Brough, USAF, the senior American officer, had insisted that the American enlisted men have their own hut. Most of the American officers would have preferred to move in too—it was difficult for them to live among foreigners—but this was not allowed, for the Japanese had ordered that officers be separated from enlisted men. The other nationalities found this hard to stomach, the Australians less so than the English.

The King was thinking about the diamond. It would not be easy to swing the deal, and this deal he had to swing. Suddenly as he approached the hut, he noticed beside the path a young man sitting on his haunches, talking rapidly in Malay to a native. The man's skin was heavily pigmented and beneath the skin the muscles showed. Wide shoulders. Slim hips. The man wore only a sarong, and the way he wore it, it seemed to belong. His face was craggy, and though he was Changi-thin, there was a grace to his movements and a sparkle about him.

The Malay—black-brown, tiny—was listening intently to the man's lilting speech; then he laughed and showed teeth abused by betel nut, and replied, accenting the melodious language with a wave of his hand. The man joined his laugh and interrupted with a flood of words, oblivious of the King's intent stare.

The King could catch only a word here and a word there, for his Malay was bad and he had to get by with a mixture of Malay and Japanese and pidgin English. He listened to the rich laugh and knew it was a rare thing. When this man was laughing, you could see that the laugh came from inside. This was very rare. Priceless.

Thoughtfully the King entered the hut. The other men looked up briefly and greeted him amiably. He returned their greetings without favour. But he knew and they knew.

Dino was lying on his bunk half asleep. He was a neat little man with dark skin and dark hair, prematurely flecked with grey, and veiled liquid eyes. The King felt the eyes and nodded and saw Dino's smile. But the eyes were not smiling.

In the far corner of the hut Kurt looked up from the pants he was trying to patch up and spat on the floor. He was a stunted, evil-looking man with yellow-brown teeth, ratlike, and he always spat on the floor and not one of them liked him, for he would never bathe. Near the centre of the hut Byron Jones III and Miller were playing their interminable chess. Both were naked. When Miller's merchant ship was torpedoed two years before, he had weighed two hundred and eighty-eight pounds. He was six feet, seven inches. Now he turned the scale at a hundred and thirty-three, and the folds of belly skin hung like a pelt over his sex. His blue eyes lit up as he reached over and took a knight. Byron Jones III quickly removed the knight, and now Miller saw that his castle was threatened.

'You've had it, Miller,' Jones said, scratching the jungle sores on his legs.

'Go to hell!'

Jones laughed. 'The Navy could always take the Merchant Marine at anything.'

'You bastards still got yourselves sunk. A battleship yet!'

'Yeah,' Jones said thoughtfully, toying with his eye patch, remembering the death of his ship, the *Houston*, and the deaths of his buddies and the loss of his eye.

The King walked the length of the hut. Max was still sitting beside his bed and the big black box that was chained to it.

'Okay, Max,' the King said. 'Thanks. You can quit now.'

'Sure.' Max had a well-used face. He came from West Side New York and he had learned the lessons of life from those streets at an early age. His eyes were brown and restless.

Automatically the King took out his tobacco box and gave Max a little of the raw tobacco.

'Gee, thanks,' Max said. 'Oh yeah, Lee told me to tell you he's done your laundry. He's getting chow today—we're on the second shift—but he told me to tell you.'

'Thanks.' The King took out his pack of Kooas and a momentary hush fell upon the hut. Before the King could get his matches out, Max was striking his native flint lighter.

'Thanks, Max.' The King inhaled deeply. Then, after a pause, he said, 'You like a Kooa?'

'Jesus, thanks,' Max said, careless of the irony in the King's voice. 'Anything else you want?'

'I'll call you if I need you.'

Max walked down the hut to sit on his string bed beside the door. Eyes saw the cigarette but mouths said nothing. It was Max's. Max had earned it. When it was their day to guard the King's possessions, well, maybe they'd get one too.

Dino smiled at Max, who winked back. They would share the cigarette after chow. They always shared what they could find or steal or make. Max and Dino were a unit.

And it was the same throughout the world of Changi. Men

ate and trusted in units. Twos, threes, rarely fours. One man could never cover enough ground, or find something edible and build a fire and cook it and eat it—not by himself. Three was the perfect unit. One to forage, one to guard what had been foraged and one spare. When the spare wasn't sick, he too foraged or guarded. Everything was split three ways: if you got an egg or stole a coconut or found a banana on a work party—or made a touch somewhere, it went to the unit. The law, like all natural law, was simple. Only by mutual effort did you survive. To withold from the unit was fatal, for if you were expelled from a unit, the word got around. And it was impossible to survive alone.

But the King didn't have a unit. He was sufficient unto himself.

His bed was in the favoured corner of the hut, under a window, set just right to catch the slightest breeze. The nearest bed was eight feet away. The King's bed was a good one. Steel. The springs were tight and the mattress filled with kapok. The bed was covered with two blankets, and the purity of sheets peeped from the top blanket near the sun-bleached pillow. Above the bed, stretched tight on posts, was a mosquito net. It was blemishless.

The King also had a table and two easy chairs, and a carpet on either side of the bed. On a shelf, behind the bed, was his shaving equipment—razor, brush, soap, blades—and beside them, his plates and cups and homemade electric stove and cooking and eating implements. On the corner wall hung his clothes, four shirts and four long pants and four short pants. Six pairs of socks, and underpants were on a shelf. Under the bed were two pairs of shoes, bathing slippers, and a shining pair of Indian chappals.

The King sat on one of the chairs and made sure that everything was still in place. He noticed that the hair he had placed so delicately on his razor was no longer there. Crummy bastards, he thought, why the hell should I risk catching their crud. But he said nothing, just made a mental note to lock it up in future.

'Hi,' said Tex. 'You busy?'

'Busy' was another password. It meant 'are you ready to take delivery?'

The King smiled and nodded and Tex carefully passed over the Ronson lighter. 'Thanks,' the King said. 'You like my soup today?'

'You bet,' Tex said and walked away.

Leisurely the King examined the lighter. As the major had said, it was almost new. Unscratched. It worked every time. And very clean. He unscrewed the flint screw and examined the flint. It was a cheap native flint and almost finished, so he opened the cigar box on the shelf and found the Ronson flint container and put in a new one. He pressed the lever and it worked. A careful adjustment of the wick and he was satisfied. The lighter was not a counterfeit and would surely bring eight hundred, nine hundred dollars.

From where he was sitting he could see the young man and the Malay. They were still hard at it, yaketty, yaketty.

'Max,' he called out quietly.

Max hurried up the length of the hut. 'Yeah?'

'See that guy,' the King said, nodding out the window.

'Which one? The Wog?'

'No. The other one. Get him for me, will you?'

Max slipped out of the window and crossed the path. 'Hey, Mac,' he said abruptly to the young man. 'The King wants to see you,' and jerked a thumb towards the hut. 'On the double.'

The man gaped at Max, then followed the line of the thumb to the American hut. 'Me?' he asked incredulously, looking back at Max.

'Yeah, you.' Max said impatiently.

'What for?'

'How the hell do I know?'

The man frowned at Max, hardening. He thought a moment, then turned to Suliman, the Malay. 'Nanti-lah,' he said.

'Bik, tuan,' said Suliman, preparing to wait. Then he added in Malay, 'Watch thyself, tuan. And go with God.'

'Fear not, my friend—but I thank thee for thy thought,' the man said, smiling. He got up and followed Max into the hut.

'You wanted me?' he asked, walking up to the King.

'Hi,' the King said, smiling. He saw that the man's eyes were guarded. That pleased him, for guarded eyes were rare. 'Take a seat.' He nodded at Max, who left. Without being asked, the

32

other men who were near moved out of earshot so the King could talk in private.

'Go on, take a seat,' the King said genially.

'Thanks.'

'Like a cigarette?'

The man's eyes widened as he saw the Kooa offered to him. He hesitated, then took it. His astonishment grew as the King snapped the Ronson, but he tried to hide it and drew deeply on the cigarette. 'That's good. Very good,' he said luxuriously. 'Thanks.'

'What's your name?'

'Marlowe. Peter Marlowe.' Then he added ironically, 'And yours?'

The King laughed. Good, he thought, the guy's got a sense of humour, and he's no ass kisser. He docketed the information, then said, 'You're English?'

'Yes.'

The King had never noticed Peter Marlowe before, but that was not unusual when ten thousand faces looked so much alike. He studied Peter Marlowe silently and the cool blue eyes studied him back.

'Kooas are about the best cigarette around,' the King said at last. ''Course they don't compare with Camels. American cigarette. Best in the world. You ever had them?'

'Yes,' Peter Marlowe said, 'but actually, they tasted a little dry to me. My brand's Gold Flake.' Then he added politely, 'It's a matter of taste, I suppose.' Again a silence fell and he waited for the King to come to the point. As he waited, he thought that he liked the King, in spite of his reputation, and he liked him for the humour that glinted behind his eyes.

'You speak Malay very well,' the King said, nodding at the Malay who waited patiently.

'Oh, not too badly, I suppose.'

The King stifled a curse at the inevitable English underplay.

'You learnt it here?' he asked patiently.

'No. In Java.' Peter Marlowe hesitated and looked around. 'You've quite a place here.'

'Like to be comfortable. How's that chair feel?'

'Fine.' A flicker of surprise showed.

'Cost me eighty bucks,' the King said proudly. 'Year ago.'

Peter Marlowe glanced at the King sharply to see if it was meant as a joke, to tell him the price, just like that, but he saw only happiness and evident pride. Extraordinary, he thought, to say such a thing to a stranger. 'It's very comfortable,' he said, covering his embarrassment.

'I'm going to fix chow. You like to join me?'

'I've just had—lunch,' Peter Marlowe said carefully.

'You could probably use some more. Like an egg?'

Now Peter Marlowe could no longer conceal his amazement, and his eyes widened. The King smiled and felt that it had been worthwhile to invite him to eat to get a reaction like that. He knelt down beside his black box and carefully unlocked it.

Peter Marlowe stared down at the contents, stunned. Half a dozen eggs, sacks of coffee beans. Glass jars of gula malacca, the delicious toffee-sugar of the Orient. Bananas. At least a pound of Java tobacco. Ten or eleven packs of Kooas. A glass jar full of rice. Another with katchang idju beans. Oil. Many delicacies in banana leaves. He had not seen treasure in such quantity for years.

The King took out the oil and two eggs and relocked the box. When he glanced back at Peter Marlowe, he saw that the eyes were once more guarded, the face composed.

'How you like your egg? Fried?'

'Well, it seems a little unfair to accept.' It was difficult for Peter Marlowe to speak. 'I mean, you don't go offering eggs, just like that.'

The King smiled. It was a good smile and warmed Peter Marlowe. 'Think nothing of it. Put it down to "hands across the sea"—lend-lease.'

A flicker of annoyance crossed the Englishman's face and his jaw muscles hardened.

'What's the matter?' the King asked abruptly.

After a pause Peter Marlowe said, 'Nothing.' He looked at the egg. He wasn't due an egg for six days. 'If you're sure I won't be putting you out, I'd like it fried.'

'Coming up,' the King said. He knew he had made a mistake somewhere, for the annoyance was real. Foreigners are weird, he thought. Never can tell how they're going to react. He lifted his electric stove onto the table and plugged it into the electric socket. 'Neat, huh?' he said pleasantly.

'Yes.'

'Max wired it for me,' he said, nodding down the hut.

Peter Marlowe followed his glance.

Max looked up, feeling eyes on him. 'You want something?'

'No,' the King said. 'Just telling him how you wired the hot plate.'

'Oh! It's working all right?'

'Sure.'

Peter Marlowe got up and leaned out of the window, calling out in Malay. 'I beg thee do not wait. I will see thee again tomorrow, Suliman.'

'Very well, tuan, peace be unto thee.'

'And upon thee.' Peter Marlowe smiled and sat down once more and Suliman walked away.

The King broke the eggs neatly and dropped them into the heated oil. The yoke was rich-gold and its circling jelly sputtered and hissed against the heat and began to set, and all at once the sizzle filled the hut. It filled the minds and filled the hearts and made the juices flow. But no one said anything or did anything. Except Tex. He forced himself up and walked out of the hut.

Many men who walked the path smelled the fragrance and hated the King anew. The smell swept down the slope and into the MP hut. Grey knew and Masters knew at once where it came from.

Grey got up, nauseated, and went to the doorway. He was going to walk around the camp to escape the aroma. Then he changed his mind and turned back.

'Come on, Sergeant,' he said. 'We'll pay a call on the American hut. Now'd be a good time to check on Sellars' story!'

'All right,' Masters said, almost ruptured by the smell. 'The bloody bastard could at least cook before lunch—not just after—not when supper's five hours away.'

'The Americans are the second shift today. They haven't eaten yet.'

Within the American hut, the men picked up the strings of time. Dino tried to go back to sleep and Kurt continued sewing and the poker game resumed and Miller and Byron Jones III resumed their interminable chess. But the sizzle destroyed the drama of an inside straight and Kurt stuck the needle in his finger and swore obscenely, and Dino's sleep-urge left him and Byron Jones III watched appalled as Miller took his queen with a lousy stinking pawn.

'Jesus H. Christ,' Byron Jones III said to no one, choked. 'I wish it would rain.'

No one answered. For no one heard anything except the crackle and the hiss.

The King too was concentrating. Over the frypan. He prided himself that no one could cook an egg better than he. To him a fried egg had to be cooked with an artist's eye, and quickly—yet not too fast.

The King glanced up and smiled at Peter Marlowe, but Peter Marlowe's eyes were on the eggs.

'Christ,' he said softly, and it was a benediction, not a curse. 'That smells so good.'

The King was pleased. 'You wait till I've finished. Then you'll see the goddamnedest egg you've ever seen.' He powdered the eggs delicately with pepper, then added the salt. 'You like cooking?' he asked.

'Yes,' said Peter Marlowe. His voice sounded unlike his real voice to him. 'I do most of the cooking for my unit.'

'What do you like to be called? Pete? Peter?'

Peter Marlowe covered his surprise. Only tried and trusted friends called you by your Christian name—how else can you tell friends from acquaintances? He glanced at the King and saw only friendliness, so, in spite of himself, he said, 'Peter.'

'Where do you come from? Where's your home?'

Questions, questions, thought Peter Marlowe. Next he'll want to know if I'm married or how much I have in the bank. His curiosity had prompted him to accept the King's summons, and he almost cursed himself for being so curious. But he was pacified by the glory of the sizzling eggs.

'Portchester,' he answered. 'That's a little hamlet on the south coast. In Hampshire.'

'You married, Peter?'

'Are you?'

'No.' The King would have continued but the eggs were done. He slipped the frypan off the stove and nodded to Peter Marlowe. 'Plates're in back of you,' he said. Then he added not a little proudly, 'Lookee here!'

36

They were the best fried eggs Peter Marlowe had ever seen, so he paid the King the greatest compliment in the English world. 'Not bad,' he said flatly. 'Not too bad, I suppose,' and he looked up at the King and kept his face as impassive as his voice and thereby added to the compliment.

'What the hell are you talking about, you son of a bitch?' the King said furiously. 'They're the best goddam eggs you've seen in your life!'

Peter Marlowe was shocked, and there was a death-silence in the hut. Then a sudden whistle broke the spell. Instantly Dino and Miller were on their feet and rushing towards the King, and Max was guarding the doorway. Miller and Dino shoved the King's bed into the corner and took up the carpets and stuffed them under the mattress. Then they took other beds and shoved them close to the King so that now, like everyone in Changi, the King had only four feet of space by six feet of space. Lieutenant Grey stood in the doorway. Behind him a nervous pace was Sergeant Masters.

The Americans stared at Grey, and after just enough of a pause to make their point they all got up. After an equally insulting pause Grey saluted briefly and said, 'Stand easy.' Peter Marlowe alone had not moved and still sat in his chair.

'Get up,' hissed the King, 'he'll throw the book at you. Get up!' He knew from long experience that Grey was hopped up now. For once Grey's eyes were not probing him, they were just fixed on Peter Marlowe, and even the King winced.

Grey walked the length of the hut, taking his time, until he stood over Peter Marlowe. He took his eyes off Peter Marlowe and stared at the eggs for a long moment. Then he glanced at the King and back to Peter Marlowe.

'You're a long way from home, aren't you, Marlowe?'

Peter Marlowe's fingers took out his cigarette box and put a little tobacco in a slip of rattan grass. He rolled a funnel-cigarette and carried it to his lips. The length of his pause was a slap in Grey's face. 'Oh, I don't know, old boy,' he said softly. 'An Englishman's at home wherever he is, don't you think?'

'Where's your armband?'

'In my belt.'

'It's supposed to be on your arm. Those are orders.'

'They're Jap orders. I don't like Jap orders,' said Peter Marlowe.

'They are also camp orders,' Grey said.

Their voices were quite calm and only a trifle irritated to American ears, but Grey knew and Peter Marlowe knew. And there was a sudden declaration of war between them. Peter Marlow hated the Japanese and Grey represented the Japanese to him, for Grey enforced camp orders which were also Japanese orders. Relentlessly. Between them there was the deeper hate, the inbred hate of class. Peter Marlowe, knew that Grey despised him for his birth and his accent, what Grey wanted beyond all things and could never have.

'Put it on!' Grey was within his right to order it.

Peter Marlowe shrugged and pulled out the band and slipped it about his left elbow. On the band was his rank. Flight Lieutenant, RAF.

The King's eyes widened, Jesus, an officer, he thought, and I was going to ask him to—

'So sorry to interrupt your lunch,' Grey was saying. 'But it seems that someone has lost something.'

'Lost something?' Jesus Christ, the King almost shouted. The Ronson! Oh my God, his fear screamed. Get rid of the goddam lighter.

'What's the matter, Corporal,' Grey said narrowly, noticing the sweat which pearled the King's face.

'It's hot, isn't it?' the King said limply. He could feel his starched shirt wilting from the sweat. He knew he had been framed. And he knew that Grey was playing with him. He wondered quickly if he dared to make a run for it, but Peter Marlowe was between him and the window and Grey could easily catch him. And to run would be to admit guilt.

He saw Grey say something and he was poised between life and death: 'What did you say, sir?' and the 'sir' was not an insult, for the King was staring at Grey incredulously.

'I said that Colonel Sellars has reported the theft of a gold ring!' Grey repeated balefully.

For a moment the King felt lightheaded. Not the Ronson at all! Panic for nothing! Just Sellars' goddam ring. He had sold it three weeks ago for Sellars—at a tidy profit. So Sellars has just reported a theft, has he? Lying son of a bitch. 'Gee,' he said, a thread of laughter in his voice, 'gee, that's tough. Stolen. Can you imagine that!'

'Yes I can,' said Grey harshly. 'Can you?'

The King did not answer. But he wanted to smile. Not the lighter! Safe!

'Do you know Colonel Sellars?' Grey was asking.

'Slightly, sir. I've played bridge with him, once or twice.' The King was quite calm now.

'Did he ever show the ring to you?' Grey said relentlessly.

The King double-checked his memory. Colonel Sellars had shown him the ring twice. Once when he had asked the King to sell it for him, and the second time when he had gone to weigh the ring. 'Oh no, sir,' he said innocently. The King knew he was safe. There were no witnesses.

'You're sure you never saw it?' Grey said.

'Oh no, sir.'

Grey was suddenly sick of the cat-and-mouse game and he was nauseated with hunger for the eggs. He would have done anything, anything for one of them.

'Have you got a light, Grey, old boy?' Peter Marlowe said. He had not brought his native lighter with him. And he needed a smoke. Badly. His dislike of Grey had dried his lips.

'No.' Get your own light, Grey thought angrily, turning to go. Then he heard Peter Marlowe say to the King, 'Could I borrow your Ronson please?' And slowly he turned back. Peter Marlowe was smiling up at the King.

The words seemed etched upon the air. Then they sped into all corners of the hut.

Appalled, groping for time, the King started to find some matches.

'It's in your left pocket,' Peter Marlowe said.

And in that moment the King lived and died and was born again. The men in the hut did not breathe. For they were to see the King chopped. They were to see the King caught and taken and put away, a thing which beyond all things was an impossibility. Yet here was Grey and here was the King and here was the man who had fingered the King—and laid him like a lamb on Grey's altar. Some of the men were horrified and some were gloating and some were sorry and Dino thought angrily, Jesus, and it was my day to guard the box tomorrow!

'Why don't you light it for him?' Grey said. The hunger had left him and in its place was only warmth. Grey knew that there was no Ronson lighter on the list.

The King took out the lighter and snapped it for Peter Marlowe. The flame that was to burn him was straight and clean.

'Thanks.' Peter Marlowe smiled, and only then did he realize the enormity of his deed.

'So,' said Grey as he took the lighter. The word sounded majestic and final and violent.

The King did not answer, for there was no answer. He merely waited, and now that he was committed, he felt no fear, he only cursed his own stupidity. A man who fails through his own stupidity has no right to be called a man. And no right to be the King, for the strongest is always the King, not by strength alone, but King by cunning and strength and luck together.

'Where did this come from, Corporal?' Grey's question was a caress.

Peter Marlowe's stomach turned over and his mind worked frantically and then he said, 'It's mine.' He knew that it sounded like the lie it was, so he added quickly, 'We were playing poker. I lost it. Just before lunch.'

Grey and the King and all the men stared at him stunned.

'You what?' said Grey.

'Lost it,' repeated Peter Marlowe. 'We were playing poker. I had a straight. You tell him,' he added abruptly to the King, tossing the ball to him to test him.

The King's mind was still in shock but his reflexes were good. His mouth opened and he said, 'We were playing stud. I had a full, and . . .'

'What were the cards?'

'Aces on twos.' Peter Marlowe interrupted without hesitation. What the hell is stud? he asked himself.

The King winced. In spite of magnificent control. He had been about to say kings on queens, and he knew that Grey had seen the shudder.

'You're lying, Marlowe!'

'Why, Grey, old chap, what a thing to say!' Peter Marlowe was playing for time. What the bloody hell is stud? 'It was pathetic,' he said, feeling the horror-pleasure of great danger. 'I

40

thought I had him. I had a straight. That's why I bet my lighter. You tell him,' he said abruptly to the King.

'How do you play stud, Marlowe?'

Thunder broke the silence, grumbling on the horizon, and the King opened his mouth but Grey stopped him.

'I asked Marlowe,' he said threateningly.

Peter Marlowe was helpless. He looked at the King and though his eyes said nothing, the King knew. 'Come on,' Peter Marlowe said quickly, 'let's show him.'

The King immediately turned for the cards and said without hesitation, 'It was my hole card—'

Grey whirled furiously. 'I said I wanted Marlowe to tell me. One more word out of you and I'll put you under arrest for interfering with justice.'

The King said nothing. He only prayed that the clue had been sufficient.

'Hole card' registered in the distance of Peter Marlowe's memory. And he remembered. And now that he knew the game, he began to play with Grey. 'Well,' he said worriedly, 'it's like any other poker game, Grey.'

'Just explain how you play the game!' Grey thought that he had them in the lie.

Peter Marlowe looked at him, his eyes flinty. The eggs were getting cold. 'What are you trying to prove, Grey? Any fool knows that it's four cards face up and one down—one in the hole.'

A sigh fled through the room. Grey knew there was nothing he could do now. It would be his word against Marlowe's, and he knew that even here in Changi he would have to do better than that. 'That's right,' he said grimly, looking from the King to Peter Marlowe. 'Any fool knows that.' He handed the lighter back to the King. 'See it's put on the list.'

'Yes, sir.' Now that it was over, the King allowed some of his relief to show.

Grey looked at Peter Marlowe a last time, and the look was both a promise and a threat. 'The old school tie would be very proud of you today,' he said with contempt, and he started out of the hut, Masters shuffling after him.

Peter Marlowe stared after Grey, and when Grey had reached the door, he said just a little louder than was necessary to the

41

King, still watching Grey, 'Can I use your lighter—my fag's out.' But Grey's stride did not falter, nor did he look back. Good man, thought Peter Marlowe grimly, good nerves—good man to have on your side in a death battle. And an enemy to cherish.

The King sat weakly in the electric silence and Peter Marlowe took the lighter from his slack hand and lit his cigarette. The King automatically found his packet of Kooas and stuck one in his lips and held it there, not feeling it. Peter Marlowe leaned across and snapped the lighter for the King. The King took a long time to focus on the flame and then he saw that Peter Marlowe's hand was as unsteady as his own. He looked down the length of the hut where the men were like statues, staring back at him. He could feel the sweat-chill on his shoulders and the wetness of his shirt.

There was a clattering of cans outside. Dino got up and looked out expectantly.

'Chow,' he called out happily. The spell shattered and the men left the hut with their eating utensils. And Peter Marlowe and the King were quite alone.

III

The two men sat for a moment, gathering themselves, then Peter Marlowe said shakily, 'God, that was close!'

'Yes,' the King said after an unhurried pause. Involuntarily, he shuddered again, then found his wallet and took out two ten-dollar bills and put them on the table. 'Here,' he said, 'this'll do for now. But you're on the payroll from here on in. Twenty a week.'

'What?'

'I'll give you twenty a week.' The King thought a moment. 'Guess you're right,' he said agreeably and smiled. 'It is worth more. We'll make it thirty.' Then his eyes noticed the armband, so he added, 'Sir.'

'You can still call me Peter,' Peter Marlowe said, his voice edged. 'And just for the books—I don't want your money.' He got up and began to leave. 'Thanks for the cigarette.'

'Hey, wait a minute,' the King said, astonished. 'What the hell's gotten into you?'

Peter Marlowe stared down at the King and the anger flickered his eyes. 'What the hell do you think I am? Take your money, and shove it.'

'Something wrong with my money?'

'No. Only your manners!'

'Since when has manners got anything to do with money?'

Peter Marlowe abruptly turned to go. The King jumped up and stood between Peter Marlowe and the door.

'Just a minute,' he said and his voice was taut. 'I want to know something. Why did you cover up for me?'

'Well, that's obvious, isn't it? I dropped you in the creek. I couldn't leave you holding the baby. What do you think I am?'

'I don't know. I'm trying to find out.'

'It was my mistake. I'm sorry.'

'You got nothing to be sorry about,' the King said sharply. 'It was my mistake, I got stupid. Nothing to do with you.'

'It makes no difference.' Peter Marlowe's face was granite like his eyes. 'But you must think me a complete shit if you expect me to let you be crucified. And a bigger one if you think I want money from you—when I'd been careless. I'm not taking that from anyone!'

'Sit down a minute. Please.'

'Why?'

'Goddammit, because I want to talk to you.'

Max hesitated at the door with the King's mess cans.

'Excuse me,' he said cautiously, 'here's your chow. You want some tea?'

'No. And Tex gets my soup today.' He took the mess can of rice and put it on the table.

'Okay,' said Max, still hesitating, wondering if the King wanted a hand to beat hell out of the son of a bitch.

'Beat it, Max. And tell the others to leave us alone for a minute.'

'Sure.' Max went out agreeably. He thought the King was very wise to have no witnesses, not when you clobber an officer.

The King looked back at Peter Marlowe. 'I'm asking you. Will you sit down a minute? Please.'

'All right,' said Peter Marlowe stiffly.

'Look,' the King began patiently. 'You got me out of the noose. You helped me—it's only right I help you, I offered you the dough because I wanted to thank you. If you don't want it, fine—but I didn't mean to insult you. If I did, I apologize.'

'Sorry,' Peter Marlowe said, softening. 'I've got a bad temper. I didn't understand.'

The King stuck out his hand. 'Shake on it.'

Peter Marlowe shook hands.

'You don't like Grey, do you?' the King said carefully.

'No.'

'Why?'

44

Peter Marlowe shrugged. The King divided the rice carelessly and handed him the larger portion. 'Let's eat.'

'But what about you?' said Peter Marlowe, gaping at the bigger helping.

'I'm not hungry. My appetite went with the birds. Jesus, that was close. I thought we'd both had it.'

'Yes,' Peter Marlowe said, with the beginning of a smile. 'It was a lot of fun, wasn't it?'

'Huh?'

'Oh, the excitement. Haven't enjoyed anything so much in years, I suppose. The danger-excitement.'

'There are a lot of things I don't understand about you,' the King said weakly. 'You mean to say you enjoyed it?'

'Certainly—didn't you? I thought it was almost as good as flying a Spit. You know, at the time it frightens you, but at the same time doesn't—and during and after you feel sort of light-headed.'

'I think you're just out of your head.'

'If you weren't enjoying it then why the hell did you try to throw me with "stud"? I bloody nearly died.'

'I didn't try to throw you. Why the hell would I want to throw you?'

'To make it more exciting and to test me.'

The King bleakly wiped his eyes and his face. 'You mean to say you think I did that deliberately?'

'Of course. I did the same to you when I passed the questioning to you.'

'Let's get this straight. You did that just to test my nerves?' the King gasped.

'Of course, old boy,' Peter Marlowe said. 'I don't understand what's the matter.'

'Jesus,' said the King, a nervous sweat beginning again. 'We're almost in the pokey and you play games!' The King paused for breath. 'Crazy, just plain crazy, and when you hesitated after I'd fed you the "hole" clue, I thought we were dead.'

'Grey thought that too. I was just playing with him. I only finished it quickly because the eggs were getting cold. And you don't see a fried egg like that every day. My word no.'

'I thought you said it wasn't any good.'

'I said it wasn't "bad".' Peter Marlowe hesitated. 'Look. Saying it's "not bad" means that it's exceptional. That's a way of paying a chap a compliment without embarrassing him.'

'You're out of your skull! You risk my neck—and your own—to add to the danger, you blow your stack when I offer you some money with no strings attached, and you say something's "not bad" when you mean it's great. Jesus,' he added, stupefied, 'I guess I'm simple or something.'

He glanced up and saw the perplexed look on Peter Marlowe's face and he had to laugh. Peter Marlowe began laughing too, and soon the two men were hysterical.

Max peered into the hut and the other Americans were close behind.

'What the hell's gotten into him?' Max said gasping. 'I thought by now he'd be beating his fugging head in.'

'Madonna,' gasped Dino. 'First the King nearly gets chopped, and now he's laughing with the guy who fingered him.'

'Don't make sense.' Max's stomach had been flapping ever since the warning whistle.

The King looked up and saw the men staring at him. He pulled out the remains of the pack of cigarettes. 'Here, Max. Pass these around. Celebration!'

'Gee, thanks.' Max took the pack. 'Wow! That was a close one. We're all so happy for you.'

The King read the grins. Some were good and he marked those. Some were false and he knew those anyway. The men echoed Max's thanks.

Max herded the men outside once more and began to divide the treasure. 'It's shock,' he said quietly. 'Must be. Like shell shock. Any moment he'll be tearing the Limey's head off.' He stared off as another burst of laughter came from the hut, then shrugged.

'He's off his head—and no wonder.'

'For God's sake,' Peter Marlowe was saying, holding his stomach. 'Let's eat. If I don't soon, I won't be able to.'

So they began to eat. Between laughter spasms. Peter Marlowe regretted that the eggs were cold, but the laughter warmed the eggs and made them superb. 'They need a little salt, don't you think?' he said, trying to keep his voice flat.

'Gee, I guess so. I thought I'd used enough.' The King

46

frowned and turned for the salt and then he saw the crinkling eyes.

'What the hell's up now?' he asked, beginning to laugh in spite of himself.

'That was a joke for God's sake. You Americans don't have much of a sense of humour, do you?'

'Go to hell! And for Chrissake stop laughing!'

When they had finished the eggs, the King put some coffee on the hot plate and searched for his cigarettes. Then he remembered he had given them away, so he reached down and unlocked the black box.

'Here, try some of this,' Peter Marlowe said, offering his tobacco box.

'Thanks, but I can't stand the stuff. It plays hell with my throat.'

'Try it. It's been treated. I learned how from some Javanese.'

Dubiously the King took the cigarette box. The tobacco was the same cheap weed, but instead of being straw-yellow it was dark golden; instead of being dry it was moist and had a texture; instead of being odourless it smelled like tobacco, sweet-strong. He found his packet of rice papers and took an overgenerous amount of the treated weed. He rolled a sloppy tube and nipped off the protruding ends, dropping the excess tobacco carelessly on the floor.

Godalmighty, thought Peter Marlowe, I said try it, not take the bloody lot. He knew he should have picked up the shreds of tobacco and put them back in the box, but he did not. Some things a chap can't do, he thought again.

The King snapped the lighter and they grinned together at the sight of it. The King took a careful puff, then another. Then a deep inhale. 'But it's great,' he said astonished. 'Not as good as a Kooa—but this's—' He stopped and corrected himself. 'I mean it's not bad.'

'It's not bad at all.' Peter Marlowe laughed.

'How the hell do you do it?'

'Trade secret.'

The King knew he had a gold mine in his hands. 'I guess it's a long and involved process,' he said delicately.

'Oh, actually it's quite easy. You just soak the raw weed in tea, then squeeze it out. Then you sprinkle a little white sugar

47

over it and knead it in, and when it's all absorbed, cook it gently in a frying pan over a low heat. Keep turning it over or it'll spoil. You've got to get it just right. Not too dry and not too moist.'

The King was surprised that Peter Marlowe had told him the process so easily—without making a deal first. Of course, he thought, he's just whetting my appetite. Can't be that easy or everyone'd be doing it. And he probably knows I'm the only one who could handle the deal.

'Just like that?' King said smiling.

'Yes. Nothing to it really.'

The King could see a thriving business. Legitimate too. 'I suppose everyone in your hut cures their tobacco the same way.'

Peter Marlowe shook his head. 'I just do it for my unit. I've been teasing them for months, telling them all sorts of stories, but they've never worked out the exact way.'

The King's smile was huge. 'Then you're the only one who knows how to do it!'

'Oh no,' said Peter Marlowe and the King's heart sank. 'It's a native custom. They do it all over Java.'

The King brightened. 'But no one here knows about it, do they?'

'I don't know. I've never really thought about it.'

The King let the smoke dribble out of his nostrils and his mind worked rapidly. Oh yes, he told himself, this *is* my lucky day.

'Tell you what, Peter. I got a business proposition for you. You show me exactly how to do it, and I'll cut you in for—' He hesitated. 'Ten per cent.'

'What?'

'All right. Twenty-five.'

'Twenty-five?'

'All right,' the King said, looking at Peter Marlowe, with new respect. 'You're a hard trader and that's great. I'll organize the whole deal. We'll buy in bulk. We'll have to set up a factory. You can oversee production and I'll look after sales.' He stuck out his hand. 'We'll be partners—split right down the middle, fifty-fifty. It's a deal.'

Peter Marlowe stared down at the King's hand. Then he looked into his face. 'Oh no it's not!' he said decisively.

48

'Goddammit,' the King exploded. 'That's the fairest offer you'll ever get. What could be fairer? I'm putting up the dough. I'll have to—' A sudden thought stopped him. 'Peter,' he said after a moment, hurt but not showing it, 'no one has to know we're partners. You just show me how to do it, and I'll see you get your share. You can trust me.'

'I know that,' Peter Marlowe said.

'Then we'll split fifty-fifty.' The King beamed.

'No we won't.'

'Jesus Christ,' the King said as he felt the screws applied. But he held his temper and thought about the deal. And the more he thought—He looked around to make sure that no one was listening. Then he dropped his voice and said hoarsely, 'Sixty-forty, and I've never offered that to anyone in my life. Sixty-forty it is.'

'No it isn't.'

'Isn't?' the King burst out, shocked. 'I've got to get something out of the deal. What the hell do you want for the process? Cash on the line?'

'I don't want anything,' said Peter Marlowe.

'Nothing?' The King sat down feebly, wrecked.

Peter Marlowe was bewildered. 'You know,' he said hesitantly, 'I don't understand why you get so excited about certain things. The process isn't mine to sell. It's a simple native custom. I couldn't possibly take anything from you. That wouldn't be right. Not at all. And anyway, I—' Peter Marlowe stopped and said quickly, 'Would you like me to show you now?'

'Just a minute. You mean to tell me you want nothing for showing me the process? When I've offered to split sixty-forty with you? When I tell you I can make money out of the deal?' Peter Marlowe nodded. 'That's crazy,' the King said helplessly. 'It's wrong. I don't understand.'

'Nothing to understand,' Peter Marlowe said, smiling faintly. 'Put it down to sunstroke.'

The King studied him a long moment. 'Will you give me a straight answer to a straight question?'

'Yes. Of course.'

'It's because of me, isn't it?'

The words hung in the heat between them.

'No,' said Peter Marlowe, breaking the silence.

And there was truth between them.

An hour later Peter Marlowe was watching Tex cook the second batch of tobacco. This time Tex was doing it without help, and the King was clucking around like an old hen.

'You sure he put in the right amount of sugar?' the King asked Peter Marlowe anxiously.

'Exactly right.'

'How long will it be now?'

'How long do you think, Tex?'

Tex smiled back at Peter Marlowe and stretched his gangling six-foot three. 'Five, maybe six minutes, thereabouts.'

Peter Marlowe got up. 'Where's the place? The loo?'

'The john? Around the back.' The King pointed. 'But can't you wait till Tex's finished? I want to make sure he's got it right.'

'Tex's doing fine,' Peter Marlowe said and walked out.

When he came back Tex took the frypan off the stove. 'Now,' he said nervously and glanced at Peter Marlowe to check if his timing was right.

'Just right,' said Peter Marlowe, examining the treated tobacco.

Excitedly the King rolled a cigarette in rice paper. So did Tex and Peter Marlowe. They lit up. With the Ronson. Another delighted laugh. Then silence as each man became a connoisseur.

'Jolly good,' said Peter Marlowe decisively. 'I told you it was quite simple, Tex.'

Tex breathed a sigh of relief.

'It's not bad,' said the King thoughtfully.

'What the hell're you talking about,' Tex said, flaring. 'It's goddam good!'

Peter Marlowe and the King were convulsed. They explained why and then Tex was laughing too.

'We got to have a brand name.' The King thought for a moment. 'I got it. How about Three Kings? One for King Royal Air Force, one for King Texas an' one for me.'

'Not bad,' Tex said.

'We'll start the factory tomorrow.'

Tex shook his head. 'I'm on a work party.'

'The hell with it! I'll get Dino to sub for you.'

'No. I'll ask him.' Tex got up and smiled at Peter Marlowe. 'Happy to know you, sir.'

'Forget the sir, will you?' Peter Marlowe said.

'Sure. Thanks.'

Peter Marlowe watched him go. 'Funny,' he said quietly to the King. 'I've never seen so many smiles in one hut before.'

'There's no point in not smiling, is there? Things could be a lot worse. You get shot down flying the hump?'

'You mean the Calcutta – Chungking route? Over the Himalayas?'

'Yeah.' The King nodded at the tobacco. 'Fill your box.'

'Thanks. I will if you don't mind.'

'Any time you're short, come and help yourself.'

'Thanks, I'll do that. You're very kind.' Peter Marlowe wanted another cigarette but he knew that he was smoking too much. If he smoked another now, then the hunger would hurt more. Better go easy. He glanced at the sun-shadow and promised that he would not smoke again until the shadow had moved two inches. 'I wasn't shot down at all. My kite—my plane got hit in an air raid in Java. I couldn't get up. Rather a bore,' he added, and tried to hide the bitterness.

'That's not so bad,' said the King. 'You might've been in it. You're alive and that's what counts. What were you flying?'

'Hurricane. Single-seat fighter. But my regular plane's a Spit—Spitfire.'

'I've heard about them—never seen one. You guys sure as hell made the Germans look sick.'

'Yes,' said Peter Marlowe softly. 'We did, rather.'

The King was surprised. 'You weren't in the Battle of Britain, were you?'

'Yes. I got my wings in 1940—just in time.'

'How old were you?'

'Nineteen.'

'Huh, I'd've thought, looking at your face, you'd be at least thirty-eight, not twenty-four!'

'Up yours, brother!' Peter Marlowe laughed. 'How old are you?'

'Twenty-five. Son of a bitch,' the King said. 'Best years of my life and I'm locked up in a stinking jail.'

51

'You're hardly locked up. And it seems to me you're doing very well.'

'We're still locked up, whichever way you figure it. How long you think it's going to last?'

'We've got the Germans on the run. That show should be over soon.'

'You believe that?'

Peter Marlowe shrugged. Careful, he told himself, you can never be too careful. 'Yes, I think so. You can never tell about rumours.'

'And our war. What about ours?'

Because the question had been asked by a friend, Peter Marlowe talked freely. 'I think ours will last forever. Oh, we'll beat the Japs. I know that now. But for us, here? I don't think we'll get out.'

'Why?'

'Well, I don't think the Japs'll ever give in. That means we'll have to land on the mainland. And when that happens, I think they'll eliminate us here, all of us. If disease and sickness haven't got us already.'

'Why the hell should they do that?'

'Oh, to save time, I suppose. I think as the net tightens on Japan, they'll start pulling in their tentacles. Why waste time over a few thousand prisoners? Japs think of life quite differently than we do. And the idea of our troops on their soil will drive them around the bend.' His voice was quite flat and calm. 'I think we've had it. Of course I hope I'm wrong. But that's what I think.'

'You're a hopeful son of a bitch,' the King said sourly, and when Peter Marlowe laughed he said, 'What the hell are you laughing about? You always seem to laugh in the wrong places.'

'Sorry, bad habit.'

'Let's sit outside. The flies're getting bad. Hey Max,' the King called out. 'You want to clean up?'

Max arrived and began tidying up and the King and Peter Marlowe slipped easily through the window. Just outside the King's window there was another small table and a bench under a canvas overhang. The King sat on the bench. Peter Marlowe squatted on his heels, native style.

'Never could do that,' said the King.

'It's very comfortable. I learned it in Java.'

'How come you speak Malay so well?'

'I lived in a village for a time.'

'When?'

'In '42. After the cease-fire.'

The King waited patiently for him to continue but nothing more came out. He waited some more, then asked, 'How come you lived in Java in a village after the cease-fire in 1942 when everyone was in a POW camp by then?'

Peter Marlowe's laugh was rich. 'Sorry. Nothing much to tell. I didn't like the idea of being in a camp. Actually, when the war ended, I got lost in the jungle and eventually found this village. They took pity on me. I stayed for six months or so.'

'What was it like?'

'Wonderful. They were very kind. I was just like one of them. Dressed like a Javanese, dyed my skin dark—you know, non-sense really, for my height and eyes would give me away—worked in the paddy fields.'

'You on your own?'

After a pause Peter Marlowe said, 'I was the only European there, if that's what you mean.' He looked out at the camp, seeing the sun beat the dust and the wind pick up the dust and swirl it. The swirl reminded him of her.

He looked away towards the east, into a nervous sky. But she was part of the sky.

The wind gathered slightly and bent the heads of the coconut palms. But she was part of the wind and the palms and the clouds beyond.

Peter Marlowe tore his mind away and watched the Korean guard plodding along beyond the fence, sweating under the lowering heat. The guard's uniform was shabby and ill-kempt and his cap as crumpled as his face, his rifle askew on his shoulders. As graceless as she was graceful.

Once more Peter Marlowe looked up into the sky, seeking distance. Only then could he feel that he was not within a box—a box filled with men, and men's smells and men's dirt and men's noises. Without women, Peter Marlowe thought helplessly, men are only a cruel joke. And he bled in the starch of the sun.

'Hey Peter!' The King was looking up the slope, his mouth agape.

Peter Marlowe followed the King's gaze and his stomach turned over as he saw Sean approaching. 'Christ!' He wanted to slip through the window out of sight, but he knew that that would make him more conspicuous. So he waited grimly, hardly breathing. He thought he had a good chance of not being seen, for Sean was deep in conversation with Squadron Leader Rodrick and Lieutenant Frank Parrish. Their heads were close together and their voices intent.

Then Sean glanced past Frank Parrish and saw Peter Marlowe and stopped.

Rodrick and Frank stopped also, surprised. When they saw Peter Marlowe they thought, Oh my God. But they concealed their anxiety.

'Hello, Peter,' Rodrick called out. He was a tall neat man with a chiselled face, as tall and neat as Frank Parrish was tall and careless.

'Hello, Rod!' Peter Marlowe called back.

'I won't be a moment,' Sean said quietly to Rodrick and walked towards Peter Marlowe and the King. Now that the first shock had worn off, Sean smiled a welcome.

Peter Marlowe felt the hackles on his neck begin to rise and he got up and waited. He could feel the King's eyes boring into him.

'Hello, Peter,' Sean said.

'Hello, Sean.'

'You're so thin, Peter.'

'Oh I don't know. No more than anyone. I'm very fit, thanks.'

'I haven't seen you for such a long time—why don't you come up to the theatre sometime? There's always a little extra around somewhere—and you know me, I never did eat much.' Sean smiled hopefully.

'Thanks,' Peter Marlowe said, raw with embarrassment.

'Well, I know you won't,' Sean said unhappily, 'but you're always welcome.' There was a pause. 'I never see you any more.'

'Oh, you know how it is, Sean. You're doing all the shows and I'm well, I'm on work parties and things.'

Like Peter Marlowe, Sean was wearing a sarong, but unlike Peter Marlowe's, which was threadbare and multifaded-colour, Sean's was new and white and the border was embroidered with blue and silver. And Sean wore a short-sleeved native baju coat, ending above the waist, cut tight to allow for the swell of breasts. The King was staring fascinated at the half-open neck of the baju.

Sean noticed the King and smiled faintly and brushed back some hair that the wind had caressed out of place and toyed with it until the King looked up. Sean smiled inside, warmed inside, as the King flushed.

'It's, er, it's getting hot, isn't it?' the King said uncomfortably.

'I suppose so,' Sean said pleasantly, cool and sweatless, as always—however intense the heat.

There was a silence.

'Oh, sorry,' Peter Marlowe said as he saw Sean looking at the King and waiting patiently. 'Do you know—'

Sean laughed. 'My God, Peter. You are in a state. Of course I know who your friend is, though we've never met.' Sean put out a hand. 'How are you? It's quite an honour to meet a King!'

'Er, thanks,' the King said, hardly touching the hand, so small against his. 'You, er, like a smoke?'

'Thanks, but I don't. But if you don't mind I will take one. In fact two, if it's all right?' Sean nodded back towards the path. 'Rod and Frank smoke and I know they'd appreciate one.'

'Sure,' the King said. 'Sure.'

'Thanks. That's very kind of you.'

In spite of himself the King felt the warmth of Sean's smile. In spite of himself he said, meaning it, 'You were great in *Othello*.'

'Thank you,' said Sean delightedly. 'Did you like *Hamlet*?'

'Yes. And I never was much on Shakespeare.'

Sean laughed. 'That's praise indeed. We're doing a new play next. Frank has written it especially and it should be a lot of fun.'

'If it's just ordinary, it'll be great,' the King said, more at ease 'and you'll be great.'

'How nice of you. Thanks.' Sean glanced at Peter Marlowe and the eyes took on an added lustre. 'But I'm afraid Peter won't agree with you.'

'Stop it, Sean,' Peter Marlowe said.

Sean did not look at Peter Marlowe, only the King, and smiled, but fury lurked beneath the smile. 'Peter doesn't approve of me.'

'Stop it, Sean,' Peter Marlowe said harshly.

'Why should I?' Sean lashed out. 'You despise deviates—isn't that what you call queers? You made that perfectly clear. I haven't forgotten!'

'Nor have I!'

'Well, that's something! I don't like to be despised—least of all by you!'

'I said stop it! This isn't the time or the place. And we've been through this before and you've said it all before. I said I was sorry. I didn't mean any harm!'

'No. But you still hate me—why? Why?'

'I don't hate you.'

'Then why do you always avoid me?'

'It's better. For God's sake, Sean, leave me be.'

Sean stared at Peter Marlowe, and then as suddenly as it had flared, the anger melted. 'Sorry, Peter. You're probably quite right. I'm the fool. It's just that I'm lonely from time to time. Lonely just for talk.' Sean reached out and touched Peter Marlowe's arm. 'Sorry. I just want to be friends again.'

Peter Marlowe could say nothing.

Sean hesitated. 'Well, I suppose I'd better be going.'

'Sean,' Rodrick called out from the path, 'we're late already.'

'I won't be a moment.' Sean still looked at Peter Marlowe, then sighed and held out a hand to the King. 'It was nice to meet you. Please forgive my bad manners.'

The King couldn't avoid touching the hand again. 'Happy to meet you,' he said.

Sean hesitated, eyes grave and searching. 'Are you Peter's friend?'

The King felt the whole world heard him when he said, stumbling, 'Er, sure, yeah, I guess so.'

'Strange, isn't it, how one word can mean so many different things. But if you are his friend, don't lead him astray, please. You've a reputation for danger, and I wouldn't like Peter hurt. I'm very fond of him.'

'Er, yes, sure.' The King's knees jellied and his backbone

melted. But the magnetism of Sean's smile pervaded him. It was unlike anything he had ever felt. 'The shows are the best thing in the camp,' he said. 'Make life worth living. And you're the best thing in them.'

'Thank you.' And then, to Peter Marlowe: 'It does make life worthwhile. I'm very happy. And I like what I'm doing. It does make things worthwhile, Peter.'

'Yes,' Peter Marlowe said, tormented. 'I'm glad all's well.'

Sean smiled hesitantly a last time, then turned quickly and was suddenly gone.

The King sat down. 'I'll be goddamned!'

Peter Marlowe sat down too. He opened his box and rolled a cigarette.

'If you didn't know he was a man, you'd swear to God that he was a woman,' the King said. 'A beautiful woman.'

Peter Marlowe nodded bleakly.

'He's not like the other fags,' the King said, 'that's for sure. No sir. Not the same at all. Jesus, there's something about him that's not—' The King stopped and groped and continued helplessly, 'Don't quite know how to put it. He's—he's a woman, goddamit! Remember when he was playing Desdemona? My God, the way he looked in the negligée, I'll bet there wasn't a man in Changi that didn't have a hard on. Don't blame a man for being tempted. I'm tempted, everyone is. Man's a liar if he says otherwise.' Then he looked at Peter Marlowe and studied him carefully.

'Oh, for the love of God,' Peter Marlowe said irritably. 'Do you think I'm a queer too?'

'No,' the King said calmly. 'I don't mind if you are. Just as long as I know.'

'Well, I'm not.'

'It sure as hell sounded like it,' the King said with a grin. 'Lover's quarrel?'

'Go to hell!'

After a minute the King said tentatively, 'You known Sean long?'

'He was in my squadron,' Peter Marlowe said at length, 'and I was sort of detailed to look after him. Got to know him very well.' He flicked the burning end of his cigarette and put the remains of tobacco back in his box. 'In fact he was my best friend. He was a very good pilot.' He looked at the King. 'I liked him a lot.'

'Was—was he like that before?'

'No.'

'Oh, I know he didn't dress like a woman all the time, but hell, it must have been obvious that he was that way.'

'Sean was never that way. He was just a very handsome, gentle chap. There was nothing effeminate about him, just a sort of . . . compassion.'

'You ever seen him without clothes on?'

'No.'

'That figures. No one else has either. Even half naked.'

Sean was allowed a tiny little room up in the theatre, a private room, which no one else in the whole of Changi had, not even the King. But Sean never slept in the room. The thought of Sean alone in a room with a lock on the door was too dangerous, because there were many in the camp whose lust swept out, and the rest were full of lust inside. So Sean always slept in one of the huts, but changed and showered in the private room.

'What's between you two?' the King asked.

'I nearly killed him. Once.'

Suddenly the conversation ceased and both men listened intently. All they could hear was a sigh, an undercurrent. The King looked around quickly. Seeing nothing extraordinary, he got up and climbed through the window, Peter Marlowe close behind. The men in the hut were listening too.

The King peered towards the corner of the jail. Nothing seemed to be wrong. Men still walked up and down.

'What do you think?' the King asked softly.

'Don't know,' said Peter Marlowe, concentrating. Men were still walking by the jail, but now an almost imperceptible quickening had been added to their walk.

'Hey, look,' Tex whispered.

Rounding the corner of the jail and heading up the slope towards them was Captain Brough. Then other officers began to appear behind him, all heading for various enlisted men's huts.

'Got to mean trouble,' Tex said sourly.

'Maybe it's a search,' Max said.

The King was on his knees in an instant, unlocking the black box. Peter Marlowe said hurriedly, 'I'll see you later.'

'Here,' the King said, throwing him a pack of Kooas, 'see you tonight if you like.'

Peter Marlowe raced out of the hut and down the slope. The King jerked out the three watches that were buried in the coffee beans and got up. He thought a moment, then he stood on his chair and stuffed the three watches into the atap thatch. He knew that all the men had seen the new hiding place but he did not care, for that could not be helped now. Then he locked the black box and Brough was at the door.

'All right, you guys, outside.'

IV

Peter Marlowe was thinking of nothing except his water bottle as he shoved through the sweating hive of men forming up on the asphalt road. He tried desperately to remember if he had filled the bottle, but he could not remember for sure.

He ran up the stairs from the street towards his hut. But the hut was already empty and a soiled Korean guard already stood in the doorway. Peter Marlowe knew that he would not be allowed to pass, so he turned back and ducked under the lee of the hut and up the other side. He ran for the other door and was beside his bunk with his water bottle in his hand before the guard saw him.

The Korean swore at him sullenly and walked over and motioned for him to put the water bottle back. But Peter Marlowe saluted with a flourish and said in Malay, which most of the guards understood, 'Greetings, sir. We may have a long time to wait, and I beg thee, let me take my water bottle with me, for I have dysentery.' As he spoke he shook the bottle. It was full.

The guard jerked the bottle out of his hands and sniffed it suspiciously. Then he poured some of the water onto the floor and shoved the bottle back at Peter Marlowe and cursed him again and pointed at the men on parade below.

Peter Marlowe bowed, weak with relief, and ran to join his group in line.

'Where the hell have you been, Peter?' Spence asked, dysentery pain adding to his anxiety.

'Never mind, I'm here.' Now that Peter Marlowe had his

60

water bottle he was giddy. 'Come on, Spence, get the bods lined up,' he said, needling him.

'Go to hell. Come on you chaps, get into line.' Spence counted the men and then said, 'Where's Bones?'

'In hospital,' Ewart said. 'Went just after breakfast. I took him myself.'

'Why the hell didn't you tell me before?'

'I've been working in the gardens all day, for Christ sake! Pick on someone else!'

'Keep your blasted shirt on!'

But Peter Marlowe wasn't listening to the curses and chatter and rumours. He hoped that the colonel and Mac had their water bottles too.

When his group was accounted for, Captain Spence walked along the road to Lieutenant-Colonel Sellars, who was in nominal charge of four huts, and saluted. 'Sixty-four, all correct, sir. Nineteen here, twenty-three in hospital, twenty-two on work parties.'

'All right, Spence.'

And as soon as Sellars had all the numbers from his four huts, he totalled them and took them up the line to Colonel Smedly-Taylor, who was responsible for ten huts. Then Smedly-Taylor took them up the line. Then the next officer took them up the line, and this procedure was repeated throughout the camp, inside and outside the jail, until totals were given to the Camp Commandant. The Camp Commandant added the figures of men inside the camp to the number of men in hospital and the number of men on work parties, and then he passed the totals over to Captain Yoshima, the Japanese interpreter. Yoshima cursed the Camp Commandant because the total was one short.

There was an aching hour of panic until the missing body was found in the cemetery. Colonel Dr. Rofer, RAMS, cursed his assistant Colonel Dr. Kennedy, who tried to explain that it was difficult to keep a tally to the instant, and Colonel Rofer cursed him anyway and said that that was his job. Then Rofer apologetically went to the Camp Commandant, who cursed his inefficiency, and then the Camp Commandant went to Yoshima and tried to explain politely that the body had been found but it was difficult to keep numbers accurate to the second. And

Yoshima cursed the Camp Commandant for inefficiency and told him that he was responsible—if he couldn't keep a simple number perhaps it was about time another officer took charge of the camp.

While the anger sped up and down the line, Korean guards were searching the huts, particularly the officers' huts. Here would be the radio they sought. The link, the hope of the men. They wanted to find the radio as they had found the one five months ago. But the guards sweltered as the men on parade sweltered, and their search was perfunctory.

The men sweated and cursed. A few fainted. The dysenteric streamed to the latrines. Those who were very sick squatted where they were or lay where they were and let the pain swirl and consummate. The fit did not notice the stench. The stench was normal and the stream was normal and the waiting was normal.

After three hours the search was completed. The men were dismissed. They swarmed for their huts and the shade, or lay on their beds gasping, or went to the showers and waited and fumed until the water cooled the ache from their heads.

Peter Marlowe walked out of the shower. He wrapped his sarong around his waist and went to the concrete bungalow of his friends, his unit.

'Puki 'mahlu!' Mac grinned. Major McCoy was a tough little Scot who carried himself neatly erect. Twenty-five years in the Malayan jungles had etched his face deeply—that and hard liquor and hard playing and bouts of fever.

''Mahlu senderis,' Peter Marlowe said, squatting happily. The Malay obscenity always delighted him. It had no absolute translation into English, though 'puki' was a four-letter part of a woman and ''mahlu' meant 'ashamed'.

'Can't you bastards speak the King's English for once?' Colonel Larkin said. He was lying on his mattress, which was on the floor. Larkin was short of breath from the heat and his head ached with the aftermath of malaria.

Mac winked at Peter Marlowe. 'We keep explaining and nothing can get through the thickness of his head. There's nae hope for the colonel!'

'Too right, cobber,' Peter Marlowe said, aping Larkin's Australian accent.'

'Why the hell I ever got in with you two,' Larkin groaned wearily, 'I'll never know.'

Mac grinned. 'Because he's lazy, eh, Peter? You and I do all the work, eh? An' he sits and pretends to be bedridden—just because he's a wee touch of malaria.'

'Puki 'mahlu. And get me some water, Marlowe!'

'Yes, sir, Colonel sir!' He gave Larkin his water bottle. When Larkin saw it he smiled through his pain.

'All right, Peter boy?' he asked quietly.

'Yes. My God, I was in a bit of a panic for a time.'

'Mac and me both.'

Larkin sipped the water and carefully handed the water bottle back.

'All right, Colonel?' Peter Marlowe was perturbed by Larkin's colour.

'My bloody oath,' Larkin said. 'Nothing a bottle of beer couldn't cure. Be all right tomorrow.'

Peter Marlowe nodded. 'At least you're over the fever,' he said. Then he took out the pack of Kooas with studied negligence.

'My God,' said Mac and Larkin in one breath.

Peter Marlowe broke the pack and gave them each a cigarette. 'Present from Father Christmas!'

'Where the hell you get them, Peter?'

'Wait till we've smoked them a bitty,' Mac said sourly, 'before we hear the bad news. He's probably sold our beds or something.'

Peter Marlowe told them about the King and about Grey. They listened with growing astonishment. He told them about the tobacco-curing process and they listened silently until he mentioned the percentages.

'Sixty-forty!' exploded Mac delightedly. 'Sixty-forty, oh my God!'

'Yes,' said Peter Marlowe, misreading Mac. 'Imagine that! Anyway, I just showed him how to do it. He seemed surprised when I wouldn't take anything in return.'

'You gave the process away?' Mac was appalled.

'Of course. Anything wrong, Mac?'

'Why?'

'Well, I couldn't go into business. Marlowes aren't tradesmen,' Peter Marlowe, said, as though talking to a child. 'It's just not done, old boy.'

'My God, you get a wonderful opportunity to make some money and you turn it down with a big fat sneer. I suppose you know that with the King behind the deal, you could have made enough to buy double rations from now until doomsday. Why the hell didn't you keep your mouth shut and tell me and let me make—'

'What are you talking about, Mac?' Larkin interrupted sharply. 'The boy did all right, and it would have been bad for him to go into business with the King.'

'But—'

'But nothing,' Larkin said.

Mac simmered down immediately, hating himself for his outburst. He forced a nervous laugh. 'Just teasing, Peter.'

'Are you sure, Mac? My God,' said Peter Marlowe unhappily. 'Have I been a fool or something? I wouldn't want to let the side down.'

'Nay, laddie, it was just my way of joking. Go on, tell us what else happened.'

Peter Marlowe told them what had happened and all the time he wondered if he had done something wrong. Mac was his best friend, and shrewd, and never lost his temper. He told them about Sean, and when he had finished he felt better. Then he left. It was his turn to feed the chickens.

When he had gone Mac said to Larkin, 'Dammit—I'm sorry. I'd no cause to fly off the handle like that.'

'Don't blame you, cobber. He's got his head in the sky. That boy's got some strange ideas. But you never can tell. Maybe the King'll have his uses yet.'

'Ay,' said Mac thoughtfully.

Peter Marlowe carried a billycan filled with scraps of leaves that had been foraged. He walked past the latrine area until he came to the runs where the camp chickens were kept.

There were big runs and small runs, runs for one scraggy hen and a huge run for one hundred and thirty hens—those that were owned by the whole camp, whose eggs went into the common pool. The other runs were owned by units, or a commune of units who had pooled their resources. Only the King owned alone.

Mac had built the chicken run for Peter Marlowe's unit. In it were three hens, the wealth of the unit. Larkin had bought the hens seven months ago when the unit had sold the last thing it possessed, Larkin's gold wedding ring. Larkin had not wanted to sell it, but Mac was sick at the time and Peter Marlowe had dysentery, and two weeks earlier the camp rations had been cut again, so Larkin sold it. But not through the King. Through one of his own men, Tiny Timse, the Aussie trader. With the money he had bought four hens through the Chinese trader who had the camp concessions from the Japanese, and along with the hens, two cans of sardines, two cans of condensed milk and a pint of orange-coloured palm oil.

The hens were good and laid their eggs on time. But one of them died and the men ate it. They saved the bones and put them into a pot with the entrails and feet and head and the green papaya that Mac had stolen on a work party and made a stew. For a whole week their bodies had felt huge and clean.

Larkin had opened one can of the condensed milk on the day they had bought it. They each had a spoonful as long as it lasted, once a day. The condensed milk did not spoil from the heat. On the day that there was no more to spoon, they boiled the can and drank the liquor. It was very good.

The two cans of sardines and the last can of condensed milk were the unit's reserve. Against a very bad run of luck. The cans were kept in a cache, which was constantly guarded by one of the unit.

Peter Marlowe looked around before he opened the lock on the chicken coop and made sure there was no one near who could see how the lock worked. He opened the door and saw two eggs.

'All right, Nonya,' he said to their prize hen, 'I'm not going to touch you.'

Nonya was sitting on a nest of seven eggs. It had taken a great amount of will for the unit to let the eggs remain beneath her, but if they were lucky and got seven chicks, and if the seven chicks lived to become hens or cocks, then their herd would be vast. Then they could spare one of the hens to sit permanently on a clutch. And they would never have to fear Ward Six.

Ward Six housed the sightless, the men blinded by beri-beri. Any vitamin strength was magic against this constant threat, and eggs were a vast source of strength, usually the only one available. Thus it was that the Camp Commandant begged and cursed and demanded more from the Overlord. But most of the time there was only one egg per man per week. Some of the men received an extra one every day, but by then it was usually too late.

Thus it was that the chickens were guarded day and night by an officer guard. Thus it was that to touch a chicken belonging to the camp, or to another, was a vast crime. Once a man had been caught with a strangled hen in his hand, and had been beaten to death by his captors. The authorities ruled it was justifiable homicide.

Peter Marlowe stood at the end of his run admiring the King's hens. There were seven, plump and giants against all others. There was a cock within the run, the pride of the camp. His name was Sunset. His sperm grew fine sons and daughters and he could be had for stud by any. At a price: choice of litter.

Even the King's hens were inviolate and guarded like the others.

Peter Marlowe watched Sunset nail a hen into the dust and mount her. The hen picked herself off the dust and ran about clucking and pecked another hen for good measure. Peter Marlowe despised himself for watching. He knew it was weakness. He knew he would think of N'ai and then his loins would ache.

He went back to the henhouse and checked to see that the lock was tight and left, holding the two eggs carefully all the way back to the bungalow.

'Peter, mon,' Mac grinned, 'this is our lucky day!'

Peter Marlowe found the pack of Kooas and divided them into three piles. 'We'll draw for the other two.'

'You take them, Peter,' Larkin said.

'No we'll draw for them. Low card loses.'

Mac lost and pretended sourness. 'Bad cess to it,' he said.

They carefully opened the cigarettes and put the tobacco in their boxes and mixed it with as much of the treated Java weed as they had. Then they split up their portions into four, and put the other three portions into another box and gave the boxes into Larkin's keeping. To have so much tobacco at one time was a temptation.

Abruptly the heavens split and the deluge began.

Peter Marlowe took off his sarong, folded it carefully and put it on Mac's bed.

Larkin said thoughtfully, 'Peter. Watch your step with the King. He could be dangerous.'

'Of course. Don't worry.' Peter Marlowe stepped out into the cloudburst. In a moment Mac and Larkin had stripped and followed him, joining the other naked men glorying in the torrent.

Their bodies welcomed the sting, lungs breathed the cooled air, heads cleared.

And the stench of Changi was washed away.

V

After the rain the men sat enjoying the fleeting coolness, waiting until it was time to eat. Water dripped from the thatch and gushed in the storm ditches, and the dust was mud. But the sun was proud in the white blue sky.

'God,' said Larkin gratefully, 'that feels better.'

'Ay,' said Mac as they sat on the veranda. But Mac's mind was up country, at his rubber plantation in Kedah, far to the north. 'The heat's more than worthwhile—makes you appreciate the coolness,' he said quietly. 'Like fever.'

'Malaya's stinking, the rain's stinking, the heat's stinking, malaria's stinking, the bugs're stinking and the flies're stinking,' Larkin said.

'Not in peacetime, mon.' Mac winked at Peter Marlowe. 'Nor in a village, eh, Peter boy?'

Peter Marlowe grinned. He had told them most of the things about his village. He knew that what he had not told them, Mac would know, for Mac had lived his adult life in the Orient and he loved it as much as Larkin hated it. 'So I understand,' he said blandly and they all smiled.

They did not talk much. All the stories had been told and retold, all the stories that they wanted to tell.

So they waited patiently. When it was time, they went to their respective lines and then returned to the bungalow. They drank their soup quickly. Peter Marlowe plugged in the home-made electric hot plate and fried one egg. They put their portions of rice into the bowl and he laid the egg on the rice with

68

a little salt and pepper. He whipped it so that the yolk and white were spread evenly throughout the rice, then divided it up and they ate it with relish.

When they had finished, Larkin took the plates and washed them, for it was his turn, and they sat once more on the veranda to wait for the dusk roll call.

Peter Marlowe was idly watching the men walk the street, enjoying the fullness in his stomach, when he saw Grey approaching.

'Good evening, Colonel,' Grey said to Larkin, saluting neatly.

''Evening Grey,' Larkin sighed. 'Who's in this time?' When Grey came to see him it always meant trouble.

Grey looked down at Peter Marlowe. Larkin and Mac sensed the hostility between them.

'Colonel Smedly-Taylor asked me to tell you, sir,' Grey said. 'Two of your men were fighting. A Corporal Townsend and Private Gurble. I've got them in jail now.'

'All right, Lieutenant,' Larkin said dourly. 'You can release them. Tell them to report to me here, after roll call. I'll give them what for!' He paused. 'You know what they were fighting about?'

'No, sir. But I think it was two-up.' Ridiculous game, thought Grey. Put two pennies on a stick and throw the coins up into the air and bet on whether the coins come down both heads, or both tails, or one head and one tail.

'You're probably right,' Larkin grunted.

'Perhaps you could outlaw the game. There's always trouble when—'

'Outlaw two-up?' Larkin interrupted abruptly. 'If I did that, they'd think I'd gone mad. They'd pay no attention to such a ridiculous order and quite right. Gambling's part of Aussie make-up, you ought to know that by now. Two-up gives the Diggers something to think about, and fighting once in a while isn't bad either.' He got up and stretched the ague from his shoulders. 'Gambling's like breathing to an Aussie. Why, everyone Down Under has a shilling or two on the Golden Casket.' His voice was edged. 'I like a game of two-up once in a while myself.'

'Yes, sir,' Grey said. He had seen Larkin and other Aussie

officers with their men, scrambling in the dirt, excited and foul-mouthed as any ranker.

'Tell Colonel Smedly-Taylor I'll deal with them. My bloody oath!'

'Pity about Marlowe's lighter, wasn't it, sir,' Grey said, watching Larkin intently.

Larkin's eyes were steady and suddenly hard. 'He should've been more careful. Shouldn't he?'

'Yes, sir,' Grey said, after enough of a pause to make his point. Well, he thought, it was worth trying. To hell with Larkin and to hell with Marlowe, there's plenty of time. He was just about to salute and leave when a fantastic thought rocked him. He controlled his excitement and said matter-of-factly, 'Oh, by the way, sir. There's a rumour going the rounds that one of the Aussies has a diamond ring.' He let the statement linger. 'Do you happen to know about it?'

Larkin's eyes were deepset under bushy eyebrows. He glanced thoughtfully at Mac before he answered. 'I've heard the rumours too. As far as I know it isn't one of my men. Why?'

'Just checking, sir,' Grey said with a hard smile. 'Of course, you'd know that such a ring could be dynamite. For its owner and a lot of people.' Then he added, 'It would be better under lock and key.'

'I don't think so, old boy,' Peter Marlowe said, and the 'old boy' was discreetly vicious. 'That'd be the worst thing to do—*if* the diamond exists. Which I doubt. If it's in a known place then a lot of chaps'd want to look at it. And anyway the Japs'd lift it once they heard about it.'

Mac said thoughtfully, 'I agree.'

'It's better where it is. In limbo. Probably just another rumour,' Larkin said.

'I hope it is,' Grey said, sure now that his hunch had been right. 'But the rumour seems pretty strong.'

'It's not one of my men.' Larkin's mind was racing. Grey seemed to know something—who would it be? Who?

'Well, if you hear anything, sir, you might let me know.' Grey's eyes swooped over Peter Marlowe contemptuously. 'I like to stop trouble before it begins.' Then he saluted Larkin correctly and nodded to Mac and walked away.

There was a long thoughtful silence in the bungalow.

Larkin glanced at Mac. 'I wonder why he asked about that?'

'Ay,' said Mac, 'I wondered too. Did ye mark how his face lit up like a beacon?'

'Too right!' Larkin said, the lines on his face etched deeper than usual. 'Grey's right about one thing. A diamond could cost a lot of men a lot of blood.'

'It's only a rumour, Colonel,' Peter Marlowe said. 'No one could keep anything like that, this long. Impossible.'

'I hope you're right.' Larkin frowned. 'Hope to God one of my boys hasn't got it.'

Mac stretched. His head ached and he could feel a bout of fever on the way. Well, not for three days yet, he thought calmly. He had had so much fever that it was as much a part of life as breathing. Once every two months now. He remembered that he had been due to retire in 1942, doctor's orders. When malaria gets to your spleen—well, then home, old fellow, home to Scotland, home to the cold climate and buy the little farm near Killin overlooking the glory of Loch Tay. Then you may live.

'Ay,' Mac said tiredly, feeling his fifty years. Then he said aloud what they were all thinking. 'But if we ha' the wee devil stone, then we could last out the never-never with nae fear for the future. Nae fear at all.'

Larkin rolled a cigarette and lit it, taking a deep puff. He passed it to Mac, who smoked and passed it to Peter Marlowe. When they had almost finished it, Larkin knocked off the burning top and put the remains of tobacco back into his box. He broke the silence. 'Think I'll take a walk.'

Peter Marlowe smiled, 'Salamat,' he said, which meant 'Peace be upon thee.'

'Salamat,' Larkin said and went out into the sun.

As Grey walked up the slope towards the MP hut, his brain churned with excitement. He promised himself that as soon as he got to the hut and released the Australians he would roll a cigarette to celebrate. His second today, even though he had only enough Java weed for three more cigarettes until payday the next week.

He strode up the steps and nodded at Sergeant Masters. 'You can let 'em out!'

Masters took away the heavy bar from the door of the

bamboo cage and the two sullen men stood to attention in front of Grey.

'You're both to report to Colonel Larkin after roll call.'

The two men saluted and left.

'Damn troublemakers,' said Grey shortly.

He sat down and took out his box and papers. This month he had been extravagant. He had bought the whole page of Bible paper, which made the best cigarettes. Though he was not a religious man, it still seemed a little blasphemous to smoke the Bible. Grey read the scripture on the fragment he was preparing to roll: 'So Satan went forth from the presence of the Lord and smote Job with sore boils from the sole of his foot unto his crown. And he took him a potsherd to scrape himself withal; and he sat down among the ashes. And then his wife said . . .'

Wife! Why the hell did I have to come across that word? Grey cursed and turned the paper over.

The first sentence on the other side was: 'Why died I not from the womb? Why did I not give up the ghost when I came out of the belly?'

Grey jerked upright as a stone hissed through the window, smashed against a wall and clattered to the floor.

A piece of newpaper was wrapped round the stone. Grey picked it up and darted to the window. But there was no one near. Grey sat down and smoothed out the paper. On the edge of it was written: *Make you a deal. I'll deliver the King on a plate—if you'll close your eyes when I trade a little in his place when you got him. If it's a deal, stand outside the hut for a minute with this stone in your left hand. Then get rid of the other cop. Guys say you're an honest cop so I'll trust you.*

'What's it say, sir?' Masters asked, staring rheumy-eyed at the paper.

Grey crumpled the paper into a ball. 'Someone thinks we work too hard for the Japs,' he said harshly.

'Bloody bastard.' Masters went to the window. 'What the hell they think'd happen if we didn't enforce discipline? The buggers'd be at each other's throats all day long.'

'That's right,' said Grey. The ball of paper felt animated in his hand. If this is a real offer, he thought, the King can be felled.

It was no easy decision to make. He would have to keep his side of the bargain. His word was his bond; he was an honest 'cop', and not a little proud of his reputation. Grey knew that he would do anything to see the King behind the bamboo cage, stripped of his finery—even close his eyes a little to a breaking of the rules. He wondered which of the Americans could be the informer. All of them hated the King, envied him—but who would play Judas, who would risk the consequences if he were to be discovered? Whoever the man was, he could never be such a menace as the King.

So he walked outside with the stone in his left hand and scrutinized the men who passed. But no one gave him a sign.

He threw the stone away and dismissed Masters. Then he sat in the hut and waited. He had given up hope when another rock sailed through the window with the second message attached: *Check a can that's in the ditch by Hut Sixteen. Twice a day, mornings and after roll call. That'll be our go-between. He's trading with Turasan tonight.*

VI

That night Larkin lay on his mattress under his mosquito net gravely concerned about Corporal Townsend and Private Gurble. He had seen them after roll call.

'What the hell were you two fighting about?' he had asked repeatedly, and each time they had both replied sullenly, 'Two-up.' But Larkin had known instinctively that they were lying.

'I want the truth,' he had said angrily. 'Come on, you two are cobbers. Now why were you fighting?'

But the two men had kept their eyes obstinately on the ground. Larkin had questioned them individually, but each in his turn scowled and said, 'Two-up.'

'All right, you bastards,' Larkin had said finally, his voice harsh. 'I'll give you one last chance. If you don't tell me, then I'll transfer you both out of my regiment. And as far as I'm concerned you won't exist!'

'But Colonel,' Gurble gasped. 'You wouldn't do that!'

'I'll give you thirty seconds,' Larkin said venomously, meaning it. And the men knew that he meant it. And they knew that Larkin's word was law in his regiment, for Larkin was like their father. To get shipped out would mean that they would not exist to their cobbers, and without their cobbers, they'd die.

Larkin waited a minute. Then he said, 'All right. Tomorrow—'

'I'll tell you, Colonel,' Gurble blurted. 'This bloody sod accused me of stealing my cobbers' food. The bloody sod said I was stealing—'

74

'An' you were, you rotten bastard!'

Only Larkin's snarl 'Stand to attention' kept them from tearing each other's throats out.

Corporal Townsend told his side of the story first. 'It's my month on the cookhouse detail. Today we've a hundred and eighty-eight to cook for—'

'Who's missing?' Larkin asked.

'Billy Donahy, sir. He went to hospital this a'ernoon.'

'All right.'

'Well, sir. A hundred and eighty-eight men at a hundred and twenty-five grams of rice a day works out at twenty-three and a half kilos. I always go up to the storehouse myself with a cobber and see the rice weighed and then I carry it back to make sure we got our bloody share. Well, today I was watching the weighing when the gut rot hit me. So I asked Gurble here to carry it back to the cookhouse. He's my best cobber so I thought I could trust him—'

'I didn't touch a bloody grain, you bastard. I swear to God—'

'We were short when I got back!' Townsend shouted. 'Near half a pound short and that's two men's rations!'

'I know, but I didn't—'

'The weights weren't wrong. I checked 'em under your bloody nose!'

Larkin went with the men and checked the weights and found them true. There was no doubt that the correct amount of rice had started down the hill, for the rations were weighed publicly every morning by Lieutenant-Colonel Jones. There was only one answer.

'As far as I'm concerned, Gurble,' Larkin said, 'you're out of my regiment. You're dead.'

Gurble stumbled away into the darkness, whimpering, and then Larkin said to Townsend, 'You keep your mouth shut about this.'

'My bloody oath, Colonel,' Townsend said. 'The Diggers'd tear him to pieces if they heard. An' rightly! Only reason I didn't tell them was that he was my best cobber.' His eyes suddenly filled with tears. 'My bloody oath, Colonel, we joined up together. We've been with you through Dunkirk an' the stinking Middle East, and all through Malaya. I've known him most of my life and I'd've bet my life—'

75

Now, thinking about it all again in the twilight of sleep, Larkin shuddered. How can a man do such a thing? He asked himself, helplessly. How? Gurble of all men, whom he had known for many years, who even used to work in his office in Sydney!

He closed his eyes and put Gurble out of his mind. He had done his duty and it was his duty to protect the many. He let his mind drift to his wife Betty cooking steak with a fried egg on top, to his home overlooking the bay, to his little daughter, to the time he was going to have afterwards. But when? When?

Grey walked quietly up the steps of Hut Sixteen like a thief in the night and headed for his bed. He stripped off his pants and slipped under the mosquito net and lay naked on his mattress, very pleased with himself. He had just seen Turasan, the Korean guard, sneak around the corner of the American hut and under the canvas overhang; he had seen the King stealthily jump out of the window to join Turasan. Grey had waited only a moment in the shadows. He was checking the spy's information, and there was no need to pounce on the King yet. No. Not yet, now that the informer was proved.

Grey shifted on the bed, scratching his leg. His practised fingers caught the bedbug and crushed it. He heard it plop as it burst and he smelled the sick sweet stench of the blood it contained—his own blood.

Around his net, clouds of mosquitos buzzed, seeking the inevitable hole. Unlike most of the officers, Grey had refused to convert his bed to a bunk, for he hated the idea of sleeping above or below someone else. Even though the added doubling up meant more space.

The mosquito nets were hung from a wire which bisected the length of the hut. Even in sleep the men were attached to each other. When one man turned or tugged at the net to tuck it more tightly under the soaking mattress, all the nets would jiggle a little, and each man knew he was surrounded.

Grey crushed another bedbug, but his mind was not on it. Tonight he was filled with happiness—about the informer, about his commitment to get the King, about the diamond ring, about Marlowe. He was very pleased, for he had solved the riddle.

It was simple, he told himself again. Larkin knows who has the diamond. The King is the only one in the camp who could arrange the sale. Only the King's contacts are good enough. Larkin would not go himself directly to the King, so he sent Marlowe. Marlowe is to be the go-between.

Grey's bed shook as dead-sick Johnny Hawkins stumbled against it, half-awake, heading for the latrines. 'Be careful, for God's sake!' Grey said irritably.

'Sorry,' Johnny said, groping for the door.

In a few minutes Johnny stumbled back again. A few sleepy curses followed in his wake. As soon as Johnny had reached his bunk it was time to go again. This time Grey did not notice his bed shake, for he was locked in his mind, forecasting the probable moves of the enemy.

Peter Marlowe was wide awake, sitting on the hard steps of Hut Sixteen under the moonless sky, his eyes and ears and mind searching the darkness. From where he sat he could watch the two roads—the one that bisected the camp and the other that skirted the walls of the jail. Japanese and Korean guards and prisoners alike used both roads. Peter Marlowe was the north sentry.

Behind him, on the other steps, he knew that Flight Lieutenant Cox was concentrating as he was, seeking the darkness for danger. Cox guarded south.

East and west were not covered because Hut Sixteen could only be approached by north or south.

From inside the hut, and all around, were the noises of the sleeping-dead—moans, weird laughs, snores, whimpers, choked half-screams—mixed with the softness of whispers of the sleepless. It was a cool good night here on the bank above the road. All was normal.

Peter Marlowe jerked like a dog pointing. He had sensed the Korean guard before his eyes picked him out of the darkness, and by the time he really saw the guard, he had already given the warning signal.

At the far end of the hut, Dave Daven did not hear the first whistle, he was so absorbed in his work. When he heard the second, more urgent one, he answered it, jerked the needles out, lay back in his bunk, and held his breath.

The guard was slouching through the camp, his rifle on his shoulder, and he did not see Peter Marlowe or the others. But he felt their eyes. He quickened his step and wished himself out of the hatred.

After an age, Peter Marlowe heard Cox give the all-clear signal, and he relaxed once more but his senses still reached out into the night.

At the far corner of the hut, Daven began breathing again. He lifted himself carefully under the thick mosquito net in the top bunk. With infinite patience, he reconnected the two needles to the ends of the insulated wire that carried the live current. After a back-breaking search, he felt the needles slip through the worm-holes in the eight-by-eight beam which served as the head crosspiece of the bunk. A bead of sweat gathered on his chin and fell on the beam as he found the other two needles that were connected to the earphone and again, after a blind, tortured search, he felt the holes for them and slipped the needles cleanly into the beam. The earphone static'd into life. ' . . . and our forces are moving rapidly through the jungle to Mandalay. That ends the news. This is Calcutta calling. To summarise the news: American and British forces are pushing the enemy back in Belgium, and on the central sector, towards St. Hubert, in driving snowstorms. In Poland, Russian armies are within twenty miles of Krakow, also in heavy blizzards. In the Philippines, American forces have driven a bridgehead across the Agno River in their thrust for Manila. Formosa was bombed in daylight by American B-29's without loss. In Burma, victorious British and Indian armies are within thirty miles of Mandalay. The next news broadcast will be at 6 A.M. Calcutta time.'

Daven cleared his voice softly and felt the live insulated wire jerk slightly and then come free as Spence, in the next bunk, pulled his set of needles out of the source. Quickly Daven disconnected his four needles and put them back in his sewing kit. He wiped the gathering sweat off his face and scratched at the biting bedbugs. Then he unscrewed the wires on the earphone, tightened the terminals carefully, and slipped it into a special pouch in his jock-strap, behind his testicles. He buttoned his pants and doubled the wire and slipped it through the belt-loops and knotted it. He found the piece of rag and wiped his hands, then carefully brushed dust over the tiny holes in the beam, glogging them, hiding them perfectly.

He lay back on the bed for a moment to regain his strength, and scratched. When he had composed himself he ducked out of the net and jumped to the floor. At this time of night he never bothered to put his leg on, so he just found his crutches and quietly swung himself to the door. He made no sign as he passed Spence's bunk. That was the rule. Can't be too careful.

The crutches creaked, wood against wood, and for the ten millionth time Daven thought about his leg. It did not bother him too much nowadays, though the stump hurt like hell. The doctors had told him that soon he would have to have it re-stumped again. He had had this done twice already, once a real operation below the knee in '42, when he had been blown up by a land mine. Once above the knee, without anaesthetics. The memory edged his teeth and he swore he would never go through that again. But this next time, the last time, would not be too bad. They had anaesthetics here in Changi. It would be the last time because there was not much left to stump.

'Oh hello, Peter,' he said as he almost stumbled over him on the steps. 'Didn't see you.'

'Hello, Dave.'

'Nice night, isn't it?' Dave carefully swung himself down the steps. 'Bladder's playing up again.'

Peter Marlowe smiled. If Daven said that, it meant that the news was good. If he said, 'It's me for a leak,' that meant nothing was happening in the world. If he said, 'My guts are killing me tonight,' that meant a bad setback somewhere in the world. If he said, 'Hold my crutch a moment,' that meant a great victory.

Though Peter Marlowe would hear the news in detail tomorrow and learn it along with Spence and tell other huts, he liked to hear how things were going tonight. So he sat back and watched Daven as he crutched towards the urinal, liking him, respecting him.

Daven creaked to a halt. The urinal was made out of a bent piece of corrugated iron Daven watched his urine trickle and meander towards the low end, then cascade frothily from the rusted spout into the large drum, adding to the scum which collected on the surface of the liquid. He remembered that tomorrow was collection day. The container would be carried away and added to other containers and taken to the gardens. The liquor would be mixed with water, then the mixture would be ladled tenderly, cup by cup, onto the roots of plants cherished and guarded by the man who grew the camp's food. This fertilizer would make the green they ate greener.

Dave hated greens. But they were food and you had to eat.

A breeze chilled the sweat on his back and brought with it the tang of the sea, three miles away, three light-years of miles away.

Daven thought about how perfectly the radio was working. He felt very pleased with himself as he remembered how he had delicately lifted a thin strip off the top of the beam and scooped beneath it a hole six inches deep. How this had all been done in secret. How it had taken him five months to build the radio, working at night and the hour of dawn and sleeping by day. How the fit of the lid was so perfect that when dust was worked into the edges its outline could not be seen, even on close inspection. And how the needle holes also were invisible when the dust was in them.

The thought that he, Dave Daven, was the first in the camp to hear the news made him not a little proud. And unique. In spite of his leg. One day he would hear that the war was over. Not just the European war. Their war. The Pacific war. Because of him, the camp was linked with the outside, and he knew that the terror and the sweat and the heartache were worth it. Only he and Spence and Cox and Peter Marlowe and two English colonels knew where the radio actually was. That was wise, for the less in the know, the less the danger.

Of course there was danger. There were always prying eyes, eyes you could not necessarily trust. There was always the possibility of informers. Or of an involuntary leak.

When Daven got back to the doorway, Peter Marlowe had already returned to his bunk. Daven saw that Cox was still sitting on the far steps, but this was only usual, for it was a rule that the sentries did not both go at the same time. Daven's stump began to itch like hell, but not really the stump, only the foot that was not there. He clambered up into his bunk, closed his eyes and prayed. He always prayed before he slept. Then the dream would not come, the vivid picture of dear old Tom Cotton, the Aussie, who had been caught with the other radio and had marched off under guard to Outram Road Jail, his coolie hat cocked flamboyantly over one eye, raucously singing 'Waltzing Matilda', and the chorus had been 'Fug the Japs'. But in Daven's dream, it was he, not Tommy Cotton who went with the guards. *He went with them*, and *he* went in abject terror.

'Oh God,' Daven said deep within himself, 'give me the peace of Thy courage. I'm so frightened and such a coward.'

The King was doing the thing he liked most in the world. He was counting a stack of brand-new notes. Profit from a sale.

Turasan was politely holding his flashlight, the beam carefully dimmed and focused on the table. They were in the 'shop' as the King called it, just outside the American hut. Now from the canvas overhang, another piece of canvas fell neatly to the ground, screening the table and the benches from ever-present eyes. It was forbidden for guards and prisoners to trade, by Japanese—and therefore camp—order.

The King wore his 'outsmarted-in-a-deal' expression and counted grimly. 'Okay,' the King sighed finally as the notes totalled five hundred. 'Ichi-bon!'

Turasan nodded. He was a small squat man with a flat moon face and a mouthful of gold teeth. His rifle leaned carelessly against the hut wall behind him. He picked up the Parker fountain pen and re-examined it carefully. The white spot was there. The nib was gold. He held the pen closer to the screened light and squinted to make sure, once more that the *14 carat* was etched into the nib.

'Ichi-bon,' he grunted at length, and sucked air between his teeth. He too wore his 'outsmarted-in-a-deal' expression, and he hid his pleasure. At five hundred Japanese dollars the pen was an excellent buy and he knew it would easily bring double that from the Chinese in Singapore.

'You goddam ichi-bon trader,' the King said sullenly. 'Next week, ichi-bon watch maybe. But no goddam wong, no trade. I got to make some wong.'

'Too plenty wong,' Turasan said, nodding to the stack of notes. 'Watch soon maybe?'

'Maybe.'

Turasan offered his cigarettes. The King accepted one and let Turasan light it for him. Then Turasan sucked in his breath a last time and smiled his golden smile. He shouldered his rifle, bowed courteously and slipped away into the night.

The King beamed as he finished his smoke. A good night's work, he thought. Fifty bucks for the pen, a hundred and fifty to the man who faked the white spot and etched the nib: three hundred profit. That the colour would fade off the nib within a week didn't bother the King at all. He knew by that time Turasan would have sold it to a Chinese.

The King climbed through the window of his hut. 'Thanks, Max,' he said quietly, for most of the Americans in the hut were already asleep. 'Here, you can quit now.' He peeled off two ten-dollar bills. 'Give the other to Dino.' He did not usually pay his men so much for such a short work period. But tonight he was full of largess.

'Gee thanks,' Max hurried out and told Dino to relax, giving him a ten-dollar note.

The King set the coffeepot on the hot plate. He stripped off his clothes, hung up his pants and put his shirt, underpants and socks in the dirty-laundry bag. He slipped on a clean sun-bleached loincloth and ducked under his mosquito net.

While he waited for the water to boil, he indexed the day's work. First the Ronson. He had beaten Major Barry down to five hundred and fifty, less fifty-five dollars, which was his ten per cent commission, and had registered the lighter with Captain Brough as a 'win in poker'. It was worth at least nine hundred, easy, so that had been a good deal. The way inflation is going, he thought, it's wise to have the maximum amount of dough in merchandise.

The King had launched the treated tobacco enterprise with a sales conference. It had gone according to plan. All the Americans had volunteered as salesmen, and the King's Aussie and English contacts had bitched. But that was only normal. He had already arranged to buy twenty pounds of Java weed from Ah Lee, the Chinese who had the concession of the camp store, and he had got it at a good discount. An Aussie cookhouse had agreed to set one of their ovens aside daily for an hour, so the whole batch of tobacco could be cooked at one time under Tex's supervision. Since all the men were working on percentage, the King's only outlay was the cost of the tobacco. Tomorrow, the treated tobacco would be on sale. The way he had set it up, he would clear a hundred per cent profit. Which was only fair.

Now that the tobacco project was launched, the King was ready to tackle the diamond . . .

The hiss of the bubbling coffeepot interrupted his contemplations. He slipped from under the mosquito net and unlocked the black box. He put three heaped spoons of coffee in the water and added a pinch of salt. As the water frothed, he took it off the stove and waited until it had subsided.

The aroma of the coffee spilled through the hut, teasing the men still awake.

'Jesus,' Max said involuntarily.

'What's the matter, Max?' the King said. 'Can't you sleep?'

'No. Got too much on my mind. I been thinking. We can make one helluva deal outta that tobacco.'

Tex shifted uneasily, soaring with the aroma. 'That smell reminds me of wildcatting.'

'How come?' The King poured in cold water to settle the grounds, then put a heaped spoonful of sugar into his mug and filled it.

'Best part of drilling's in the mornings. After a long sweaty night's shift on the rig. When you set with your buddies over the first steaming pot of Java, about dawn.' An' the coffee's steamy hot and sweet, an' at the same time a bit bitter. An' maybe you look out through the maze of oil derricks at the sun rising over Texas.' There was a long sigh. 'Man, that's living.'

'I've never been to Texas,' the King said. 'Been all over but not Texas.'

'That's God's country.'

'You like a cup?'

'You know it.' Tex was there with his mug. The King poured himself a second cup. Then he gave Tex half a cup.

'Max?'

Max got half a cup too. He drank the coffee quickly. 'I'll fix this for you in the morning,' he said, taking the pot with its bed of grounds.

'Okay. 'Night, you guys.'

The King slipped under the net once more and made sure it was tight and neat under the mattress. Then he lay back gratefully between the sheets. Across the hut he saw Max add some water to the coffee grounds and set it beside the bunk to marinate. He knew that Max would rebrew the grounds for breakfast. Personally the King never liked rebrewed coffee. It was too bitter. But the boys said it was fine. If Max wanted to rebrew it, great, he thought agreeably. The King did not approve of waste.

He closed his eyes and turned his mind to the diamond. At last he knew who had it, how to get it, and now that luck had brought Peter Marlowe to him, he knew how the vastly complicated deal could be arranged.

Once you know a man, the King told himself contentedly, know his Achilles heel, you know how to play him, how to work him into your plans. Yep, his hunch had paid off when he had first seen Peter Marlowe squatting Woglike in the dirt, chatting Malay. You got to play hunches in this world.

Now, thinking about the talk he had had with Peter Marlowe after dusk roll call, the King felt the warmth of anticipation spread over him.

'Nothing happens in this lousy dump,' the King had said innocently as they sat in the lee of the hut under a moonless sky.

'That's right,' Peter Marlowe said. 'Sickening. One day's just like the rest. Enough to drive you around the bend.'

The King nodded. He squashed a mosquito. 'I know a guy who has all the excitement he can use, and then some.'

'Oh? What does he do?'

'He goes through the wire. At night.'

'My God. That's asking for trouble. He must be mad!'

But the King had seen the flicker of excitement in Peter Marlowe's eyes. He waited in silence, saying nothing.

'Why does he do it?'

'Most times, just for kicks.'

'You mean excitement?'

The King nodded.

Peter Marlowe whistled softly. 'I don't think I'd have that amount of nerve.'

'Sometimes this guy goes to the Malay village.'

Peter Marlowe looked out of the wire, seeing in his mind the village that they all knew existed on the coast three miles away. Once he had gone to the topmost cell in the jail and had clambered up to the tiny barred window. He had looked out

84

and seen the panorama of jungle and the village, nestling the coast. There were ships in the waters that day. Fishing ships, and enemy warships—big ones and little ones—set like islands in the glass of the sea. He had stared out, fascinated with the sea's closeness, hanging to the bars until his hands and arms were tired. After resting awhile he was going to jump up and look out again. But he did not look again. Ever. It hurt too much. He had always lived near the sea. Away from it, he felt lost. Now he was near it again. But it was beyond touch.

'Very dangerous to trust a whole village,' Peter Marlowe said.

'Not if you know them.'

'That's right. This man really goes to the village?'

'So he told me.'

'I don't think even Suliman would risk that.'

'Who?'

'Suliman. The Malay I was talking to. This afternoon.'

'It seems more like a month ago,' the King said.

'It does, doesn't it?'

'What the hell's a guy like Suliman doing in this dump? Why didn't he just take off when the war ended?'

'He was caught in Java. Suliman was a rubber tapper on Mac's plantation. Mac's one of my unit. Well, Mac's battalion, the Malayan Regiment, got out of Singapore and were sent to Java. When the war ended, Suliman had to stick with the battalion.'

'Hell, he could've got lost. There are millions of them in Java . . .'

'The Javanese would have recognized him instantly, and probably turned him in.'

'What about the co-prosperity sphere yak? You know, Asia for the asiatics?'

'I'm afraid that doesn't mean much. It didn't do the Javanese much good, either. Not if they didn't obey.'

'How do you mean?'

'In '42, autumn of '42, I was in a camp just outside Bandung,' Peter Marlowe said. 'That's up in the hills of Java, in the centre of the island. At that time there were a lot of Ambonese, Menadonese and a number of Javanese with us—men who were in the Dutch army. Well, the camp was tough on the

Javanese because many of them were from Bandung, and their wives and children were living just outside the wire. For a long time they used to slip out and spend the night, then get back into the camp before dawn. The camp was lightly guarded, so it was easy. Very dangerous for Europeans though, because the Javanese'd turn you over to the Japs and that'd be your lot. One day the Japs gave out an order that anyone caught outside would be shot. Of course the Javanese thought it applied to everyone except them—they had been told that in a couple of weeks they were all to go free anyway. One morning seven of them got caught. We were paraded the next day. The whole camp. The Javanese were put up against a wall and shot. Just like that, in front of us. The seven bodies were buried—with military honours—where they fell. Then the Japs made a little garden around the graves. They planted flowers and put a tiny white rope fence around the whole area and put up a sign in Malay, Japanese and English. It said, *These men died for their country*.'

'You're kidding!'

'No I'm not. But the funny thing about it was that the Japs posted an honour guard at the grave. After that, every Jap guard, every Jap officer who passed the 'shrine', saluted. Everyone. And at that time POW's had to get up and bow if a Jap private came within seeing distance. If you didn't you got the thick end of a rifle butt around your head.'

'Doesn't make sense. The garden and saluting.'

'It does to them. That's the Oriental mind. To them that's complete sense.'

'It sure as hell isn't. Nohow!'

'That's why I don't like them,' Peter Marlowe said thoughtfully. 'I'm afraid of them, because you've no yardstick to judge them. They don't react the way they should. Never.'

'I don't know about that. They know the value of a buck and you can trust them most times.'

'You mean in business?' Peter Marlowe laughed. 'Well, I don't know about that. But as far as the people themselves . . . Another thing I saw. In another camp in Java—they were always shifting us around there, not like in Singapore—it was also in Bandung. There was a Jap guard, one of the better ones. Didn't pick on you like most of them. Well, this man, we used to call him Sunny because he was always smiling. Sunny loved dogs. And he always had half a dozen with him as he went around the camp. His favourite was a sheepdog—a bitch. One day the bitch had a litter of puppies, the cutest dogs you ever saw, and Sunny was just about the happiest Jap in the whole world, training the puppies, laughing and playing with them. When they could walk he made leads for them out of string and he'd walk around the camp with them in tow. One day he was pulling the pups around—one of them sat on its haunches. You know how pups are, they get tired, and they just sit. So Sunny dragged it a little way, then gave it a real jerk. The pup yelped but stuck its feet in.'

Peter Marlowe paused and made a cigarette. Then he continued. 'Sunny took a firm grip on the string and started swinging the pup around his head on the end of the rope. He whirled it maybe a dozen times, laughing as though this was the greatest joke in the world. Then as the screaming pup gathered momentum, he gave it a final whirl and let go of the string. The pup must have gone fifty feet into the air. And when it fell on the iron-hard ground, it burst like a ripe tomato.'

'Bastard!'

After a moment Peter Marlowe said, 'Sunny went over to the pup. He looked down at it, then burst into tears. One of our chaps got a spade and buried the remains and, all the time, Sunny tore at himself with grief. When the grave was smoothed over, he brushed away his tears, gave the man a pack of cigarettes, cursed him for five minutes, angrily shoved the butt of the rifle in the man's groin, then bowed to the grave, bowed to the hurt man, and marched off, beaming happily, with the other pups and dogs.'

The King shook his head slowly. 'Maybe he was just crazy. Syphilitic.'

'No, Sunny wasn't. Japs seem to act like children—but they've men's bodies and men's strength. They just look at things as a child does. Their perspective is oblique—to us—and distorted.'

'I heard thing were rough in Java, after the capitulation,' the King said to keep him talking. It had taken him almost an hour to get Peter Marlowe started and he wanted him to feel at home.

'In some ways. Of course in Singapore there were over a

hundred thousand troops, so the Japs had to be a little careful. The chain of command still existed, and a lot of units were intact. The Japs were pressing hard in the drive to Australia, and didn't care too much so long as the POW's behaved themselves and got themselves organized into camps. Same thing in Sumatra and Java for a time. Their idea was to press on and take Australia, then we were all going to be sent down there as slaves.'

'You're crazy,' said the King.

'Oh no. A Jap officer told me after I was picked up. But when their drive was stopped in New Guinea, they started cleaning up their lines. In Java there weren't too many of us, so they could afford to be rough. They said we were without honour— the officers—because we had allowed ourselves to be captured. So they wouldn't consider us POW's. They cut off our hair and forbade us to wear officers' insignia. Eventually they allowed us to 'become' officers again, though they never allowed us back our hair.' Peter Marlowe smiled. 'How did you get here?'

'The usual foul-up. I was in an airstrip building outfit. In the Philippines. We had to get out of there in a hurry. The first ship we could get was heading here, so we took it. We figured Singapore'd be safe as Fort Knox. By the time we got here, the Japs were almost through Johore. There was a last-minute panic, and all the guys got on the last convoy out. Me, I thought that was a bad gamble, so I stayed. The convoy got blown out of the sea. I used my head—and I'm alive. Most times, only suckers get killed.'

'I don't think I would have had the wisdom not to go—if I had had the opportunity,' Peter Marlowe said.

'You got to look after number one, Peter. No one else does.'

Peter Marlowe thought about that for a long time. Snatches of conversation fled through the night. Occasionally a burst of anger. Whispers. The constant clouds of mosquitoes. From afar there was the mournful call of ship-horn to ship-horn. The palms, etched against the dark sy, rustled. A dead frond fell away from the crest of a palm and crashed to the jungle bed.

Peter Marlowe broke the silence. 'This friend of yours. He really goes to the village?'

The King looked into Peter Marlowe's eyes. 'You like to come?' he asked softly. 'The next time I go?'

A faint smile twisted Peter Marlowe's lips. 'Yes . . .'

A mosquito buzzed the King's ear with sudden crescendo. He jerked up, found his flashlight and searched the inside of the net. At length the mosquito settled on the curtain. Deftly, the King crushed it. Then he double-checked to make certain that there were no holes in the net, and lay back once again.

In a moment he dismissed all things from his mind. Sleep came quickly and peacefully to the King.

Peter Marlowe still lay awake on his bunk, scratching bedbug bites. Too many memories had been triggered by what the King had said . . .

He remembered the ship that had brought him and Mac and Larkin from Java a year ago.

The Japanese had ordered the Commandant of Bandung, one of the camps in Java, to provide a thousand men for a work party. The men were to be sent to another camp nearby for two weeks with good food—double rations—and cigarettes. Then they would be transferred to another place. Fine working conditions.

Many of the men had offered to go because of the two weeks. Some were ordered. Mac had volunteered himself, Larkin and Peter Marlowe. 'Never can tell, laddies,' he had reasoned when they had cursed him. 'If we can get to a wee island, well Peter and I know the language. Ay, an' the place cannot be worse than here.'

So they had decided to change the evil they knew for the evil that was to come.

The ship was a tiny tramp steamer. At the foot of the gangway there were many guards and two Japanese dressed in white with white face masks. On their backs were large containers, and in their hands, were spray guns which connected with the containers. All prisoners and their possessions were spray-sterilized against carrying Javanese microbes onto the clean ship.

In the small hold aft there were rats and lice and faeces, and there was a space twenty feet by twenty feet in the centre of the hold. Around the hold, joined to the hull of the ship from the deck to the ceiling, were five tiers of deep shelves. The height between the shelves was three feet, and their depth ten feet.

A Japanese sergeant showed the men how to sit in the shelves, cross-legged. Five men in column, then five men in column beside them, then five men in column beside them. Until all the shelves were packed.

When panic protests began, the sergeant said that this was the way Japanese soldiers were trans-shipped, and if this was good enough for the glorious Japanese Army, it was good enough for white scum. A revolver fled the first five men, gasping, into the claustrophic darkness, and the press of the men clambering down into the hold forced the others to get out of the the shoving mass into the shelves. They, in turn, were forced by others. Knee to knee, back to back, side to side. The spillover of men—almost a hundred—stood numbly in the small twenty-foot by twenty-foot area, blessing their luck that they were not in the shelves. The hatches were still off, and the sun poured down into the hold.

The sergeant led a second column which included Mac, Larkin, and Peter Marlowe to the fore hold and that too began to fill up.

When Mac got to the steamy bottom he gasped and fainted. Peter Marlowe and Larkin caught him, and above the din they fought and cursed their way back up the gangway to the deck. A guard tried to shove them back. Peter Marlowe shouted and begged and showed him Mac's quivering face. The guard shrugged and let them pass, nodding towards the bow.

Larkin and Peter Marlowe shoved and swore a space for Mac to lie down.

'What'll we do?' Peter Marlowe asked Larkin.

'I'll try and get a doctor.'

Mac's hand caught Larkin. 'Colonel.' His eyes opened a fraction and he whispered quickly, 'I'm all right. Had to get us out of there somehow. For Christ's sake look busy and don't be afraid if I pretend a fit.'

So they held on to Mac as he whimpered deliriously and fought and vomited the water they pressed to his lips. He kept it up until the ship cast off. Now even the decks of the ship were packed with men.

There was not enough space for all the men aboard to sit at the same time. But as there were lines to join—lines for water,

lines for rice, lines for the latrines—each man could sit part ᴏf
the time.

That night a squall lashed the ship for six hours. Those in the
hold tried to escape the vomit and those on deck tried to escape
the torrent.

The next day was calm under a sun-bleached sky. A man fell
overboard. Those on deck—men and guards—watched a long
time as he drowned in the wake of the ship. After that no one
else fell overboard.

On the second day three men were given to the sea. Some
Japanese guards fired their rifles to make the funeral more
military. The service was brief—there were lines to be joined.

The voyage lasted four days and five nights. For Mac and
Larkin and Peter Marlowe it was uneventful . . .

Peter Marlowe lay on his sodden mattress aching for sleep. But
his mind raced uncontrolled, dredging up terrors of the past
and fears of the future. And memories better not remembered.
Not now, not alone. Memories of her.

Dawn had already nudged the sky when at last he slept. But
even then his sleep was cruel.

VII

Days succeeded days, days in a monotony of days.

Then one night the King went to the camp hospital looking for Masters. He found him on the veranda of one of the huts. He was lying in a reeking bed, half conscious, his eyes staring at the atap wall.

'Hi, Masters,' the King said after he made sure that no one was listening. 'How do you feel?'

Masters stared up, not recognizing him. 'Feel?'

'Sure.'

A minute passed, then Masters mumbled, 'I don't know.' A trickle of saliva ran down his chin.

The King took out his tobacco box and filled the empty box which lay on the table beside the bed.

'Masters,' the King said. 'Thanks for sending me the tip.'

'Tip?'

'Telling me what you'd read on the piece of newspaper. I just wanted to thank you, give you some tobacco.'

Masters strained to remember. 'Oh! Not right for a mate to spy on a mate. Rotten, copper's nark!' And then he died.

Dr. Kennedy came over and pulled the coarse blanket neatly over Masters' head. 'Friend of yours?' he asked the King, his tired eyes frost under a mattress of shaggy eyebrows.

'In a way, Colonel.'

'He's lucky,' the doctor said. 'No more aches now.'

'That's one way of looking at it, sir,' the King said politely. He picked up the tobacco and put it back in his own box; Masters would not need it now. 'What'd he die of?'

'Lack of spirit.' The doctor stifled a yawn. His teeth were stained and dirty, and his hair lank and dirty, and his hands pink and spotless.

'You mean will to live?'

'That's one way of looking at it.' The doctor glowered up at the King. 'That's one thing you won't die of, isn't it?'

'Hell no. Sir.'

'What makes you so *invincible*?' Dr. Kennedy asked, hating this huge body which exuded health and strength.

'I don't follow you. Sir.'

'Why are you all right, and all the rest not?'

'I'm just lucky,' the King said and started to leave. But the doctor caught his shirt.

'It can't be just luck. It can't. Maybe you're the devil sent to try us further! You're a vampire and a cheat and a thief . . .'

'Listen, you. I've never thieved or cheated in my life and I won't take that from anyone.'

'Then just tell me how you do it? How? That's all I want to know. Don't you see? You're the answer for all of us. You're either good or evil and I want to know which you are.'

'You're crazy,' the King said, jerking his arm away.

'You can help us . . .'

'Help yourself. I'm worrying about me. You worry about you.' The King noticed how Dr. Kennedy's white coat hung away from his emaciated chest. 'Here,' he said, giving him the remains of a pack of Kooas. 'Have a cigarette. Good for the nerves. Sir.' He wheeled around and strode out, shuddering. He hated hospitals. He hated the stench and the sickness and the impotence of the doctors.

The King despised weakness. That doctor, he thought, he's for the big jump, the son of a bitch. Crazy guy like that won't last long. Like Masters, poor guy! Yet maybe Masters wasn't a poor guy—he was Masters and he was weak and therefore no goddamned good. The world was jungle, and the strong survived and the weak should die. It was you or the other guy. That's right. There is no other way.

Dr. Kennedy stared at the cigarettes blessing his luck. He lit one. His whole body drank the nicotine sweet. Then he went into the ward, over to Johnny Carstairs, DSO, Captain, 1st Tank Regiment, who was almost a corpse.

'Here,' he said, giving him the cigarette.

'What about you, Dr. Kennedy?'

'I don't smoke, never have.'

'You're lucky.' Johnny coughed as he took a puff, and a little blood came up with the phlegm. The strain of the cough contracted his bowels and blood-liquid gushed out of him, for his anus muscles had long since collapsed.

'Doc,' Johnny said. 'Put my boots on me, will you, please? I've got to get up.'

The old man looked all around. It was hard to see, for the ward's night light was dimmed and carefully screened.

'There aren't any,' he said, peering myopically back at Johnny as he sat on the edge of the bed.

'Oh. Well, that's that then.'

'What sort of boots were they?'

A thin rope of tears welled from Johnny's eyes. 'Kept those boots in good shape. Those boots marched me a lifetime. Only thing I had left.'

'Would you like another cigarette?'

'Just finishing, thanks.'

Johnny lay back in his own filth.

'Pity about my boots,' he said.

Dr. Kennedy sighed and took off his laceless boots and put them on Johnny's feet. 'I've got another pair,' he lied, then stood up barefoot, an ache in his back.

Johnny wriggled his toes enjoying the feel of the roughed leather. He tried to look at them but the effort was too much.

'I'm dying,' he said.

'Yes,' the doctor said. There was a time—was there ever a time?—when he would have forced his best bedside manner. No reason now.

'Pretty pointless, isn't it, Doc? Twenty-two years and nothing. From nothing, into nothing.'

An air current brought the promise of dawn into the ward.

'Thanks for the loan of your boots,' Johnny said. 'Something I always promised myself. A man's got to have boots.'

He died.

Dr. Kennedy took the boots off Johnny and put them back on his own feet. 'Orderly,' he called out as he saw one on the veranda.

'Yes, sir?' Steven said brightly, coming over to him, a pail of diarrhoea in his left hand.

'Get the corpse detail to take this one. Oh yes, and you can take Sergeant Masters' bed as well.'

'I simply can't do everything, Colonel,' Steven said, putting down the pail. 'I've got to get three bedpans for Bed Ten, Twenty-three and Forty-seven. And poor Colonel Hutton is so uncomfortable, I've just got to change his dressing.' Steven looked down at the bed and shook his head. 'Nothing but dead—'

'That's the job, Steven. The least we can do is bury them. And the quicker the better.'

'I suppose so. Poor boys.' Steven sighed and daintily patted the perspiration from his forehead with a clean handkerchief. Then he replaced the handkerchief in the pocket of his white medical overalls, picked up the pail, staggered a little under its weight, and walked out the door.

Dr. Kennedy despised him, despised his oily black hair, his shaven armpits and shaven legs. At the same time, he could not blame him. Homosexuality was one way to survive. Men fought over Steven, shared their rations with him, gave him cigarettes—all for the temporary use of his body. And what, the doctor asked himself, what's so disgusting about it anyway? When you think of 'normal sex', well, clinically it's just as disgusting.

His leathery hand absently scratched his scrotum, for the itch was bad tonight. Involuntarily he touched his sex. It was feelingless. Gristle.

He remembered that he had not had an erection for months. Well, he thought, it's only the low nutriment diet. Nothing to worry about. As soon as we get out and get regular food, then everything will be all right. A man of forty-three is still a man.

Steven came back with the corpse detail. The body was put on a stretcher and taken out. Steven changed the single blanket. In a moment another stretcher was carried in and the new patient helped into bed.

Automatically Dr. Kennedy took the man's pulse.

'The fever'll break tomorrow,' he said. 'Just malaria.'

'Yes, Doctor.' Steven looked up primly. 'Shall I give him some quinine?'

'Of course you give him quinine!'

'I'm sorry, Colonel,' Steven said tartly, tossing his head. 'I was just asking. Only doctors are supposed to authorize drugs.'

'Well, give him quinine and for the love of God, Steven, stop trying to pretend you're a blasted woman.'

'Well!' Steven's link bracelets jingled as he bridled and turned back to the patient. 'It's quite unfair to pick on a person, Dr. Kennedy, when one's trying to do one's best.'

Dr. Kennedy would have ripped into Steven, but at that moment Dr. Prudhomme walked into the ward.

'Evening, Colonel.'

'Oh, hello.' Dr. Kennedy turned to him thankfully, realizing it would have been stupid to tear into Steven. 'Everything all right?'

'Yes. Can I see you a moment?'

'Certainly.'

Prudhomme was a small serene man—pigeon-chested—his hands stained with years of chemicals. His voice was deep and gentle. 'There are two appendices for tomorrow. One's just arrived in Emergency.'

'All right. I'll see them before I go off.'

'Do you want to operate?' Prudhomme glanced at the far end of the ward, where Steven was holding a bowl for a man to vomit into.

'Yes. Give me something to do,' Kennedy said. He peered into the dark corner. In the half light of the shielded electric lamp Steven's long slim legs were accentuated. So was the curve of his buttocks straining against his tight short pants.

Feeling their scrutiny, Steven looked up. He smiled. 'Good evening, Dr. Prudhomme.'

'Hello, Steven,' Prudhomme said gently.

Dr. Kennedy saw to his dismay that Prudhomme was still looking at Steven.

Prudhomme turned back to Kennedy and observed his shock and loathing. 'Oh, by the way, I finished the autopsy on that man who was found in the borehole. Death from suffocation,' he said agreeably.

'If you find a man head first halfway down a borehole, it's more than likely that death will be due to suffocation.'

96

'True, Doctor,' Prudhomme said lightly. 'I wrote on the death certificate "Suicide while the balance of his mind was disturbed".'

'Have they identified the body?'

'Oh yes. This afternoon. It was an Australian. A man called Gurble.'

Dr. Kennedy rubbed his face. 'Not the way I'd commit suicide. Ghastly.'

Prudhomme nodded and his eyes strayed back to Steven. 'I quite agree. Of course, he might have been put into the borehole.'

'Were there any marks on the body?'

'None.'

Dr. Kennedy tried to stop noticing the way Prudhomme looked at Steven. 'Oh well, murder or suicide, it's a horrible way. Horrible! I suppose we'll never know which it was.'

'They held a quiet court of inquiry this afternoon, as soon as they knew who it was. Apparently a few days ago this man was caught stealing some hut rations.'

'Oh! I see.'

'Either way, I'd say he deserved it, wouldn't you?'

'I suppose so.' Dr. Kennedy wanted to continue the conversation, for he was lonely, but he saw that Prudhomme was interested only in Steven.

'Well,' he said, 'I'd better make my rounds. Would you like to come along?'

'Thanks, but I have to prepare the patients for operation.'

As Dr. Kennedy left the ward, from the corner of his eye he saw Steven brush past Prudhomme and he saw Prudhomme's furtive caress. He heard Steven's laugh and saw him return the caress openly and intimately.

Their obscenity overwhelmed him and he knew that he should go back into the ward and order them apart and court-martial them. But he was too tired, so he just walked to the far end of the veranda.

The air was still, the night dark and leafless, the moon like a giant arc light hanging from the rafters of the heavens. Men still walked the path, but they were all silent. Everything was awaiting the coming of dawn.

Kennedy looked up into the stars, trying to read from them

an answer to his constant question. When, oh God, when will this nightmare end?

But there was no answer.

Peter Marlowe was at the officer's latrine enjoying the beauty of a false dawn and the beauty of a contented bowel movement. The first was frequent, the second rare.

He always picked the back row when he came to the latrines, partly because he still hated to relieve himself in the open, partly because he hated anyone behind him, and partly because it was entertaining to watch others.

The boreholes were twenty-five feet deep and two feet in diameter and six feet apart. Twenty rows heading down the slope, thirty to a row. Each had a wooden cover and a loose lid.

In the centre of the area was a single throne made out of wood. A conventional one-holer. This was the prerogative of colonels. Everyone else had to squat, native style, feet either side of the hole. There were no screens of any sort and the whole area was open to the sky and camp.

Seated in lonely splendour on the throne was Colonel Samson. He was naked but for his tattered coolie hat. He always wore his hat, a quirk with him. Except when he was shaving his head or massaging it or rubbing in coconut oil or weird ointments to recover his hair. He had caught some unknown disease and all his head hair had fallen out one day—eyebrows and lashes too. The rest of him was furry as a monkey.

Other men were dotted around the area, each as far from the next man as possible. Each with a bottle of water. Each waving at the constant swarming flies.

Peter Marlowe told himself again that a squatting naked man relieving himself is the ugliest creature in the world—perhaps the most pathetic.

As yet there was only the promise of day, a lightening haze, fingers of gold spreading the velvet sky. The earth was cool, for the rains had come in the night, and the breeze was cool and delicate with sea-salt and frangipani.

Yes, Peter Marlowe thought contentedly, it's going to be a good day.

When he had finished, he tilted the bottle of water while he still squatted and washed away the traces of faeces, deftly using the fingers of his left hand. Always the left. The right is the eating hand. The natives have no word for left hand or right hand, only dung hand and eating hand. And all men used water, for paper, any paper, was too valuable. Except the King. He had real toilet paper. *He* had given Peter Marlowe a piece and Peter Marlowe had shared it amongst the unit, for it made superb cigarette paper.

Peter Marlowe stood up and retied his sarong and headed back to his hut, anticipating breakfast. It would be rice pap and weak tea as always, but today the unit also had a coconut—another present from the King.

In the few short days he had known the King, a rare friendship had developed. The bonds were part food and part tobacco and part help—the King had cured the tropical ulcers on Mac's ankles with salvarsan, cured them in two days, that which had suppurated for two years. Peter Marlowe knew, too, that though all three of them welcomed the King's wealth and help, their liking for him was due mainly to the man himself. When you were with him he poured out strength and confidence. You felt better and stronger yourself—for you seemed to be able to feed on the magic that surrounded him.

'He's a witch doctor!' Involuntarily, Peter Marlowe said it aloud.

Most of the officers in Hut Sixteen were still asleep, or lying on their bunks waiting for breakfast, when he entered. He pulled the coconut from under his pillow and picked up the scraper and parang machete. Then he went outside and sat on a bench. A deft tap with the parang split the coconut in two perfect halves and spilled the milk into a billycan. Then he carefully began scraping one half of the coconut. Shreds of white meat fell into the milk.

The other half coconut he scraped into a separate container. He put this coconut meat into a piece of mosquito curtain and carefully squeezed the thick-sweet sap into a cup. Today it was Mac's turn to add the sap to his breakfast rice pap.

Peter Marlowe thought again what a marvellous food the residue of coconut was. Rich in protein and perfectly tasteless. Yet a sliver of garlic in it, and it was all garlic. A quarter of a sardine, and the whole became sardine, and the body of it would flavour many bowls of rice.

Suddenly he was famished for the coconut. He was so hungry that he did not hear the guards approaching. He did not feel their presence until they were already standing ominously in the doorway of the hut and all the men were on their feet.

Yoshima, the Japanese officer, shattered the silence. 'There is a radio in this hut.'

VIII

Yoshima waited five minutes for someone to speak. He lit a cigarette and the sound of the match was a thunderclap.

Dave Daven's first reaction was, Oh my God, who's the bastard who gave us away or made the slip? Peter Marlowe? Cox? Spence? The colonels? His second reaction was terror—terror incongruously mixed with relief—that *the* day had come.

Peter Marlowe's fear was just as choking. Who leaked? Cox? The colonels? Why, even Mac and Larkin don't know that I know! Christ! Outram Road!

Cox was petrified. He leaned against the bunk looking from slant eyes to slant eyes, and only the strength of the posts kept him from falling.

Lieutenant-Colonel Sellars was in nominal charge of the hut, and his pants were slimed with fear as he entered the hut with his adjutant, Captain Forest.

He saluted, his dewlapped face flushed and sweating.

'Good morning, Captain Yoshima . . .'

'It is not a good morning. There is a radio here. A radio is against orders of the Imperial Nipponese Army.' Yoshima was small, slight and very neat. A samurai sword hung from his thick belt. His knee boots shone like mirrors.

'I don't know anything about it. No. Nothing,' Sellars blustered. 'You!' A palsied finger pointed at Daven. 'Do you know anything about it?'

'No, sir.'

Sellars turned around and faced the hut. 'Where's the wireless?'

Silence.

'Where is the wireless?' He was almost hysterical. *'Where is the wireless*? I order you to hand it over instantly. You know we're all responsible for orders of the Imperial Army.'

Silence.

'I'll have the lot of you court-martialled,' he screamed, his jowls shaking. 'You'll all get what you deserve. You! What's your name?'

'Flight Lieutenant Marlowe, sir.'

'Where's the wireless?'

'I don't know, sir.'

Then Sellars saw Grey. 'Grey! You're supposed to be Provost Marshal. If there's a wireless here it's your responsibility and no one else's. You should have reported it to the authorities. I'll have you court-martialled and it'll show on your record . . .'

'I know nothing about a wireless, sir.'

'Then, by God you should,' Sellars screamed at him, his face contorted and purple. He stormed up the hut to where the five American officers bunked. 'Brough! What do you know about this?'

'Nothing. And it's *Captain* Brough, Colonel!'

'I don't believe you. It's just the sort of trouble you bloody Americans'd cause. You're nothing but an ill-disciplined rabble . . .'

'I'm not taking that goddam crap from you!'

'Don't you talk to me like that. Say "Sir" and stand to attention.'

'I'm the senior American officer and I'm not taking insults from you or anyone else. There's no radio in the American contingent that I know of. There's no radio in this hut that I know of. And if there was, I sure as hell wouldn't tell you. Colonel!'

Sellars turned and panted to the centre of the hut. 'Then we'll search the hut. Everyone stand by their beds! Attention! God help the man who has it. *I'll personally see he's punished to the limit of the law*, you mutinous swine . . .'

'Shut up, Sellars.'

Everyone stiffened as Colonel Smedly-Taylor entered the hut.

'There's a wireless here and I was trying—'

102

'Shut up.'

Smedly-Taylor's well-used face was taut as he walked over to Yoshima, who had been watching Sellars with astonishment and contempt. 'What's the trouble, Captain?' he asked, knowing what it was.

'There's a radio in the hut.' Then Yoshima added with a sneer, 'According to the Geneva Convention governing prisoners of war . . .'

'I know the code of ethics quite well,' Smedly-Taylor said, keeping his eyes off the eight-by-eight beam. 'If you believe there is a wireless here, please make a search for it. Or if you know where it is, please take it and be done with the affair. I've a lot to do today.'

'Your job is to enforce the law . . .'

'My job is to enforce civilized law. If you want to cite law, then obey it yourselves. Give us the food and medical supplies to which we are entitled!'

'One day you will go too far, Colonel.'

'One day I'll be dead. Perhaps I'll die of apoplexy trying to enforce ridiculous rules imposed by incompetent administrators.'

'I'll report your impertinence to General Shima.'

'Please do so. Then ask him who gave the order that each man in camp should catch twenty flies a day, that they are to be collected and counted and delivered daily to your office by me.'

'You senior officers are always whining about the dysenteric death rate. Flies spread dysentery—'

'You don't have to remind me about flies or death rate,' Smedly-Taylor said harshly. 'Give us chemicals, and permission to enforce hygiene in the surrounding areas, and we'll have the whole of Singapore Island under control.'

'Prisoners are not entitled . . .'

Your dysenteric rate is uneconomic. *Your* malaria rate is high. Before you came here Singapore was malaria-free.'

'Perhaps. But we conquered you in your thousands and we captured you in your thousands. No man of honour would allow himself to be captured. You are all animals and should be treated as such.'

'I understand that quite a few Japanese prisoners are being taken in the Pacific.'

'Where did you get that information?'

'Rumours, Captain Yoshima. You know how it is. Obviously incorrect. And incorrect that the Japanese fleets are no longer on the seas, or that Japan is being bombed, or that the Americans have captured Guadalcanal, Guam and Rabaul and Okinawa, and are presently poised for an attack on the Japanese mainland—'

'*Lies*!' Yoshima's hand was on the samurai sword at his waist and he jerked it an inch out of the scabbard. 'Lies! The Imperial Japanese Army is winning the war and will soon have dominated Australia and America. New Guinea is in our hands and a Japanese armada is at this very moment off Sydney.'

'Of course.' Smedly-Taylor turned his back on Yoshima and looked down the length of the hut. White faces stared back at him. 'Everyone outside, please,' he said quietly.

His order was silently obeyed.

When the hut was empty, he turned back to Yoshima. 'Please make your search.'

'And if I find the radio?'

'That is in the hands of God.'

Suddenly Smedly-Taylor felt the weight of his fifty-four years. He shuddered under the responsibility of his burden, for though he was glad to serve, and glad to be here in a time of need, and glad to do his duty, now he had to find the traitor. When he found the traitor he would have to punish him. Such a man deserved to die, as Daven would die if the wireless was found. Pray God it is not found, he thought despairingly, it's our only line with sanity. If there is a God in heaven, let it not be found! Please.

But Smedly-Taylor knew that Yoshima was right about one thing. He should have had the courage to die like a soldier—on the battlefield or in escape. Alive, the cancer of memory ate him—the memory that greed, power lust, and bungling had caused the rape of the East, and countless hundred thousand useless deaths.

But then, he thought, if I had died, what of my darling Maisie, and John—my Lancer son—and Percy—my Air Force son—and Trudy, married so young and pregnant so young and widowed so young, what of them? Never to see or touch them, or feel the warmth of home again.

104

'That is in the hands of God,' he said again, but, like him, the words were old and very sad.

Yoshima snapped orders at the four guards. They pulled the bunks from the corners of the hut and made a clearing. Then they pulled Daven's bunk into the clearing. Yoshima went into the corner and began to peer at the rafters, at the atap thatch, and at the rough boards beneath. His search was careful, but Smedly-Taylor suddenly realized that this was only for his benefit—that the hiding place was known.

He remembered the night months upon months ago when they had come to him. 'It's on your own heads,' he had said. 'If you get caught, you get caught, and that's the end of it. I can do nothing to help you—nothing.' He had singled out Daven and Cox and said quietly: 'If the wireless is discovered—try not to implicate the others. You must try for a little while. Then you are to say that I authorized this wireless. I ordered you to do it.' Then he had dismissed them and blessed them in his own way and wished them luck.

Now they were all steeped in unluck.

He waited impatiently for Yoshima to get to work on the beam, hating the cat-and-mouse agony. He could hear the undercurrent of despair from the men outside. There was nothing he could do but wait.

Finally Yoshima tired of the game too. The stench of the hut bothered him. He walked to the bunk and made a perfunctory search. Then he studied the eight by eight. But his eyes could not find the cuts. Scowling, he examined it closer, his long sensitive fingers plying the wood. Still he could not find it.

His first reaction was that he had been misinformed. But this he could not believe, for the informer had not yet been paid.

He grunted a command and a Korean guard unsnapped his bayonet and gave it to him haft first.

Yoshima tapped the beam, listening for the hollow sound. Ah, now he had it! Again he tapped. Again the hollow sound. But he could not find the cracks. Angrily he jabbed the bayonet into the wood.

The lid came free.

'So.'

Yoshima was proud that he had found the radio. The general would be pleased. Pleased enough, perhaps to assign him a combat unit, for his *Bushido* revolted at paying informers and dealing with these animals.

Smedly-Taylor moved forward, awed by the ingenuity of the hiding place and the patience of the man who made it. I must recommend Daven, he thought. This is duty above and beyond the call of duty. But recommend him for what?

'Who belongs to this bunk?' Yoshima asked.

Smedly-Taylor shrugged and went through the same pretence of finding out.

Yoshima was sorry, truly sorry that Daven had only one leg. 'Would you like a cigarette?' he said, offering the pack of Kooas.

'Thank you.' Daven took the cigarette and accepted a light but did not taste the smoke.

'What is your name?' Yoshima asked courteously.

'Captain Daven, Infantry.'

'How did you lose your leg, Captain Daven?'

'I—I was blown up by a mine. In Johore—just north of the causeway.'

'Did you make the radio?'

'Yes.'

Smedly-Taylor thrust away his own fear-sweat. 'I ordered Captain Daven to make it. It's my responsibility. He was following my orders.'

Yoshima glanced at Daven. 'Is this true?'

'No.'

'Who else knows about the radio?'

'No one. It was my idea and I made it. Alone.'

'Please sit down, Captain Daven.' Then Yoshima nodded contemptuously towards Cox, who sat sobbing with terror. 'What's his name?'

'Captain Cox,' Daven said.

'Look at him. Disgusting.'

Daven drew on the cigarette. 'I'm just as afraid as he is.'

'You are in control. You have courage.'

'I'm more afraid than he is.' Daven hobbled awkwardly over to Cox, laboriously sat beside him. 'It's all right, Cox, old boy,' he said compassionately, putting his hand on Cox's shoulder. 'It's all right.' Then he looked up at Yoshima. 'Cox earned the Military Cross at Dunkirk before he was twenty. He's another man now. Constructed by you bastards over three years.'

Yoshima quelled an urge to strike Daven. Before a *man*, even an enemy, there was a code. He turned to Smedly-Taylor and ordered him to get the six men from the bunks nearest to Daven's, and told him to keep the rest on parade, under guard, until further orders.

The six men stood in front of Yoshima. Only Spence knew of the radio, but he, like all of them, denied the knowledge.

'Pick up the bunk and follow me,' Yoshima ordered.

When Daven groped for his crutch, Yoshima helped him to his feet.

'Thank you,' Daven said.

'Would you like another cigarette?'

'No thank you.'

Yoshima hesitated. 'I would be honoured if you would accept the packet.'

Daven shrugged and took it, then hobbled to his corner and reached down for his iron leg.

Yoshima snapped out a command and one of the Korean guards picked up the leg and helped Daven sit down.

His fingers were steady as he attached the leg, then he stood, picked up his crutches, and stared at them a moment. Then he threw them into the corner of the hut.

He clomped to the bunk and looked at the radio. 'I'm very proud of that,' he said. He saluted Smedly-Taylor, then moved out of the hut.

The tiny procession wove through the silence of Changi. Yoshima led and timed the speed of the march to Daven's progress. Beside him was Smedly-Taylor. Then came Cox, tear-streamed and oblivious to the tears. The other two guards waited with the men of Hut Sixteen.

They waited eleven hours.

Smedly-Taylor returned, and the six men returned. Daven and Cox did not return. They remained in the guardhouse and tomorrow they were going to Outram Road Jail.

The men were dismissed.

Peter Marlowe had a blinding headache from the sun. He stumbled back to the bungalow, and after a shower, Larkin and Mac massaged his head and fed him. When he had finished

Larkin went out and sat beside the asphalt road. Peter Marlowe squatted in the doorless door, his back to the room.

Night was gathering beyond the horizon. There was an immense solitude in Changi and the men who walked up and down seemed more than ever lost.

Mac yawned. 'Think I'll turn in now, laddie. Get an early night.'

'All right, Mac.'

Mac settled the mosquito net around his bed and tucked it under the mattress. He wrapped a sweat-rag around his fore-head, then slipped Peter Marlowe's water-bottle from its felt case and unclipped the false base plate. He took the covers and bases off his own water bottle and Larkin's, then carefully put them on top of one another. Within each of the bottles was a maze of wire, condenser and tube.

From the top bottle he carefully pulled out a six-pronged male-joint and its complex of wire and fitted it deftly into the female in the middle water bottle. Then he took a four-pronged male-joint from the middle one and fitted it into its appointed socket in the last.

His hands were shaking and his knees quivered, for to do this in the half light, lying propped on one elbow, screening the bottles with his body, was very awkward.

Night swarmed across the sky, adding to the closeness. Mosquitoes began to attack.

When all the bottles were joined together, Mac stretched the ache from his back and dried his slippery hands. Then he pulled out the earphone from its hiding place in the top bottle and checked the connections to make sure they were tight. The insulated source wire was also in the top bottle. He unrolled it and checked that the needles were still tightly soldered to the ends of the wire. Again he wiped away his sweat and rapidly rechecked all the joining connections, thinking as he did that the radio still looked as pure and clean as when he had finished it secretly in Java—while Larkin and Peter Marlowe guarded—two years ago.

It had taken six months to design and make.

Only the lower half of the bottle could be used—the top half had to contain water—so he not only had to compress the radio into three tiny rigid units, but also had to set the units into leakless containers, then solder the containers into the water bottles.

The three of them had carried the bottles for eighteen months. Against such a day as this.

Mac got to his knees and stuck two needles into the guts of the wires that joined the ceiling light to its source. Then he cleared his throat.

Peter Marlowe got up and made sure no one was near. He quickly unsnapped the light bulb and turned the light switch on. Then he went back to the doorway and stood guard there. He saw that Larkin was still in position guarding the other side, and gave the all-clear signal.

When Mac heard it, he turned up the volume and picked up the earphone and listened.

Seconds mounted into minutes. Peter Marlowe jerked around, suddenly frightened, as he heard Mac moan.

'What's the matter, Mac?' he whispered.

Mac stuck his head out of the mosquito net, his face ashen. 'It does na' work, mon,' he said. 'The fugging thing does na' work.'

BOOK TWO

IX

Six days later Max cornered a rat. In the American hut. 'Look at that son of a bitch,' the King gasped. 'That's the biggest rat I've ever seen!'

'My God,' Peter Marlowe said. 'Watch out it doesn't bite your arm off!'

They were all surrounding the rat. Max was gloating, a bamboo broom in his hands. Tex had a baseball bat, Peter Marlowe another broom. The rest wielded sticks and knives.

Only the King was unarmed, but his eyes were on the rat and he was ready to jump out of the way. He had been in his corner, chatting with Peter Marlowe, when Max first shouted, and he had leaped up with the others. It was just after breakfast.

'Look out!' he shouted as he anticipated the rat's sudden dash for freedom.

Max swiped at it savagely and missed. Another broom caught it a glancing blow, turning it on its back for an instant. But the rat whirled to its feet and ran back into the corner and turned, hissing and spitting and working its lips from its needle teeth.

'Jesus,' said the King. 'Thought the bastard got away that time.'

The rat was nearly a hairy foot long. Its tail was another foot in length and as thick at the base as a man's thumb and hairless. Small beady eyes darting left and right seeking escape. Brown and dirt-obscene. Head tapering to a sharp muzzle, mouth narrow, large—very large—incisor teeth. Total weight near two pounds. Vicious and very dangerous.

Max was breathing hard from the exertion and his eyes were

113

on the rat. 'Chrissake,' he spat, 'I hate rats, I hate even looking at it. Let's kill it. Ready?'

'Wait a second, Max,' the King said. 'There's no hurry. It can't get away now. I want to see what it does.'

'It'll make another break, that's what,' Max said.

'So we'll stop it. What's the hurry?' The King looked back at the rat and grinned. 'You're clobbered, you son of a bitch. Dead.'

Almost as though the rat understood, it made a dart at the King, teeth bared. Only the wild flurry of blows and shouts drove it back again.

'That bastard'd tear you to pieces if it got its teeth in you,' the King said. 'Never knew they'd be so fast.'

'Hey,' Tex said. 'Maybe we should keep it.'

'What're you talking about?'

'We could keep it. A mascot maybe. Or when we had nothing to do, we could let it out and chase it.'

'Hey, Tex,' said Dino. 'Maybe you got something there. You mean like they did in the old days. With foxes?'

'That's a lousy idea,' said the King. 'It's okay to kill the bastard. No need to torture it, even if it is a rat. It never did you any harm.'

'Maybe. But rats're vermin. They got no right to be alive.'

'Sure they have,' said the King. 'If it wasn't for them, well, they're scavengers, like microbes. Weren't for rats, why the whole world'd be a stink-pile.'

'Hell,' Tex said. 'Rats ruin the crops. Maybe this's the bastard that ate the bottom out of the rice sack. Its belly's big enough.'

'Yeah,' Max said malevolently. 'They got away with near thirty pounds one night.'

Again the rat stabbed for freedom. It broke the circle and fled down the hut. Only through luck was it cornered again. Once more the men surrounded it.

'We'd better finish it off. Next time we mayn't be so lucky,' wheezed the King. Then suddenly he had an inspiration. 'Wait a minute,' he said as they all began to close on the corner.

'What?'

'I got an idea.' He whipped round to Tex. 'Get a blanket, Quick.'

Tex jumped for his bed and ripped off the blanket.

114

'Now,' the King said, 'you and Max get the blanket and trap the rat.'

'Huh?'

'I want it alive. Come on, get the lead out,' the King snapped.

'With *my* blanket? You crazy? It's the only one I got!'

'I'll get you another. Just catch the bastard.'

They all gawked at the King. Then Tex shrugged. He and Max took hold of the blanket, using it as a screen, and began to converge on the corner. The others held their brooms ready to make sure the rat would not escape around the edges. Then Tex and Max made a sudden dive and the rat was caught in the folds of the material. Its teeth and claws ripped for an escape, but in the uproar Max rolled the blanket up and the blanket became a squirming ball. The men were excited and shouting at the capture.

'Keep it quiet,' the King ordered. 'Max, you hold it. And make sure it doesn't get out. Tex, put on the Java. We'll all have some coffee.'

'What's this idea?' Peter Marlowe asked.

'It's too good to let out, just like that. We'll have the coffee first.'

While they were drinking their coffee, the King stood up. 'All right, you guys. Now listen. We've got a rat, right?'

'So?' Miller was perplexed as they all were.

'We've no food, right?'

'Sure, but—'

'Oh my God,' Peter Marlowe said aghast. 'You don't mean you're suggesting we eat it?'

'Of course not,' the King said. Then he beamed seraphically. '*We're* not going to. But there's plenty who'd like to buy some meat—'

'Rat meat?' Byron Jones III's eye popped majestically.

'You're outta your mind. You think someone'd buy rat meat? Course they wouldn't,' Miller said impatiently.

'Of course no one'll buy the meat if they know it's rat. But say they don't know, huh?' The King let the words settle, then continued benignly, 'Say we don't tell anyone. The meat'll look like any other meat. We'll say it's rabbit—'

'There aren't any rabbits in Malaya, old chap,' Peter Marlowe said.

'Well, think of an animal that is, about the same size.'

'I suppose,' Peter Marlowe said after a moment's reflection, 'that you could call it squirrel—or, I know,' he brightened. 'Deer. That's it, deer—'

'For Chrissake, a deer's much bigger,' Max said, still holding the squirming blanket. 'I shot one up in the Alleghenies—'

'I don't mean that type of deer. I mean *Rusa tikas*. They're tiny, about eight inches high and weigh perhaps a couple of pounds. About the size of the rat. The natives consider them a delicacy.' He laughed. '*Rusa tikus* translated means "mouse deer".'

The King rubbed his hands, delighted. 'Very good, old chap!' He looked around the room. 'We'll sell *Rusa tikus* haunches. And that ain't gonna be a lie either.'

They all laughed.

'Now we've had the laugh, let's kill the goddam rat and sell the goddam legs,' Max said. 'The bastard's gonna get out any minute. And I'm godamned if I'm gonna get bit.'

'We got one rat,' the King said ignoring him. 'All we've got to do is find out if it's a male or female. Then we get the opposite one. We put 'em together. Presto, we're in business.'

'Business?' Tex said.

'Sure.' The King looked around happily. 'Men, we're in the breeding business. We're going to make us a rat farm. With the dough we make, we'll buy chicken—and the peasants can eat the *tikus*. So long as no one opens his goddam mouth, it's a natural.'

There was an appalled silence. Then Tex said weakly: 'But where we gonna keep the rats while they're breeding?'

'In the slit trench. Where else?'

'But say there's an air raid. We might wanna use the trench.'

'We'll fence off one end. Just enough to keep the rats in.' The King's eyes sparkled. 'Just think. Fifty of these big bastards a week to sell. Why, we've got a gold mine. You know the old saying, breed like rats . . .'

'How often do they breed?' Miller asked, absently scratching his pelt.

'I don't know. Anybody know?' The King waited, but they all shook their heads. 'Where the hell we gonna find out about their habits?'

116

'I know,' Peter Marlowe said. 'Vexley's class.'

'Huh?'

'Vexley's class. He teaches botany, zoology, that sort of thing. We could ask him.'

They looked at one another thoughtfully. Then suddenly they began to cheer. Max almost dropped the fighting blanket amid cries of 'Mind the gold, you clumsy bastard,' 'Don't let go, for Pete's sake,' 'Watch it, Max!'

'All right, I got the bastard.' Max drowned out the catcalls, then nodded at Peter Marlowe.

'For an officer, you're all right. So we'll go to school.'

'Oh no you won't,' said the King crisply. 'You got work to do.'

'Like what?'

'Like liberate another rat. Whichever sex this one isn't. Peter and I'll get the info. Now let's get with it!'

Tex and Byron Jones III prepared the slit trench. It was directly under the hut, six feet deep, four feet wide and thirty feet long.

'Great,' Tex said excitedly. 'Room for a thousand of the bastards!'

It took them a few minutes to devise an efficient gate. Tex went to steal chicken wire while Byron Jones III went to steal wood. Jones grinned as he remembered some fine pieces belonging to a bunch of Limeys who weren't too careful about guarding it, and by the time Tex returned, he had the framework already made. Nails came from the roof of the hut, the hammer had also been 'borrowed' from some careless mechanic up in the garage months ago, along with the wrenches, screwdrivers, and a lot of useful things.

Once the gate was in position and neat, Tex fetched the King.

'Good,' the King said as he inspected it. 'Very good.'

'Damned if I know how you do it,' Peter Marlowe said. 'You work so fast.'

'You got something to do, you do it. That's American style.' The King nodded for Tex to get Max.

Max crawled under the hut to join them. He gingerly dropped the rat into its section. The rat whirled and frantically sought an escape. When there was none to be found, it backed into a corner and hissed at them violently.

117

'It looks healthy enough,' the King grinned.

'Hey, we got to give it a name,' Tex said.

'That's easy. It's Adam.'

'Yeah, but say it's a girl.'

'Then it's Eve.' The King crawled from under the hut. 'Come on, Peter, let's get with it.'

Squadron Leader Vexley's class had already begun when at length they tracked him down.

'Yes?' asked Vexley, astonished to see the King and a young officer standing near the hut in the sun, watching him.

'We thought,' began Peter Marlowe self-consciously, 'we thought we might, er, join the class. If, of course, we're not interrupting,' he added quickly.

'Join the class?' Vexley was bewildered. He was a bleak, one-eyed man with a face of stretched parchment, mottled and scarred by the flames of his final bomber. His class had only four pupils and they were idiots who had no interest in his subject. He knew that he only continued the class as a sop to indecision; it was easier to pretend that it was a success than to stop. In the beginning he had been enthusiastic but now he knew it was a pretence. And if he stopped the class he would have no purpose in life.

A long time ago the camp had started a university. The University of Changi. Classes were organized. The Brass had ordered it. 'Good for the troops,' they had said. 'Give them something to do. *Make* them better themselves. *Force* them to be busy, then they won't get into trouble.'

There were courses in languages and art and engineering—for among the original hundred thousand men there was at least one man who knew any subject.

The knowledge of the world. A great opportunity. Broaden horizons. Learn a trade. Prepare for the Utopia that would come to pass once the goddam war ended and things were back to normal. And the university was Athenian. No classrooms. Only a teacher who found a place in the shade and grouped his students around him.

But the prisoners of Changi were just ordinary men, so they sat on their butts and said, 'Tomorrow I'll join a class.' Or they joined and when they discovered that knowledge comes hard they would miss a class and another class and then they would

118

say, 'Tomorrow I'll rejoin. Tomorrow I'll start to become what I want to be afterwards. Musn't waste time. Tomorrow I'll really start.'

But in Changi, as elsewhere, there was only today.

'You really want to join my class?' Vexley repeated incredulously.

'You sure we won't be putting you to any trouble, sir?' the King asked cordially.

Vexley got up with quickening interest and made a space for them in the shade.

He was delighted to see new blood. And the King! My God what a catch! The King in *his* class! Maybe he'll have some cigarettes . . . 'Delighted, my boy, delighted.' He shook the King's extended hand warmly. 'Squadron Leader Vexley!'

'Happy to know you, sir.'

'Flight Lieutenant Marlowe,' Peter Marlowe said as he also shook hands and sat down in the shade.

Vexley waited nervously till they were seated and absently pressed his thumb into the back of his hand, counting the seconds till the indentation in the skin slowly filled. Pellagra had its compensations, he thought. And thinking of skin and bone reminded him of whales and his pop-eye brightened. 'Well, today I was going to talk about whales. Do you know about whales?—Ah,' he said ecstatically as the King brought out a pack of Kooas and offered him one. The King passed the pack around the whole class.

The four students accepted the cigarettes and moved to give the King and Peter Marlowe more space. They wondered what the hell the King was doing there, but they didn't really care—he'd given them a real tailor-made cigarette.

Vexley started to continue his lecture on whales. He loved whales. He loved them to distraction.

'Whales are without a doubt the highest form that nature has aspired to,' he said, very pleased with the resonance of his voice. He noticed the King's frown. 'Did you have a question?' he asked eagerly.

'Well, yes. Whales are interesting, but what about rats?'

'I beg your pardon,' Vexley said politely.

'Very interesting what you were saying about whales, sir,' the King said. 'I was just wondering about rats, that's all.'

'What about rats?'

'I was just wondering if you knew anything about them,' the King said. He had a lot to do and didn't want to screw around.

'What he means,' Peter Marlowe said quickly, 'is that if whales are almost human in their reflexes, isn't that true of rats, too?'

Vexley shook his head and said distastefully, 'Rodents are entirely different. Now about whales . . .'

'How are they different?' asked the King.

'I cover the rodents in the spring seminar,' Vexley said testily. 'Disgusting beasts. Nothing about them to like. Nothing. Now you take the sulphur-bottom whale,' Vexley hastily launched off again. 'Ah, now there's the giant of all whales. Over a hundred feet long and it can weigh as much as a hundred and fifty tons. The biggest creature alive—that has ever lived—on earth. The most powerful animal in existence. And its mating habits,' Vexley added quickly, for he knew that a discussion of the sex life always kept the class awake.

'It's mating is marvellous. The male begins his titilation by blowing glorious clouds of spray. He pounds the water with his tail near the female, who waits with patient lust on the ocean's surface. Then he will dive and soar up, out of the water, huge, vast, enormous, and crash back with thundering flukes, churning the water into foam pounding at the surface.' He dropped his voice sensuously. 'Then he slides up to the female and starts tickling her with his flippers . . .'

In spite of his anxiety about rats, even the King began to listen attentively.

'Then he will break off the seduction and dive again, leaving the female panting on the surface—leaving her perhaps for good.' Vexley made a dramatic pause. 'But no. He doesn't leave her. He disappears for perhaps an hour, into the depths of the ocean, gathering strength, and then he soars up once more and bursts clear of the water and falls like a clap of thunder in a monstrous cloud of spray. He whirls over and over on to his mate, hugging her tight with both flippers and has his mighty will of her to exhaustion.'

Vexley was exhausted, too, at the magnificence of the spectacle of mating giants. Ah, to be so lucky as to witness it, to be there, an insignificant human . . .

He rushed on: 'Mating takes place about July, in warm waters. The baby weighs five tons at birth and is about thirty feet long.' His laugh was practised. 'Think of that.' There were polite smiles, and then Vexley came in with the clincher, always good for a deep chuckle. 'And if you think of that and the size of the calf, just think about the whale's jolly old John Thomas, what?' Again there were courteous smiles—the regular members had heard the story many times.

Vexley went on to describe how the calf is nursed for seven months by the mother, who supplies the calf with milk from two monstrous teats towards the ass end of her underside. 'As you can no doubt imagine,' he said ecstatically, 'prolonged suckling underwater has its problems.'

'Do rats suckle their young?' The King jumped in quickly.

'Yes,' the squadron leader said miserably. 'Now about ambergris . . .'

The King sighed, beaten, and listened to Vexley expound about ambergris and sperm whales and toothed whales and white whales and goose-beaked whales and pygmy whales and beaked whales and narwhales and killer whales and humpback whales and bottle-nosed whales and whalebone whales and grey whales and right whales and finally bowhead whales. By this time all the class except Peter Marlowe, and the King had left. When Vexley had finished, the King said simply:

'I want to know about rats.'

Vexley groaned. 'Rats?'

'Have a cigarette,' said the King benignly.

X

'All right, you guys, sort yourselves out,' the King said. He waited until there was quiet in the hut and the lookout at the doorway was in position. 'We got problems.'

'Grey?' asked Max.

'No. It's about our farm.' The King turned to Peter Marlowe, who was sitting on the edge of a bed. 'You tell 'em, Peter.'

'Well,' began Peter Marlowe, 'it seems that rats—'

'Tell 'em it from the beginning.'

'All of it?'

'Sure. Spread the knowledge, then we can all figure angles.'

'All right. Well, we found Vexley. He told us, quote: "The *Rattus norvegicus*, or Norwegian rat—sometimes called the *Mus decumanus*—"'

'What sort of talk is that?' Max asked.

'Latin, for Chrissake. Any fool knows that,' Tex said.

'You know Latin, Tex?' Max gaped at him.

'Hell no, but those crazy names're always Latin—'

'For Chrissake, you guys,' the King said. 'You want to know or don't you?' Then he nodded for Peter Marlowe to continue.

'Well, anyway, Vexley described them in detail, hairy, no hair on the tail, weight up to four pounds, the usual is about two pounds in this part of the world. Rats mate promiscuously at any time—'

'What the hell does that mean?'

'The male'll screw any female irrespective,' the King said impatiently, 'and there ain't no season.'

'Just like us, you mean?' Jones said agreeably.

'Yes. I suppose so,' said Peter Marlowe. 'Anyway, the male rat will mate at any season and the female can have up to twelve litters per year, around twelve per litter, but perhaps as many as fourteen. The young are born blind and helpless twenty-two days after—contact.' He picked the word delicately. 'The young open their eyes after fourteen to seventeen days and become sexually mature in two months. They cease breeding at about two years and are old at three years.'

'Holy cow' Max said delightedly in the awed silence. 'We sure as hell've problems. Why, if the young'll breed in two months, and we got twelve—say for round figures ten a litter—figure it for yourself. Say we get ten young on Day One. Another ten on Day Thirty. By Day Sixty the first pair've bred, and we get fifty. Day Ninety we got another five pairs breeding and another fifty. Day One-twenty, we got two-fifty plus another fifty and another fifty and a new batch of two-fifty. For Chrissake, that makes sixty-five rats in five months. The next month we got near six thousand five hundred—'

'Jesus, we got us a gold mine!' Miller said, scratching furiously.

'The hell we have,' the King said. 'Not without some figuring. Number one, we can't put 'em all together. They're cannibals. That means we got to separate the males and females except when we're mating them. Another thing they'll fight among themselves, all the time. So that means separating males from males and females from females.'

'So we separate them. What's so tough about that?'

'Nothing, Max,' said the King patiently. 'But we got to have cages and get the thing organized. It isn't going to be easy.'

'Hell,' Tex said. 'We can build a stock of cages, no sweat in that.'

'You think, Tex, we can keep the farm quiet? While we're building up the stock?'

'Don't see why not!'

'Oh, another thing,' the King said. He was feeling pleased with the men and more than pleased with the scheme. It was a business after his own heart—nothing to do except wait. 'They'll eat anything, alive or dead. Anything. So we've no logistics problem.'

'But they're filthy creatures and they'll stink to the skies,'

123

Byron Jones III said. 'We've enough stench around here as it is without putting more under our own hut. And rats are also plague carriers!'

'Maybe that's a special type of rat, like a special mosquito carries malaria,' Dino said hopefully, his dark eyes roving the men.

'Rats can carry plague, sure,' the King said, shrugging. 'And they carry a lot of human diseases. But that don't mean nothing. We got a fortune in the making and all you bastards do is figure negatives! It's un-American!'

'Well, Jesus, this plague bit. How do we know if they'll be clean or not?' Miller said queasily.

The King laughed. 'We asked Vexley that an' he said, quote, "You'd find out soon enough. You'd be dead." Unquote. Hell, it's just like chickens. Keep 'em clean and feed 'em good and you got good stock! Nothing to worry about.'

So they talked about the farm, its dangers and its potentials—and they could all appreciate the potentials—provided *they* didn't have to eat the produce—and they discussed the problems connected with such a large-scale operation. Then Kurt came into the hut and in his hands was a squirming blanket.

'I got another,' he said sourly.

'You have?'

'Sure I have. While you bastards're talkin' I'm out doing'. It's a bitch.' Kurt spat on the floor.

'How do you know?'

'I looked. I seed enough rats in the Merchant Marine to know. An' the other's a male. An' I looked too.'

They all climbed under the hut and watched Kurt put Eve into the trench. Immediately the two rats stuck together viciously, and the men were hard put not to cheer. The first litter was on its way. The men voted that Kurt was to be in charge and Kurt was happy.

That way he knew he would get his share. Sure he'd look after the rats. Food was food. Kurt knew he was going to survive if any bastard did.

XI

Twenty-two days later Eve gave birth. In the next cage, Adam tore at the wire netting to get at the living food and almost got through but Tex spotted the rent just in time. Eve suckled the young. There were Cain and Abel and Grey and Alliluha; Beulah and Mabel and Junt and Princess and Little Princess and Big Mabel and Big Junt and Big Beaulah. Naming the males was easy. But none of the men wanted their girl's names or their sister's or their mother's names attached to the females. Even mother-in-law names were some other man's passion or relation of the past. It had taken them three days to agree on Beulah and Mabel.

When the young were fifteen days old, they were put into separate cages. The King, Peter Marlowe, Tex and Max gave Eve until noon to recover, then put her back with Adam. The second litter was launched.

'Peter,' the King said benignly as they climbed through the trap-door into the hut, 'our fortune's made.'

The King had decided on the trapdoor because he knew that so many trips under the hut would excite curiosity. It was vital to the success of the farm that it should remain secret. Even Mac and Larkin knew nothing about it.

'Where's everyone today?' Peter Marlowe asked, closing the trapdoor. Only Max was in the hut, lying on his bunk.

'Poor slobs got caught for a work party. Tex's in hospital. The rest are out liberating.'

'Think I'll go and liberate too. Give me something to think about.'

125

The King lowered his voice. 'I got something for you to think about. Tomorrow night we're going to the village.' Then he yelled to Max, 'Hey, Max, you know Prouty? The Aussie major? Up in Hut Eleven?'

'The old guy? Sure.'

'He's not old. Can't be more'n forty.'

'From where I'm at forty's old as God. It'll take me eighteen years to get that old.'

'You should be so lucky,' the King said. 'Go see Prouty. Tell him I sent you.'

'And?'

'And nothing. Just go see him. And make sure Grey isn't around—or any of his eyes.'

'On my way,' Max said reluctantly and left them alone.

Peter Marlowe was looking over the wire, seeking to the coast. 'I was beginning to wonder if you'd changed your mind.'

'About taking you along?'

'Yes.'

'No need for you to worry, Peter.' The King got out the coffee and handed a mug to Peter Marlowe. 'You want to have lunch with me?'

'I don't know how the hell you do it,' Peter Marlowe grunted. 'Everyone's starving and you invite me to lunch.'

'I'm having some katchang idju.'

The King unlocked his black chest and took out the sack of little green beans and handed them to Peter Marlowe. 'You like to fix them?'

As Peter Marlowe took them out to the tap to begin washing them, the King opened a can of bully and carefully eased the contents onto a plate.

Peter Marlowe came back with the beans. They were well washed and no husks floated on the clean water. Good, the King thought. Don't have to tell Peter twice. And the aluminium container had exactly the right amount of water—six times the height of the beans.

He set it on the hot plate and added a large spoonful of sugar and two pinches of salt. Then he added half the can of bully. 'Is it your birthday?' Peter Marlowe asked.

'Huh?'

'Katchang idju *and* bully in one meal?'

126

'You just don't live right.'

Peter Marlowe was tantalized by the aroma and the bubble of the stew. The last weeks had been rough. The discovery of the radio had hurt the camp. The Japanese Commandant had "regretfully" cut the camp's rations due to "bad harvests", so even the tiny desperation stocks of the units had gone. Miraculously, there had been no other repercussions. Except the cut in food.

In Peter Marlowe's unit, the cut had hit Mac the worst. The cut and the uselessness of their water-bottled radio.

'Dammit,' Mac had sworn after weeks of trying to trace the trouble. 'It's nae use, laddies. Without taking the bleeding thing apart I canna do a thing. Everything seems correct. Without some tools an' a battery of sorts, I canna find the fault.'

Then Larkin had somehow acquired a tiny battery and Mac had gathered his waning strength and gone back to testing, checking and rechecking. Yesterday, while he was testing, he had gasped and fainted, deep in a malarial coma. Peter Marlowe and Larkin had carried him up to the hospital and laid him on a bed. The doctor had said that it was just malaria, but with such a spleen, it could easily become very dangerous.

'What's a matter, Peter?' the King asked, noticing his sudden gravity.

'Just thinking about Mac.'

'What about him?'

'We had to take him up to the hospital yesterday. He's not so hot.'

'Malaria?'

'Mostly.'

'Huh?'

'Well, he's got fever all right. But that's not the main trouble. He goes through periods of terrible depression. Worry—about his wife and son.'

'All married guys've the same sweat.'

'Not quite like Mac,' Peter Marlowe said sadly. 'You see, just before the Japs landed on Singapore, Mac put his wife and son on a ship in the last real convoy out. Then he and his unit took off for Java in a coastal junk. When he got to Java he heard the whole convoy had got shot out of the water or captured. No proof either way—only rumours. So he doesn't know if they got through. Or if they're dead. Or if they're alive. And if they are—where they are. His son was just a baby—only four months old.'

'Well, now the kid's three years and four months,' the King said confidently. 'Rule Two: Don't worry about nothing you can't do nothing about.' He took a bottle of quinine out of his black box and counted out twenty tablets and gave them to Peter Marlowe. 'Here. These'll fix his malaria.'

'But what about you?'

'Got plenty. Think nothing of it.'

'I don't understand why you're so generous. You give us food and medicine. And what do we give you? Nothing. I don't understand it.'

'You're a friend.'

'Christ, I feel embarrassed accepting so much.'

'Hell with it. Here.' The King began spooning out the stew. Seven spoons for him and seven spoons for Peter Marlowe. There was about a quarter of the stew left in the mess can.

They ate the first three spoons quickly to allay the hunger, then finished the rest slowly, savouring its excellence.

'Want some more?' The King waited. How well do I know you, Peter? I know you could eat a ton more. But you won't. Not if your life depended on it.

'No thanks. Full. To the brim.'

It's good to know your friend, the King thought to himself. You've got to be careful. He took another spoonful. Not because he wanted it. He felt he had to or Peter Marlowe would be embarrassed. He ate it and put the rest aside.

'Fix me a smoke, will you?'

He tossed over the makings and turned away. He put the rest of the bully in the remains of the stew and mixed it up. Then he divided this into two mess kits and covered them and set them aside.

Peter Marlowe handed handed him the rolled cigarette.

'Make yourself one,' said the King.

'Thanks.'

'Jesus, Peter, don't wait to be asked. Here, fill your box.'

He took the box out of Peter Marlowe's hands and stuffed it full of the Three Kings Tobacco.

'What're you going to do about Three Kings? With Tex in hospital?' asked Peter Marlowe.

'Nothing.' The King exhaled. 'That idea's milked. The Aussies have found out the process and they've undercut us.'

'Oh, that's too bad. How do you think they found out?'

The King smiled. 'It was an in and out anyway.'

'I don't understand.'

'In and out? You get in and out fast. A small investment for a quick profit. I was covered in the first two weeks.'

'But you said it would take you months to get back the money you put out.'

'That was a sales pitch. That was for outside consumption. A sales pitch is a gimmick. A way of making people believe something. People always want something for nothing. So you have to make 'em believe they're stealing from you, that you're the sucker, that they—the buyers—are a helluva lot smarter than you. For example. Three Kings. The sales force, the first buyers, believed they were in my debt, they believed that if they worked hard for the first month, they could be my partners and coast forever after—on my money. They thought I was a fool to give them such a break after the first month. But I knew that the process would leak and that the business wouldn't last.'

'How did you know that?'

'Obvious. And I planned it that way. I leaked the process myself.'

'You what?'

'—Sure. I traded the process for a little information.'

'Well, I can understand that. It was yours to do as you pleased. But what about all the people who were working, selling the tobacco?'

'What about them?'

'It seems that you sort of took advantage of them. You made them work for a month, more or less for nothing, and then pulled the rug from under them.'

'The hell I did. They made a few bucks out of it. They were playing me for a sucker and I just outsmarted them, that's all. That's business.' He lay back on the bed, amused at the naïveté of Peter Marlowe.

Peter Marlowe frowned, trying to understand. 'When anyone starts talking about business, I'm afraid I'm right out of my depth,' he said. 'I feel such an idiot.'

'Listen. Before you're very much older, you'll be horse-trading with the best of them.' The King laughed.

'I doubt that.'

'You doing anything tonight? Oh, about an hour after dusk?'

'No, why?'

'Would you interpret for me?'

'Gladly. Who, a Malay?'

'A Korean.'

'Oh!' Then Peter Marlowe added, covering at once, 'Certainly.'

The King had marked Peter Marlowe's aversion but didn't mind. A man's a right to his opinions, he'd always said. And so long as those opinions didn't conflict with his own purposes, well, that was all right too.

Max entered the hut and crumpled on his bunk. 'Couldn't find the son of a bitch for a goddam hour. Then I tracked him down in the vegetable patch. Jesus, with all that piss they use for fertilizer, that son-of-a-bitching place stinks like a Harlem brothel on a summer's day.'

'You're just the sort of bastard who'd use a Harlem brothel.'

The King's snarl and the raw grate of his voice startled Peter Marlowe.

Max's smile and fatigue vanished just as suddenly. 'Jesus, I didn't mean anything. It's just a saying.'

'Then why pick on Harlem? You wanna say it stinks like a brothel, great. They all stink the same. No difference because one's black and another's white.' The King was hard and mean and the flesh on his face was tight and masklike.

'Take it easy. I'm sorry. I didn't mean nothin'.'

Max had forgotten that the King was touchy about talking crossways about Negroes. Jesus, when you live in New York, you get Harlem with you, whichever way you look at it. And there are brothels there, an' a piece of coloured tail's goddam good once in a while. All the same, he thought bitterly, I'm goddamned if I know why he's so goddam touchy about nigs.

'I didn't mean nothin',' Max said again, trying hard to keep his eyes off the food. He had smelled it all the way up the hut. 'I tracked him down and tol' him what you said.'

'So?'

'He, er, gave me something for you,' Max said and looked at Peter Marlowe.

'Well, hand it over for Chrissake!'

Max waited patiently while the King looked at the watch closely, wound it up and held it close to his ear.

'What do you want, Max?'

'Nothin'. Er, you like me to wash up for you?'

'Yeah. Do that, then get to hell out of here.'

'Sure.'

Max collected the dirty dishes and meekly took them outside, telling himself by Jesus one day he'd get the King. Peter Marlowe said nothing. Strange, he thought. Strange and wild. The King's got a temper. A temper is valuable but most times dangerous. If you go on a mission it's important to know the value of your wingman. On a hairy mission, like the village perhaps, it's wise to be sure who guards your back.

The King carefully unscrewed the back of the watch. It was a waterproof, stainless steel.

'Uh-huh!' the King said. 'I thought so.'

'What?'

'It's a phoney. Look.'

Peter Marlowe examined the watch carefully. 'It looks all right to me.'

'Sure it is. But it's not what it's supposed to be. An Omega. The case is good but the insides are old. Some bastard has substituted the guts.'

The King screwed the case back on, then tossed it up in his hand speculatively. 'Y'see Peter. Just what I was telling you. You got to be careful. Now, say I sell this as an Omega and *don't* know it's a fake, then I could be in real trouble. But so long as I know in advance, then I can cover myself. You can't be too careful.'

He smiled. 'Let's have another cup of Joe, business is looking up.'

His smile faded as Max returned with the cleaned mess cans and put them away. Max didn't say anything, just nodded obsequiously and then went out again.

'Son of a bitch,' the King said.

Grey had not yet recovered from the day Yoshima had found the radio. As he walked up the broken path towards the supply hut he brooded about the new duties imposed on him by the Camp Commandant in front of Yoshima and later elaborated by Colonel Smedly-Taylor. Grey knew that although officially he was to carry out the new orders, actually he was to keep his eyes shut and do nothing. Mother of God, he thought, whatever I do, I'm wrong.

Grey felt a spasm building in his stomach. He stopped as it came and passed. It wasn't dysentery, only diarrhoea; and the slight fever on him wasn't malaria, only a touch of dengue, a slighter but more insidious fever which came and went by whim. He was very hungry. He had no stocks of food, no last can and no money to buy any with. He had to subsist on rations with no extras, and the rations were not enough, not enough.

When I get out, he thought, I swear by God that I'll never be hungry again. I'll have a thousand eggs and a ton of meat and sugar and coffee and tea and fish. We'll cook all day, Trina and I, and when we're not cooking, or eating we'll be making love. Love? No, just making pain. Trina, that bitch, with her 'I'm too tired' or 'I've got a headache' or 'For the love of God, what, again?' or 'All right, I suppose I'll have to' or 'We can make love now, if *you* want to' or 'Can't you leave me in peace for once', when it wasn't so often and most times he had restrained himself and suffered, or the angry 'Oh, all right,' and then the light would be snapped on and she would get out of bed and storm off to the bathroom to 'get ready' and he would only see the glory of her body through the sheer fabric until the door had closed and then he would wait and wait and wait until the bathroom light was snapped off and she came back into their room. It always took an eternity for her to cross from the door to the bed and he saw only the pure beauty of her under the silk and felt only the cold in her eyes as she watched him and he could not meet her eyes and loathed himself. Then she would be beside him and soon it would be silently over and she would get up and go to the bathroom and clean herself as though his love was dirt, and the water would run and when she came back she would be freshly perfumed and he loathed himself afresh, unsatisfied, for taking her when she didn't want to be taken. It had always been thus. In their six months of married life—twenty-one days of leave, being together—they had made pain nine times. And never once had he touched her.

He had asked her to marry him a week after he had met her. There had been difficulties and recriminations. Her mother hated him for wanting her only daughter just when her career was launched and she was so young. Only eighteen. His parents said wait, the war may be over soon and you've no money and, well, she's not exactly from a *good* family, and he had looked around his home, a tired building joined to a thousand other tired buildings amid the twisted tramlines of Streatham, and he saw that the rooms were small and the minds of his parents were small and lower class and their love was twisted like the tramlines.

They were married a month later. Grey looked smart in his uniform and sword (hired by the hour). Trina's mother didn't come to the drab ceremony, performed in haste between air raid alerts. His parents wore disapproving masks and their kisses were perfunctory and Trina had dissolved into tears and the marriage licence was wet with tears.

That night Grey discovered that Trina wasn't a virgin. Oh, she acted as though she was, and complained for many days that, please darling, I'm so sore, be patient. But she wasn't a virgin and that hurt Grey, for she had implied it many times. But he pretended that he didn't know she had cheated him.

The last time he saw Trina was six days before he embarked for overseas. They were in their flat and he was lying on the bed watching her dressing.

'Do you know where you're going?' she asked.

'No,' Grey said. The day had been bad and the quarrel of the night before bad, and the lack of her and the knowledge that his leave was up today was heavy on him.

He got up and stood behind her, slipping his hands into her bosom, moulding the tautness of her, loving her.

'Don't!'

'Trina, could we—'

'Don't be foolish. You know the show starts at eight-thirty.'

'There's plenty of time—'

'For the love of God, Robin, don't! You'll mess up my make-up!'

'To hell with your make-up,' he said. 'I won't be here tomorrow.'

'Perhaps that just as well. I don't think you're very kind or very thoughtful.'

'What do you expect me to be like? Is it wrong for a husband to want his wife?'

'Stop shouting. My God, the neighbours will hear you.'

'Let 'em, by God! He went towards her, but she slammed the bathroom door in his face.

When she came back into the room she was cold and fragrant. She wore a bra and half slip and panties under the slip, and stockings held by a tiny belt. She picked up the cocktail dress and began to step into it.

'Trina,' he began.

'No.'

He stood over her, and his knees had no strength in them. 'I'm sorry I-I shouted.'

'It doesn't matter.'

He bent to kiss her shoulders, but she moved away.

'I see you've been drinking again,' she said, wrinkling her nose.

Then his rage burst. 'I only had one drink, damn you to hell,' he shouted and spun her around and ripped the dress off her and ripped the bra off her and thew her on the bed. And he ripped at her clothes until she was naked but for the shreds of stockings clinging to her legs. And all the time she lay still, staring up at him.

'Oh, God, Trina, I love you,' he croaked helplessly, then backed away, hating himself for what he had done and what he had nearly done.

Trina picked up the shreds of the clothes. As though in a dream, he watched as she went back to the mirror and sat before it and began to repair her make-up and started to hum a tune, over and over.

Then he slammed the door and went back to his unit and the next day he tried to phone her. There was no answer. It was too late to go back to London, in spite of his desperate pleading. The unit moved to Greenock for embarkation and every day, every minute of every day, he phoned her, but there was no answer, and no answer to his frantic telegrams, and then the coast of Scotland was swallowed up by the night, and the night was only ship and sea, and he was only tears.

Grey shuddered under the Malayan sun. Ten thousand miles away. It wasn't Trina's fault, he thought weak with self-disgust. It wasn't her, it was me. I was too anxious. Maybe I'm insane. Maybe I should see a doctor. Maybe I'm oversexed. It's got to be me, not her. Oh Trina, my love.

'Are you all right, Grey?' Colonel Jones asked.

'Oh, yes, sir, thank you.' Grey came to and discovered that he was leaning weakly against the supply hut. 'It was—was just a touch of fever.'

'You don't look too good. Sit down for a minute.'

'It's all right, thank you. I'll just get some water.'

Grey went over to the tap and took off his shirt and dunked his head under the stream of water. Bloody fool, to let yourself go like that! he thought. But in spite of his resolve, inexorably his mind returned to Trina. Tonight, tonight I'll let myself think of her, he promised. Tonight, and every night. To hell with trying to live without food. Without hope. I want to die. How much I want to die.

Then he saw Peter Marlowe walking up the hill. In his hands was an American mess can and he was holding it carefully.

'Marlowe!' Grey moved in front of him.

'What the hell do you want?'

'What's in there?'

'Food.'

'No contraband?'

'Stop picking on me, Grey.'

'I'm not picking on you. Judge a man by his friends.'

'Just stay away from me.'

'I can't, I'm afraid, old boy. It's my job. I'd like to see that. Please.'

Peter Marlowe hesitated. Grey was within his right to look and within his right to take him to Colonel Smedly-Taylor if he stepped out of line. And in his pocket were the twenty quinine tablets. No one was supposed to have private stores of medicine. If they were discovered he would have to tell where he had got them and then the King would have to tell where he got them. And, anyway, Mac needed them *now*. So he opened the can.

The katchang idju-bully gave off an unearthly fragrance to Grey. His stomach turned over and he tried to keep from showing his hunger. He tipped the mess can carefully so that he could see the bottom. There was nothing in it other than the bully and the katchang idju, delicious.

'Where did you get it?'

'I was given it.'

'Did he give it to you?'

'Yes.'

'Where are you taking it?'

'To the hospital.'

'For whom?'

'For one of the Americans.'

'Since when does a Flight Lieutenant DFC run errands for a corporal?'

'Go to hell!'

'Maybe I will. But before I do I'm going to see you and him get what's coming to you.'

Easy, Peter Marlowe told himself, easy. If you take a sock at Grey you'll really be up the creek.

'Are you finished with the questions, Grey?'

For the moment. But remember—' Grey went a pace closer and the smell of the food tortured him. 'You and your damned crook friend are on the list. I haven't forgotten about the lighter.'

'I don't know what you're talking about. I've done nothing against orders.'

'But you will, Marlowe. If you sell your soul, you've got to pay sometime.'

'You're out of your head!'

'He's a crook, a liar and a thief—'

'He *is* my friend, Grey. He's not a crook and not a thief . . .'

'But he is a liar.'

'Everyone's a liar. Even you. You denied the wireless. You've got to be a liar to stay alive. You've got to do a lot of things . . .'

'Like kissing a corporal's arse to get food?'

The vein in Peter Marlowe's forehead swelled like a thin black snake. But his voice was soft and the venom honey-coated. 'I ought to thrash you, Grey. But it's so ill-bred to brawl with the lower class. Unfair, you know.'

'By God, Marlowe—' began Grey, but he was beyond speech, and the madness in him rose up and choked him.

Peter Marlowe looked deep into Grey's eyes and knew that he had won. For a moment he gloried in the destruction of the man, and then his fury evaporated and he stepped around Grey and walked up the hill. No need to prolong a battle once it's won. That's ill-bred, too.

By the Lord God, Grey swore brokenly, I'll make you pay for that. I'll have you on your knees begging my forgiveness. And I'll not forgive you. Never!

Mac took six of the tablets and winced as Peter Marlowe helped him up a little to drink the water held to his lips. He swallowed and sank back.

'Bless you, Peter,' he whispered. 'That'll do the trick. Bless you, laddie.' He lapsed into sleep, his face burning, his spleen stretched to bursting, and his brain took flight in nightmares. He saw his wife and son floating in the ocean depths, eaten by fish and screaming from the deep. And he saw himself there, in the deep, tearing at the sharks, but his hands were not strong enough and his voice not loud enough, and the sharks tore huge pieces of the flesh of his flesh and there were always more to tear. And the sharks had voices and their laughter was of demons, but angels stood by and told him to hurry, hurry, Mac, hurry or you'll be too late. Then there were no sharks, only yellow men with bayonets and gold teeth, sharpened to needles, surrounding him and his family on the bottom of the sea. Their bayonets huge, sharp. Not them, me! he screamed. Me, kill me! And he watched, impotent, while they killed his wife and killed his son and then they turned on him and the angels watched and whispered in chorus, Hurry, Mac, hurry. Run. Run. Run away and you'll be safe. And he ran, not wanting to run, ran away from his son and his wife and their blood-filled sea, and he fled through the blood and strangled. But he still ran and they chased him, the sharks with slant eyes and gold needle teeth with their rifles and bayonets, tearing at his flesh until he was at bay. He fought and he pleaded, but they would not stop and now he was surrounded. And Yoshima shoved the bayonet deep into his guts. And the pain was huge. Beyond agony. Yoshima jerked the bayonet out and he felt his blood

137

pour out of him, through the jagged hole, through all the openings of his body, through the very pores of his skin until only the soul was left in the husk. Then, at last, his soul sped forth and joined with the blood of the sea. A great, exquisite relief filled him, infinite, and he was glad that he was dead.

Mac opened his eyes. His blankets were soaked. His fever had passed. And he knew that he was alive once more.

Peter Marlowe was still sitting beside the bed. Night somewhere behind him.

'Hello, laddie.' The words were so faint that Peter Marlowe had to bend forward to catch them.

'You all right, Mac?'

'All right, laddie. It's almost worth the fever, to feel so good. I'll sleep now. Bring me some food tomorrow.'

Mac closed his eyes and was asleep. Peter Marlowe pulled the blankets off him and dried the husk of the man.

'Where can I get some dry blankets, Steven?' he asked, as he caught sight of the orderly hurrying through the ward.

'I don't know, sir,' Steven said. He had seen this young man many times. And liked him. Perhaps—but no, Lloyd would be terribly jealous. Another day. There's plenty of time. 'Perhaps I can help you, sir.'

Steven went over to the fourth bed and took the blanket off the man, then deftly slid the bottom blanket off and came back. 'Here,' he said. 'Use these.'

'What about him?'

'Oh,' Steven said with a gentle smile. 'He doesn't need them any more. The detail's due. Poor boy.'

'Oh!' Peter Marlowe looked across to see who it was, but it was a face he didn't know. 'Thanks,' he said and began to fix the bed.

'Here,' Steven said. 'Let me. I can do it much better than you.' He was proud of the way he could make a bed without hurting the patient.

'Now, don't you worry about your friend,' he said, 'I'll see that he's all right.' He tucked Mac in like a child. 'There.' He stroked Mac's head for a moment, then took out a handkerchief and wiped the remains of the sweat off Mac's forehead. 'He'll be fine in two days. If you have some extra food—' but he stopped and looked at Peter Marlowe and the tears gathered in his eyes. 'How silly of me. But don't you fret, Steven will find something for him. Now don't you worry. There's nothing more you can do tonight. You go off and have a good night's rest. Go on, there's a good boy.'

Speechless, Peter Marlowe allowed himself to be led outside. Steven smiled good night and went back inside.

From the darkness Peter Marlowe watched Steven smooth a fevered brow and hold an agued hand, and caress away the night-devils and soften the night-cries and adjust the covers and help a man to drink and help a man to vomit, and all the time sang a lullaby, delicate and sweet. When Steven came to Bed Four, he stopped and looked down on the corpse. He straightened the limbs and crossed the hands, then took off his smock and covered the body, his touch a benediction. Steven's slim smooth torso and slim smooth legs glowed in the glittering half light.

'You poor boy,' he whispered and looked around the tomb. 'Poor boys. Oh, my poor boys,' and he wept for them all.

Peter Marlowe turned away into the night, filled with pity, ashamed that Steven had once upon a time disgusted him.

XII

As Peter Marlowe neared the American hut he was full of misgivings. He was sorry that he had agreed so readily to interpret for the King, and at the same time upset that he was unhappy about doing it. You're a fine friend, he told himself, after all he's done for you.

The sinking in his stomach increased. Just like before you go up for a mission, he thought. No, not like that. This feeling's like when you've been sent for by the headmaster. The other's just as painful, but at the same time mixed with pleasure. Like the village. That makes your heart take flight. To take such a chance, just for the excitement—or in truth for the food or the girl that might be there.

He wondered for the thousandth time just why the King went and what he did there. But to ask would be impolite and he knew that he only had to have a little patience to find out. There was another reason he liked the King. The way that he volunteered nothing and kept most of his thoughts to himself. That's the English way, Peter Marlowe told himself contentedly. Just let out a little at a time, when you're in the mood. What you are or who you are is your own affair—until you wish to share with a friend. And a friend never asks. It has to be freely given or not at all.

Like the village. My God, he thought, that shows how much he thinks of you, to open up like that. Just to come out and say do you want to come along, the next time *I* go.

Peter Marlowe knew that it was an insane thing to do. To go to the village. But perhaps not so insane now. Now there was a real reason. An important reason. To try to get a part to fix the wireless—or to get a wireless, a whole one. Yes. This makes the risk worthwhile.

But at the same time he knew that he would have gone just because he had been asked to go, and because of the might-be-food and might-be-girl.

He saw the King deep in shadow, beside a hut, talking to another shadow. Their heads were close together and their voices were inaudible. So intent were they that Peter Marlowe decided to pass the King by, and he began to mount the stairs into the American hut, crossing the shaft of light.

'Hey, Peter,' the King called out.

Peter Marlowe stopped.

'Be right with you, Peter.' The King turned back to the other figure. 'Think you'd better wait here, Major. Soon as he arrives I'll give you the word.'

'Thank you,' the small man said, his voice wet with embarrassment.

'Have some tobacco,' the King said, and it was accepted avidly. Major Prouty backed deeper into the shadows but kept his eyes on the King as he walked the space to his own hut.

'Missed you, buddy,' the King said to Peter Marlowe and punched him playfully. 'How's Mac?'

'He's all right, thanks.' Peter Marlowe wanted to get out of the shaft of light. Dammit, he thought. I'm embarrassed being seen with my friend. And that's rotten. Very rotten.

But he could not help feeling the major's eyes watching—or stop the wince as the King said, 'C'mon. Won't be long, then we can go to work!'

Grey went to the hiding place just in case there was a message for him in the can. And there was. *Major Prouty's watch. Tonight. Marlowe and him.*

Grey tossed the can back into the ditch as casually as he had picked it up. Then, stretching, he got up and walked back towards Hut Sixteen. But all the time his mind worked with computer speed.

Marlowe and the King. They'll be in the 'shop' behind the American hut. Prouty. Which one? Major! Is he the one with the Artillery? Or the Aussie? Come on, Grey, he asked himself irritably, where's the card index mind you're so proud of? Got him! Hut Eleven! Little man! Pioneers! Aussie!

Is he connected with Larkin? No. Not to my knowledge. An Aussie. Then why not through the Aussie black-marketeer Tiny Timsen? Why the King? Maybe it's too big for Timsen to handle. Or maybe it's stolen property—more likely, for then Prouty wouldn't use regular Aussie channels. That's more like it.

Grey glanced at his watch. He did it instinctively, even though he had not had a watch for three years, even though he needed no watch to tell the time or gauge the hour of the night. Like all of them, he knew the time, as much of time as it was necessary to know.

It's too early yet, he thought. The guards don't change yet awhile. And when they did, from his hut he would be able to see the old guard plod the camp, way up the road, past his hut towards the guardhouse. The man to watch'll be the new guard. Who is it? Who cares? I'll know soon enough. Safer to wait and wait until the time, then swoop. Carefully. Just interrupt them politely. See the guard with the King and Marlowe. Better to see them when the money changes hands or when the King hands over the money to Prouty. Then a report to Colonel Smedly-Taylor: 'Last night I witnessed an interchange of money,' or just as good: 'I saw the American corporal and Flight Lieutenant Marlowe, DFC—Hut Sixteen—with a Korean guard. I have reason to believe that Major Prouty, Pioneers, was involved and provided the watch for sale.'

That would do it. The regulations, he thought happily, were clear and defined. 'No sales to guards!' Caught in the act. Then there would be a court-martial.

A court-martial to begin with. Then my jail, my little jail. With no extras and no katchang idju-bully. No nothing. Only caged, caged like the rats you are. Then to be let go—angry and hating. And angry men make mistakes. And the next time, perhaps Yoshima would be waiting. Better let the Japs do their own work—to help them isn't right. Perhaps in this case it would be all right. But no. Just a nudge, perhaps?

I'll pay you back, Peter Bloody Marlowe. Maybe sooner than I'd hoped. And my revenge on you and that crook will be ecstasy.

142

The King glanced at his watch. Nine-four. Any second now. One thing about the Japs, you always knew to the instant what they were going to do, for once a timetable had been set, it was set.

Then he heard the footsteps. Torusumi rounded the corner of the hut and came quickly under the lee of the curtain. The King rose to greet him. Peter Marlowe, also under the curtain, got up reluctantly, hating himself.

Torusumi was a character among the guards. Quite well-known. Dangerous and unpredictable. He had a face where most of them were faceless. He had been with the camp for a year or more. He liked to work the POW's hard and keep them in the sun and shout at them and kick them when the mood was on him.

'Tabe,' said the King, grinning. 'Like smoke?' He offered some raw Java tobacco.

Torusumi showed his gold-proud teeth and handed Peter Marlowe his rifle and sat down. He pulled out a pack of Kooas and offered them to the King, who accepted one. Then the Korean looked at Peter Marlowe.

'Ichi-bon friend,' said the King.

Torusumi grunted, showed teeth, sucked his breath in and offered a cigarette.

Peter Marlowe hesitated. 'Take it, Peter,' the King said.

Peter Marlowe obeyed, and the guard sat down at the little table.

'Tell him,' said the King to Peter Marlowe, 'that he's welcome.'

'My friend says that thou art welcome and he is pleasured to see thee here.'

'Ah, I thank thee. Does my worthy friend have anything for me?'

'He asks have you anything for him?'

'Tell him exactly what I say, Peter. Be exact.'

'I'll have to put it in the vernacular. You can't translate exactly.'

'That's okay—but make sure it's right—and take your time.'

The King passed over the watch. Peter Marlowe noticed with surprise that it was like new, freshly burnished, a new plastic watch face, and in a neat little chamois leather case.

'Tell him this—a guy I know wants to sell it. But it's expensive, and maybe not what he wants.'

Even Peter Marlowe saw the glint of avarice in the Korean's eyes as he took the watch out of the case and held it to his ear, grunted casually and put it back on the table.

Peter Marlowe translated the Korean's reply. 'Hast thou something else? I regret that Omegas are not bringing much in Singapore these days.'

'Thy Malay is exceptionally good, sir,' Torusumi added to Peter Marlowe, politely sucking the air past his teeth.

'I thank thee,' Peter Marlowe said grudgingly.

'What'd he say, Peter?'

'Just that I spoke Malay well, that's all.'

'Oh! Well, tell him I'm sorry, but that's all I've got.'

The King waited until this had been translated, then smiled and shrugged and picked up the watch and put it into its case and back in his pocket, and got up. 'Salamat!' he said.

Torusumi showed his teeth once more, then indicated that the King should sit. 'It is not that I want the watch,' he said to the King. But because thou are my friend and thou hast taken much trouble, I should inquire what does the man who owns this insignificant watch want for it?'

'Three thousand dollars,' the King replied. 'I'm sorry it's over-priced.'

'Truly it is overpriced. The owner has sickness in his head. I am a poor man, only a guard, yet because we have done business in the past and to do thee a favour I will offer three hundred dollars.'

'I regret. I dare not. I have heard that there are other buyers who would pay a more reasonable price through other intermediaries. I agree that thou art a poor man and should not offer money for so insignificant a watch. Of course, Omegas are not worth much money, but in deference to the owner thou wouldst understand it would be an insult to offer him anything less than a second-class watch is worth.'

'That is true. Perhaps I should increase the price, for even a poor man has honour, and it would be honourable to try to alleviate any man's suffering in these trying times. Four hundred.'

'I thank your concern for my acquaintance. But this watch—

144

being an Omega—and being that the price of Omegas has fallen from their accepted high place previously, obviously there is a more definite reason for thou not wanting to do business with me. A man of honour is always honourable—'

'I too, am a man of honour. I had no wish to impugn thy reputation and the reputation of your acquaintance who owns the watch. Perhaps I should risk my reputation and try to see if I could persuade those miserable Chinese merchants with whom I have to deal to give a fair price once in their miserable existences. I'm sure that thou wilt agree, five hundred would be the maximum a fair and honourable man could go for an Omega, even before their price dropped.'

'True, my friend. But I have a thought for thee. Perhaps the prices of Omegas have not dropped from their ichi-bon position. Perhaps the miserly Chinese are mistakenly taking advantage of a man of honour. Why, only last week another of thy Korean friends came to me and bought such a watch and paid three thousand dollars for it. I only offered it to thee because of my long friendship and trust that pertains as between associates of long standing.'

'Dost thou tell me truly?' Torusumi spat vehemently on the floor, and Peter Marlowe readied himself for the blow which had followed such outbursts before.

The King sat unperturbed. God, thought Peter Marlowe, he's got nerves of steel. The King pulled out some shreds of tobacco and began to roll himself a cigarette. When Torusumi saw this, he stopped raving and offered the pack of Kooas and cooled.

'I am astonished that the miserable Chinese merchants for whom I risk my life are so corrupt. I am horrified to hear what thou, my friend, has told me. Worse, I am appalled. To think that they have abused my trust. For a year I have been dealing with the same man. And to think that he has cheated me for so long. I think I will kill him.'

'Better,' said the King, To outsmart him.'

'How? I would dearly like my friend to tell me.'

'Curse him with thy tongue. Tell him that information has been given thee to prove that he is a cheat. Tell him if he does not give thee a fair price in future—a fair price plus twenty per cent, to pay thee back for all his past errors—then thou mayest whisper in the ear of the authorities. Then they will take him and take his women and take his children and abuse them to thy satisfaction.'

'It is superb advice. I am happy with the thought of my friend. Because of his thought and the friendship I hold for him, let me offer fifteen hundred dollars. It is all the money I have in the world, plus some money entrusted to me by my friend who is with the sickness of women in the stink-house called a hospital and who cannot work for himself.'

The King bent down and slapped at the clouds of mosquitoes on his ankles. That's more like it, boy, he thought. Let's see. Twenty would be high. Eighteen okay. Fifteen not bad.

'The King begs thee to wait,' Peter Marlowe translated. 'He must consult with the miserable man who wishes to sell thee an over-priced commodity.'

The King climbed through the window and walked down the length of the hut, checking. Max was in place. Dino down the path to one side. Byron Jones III to the other.

He found Major Prouty, sweating with anxiety in the shadow of the hut next to the American hut.

'Gee, I'm sorry, sir,' the King whispered unhappily. 'The guy's not anxious at all.'

Prouty's anxiety intensified. He had to sell. Oh God, he thought, just my luck. Got to get some money somehow.

'Won't he offer anything?'

'Best I could do was four hundred.'

'Four hundred! Why everyone knows that an Omega's worth at least two thousand.'

'I'm afraid that's a story, sir. He, well, he seems suspicious. That it's not an Omega.'

'He's out of his mind. Of course it's an Omega.'

'I'm sorry, sir,' said the King, stiffening slightly. 'I'm only reporting . . .'

'My fault, Corporal. I didn't mean to pick on you. These yellow bastards are all the same.' Now what do I do? Prouty asked himself. If I don't sell it through the King we won't sell it at all, and the unit needs the money and all our work will be for nothing. What do I do?

Prouty thought a minute, then said, 'See what you can do, Corporal. I couldn't take less than twelve hundred. I just couldn't.'

146

'Well, sir. I don't think I can do much, but I'll try.'

'There's a good fellow. I'm relying on you. I wouldn't let it go so low, but well, food's been so short. You know how it is.'

'Yes, sir,' said the King politely. 'I'll try, but I'm afraid I can't push him up much. He says the Chinese aren't buying like they used to. But I'll do what I can.'

Grey had marked Torusumi walking the camp and he knew that the time would soon be ripe. He had waited enough and now it was time. He got up and walked out of the hut, adjusting his armband and straightening his hat. No need for another witness, his word was enough. So he went alone.

His heart thumped pleasantly. It always did when he was preparing an arrest. He crossed the line of huts, walked down the steps onto the main street. This was the long way around. He chose it deliberately for he knew the King kept guards out whenever he was transacting business. But he knew their positions. And he knew there was one way, through the human mine field.

'Grey!'

He looked over. Colonel Samson was walking over to him.

'Yes, sir?'

'Ah, Grey, nice to see you. How are things going?'

'Fine, thank you, sir,' he replied, surprised to be greeted in such a friendly way. In spite of his eagerness to be away, he was not a little pleased.

Colonel Samson had a special place in Grey's future. Samson was Brass, but real Brass. War Office. And very well connected. A man like that would be more than useful—afterwards. Samson was on the General Staff of the Far East and had some vague but important job—G something or other. He knew all the generals and talked about how he entertained them social-ly—out at his 'country seat' in Dorset and how the gentry came shooting, and the garden parties and the hunt balls he orga-nized. A man like Samson could perhaps balance the scales against Grey's lack of record. And his class.

'I wanted to talk to you, Grey,' Samson said. 'I have an idea that you might think worth working on. You know I'm compil-ing the official history of the campaign. Of course,' he added with good humour, 'it's not *the* official one yet, but who knows, maybe it will be. General Sonny Wilkinson is historian in charge at the War Office, you know, and I'm sure Sonny'll be interested in an on-the-spot version. I wondered if you would be interested in checking a few facts for me. About your regiment?'

Like to, Grey thought. Like to! I'd give anything to. But not now.

'I'd love to, sir. I'm flattered that you'd think my views'd be worthwhile. Would tomorrow be all right? After breakfast.'

'Oh,' said Samson, 'I had hoped we could talk a little now. Well, perhaps another day. I'll let you know . . .'

And Grey knew instinctively that if it wasn't now, it was never. Samson had never said much to him before. Perhaps, he thought desperately, perhaps I can give him enough to start him off and I can still catch them. Deals took hours sometimes. Worth the risk!

'Be glad to now, if you wish, sir. But not too long, if you don't mind. I've a little headache. A few minutes if you don't mind.'

'Good.' Colonel Samson was very happy. He took Grey's arm and led him back towards the hut. 'You know, Grey, your regiment was one of my favourites. Did an excellent job. You got a mention in dispatches, didn't you? At Kota Bharu?'

'No, sir,' By God, I should have though. 'There was no time to send in requests for decorations. Not that I was entitled to one any more than anyone.' He meant it. Lot of the men deserved VCs and they would never get so much as a mention. Not now.

'You never can tell, Grey,' said Samson. 'Perhaps after the war we can rehash a lot of things.'

He sat Grey down. Now, just what was the state of the battle lines when you arrived in Singapore?'

'I regret to tell my friend,' Peter Marlowe said for the King, that the miserable owner of this watch laughed at me. He told me that the very least he would take was twenty-six hundred dollars. I am even ashamed to tell it to thee, but because thou art my friend of necessity I must tell it.'

Torusumi was obviously chagrined. Through Peter Marlowe, they talked about the weather and the lack of food, and Torusumi showed them a creased and battered photo of his wife and three children and told them a little about his life in his village

148

just outside Seoul and how he earned his living as a farmer, even though he had a minor university degree, and how he hated war. He told them how he himself hated the Japanese, how all the Koreans hated their Japanese overlords. Koreans are not even allowed in the Japanese Army, he said. They're second-class citizens and have no voice in anything and can be kicked about at the whim of the lowest Japanese.

And so they talked until at length Torusumi got up. He took his rifle back from Peter Marlowe, who all the time had held it, obsessed with the thought that it was loaded and how easy it would be to kill. But for what reason? And what then?

'I will tell my friend one last thing, because I don't like to see thee empty-handed with no profit on this stench-filled night, and would ask thee to consult with the greedy owner of this miserable watch. Twenty-one hundred!'

'But with respect, I must remind my friend that the miserable owner, who is a colonel, and as such a man of no humour, said he would only take twenty-six. I know you would not wish for him to spit upon me.'

'True. But with deference I would suggest that at least thou shouldst allow him the opportunity to refuse a last offer, given in true friendship, wherein I have no profit myself. And perhaps give him the opportunity to recant his uncouthness.'

'I will try because thou art my friend.'

The King left Peter Marlowe and the Korean. The time passed and they waited. Peter Marlowe listened to the story of how Torusumi was pressed into the service and how he had no stomach for war.

Then the King climbed down from the window.

'The man is a pig, a whore of no honour. He spat upon me and said he would spread the word that I was a bad business-man, that he would put me in jail before he would accept less than twenty-four—'

Torusumi raved and threatened. The King sat quietly and thought, Jesus, I've lost my touch, I pushed him too far this time, and Peter Marlowe thought, Christ, why the hell did I have to get mixed up in this?

Twenty-two,' Torusumi spat.

The King shrugged helplessly, beaten.

'Tell him okay,' he grumbled to Peter Marlowe. 'He's too

tough for me. Tell him I'll have to give up my goddamned commission to make up the difference. The son of a bitch won't accept a penny less. But where the hell's my profit in that?'

'Thou art a man of iron,' Peter Marlowe said for the King. 'I will tell the miserable owner Colonel that he can have his price, but to do this I will have to give up my commission to make up the difference between the price that thou hast offered and the price that he, miserable man, will accept. But where is my profit in that? Business is honourable, but even between friends there should be profit on both sides.'

'Because thou art my friend, I will add one hundred. Then thy face is saved and the next time thou needst not take the business of so avaricious and miserly a patron.'

'I thank thee. Thou art cleverer than I.'

The King handed over the watch in its little chamois case and counted the money from the huge roll of new counterfeit bills. Twenty-two hundred were in a neat pile. Then Torusumi handed over the extra hundred. Smiling. He had outsmarted the King, whose reputation as a fine businessman was common knowledge among all the guards. He could sell the Omega easily for five thousand dollars. Well, at least three-five. Not a bad profit for one guard duty.

Torusumi left the opened pack of Kooas and another full pack as compensation for the bad deal the King had made. After all, he thought there's a long war ahead, and business is good. And if the war is short—well, either way, the King would be a useful ally.

'You did very well, Peter.'

'I thought he was going to bust.'

'So did I. Make yourself at home, I'll be back in a minute.'

The King found Prouty still in the shadows. He gave him nine hundred dollars, the amount that the bitterly unhappy major had reluctantly agreed to, and collected his commission, ninety dollars.

'Things are getting tougher every day,' the King said.

Yes, they are, you bastard, Prouty thought to himself. Still, eight-ten isn't too bad for a phoney Omega. He chuckled to himself that he'd taken the King.

'Terribly disappointed, Corporal. Last thing I owned.' Let's see, he thought happily, it'll take us a couple of weeks to get another in shape. Timsen, the Aussie, can handle the next sale.

Suddenly Prouty saw Grey approaching. He scuttled into the maze of huts, melting with the shadows, safe. The King vaulted through a window into the American hut and joined the poker game and hissed at Peter Marlowe, 'Pick up the cards for Chrissake.' The two men whose places they had taken calmly kibitzed the game and watched the King deal out the stack of bills until there was a small pile in front of each man, and Grey stood in the doorway.

No one paid him any attention until the King looked up pleasantly. 'Good evening. Sir.'

'Evening.' The sweat was running down Grey's face. 'That's a lot of money.' Mother of God, I haven't seen so much money in my life. Not all in one place. And what I couldn't do with just a portion of it.

'We like to gamble, sir.'

Grey turned back into the night. God damn Samson to hell!

The men played a few hands until the all-clear was sounded. Then the King scooped up the money and gave each man a ten and they chorused their thanks. He gave Dino ten for each of the outside guards, jerked his head at Peter, and together they went back to his end of the hut.

'We deserve a cuppa Joe.' The King was a little tired. The strain of being on top was fatiguing. He stretched out on the bed and Peter Marlowe made the coffee.

'I feel I didn't bring you much luck,' Peter Marlowe said quietly.

'Huh?'

'The sale. It didn't go too well, did it?'

The King roared. 'According to plan. Here,' he said, and peeled off a hundred and ten dollars and gave them to Peter Marlowe. 'You owe me two bucks.'

'Two bucks?' He looked at the money. 'What's this for?'

'It's your commission.'

'For what?'

'Jesus, you don't think I'd put you to work for nothing, do you? What d'you take me for?'

'I said I was happy to do it. I'm not entitled to anything just for interpreting.'

151

'You're crazy. A hundred and eight bucks—ten per cent. It isn't a handout. It's yours. You earned it.'

'You're the one who's crazy. How in the hell can I earn a hundred and eight dollars from a sale of two thousand, two hundred dollars when that was the total price and there was no profit? I'm not taking the money he gave you.'

'You can't use it? You or Mac or Larkin?'

'Of course I can. But that's not fair. And I don't understand why a hundred and eight dollars.'

'Peter, I don't know how you've survived in this world up to now. Look. I'll make it simple for you. I made ten hundred and eighty bucks on the deal. Ten per cent is one hundred and eight. A hundred and ten less two is one hundred and eight. I gave you one hundred and ten. You owe me two bucks.'

'How in the hell did you make all that when—'

'I'll tell you. Lesson number one in business. You buy cheap and sell dear, if you can. Take tonight, for instance.' The King happily explained how he had outfoxed Prouty. When he finished, Peter Marlowe was silent for a long time. Then he said, 'It seems—well, that seems dishonest.'

'Nothing dishonest about it, Peter. All business is founded on the theory that you sell higher than you buy—or it costs you.'

'Yes. But doesn't your—profit margin seem a little high?'

'Hell, no. We all knew the watch was a phoney. Except Torusumi. You don't mind screwing him, do you? Though he can off-load it on a Chinese, easy, for a profit.'

'I suppose not.'

'Right. Take Prouty. He was selling a phoney. Maybe he'd stolen it, hell, I don't know. But he got a poor price 'cause he wasn't a good trader. If he'd had the guts to take the watch back and start down the street, then I'd have stopped him and upped the price. He could have bartered me. He doesn't give a goddam in hell about me if the watch backfires. Part of the deal is that I always protect my customers—so Prouty's safe and knows it—when I may be out on a limb.'

'What'll you do when Torusumi finds out and does come back?'

'He'll come back,' the King grinned suddenly and the warmth of it was a joy to see, 'but not to scream. Hell, if he did that he'd be losing face. He'd never dare admit that I'd out-smarted him in a deal. Why, his pals'd rib him to death if I spread the word. He'll come back, sure but to try to outsmart me next time.'

He lit a cigarette and gave one to Peter Marlowe.

'So,' he continued blithely, 'Prouty got nine hundred less my ten per cent, commission. Low but not unfair, and don't forget, you and I were taking *all* the risks. Now as to our costs. I had to pay a hundred bucks to get the watch burnished and cleaned and get a new glass. Twenty for Max, who heard about the prospective sale, ten apiece for the four guards and another sixty for the boys for covering with the game. That totals eleven twenty. Eleven twenty from twenty-two hundred is a thousand and eighty bucks even. Ten per cent of that is one hundred and eight. Simple.'

Peter Marlowe shook his head. So many figures and so much money and so much excitement. One moment they were just talking to a Korean, and the next he had a hundred and ten—a hundred and eight—dollars handed to him as simple as that. Holy mackerel! he thought exultantly. That's twenty-odd coco-nuts or lots of eggs. Mac! Now we can give him some food. Eggs, eggs are the thing!

Suddenly he heard his father talking, heard him as clearly as though he were beside him. And he could see him, erect and thickset in his Royal Navy uniform. 'Listen, my son. There is such a thing as honour. If you deal with a man, tell him the truth and then he must of necessity tell you the truth or he has no honour. Protect another man as you expect him to protect you. And if a man has no honour, do not associate with him for he will taint you. Remember, there are honourable people and dirty people. There is honourable money and dirty money.'

'But this isn't dirty money,' he heard himself answer, 'not the way the King has just explained it. They were taking him for a sucker. He was cleverer than they.'

'True. But it is dishonest to sell the property of a man and tell him that the price was so far less than the real price.'

'Yes, but . . .'

'There are no buts, my son. True there are degrees of hon-our—but one man can have only one code. Do what you like. It's your choice. Some things a man must decide for himself.

Sometimes you have to adapt to circumstances. But for the love of God guard yourself and your conscience—no one else will—and know that a bad decision at the right time can destroy you far more surely than any bullet!'

Peter Marlowe weighed the money and pondered what he could do with it, he, Mac and Larkin. He struck a balance and the scales were heavy on one side. The money rightly belonged to Prouty and his unit. Perhaps it was the last thing they possessed in the world. Perhaps because of the stolen money, Prouty and his unit, none of whom he knew, perhaps they would die. All because of his greed. Against this was Mac. His need was now. And Larkin's and mine. Mine too, don't forget me. He remembered the King saying, 'No need to take a handout,' and he had been taking handouts. Many of them.

What to do, dear God, what to do? But God didn't answer.

'Thanks. Thanks for the money,' Peter Marlowe said. He put it away. And all of him was conscious of its burn.

'Thanks nothing. You earned it. It's yours. You worked for it. I didn't give you anything.'

The King was jubilant and his joy smothered Peter Marlowe's self-disgust. 'C'mon,' he said. 'We got to celebrate our first deal together. With my brains and your Malay, why, we'll live a life of Riley yet!' And the King fried some eggs.

While they ate, the King told Peter Marlowe how he had sent the boys out to buy extra stocks of food when he heard that Yoshima had found the radio.

'Got to gamble in this life, Peter boy. Sure. I figured that the Japs'd make life tough for a while. But only for those who weren't prepared to figure an angle. Look at Tex. Poor son of a bitch hadn't any dough to buy a lousy egg. Look at you and Larkin. Wasn't for me Mac'd still be suffering, poor bastard. Of course, I'm happy to help. Like to help my friends. A man's got to help his friends or there's no point in anything.'

'I suppose so,' Peter Marlowe replied. What an awful thing to say. He was hurt by the King and did not understand that the American mind is simple in some things, as simple as the English mind. An American is proud of his money-making capability, rightly so. An Englishman, such as Peter Marlowe, is proud to get killed for the flag. Rightly so.

He saw the King glance out of the window and saw the snap

of the eyes. He followed the glance and saw a man coming up the path. As the man walked into the shaft of light Peter Marlowe recognised him. Colonel Samson.

When Samson saw the King, he waved amicably. 'Evening, Corporal,' he said, and continued his walk past the hut.

The King peeled off ninety dollars and handed it to Peter Marlowe.

'Do me a favour, Peter. Put a ten with this and give it to that guy.'

'Samson? Colonel Samson?'

'Sure. You'll find him up near the corner of the jail.'

'Give him the money? Just like that? But what do I say to him?'

'Tell him it's from me.'

My God, thought Peter Marlowe, appalled, is Samson on the payroll? He can't be! I can't do it. You're my friend, but I can't go up to a colonel and say here's a hundred bucks from the King. I can't!

The King saw through his friend. Oh Peter, he thought, you're such a goddam child. Then he added, To hell with you! But he threw the last word away and cursed himself. Peter was the only guy in the camp he had ever wanted for his friend, the only guy he needed. So he decided to teach him the facts of life. It's going to be tough, Peter boy, and it may hurt you a lot, but I'm going to teach you if I have to break you. You're going to survive and you're going to be my partner.

'Peter,' he said, 'there are times when you have to trust me. I'll never put you behind the eightball. As long as you're my friend, trust me. If you don't want to be my friend, fine. But I'd like you to be my friend.'

Peter Marlowe knew that here was another moment of truth. Take the money in trust—or leave it and be gone.

A man's life is always at a crossroads. And not his life alone, not if he's a *man*. Always others in the balance.

He knew that one path risked Mac's and Larkin's lives, along with his own, for without the King they were as defenceless as any in the camp; without the King there was no village, for he knew that he would never risk it alone—even for the wireless. The other path would jeopardize a heritage or destroy a past. Samson was a power in the Regular Army, a man of caste, position and wealth, and Peter Marlowe was born to be an officer—as his father before him and his son after him—and such an accusation could never be forgotten. And if Samson was a hireling, then everything he had been taught to believe would have no value.

Peter Marlowe watched himself as he took the money and went into the night and walked up the path and found Colonel Samson, and heard the man whisper, 'Oh hello, you're Marlowe, aren't you?'

He saw himself hand over the money. 'The King asked me to give you this.'

He saw the mucoused eyes light up as Samson greedily counted the money and tucked it away in his threadbare pants.

'Thank him,' he heard Samson whisper, 'and tell him I stopped Grey for an hour. That was as long as I could hold him. That was long enough, wasn't it?'

'It was enough. Just enough.' Then he heard himself say, 'Next time keep him longer, or send word, you stupid bugger!'

'I kept him as long as I could. Tell the King I'm sorry. I'm truly sorry and it won't happen again. I promise. Listen, Marlowe. You know how it is sometimes. It gets a bit difficult.'

'I'll tell him you're sorry.'

'Yes, yes, thank you, thank you, Marlowe. I envy you Marlowe. Being so close to the King. You're lucky.'

Peter Marlowe returned to the American hut. The King thanked him and he thanked the King again and walked out into the night.

He found a small promontory overlooking the wire and wished himself into his Spitfire soaring the sky alone, up, up, up in the sky, where all is clean and pure, where there are no lousy people—like me—where life is simple and you can talk to God and be of God, without shame.

XIII

Peter Marlowe lay on his bunk drifting in half sleep. Around him men were waking, getting up, going to relieve themselves, preparing for work parties, going and coming from the hut. Mike was already grooming his moustache, fifteen inches from tip to tip; he had sworn never to cut it until he was released. Barstairs was already standing on his head practising Yoga, Phil Mint already picking his nose, the bridge game already started, Raylins already doing his singing exercises, Myner already doing scales on his wooden keyboard, Chaplain Grover already trying to cheer everyone up, and Thomas was already cursing the lateness of breakfast.

Above Peter Marlowe, Ewart, who had the top bunk, groaned out of sleep and hung his legs over the bunk. ''Mahlu on the night!'

'You were kicking like hell.' Peter Marlowe had said the same remark many times, for Ewart always slept restlessly.

'Sorry.'

Ewart always said, Sorry. He jumped down heavily. He had no place in Changi. His place was five miles away, in the civilian camp, where his wife and family were—perhaps were. No contact had ever been allowed between the camps.

'Let's burn the bed after we've showered,' he said yawning. He was short and dark and fastidious.

'Good idea.'

'Never think we did it three days ago. How did you sleep?'

'Same as usual.' But Peter Marlowe knew that nothing was the same, not after accepting the money, not after Samson.

157

The impatient line for breakfast was already forming as they carried the iron bunk out of the hut. They lifted the top bed off and pulled out the iron posts which fitted into slots on the lower one. Then they got coconut husks and twigs from their section under the hut and built fires under the four legs.

While the legs were heating, they took burning fronds and held them under the longitudinal bars and under the springs. Soon the earth beneath the bed was black with bedbugs.

'For Christ's sake, you two,' Phil shouted at them. 'Do you have to do that before breakfast?' He was a sour, pigeon-chested man with violent red hair.

They paid no attention. Phil always shouted at them, and they always burned their bunk before breakfast.

'God, Ewart,' Peter Marlowe said. 'You'd think the buggers could pick up the bunk and walk away with it.'

'Damn nearly threw me out of bed last night. Stinking things.' In a sudden flurry of rage Ewart beat the myriads of bugs.

'Easy, Ewart.'

'I can't help it. They make my skin crawl.'

When they had completed the bed they left it to cool and cleaned their matresses. This took half an hour. Then the mosquito nets. Another half an hour.

By that time the beds were cool enough to handle. They put the bunk together and carried it back and set it in the four tins—carefully cleaned and filled with water—and made sure the edges of the tins did not touch the iron legs.

'What's today, Ewart?' Peter Marlowe said absently as they waited for breakfast.

'Sunday.'

Peter Marlowe shuddered, remembering that other Sunday.

It was after the Japanese patrol had picked him up. He was in hospital in Bandung that Sunday. That Sunday, the Japanese had told all the prisoner of war patients to pick up their belongings and march because they were going to another hospital.

They had lined up in their hundreds in the courtyard. Only senior officers did not go. They were being sent to Formosa, so the rumour said. The General stayed too, he who was *the* senior officer, he who openly walked the camp communing with the

Holy Ghost. The General was a neat man, square-shouldered, and his uniform was wet with the spit of the conquerors.

Peter Marlowe remembered carrying his mattress through the streets of Bandung under a heated sky, streets lined with shouting silent people, dressed multihued. Then throwing away the mattress. Too heavy. Then falling but getting up. Then the gates of the prison had opened and the gates of the prison had closed. There was enough room to lie down in the courtyard. But he and a few others were locked alone into tiny cells. There were chains on the walls and a small hole in the ground which was the toilet, and around the toilet were faeces of years. Stench-straw matted the earth.

In the next cell was a maniac, a Javanese who had run amok and killed three women and two children before the Dutch had overpowered him. Now it was not the Dutch who were the jailers. They were jailed too. All the days and all the nights the maniac banged his chains and screamed.

There was a tiny hole in Peter Marlowe's door. He lay on the straw and looked out at the feet and waited for food and listened to the prisoners cursing and dying, for there was plague.

He waited forever.

Then there was peace and clean water and there was no longer just a tiny hole for the world, but the sky was above and there was cool water sponging him, washing away the filth. He opened his eyes and saw a gentle face and it was upside down and there was another face and both were filled with peace and he thought that he was truly dead.

But it was Mac and Larkin. They had found him just before they left the prison for another camp. They had thought that he was a Javanese, like the maniac next door, who still howled and rattled his chains, for he too had been shouting in Malay and looked like the Javanese . . .

'Come on, Peter,' Ewart said again. 'Grub's up!'

'Oh, thanks.' Peter Marlowe collected his mess cans.

'You feeling all right?'

'Yes.' After a moment he said, 'It's good to be alive, isn't it?'

In the middle of the morning the news flared through Changi. The Japanese Commandant was going to return the camp to the standard ration of rice, to celebrate a great Japanese victory at sea. The Commandant had said that a United States task force had been totally destroyed, that the probe to the Philippines was therefore halted, that even now Japanese forces were regrouping for the invasion of Hawaii.

Rumours and counter-rumours. Opinions and counter-opinions.

'Bloody nonsense! Just put out to cover a defeat.'

'I don't think so. They've never given us an increase to celebrate a defeat.'

'Listen to him! Increase! We're only getting back something we just lost. No, old chap. You take my word for it. The bloody Japs are getting their come-uppance. You take it from me!'

'What the hell do you know that we don't? You've a wireless, I suppose?'

'If I had, as sure as God made little apples, I wouldn't tell you.'

'By the way, what about Daven?'

'Who?'

'The one who had the wireless.'

'Oh, yes, I remember. But I didn't know him. What was he like?'

'Regular sort of bloke, I hear. Pity he got caught.'

'I'd like to find the bastard who gave him away. Bet he was an Air Force type. Or an Australian. Those bastards'd sell their souls for a halfpenny!'

'I'm Australian, you Pommy bastard.'

'Oh. Take it easy. Just a joke!'

'You've a funny sense of humour, you bugger.'

'Oh, take it easy, you two. It's too hot. Anyone lend me a smoke?'

'Here, take a puff.'

'Gee whiz, that tastes rough.'

'Papaya leaves. Cured it myself. It's all right once you get used to it.'

'Look over there!'

'Where?'

Going up the road. Marlowe!'

'That him? I'll be damned! I hear he's taken up with the King.'

160

'That's why I pointed him out, you idiot. Whole camp knows about it. You been sleeping or something?'

'Don't blame him. I would if I had half the chance. They say the King's got money and gold rings and food to feed an army.'

'I hear he's a homo. That Marlowe's his new girl.'

'That's right.'

'The hell it is. The King's no homo, just a bloody crook.'

'I don't think he's a homo either. He's certainly smart, I'll say that for him. Miserable bastard.'

'Homo or not, I wish I was Marlowe. Did you hear he's got a whole stack of dollars? I heard that he and Larkin were buying some eggs and a whole chicken.'

'You're crazy. No one's got that amount of money—except the King. They've got chickens of their own. Probably one died, that's all! That's another of your bloody stories.'

'What do you think Marlowe's got in that billy?'

'Food. What else? You don't need to know anything to know that it's food.'

Peter Marlowe headed towards the hospital.

In his mess can was the breast of a chicken, and the leg and the thigh. Peter Marlowe and Larkin had bought it from Colonel Foster for sixty dollars and some tobacco and the promise of a fertile egg from the clutch that Rajah, the son of Sunset, would soon fertilize through Nonya. They had decided, with Mac's approval, to give Nonya another chance, not to kill her as she deserved, for none of the eggs had hatched. Perhaps it wasn't Nonya, Mac had said, perhaps the cock, which had belonged to Colonel Foster, was no damned good—and all the flurry of wings and pecking and jumping the hens was merely show.

Peter Marlowe sat with Mac while he consumed the chicken.

'God, laddie, I haven't felt so good or so full for almost as long as I can remember.'

'Fine. You look wonderful, Mac.'

Peter Marlowe told Mac where the money for the chicken had come from, and Mac said, 'You were right to take the money. Like as not that Prouty laddie stole the thing or made the thing. He was wrong to try to sell a bad piece of merchandise. Remember laddie, *Caveat emptor.*'

'Then why is it,' Peter Marlowe asked, 'why is it I feel so

damned guilty? You and Larkin say it was right. Though I think Larkin was not so sure as you are—'

'It's business laddie. Larkin's an accountant. He's not a real businessman. Now, I know the way of the world.'

'You're just a miserable rubber planter. What the hell do you know about business? You've been stuck on a plantation for years!'

'I'll ha' you know,' Mac said, his feathers ruffled, 'most of planting is being a businessman. Why, every day you have to deal with the Tamils or the Chinese—now there are a race of businessmen. Why, laddie, they invented every trick there was.'

So they talked to one another, and Peter Marlowe was pleased that Mac reacted once more to his jibes. Almost without noticing it, they lapsed into Malay.

Then Peter Marlowe said casually, 'Knowest thou the thing that is of three things?' For safety he spoke about the radio in parables.

Mac glanced around to make sure they were not being overheard. 'Truly. What of it?'

'Art thou sure now of its particular sickness?'

'Not sure—but almost sure. Why dost thou inquire of it?'

'Because the wind carries a whisper which spoke of medicine to cure the sickness of various kinds.'

Mac's face lit up. 'Wah-lah,' he said. 'Thou has made an old man happy. In two days I will be out of this place. Then thou wilt take me to this whisper.'

'No. That is not possible. I must do this privately. And quickly.'

'I would not have thee in danger,' Mac said thoughtfully.

'The wind carried hope. As it is written in the Koran, without hope, man is but an animal.'

'It might be better to wait than to seek thy death.'

'I would wait, but the knowledge I seek I must know today.'

'Why?' Mac said abruptly in English. 'Why today, Peter?'

Peter Marlowe cursed himself for falling into the trap he had so carefully planned to avoid. He knew that if he told Mac about the village, Mac would go out of his head with worry. Not that Mac could stop him, but he knew he would not go if Mac and Larkin asked him not to go. What the hell do I do now?

Then he remembered the advice of the King. Today, tomorrow, it doesn't matter. Just interested,' he said and played his trump. He got up. The oldest trick in the book. 'Well, see you tomorrow, Mac. Maybe Larkin and I'll drop around tonight.'

'Sit down, laddie. Unless you've something to do.'

'I've nothing to do.'

Mac testily switched to Malay. 'Thou speakest truly? That "today" means nothing? The spirit of my father whispered that those who are young will take risks which even the devil would pass by.'

'It is written, the scarcity of years does not necessitate lack of wisdom.'

Mac studied Peter Marlowe speculatively. Is he up to something? Something with the King? Well, he thought tiredly, Peter's already in the radio-danger up over his head, and he did carry a third of it all the way from Java.

'I sense danger for thee,' he said at length.

'A bear can take the honey of hornets without danger. A spider can seek safely under rocks, for it knows where and how to seek.' Peter Marlowe kept his face bland. 'Do not fear for me, Old One. I seek only under rocks.'

Mac nodded, satisfied. 'Knowest thou my container?'

'Assuredly.'

'I believe it became sick when a raindrop squeezed through a hole in its sky and touched a thing and festered it like a fallen tree in the jungle. The thing is small, like a tiny snake, thin as an earthworm, short as a cockroach.' He groaned and stretched. 'My back's killing me,' he said in English. 'Fix my pillow, will you, laddie?'

As Peter Marlowe bent down, Mac lifted himself and whispered in his ear, 'A coupling condenser, three hundred microfarads.'

'That better?' Peter Marlowe asked as Mac settled back.

'Fine, laddie, a lot better. Now be off with you. All that nonsense talk has tired me out.'

'You know it amuses you, you old bugger.'

'Less of the old, puki'mahlu!'

'Senderis!' said Peter Marlowe, and he walked into the sun. A coupling condenser, three hundred microfarads. What the hell's a microfarad?

163

He was windward of the garage and smelled the sweet gasoline-laden air, heavy with oil and grease. He squatted down beside the path on a patch of grass to enjoy the aroma. My God, he thought, the smell of petrol brings back memories. Planes and Gosport and Farnborough and eight other airfields, and Spitfires and Hurricanes.

But I won't think about them now, I'll think about the wireless.

He changed his position and sat in the lotus seat, right foot on left thigh, left foot on right thigh, hands in his lap, knuckles touching and thumbs touching and fingers pointing to his navel. Many times he had sat thus. It helped him to think, for once the initial pain had passed, there was a quietude pervading the body and the mind soared free.

He sat quietly and men passed by, hardly noticing him. There was nothing strange in seeing a man sitting thus in the heat of the noon sun, cinder-burned, in a sarong. Nothing strange at all.

Now I know what has to be obtained. Somehow. There's bound to be a wireless in the village. Villages are like magpies— they collect all sorts of things; and he laughed, remembering *his* village in Java.

He had found it, stumbling in the jungle, exhausted and lost, more dead than alive, far from the threads of road that crisscrossed Java. He had run many miles and the date was March 11. The island forces had capitulated on March 8, and the year was 1942. For three days he had wandered the jungle, eaten by bugs and flies and ripped by thorns and bloodsucked by leeches and soaked by rains. He had seen no one, heard no one since he had left the airfield north, the fighter 'drome at Bandung. He had left his squadron, what remained of it, and left his Hurricane. But before he had run away, he had made his dead airplane—twisted, broken by bomb and tracer—a funeral pyre. A man could do no less than cremate his friend.

When he came upon the village it was sunset. The Javanese who surrounded him were hostile. They did not touch him, but the anger in their faces was clear to see. They stared at him silently, and no one made a move to succour him.

'Can I have some food and water?' he asked.

No answer.

Then he had seen the well and gone over to it, followed by angry eyes, and had drunk deep from it. Then he had sat down and had begun to wait.

The village was small, well hidden. It seemed quite rich. The houses, built around a square, were on stilts and made of bamboo and atap. And under the houses were many pigs and chickens. Near a larger house was a corral and in it were five water buffalo. That meant the village was well-to-do.

At length he was led to the house of the headman. The silent natives followed up the steps but did not enter the house. They sat on the veranda and listened and waited.

The headman was old, nut-brown and withered. And hostile. The house, like all their houses, was one large room partitioned by atap screens into small sections.

In the centre of the section devoted to eating, talking, and thinking was a porcelain toilet bowl, complete with a seat and lid. There were no water connections and the toilet sat in a place of honour on a woven carpet. In front of the toilet bowl on another mat the headman sat on his haunches. His eyes were piercing.

'What do you want? Tuan!' and the 'Tuan' was an accusation.

'I just wanted some food and water, sir, and—perhaps I could stay for a little while until I've caught up with myself.'

'You call me sir, when three days ago you and the rest of the whites were calling us Wogs and were spitting upon us?'

'I never called you Wogs. I was sent here to try to protect your country from the Japanese.'

'They have liberated us from the pestilential Dutch! As they will liberate the whole of the Far East from the white imperialists!'

'Perhaps. But I think you'll regret the day they came!'

'Get out of my village. Go with the rest of the imperialists. Go before I call the Japanese themselves.'

'It is written, "If a stranger comes to thee and asks for hospitality, give it to him that thou find favour in the sight of Allah."'

The headman had looked at him aghast. Nut-brown skin, short baju coat, multi-coloured sarong and the decorating head cloth in the gathering darkness.

'What do you know of the Koran and the words of the Prophet?'

'On whose name be praise,' Peter Marlowe said. 'The Koran has been translated into English for many years by many men.' He was fighting for his life. He knew that if he could stay in the village he might be able to get a boat to sail to Australia. Not that he knew how to sail a boat, but the risk was worthwhile. Captivity was death.

'Are you one of the Faithful?' the astonished headman asked.

Peter Marlowe hesitated. He could easily pretend to be a Mohammedan. Part of his training had been to study the Book of Islam. Officers of His Majesty's forces had to serve in many lands. Hereditary officers are trained in many things over and apart from formal schooling.

If he said yes, he knew he would be safe, for Java was mostly the domain of Mohammed.

'No. I am not one of the Faithful.' He was tired and at the end of his run. 'At least I don't know. I was taught to believe in God. My father used to tell us, my sisters and I, that God has many names. Even Christians say that there is a Holy Trinity—that there are parts of God.

'I don't think it matters what you call God. God won't mind if he is recognized as Jesus or Allah, or Buddha or Jehovah, or even you!—because if he is God, then he knows that we are only finite and don't know too much about anything.

'I believe Mohammed was a man of God, a Prophet of God. I think Jesus was of God, as Mohammed calls him in the Koran, the "most blameless of the Prophets." That Mohammed is the last of the Prophets as he claimed, I don't know. I don't think that we, humans, can be certain about anything to do with God.

'But I do not believe that God is an old man with a long white beard who sits on a golden throne far up in the sky. I do not believe, as Mohammed promised, that the Faithful will go to paradise, where they will lie on silken couches and drink wine and have many beautiful maids to serve them, or that paradise will be a garden with an abundance of green foliage and pure streams and fruit trees. I do not believe that angels have wings growing from their backs.'

Night swooped over the village. A baby cried and was gentled back to sleep.

166

'One day I will know for certain by what name to call God. The day I die.' The silence gathered. 'I think it would be very depressing to discover there was no God.'

The headman motioned for Peter Marlowe to sit.

'You may stay. But there are conditions. You will swear to obey our laws and be one of us. You will work in the paddy and work in the village, the work of a man. No more and no less than any man. You will learn our language and speak only our language and wear our dress and dye the colour of your skin. Your height and the colour of your eyes will shout that you are a white man, but perhaps colour, dress and language may protect you for a time; perhaps it can be said that you are half Javanese, half white. You will touch no woman here without permission. And you will obey me without question.'

'Agreed.'

'There is one other thing. To hide an enemy of the Japanese is dangerous. You must know that when the time comes for me to choose between you and my people to protect my village, I will choose my village.'

'I understand. Thank you, sir.'

'Swear by your God—' a flicker of a smile swept the features of the old man—'swear by God that you will obey and agree to these conditions.'

'I swear by God I agree and will obey. And I'll do nothing to harm you while I'm here.'

'You harm us by your very presence, my son,' the old man replied.

After Peter Marlowe had had the food and drink, the headman said, 'Now you will speak no more English. Only Malay. From this moment on. It is the only way for you to learn quickly.'

'All right. But first may I ask you one thing?'

'Yes.'

'What is the significance of the toilet bowl? I mean, it hasn't any pipes attached to it.'

'It has no significance, other than it pleases me to watch the faces of my guests and hear them thinking, "What a ridiculous thing to have as an ornament in a house."'

And huge waves of laughter engulfed the old man and the tears ran down his cheeks and his whole household was in an uproar and his wives came in to succour him and rub his back and stomach, and then they too were shrieking and so was Peter Marlowe.

Peter Marlowe smiled again, remembering. Now that was a man! Tuan Abu. But I won't think any more today about my village, or my friends of the village, or N'ai, the daughter of the village they gave me to touch. Today I'll think about the wireless and how I'm going to get the condenser and sharpen my wits for the village tonight.

He unwound himself from the lotus seat, then waited patiently till the blood began to flow in his veins once more. Around him was the sweet gasoline smell, carried by a breeze. Also on the breeze came voices raised in hymn. They came from the open air theatre, which today was the Church of England. Last week it was a Catholic Church, the week before the Seventh-day Adventist, the week before another denomination. They were tolerant in Changi.

There were many parishioners crowding the rough seats. Some were there because of a faith, some were there for lack of a faith. Some were there for something to do, some were there because there was nothing else to do. Today Chaplain Drinkwater was conducting the service.

Chaplain Drinkwater's voice was rich and round. His sincerity poured from him and the words of the Bible sprang to life, and gave you hope, and made you forget that Changi was fact, that there was no food in your belly.

Rotten hypocrite, Peter Marlowe thought, despising Drinkwater, remembering once again . . .

'Hey, Peter,' Dave Daven had whispered that day, 'look over there.'

Peter Marlowe saw Drinkwater talking with a withered RAF corporal called Blodger. Drinkwater's bunk had a favoured spot near the door of Hut Sixteen.

'That must be his new batman,' Daven said. Even in the camp the age-old tradition was kept.

'What happened to the other one?'

'Lyles? My man told me he was up in hospital. Ward Six.'

Peter Marlowe got to his feet. 'Drinkwater can do what he likes with Army types, but he's not getting one of mine.'

He walked the four bunk lengths. 'Blodger!'

'What do you want, Marlowe?' Drinkwater said.

Peter Marlowe ignored him. 'What're you doing here, Blodger?'

'I was just seeing the chaplain, sir. I'm sorry, sir,' he said moving closer, 'I don't see you too well.'

'Flight Lieutenant Marlowe.'

'Oh. How're you, sir? I'm the chaplain's new batman, sir.'

'You get out of here, and before you take a job as a batman, you come and ask me first!'

'But sir—'

'Who do you think you are, Marlowe?' Drinkwater snapped. 'You've no jurisdiction over him.'

'He's not going to be your batman.'

'Why?'

'Because I say so. You're dismissed, Blodger.'

'But sir, I'll look after the chaplain fine, I really will. I'll work hard—'

'Where'd you get that cigarette?'

'Now look here, Marlowe—' Drinkwater began.

Peter Marlowe whirled on him. 'Shut up!' Others in the hut stopped what they were doing and began to collect.

'Where did you get that cigarette, Blodger?'

'The chaplain gave it to me,' whimpered Blodger, backing away, frightened by the edge to Peter Marlowe's voice. 'I gave him my egg. He promised me tobacco in exchange for my daily egg. I want the tobacco and he can have the eggs.'

'There's no harm in that,' Drinkwater blustered, 'no harm in giving the boy some tobacco. He asked me for it. In exchange for an egg.'

'You been up to Ward Six recently?' Peter Marlowe asked. 'Did you help them admit Lyles? Your last batman? He's got no eyes now.'

'That's not my fault. I didn't do anything about him.'

'How many of his eggs did you have?'

'None. I had none.'

Peter Marlowe snatched a Bible and thrust it into Drinkwater's hands. 'Swear it, then I'll believe you. Swear it or by God I'll do you!'

'I swear it!' Drinkwater moaned.

'You lying bastard,' Daven shouted. 'I've seen you take Lyle's eggs. We all have.'

Peter Marlowe grabbed Drinkwater's mess can and found the egg. Then he smashed it against Drinkwater's face, cramming the egg shell into his mouth. Drinkwater fainted.

Peter Marlowe dashed a bowl of water in his face, and he came to.

'Bless you, Marlowe,' he had whispered. 'Bless you for showing me the error of my ways.' He had knelt beside the bunk. 'Oh God, forgive this unworthy sinner. Forgive me my sins . . .'

Now, on this sun-kissed Sunday, Peter Marlowe listened as Drinkwater finished the sermon. Blodger had long since gone to Ward Six, but whether Drinkwater had helped him there, Peter Marlowe could never prove. Drinkwater still got many eggs from somewhere.

Peter Marlowe's stomach told him it was time for lunch.

When he got back to his hut, the men were already waiting, mess cans in hands, impatient. The extra was not going to arrive today. Or tomorrow according to rumour. Ewart had already checked the cookhouse. Just the usual. That was all right too, but why the hell don't they hurry up?

Grey was sitting on the end of his bed.

'Well, Marlowe,' he said, 'you eating with us these days? Such a pleasant surprise.'

'Yes, Grey, I'm still eating here. Why don't you just run along and play cops and robbers? You know, pick on someone who can't hit back!'

'Not a chance, old man. Got my eye on bigger game.'

'Jolly good luck.' Peter Marlowe got his mess cans ready. Across the way from him Brough, kibitzing a game of bridge, winked.

'Cops!' he whispered. 'They're all the same.'

'That's right.'

He joined Peter Marlowe. 'Hear you've a new buddy.'

'That's right.' Peter Marlowe was on his guard.

'It's a free country. But sometimes a guy's got to get out on a limb and make a point.'

'Oh?'

170

'Yeah. Fast company can sometimes get out of hand.'

'That's true in any country.'

'Maybe,' Brough grinned, 'maybe you'd like to have a cuppa Joe sometime and chew that fat.'

'I'd like that. How about tomorrow? After chow—' Involuntarily he used the King's word. But he didn't correct himself. He smiled and Brough smiled back.

'Hey, grub's up!' Ewart called out.

'Thank God for that,' Phil groaned. 'How about a deal, Peter? Your rice for my stew?'

'You've got a hope!'

'No harm in trying.'

Peter Marlowe went outside and joined the mess line. Raylins was serving out the rice. Good, he thought, no need to worry today.

Raylins was middle-aged and bald. He had been a junior manager in the Bank of Singapore and, like Ewart, one of the Malayan Regiment. In peacetime it was a great organization to belong to. Lots of parties, cricket, polo. A man had to be in the Regiment to be anyone. Raylins also looked after the mess fund, and banqueting was his speciality. When they gave him a gun and told him he was in the war and ordered him to take his platoon across the causeway and fight the Japanese, he had looked at the colonel and laughed. His job was accounts. But it hadn't helped him, and he had to take twenty men, as untrained as himself, and march up the road. He had marched then suddenly his twenty men were three. Thirteen had been killed instantly in the ambush. Four were only wounded. They were lying in the middle of the road screaming. One had his hand blown off and he was staring at the stump stupidly, catching his blood in his only hand, trying to pour it back into his arm. Another was laughing, laughing as he crammed his entrails back into the gaping hole.

Raylins had stared stupidly as the Japanese tank came down the road, guns blazing. Then the tank was past and the four were merely stains on the asphalt. He had looked at his remaining three men—Ewart was one of them. They had looked back at him. Then they were running, running terror-stricken into the jungle. Then they were lost. Then he was alone, alone in a horror night of leeches and noises, and the only thing that

171

saved him from insanity was a Malay child who had found him babbling and had guided him to a village. He had sneaked into the building where remnants of an army were collected. The next day the Japanese shot two of every ten. He and a few others were kept in the building. Later they were put into a truck and sent to a camp and he was among his own people. But he could never forget his friend Charles, the one with his intestines hanging out.

Raylins spent most of his time in a fog. For the life of him he could not understand why he wasn't in his bank counting his figures, clean neat figures, and why he was in a camp where he excelled at one thing. He could deal an unknown amount of rice into exactly the right number of parts. Almost to the grain.

'Ah Peter,' Raylins said, giving him his share, 'You knew Charles, didn't you?'

'Oh yes, nice fellow.' Peter Marlowe didn't know him. None of them did.

'Do you think he ever got them back in?' Raylins asked.

'Oh yes. Certainly.' Peter Marlowe took his food away as Raylins turned to the next in the line.

'Ah, Chaplain Grover, it's a warm day, isn't it? You knew Charles didn't you?'

'Yes,' the Chaplain said, eyes on the measure of rice. 'I'm sure he did, Raylins.'

'Good, good. I'm glad to hear it. Funny place to find your insides, on the outside, just like that.'

Raylins' mind wandered to his cool, cool bank and to his wife, whom he would see tonight, when he left the bank, in their neat little bungalow near the racecourse. Let me see, he thought, we'll have lamb for dinner tonight. Lamb! And a nice cool beer. Then I'll play with Penelope, and the missus'll be content to sit on the veranda and sew.

'Ah,' he said, happily recognizing Ewart. 'Would you like to come to dinner tonight, Ewart old boy? Perhaps you'd like to bring the missus.'

Ewart mumbled through clenched teeth. He took his rice and stew and turned away.

'Take it easy, Ewart,' Peter Marlowe cautioned him.

'Take it easy yourself! How do you know what it feels like? I swear to God I'll kill him one day.'

'Don't worry—'

'Worry! They're dead. His wife and child are dead. I saw them dead. But my wife and two children? Where are they, eh? Where? Somewhere dead too. They've got to be after all this time. Dead!'

'They're in the civilian camp—'

'How in Christ's name do you know? You don't, I don't, and it's only five miles away. They're dead! Oh my God,' and Ewart sat dow and wept, spilling his rice and stew on the ground. Peter Marlowe scooped up the rice and the leaves that floated in the stew and put them in Ewart's mess can.

'Next week they'll let you write a letter. Or maybe they'll let you visit. The Camp Commandant's always asking for a list of the women and children. Don't worry, they're safe.' Peter Marlowe left him slobbering his rice into his face, and took his own rice and went down to the bungalow.

'Hello, cobber,' Larkin said. 'You been up to see Mac?'

'Yes. He looks fine. He even started getting ruffled about his age.'

'It'll be good to get old Mac back.' Larkin reached under his mattress and brought out a spare mess can. 'Got a surprise!' He opened the mess can and revealed a two-inch square of brownish putty-like substance.

'By all that's holy! Blachang! Where the devil did you get it?'

'Scrounged it, of course.'

'You're a genius, Colonel. Funny, I didn't smell it.' Peter Marlowe leaned over and took a tiny piece of the blachang. 'This'll last us a couple of weeks.'

Blachang was a native delicacy, easy to make. When the season was right, you went to the shore and netted the myriads of tiny sea creatures that hovered in the surf. You buried them in a pit lined with seaweed, then covered it with more seaweed and forgot about it for two months.

When you opened the pit, the fishes had decayed into a stinking paste, the stench of which would blow your head off and destroy your sense of smell for a week. Holding your breath, you scooped up the paste and fried it. But you had to stay to windward or you'd suffocate. When it cooled, you shaped it into blocks and sold it for a fortune. Pre-war, ten cents a cube. Now maybe ten dollars a sliver. Why a delicacy? It was pure protein. And a tiny fraction would flavour a whole bowl of rice. Of course you could easily get dysentery from it. But if it'd been aged right and cooked right and hadn't been touched by flies, it was all right.

But you never asked. You just said, 'Colonel, you're a genius,' and spooned it into your rice and enjoyed it.

'Take some up to Mac, eh?'

'Good idea. But he's sure to complain it's not cooked enough.'

'Old Mac'd complain if it was cooked to perfection—' Larkin stopped. 'Hey, Johnny,' he called to the tall man walking past, leading a scrawny mongrel on a tether. 'Would you like some blachang, cobber?'

'Would I?'

They gave him a portion on a banana leaf and talked of the weather and asked how the dog was. John Hawkins loved his dog above all things. He shared his food with it—astonishing the things a dog would eat—and it slept on his bunk. Rover was a good friend. Made a man feel civilized.

'Would you like some bridge tonight? I'll bring a fourth,' Hawkins said.

'Can't tonight,' Peter Marlowe said, maiming flies.

'I can get Gordon, next door,' suggested Larkin.

'Great. After dinner?'

'Good-oh, see you then.'

'Thanks for the blachang,' Hawkins said as he left, Rover yapping happily beside him.

'How the hell he gets enough to feed himself and that dingo, damned if I know,' Larkin said. 'Or kept him out of some bugger's billy can for that matter!'

Peter Marlowe stirred his rice, mixing the blachang carefully. He wanted very much to share the secret of his trip tonight with Larkin. But he knew it was too dangerous.

174

XIV

Getting out of the camp was too simple. Just a short dash to a shadowed part of the six-wire fence, then easily through and a quick run into the jungle. When they stopped to catch their breath, Peter Marlowe wished he were safely back talking to Mac or Larkin or even Grey.

All this time, he told himself, I've been wanting to be out, and now when I am, I'm frightened to death.

It was weird—on the outside, looking in. From where they were they could see into the camp. The American hut was a hundred yards away. Men were walking up and down. Hawkins was walking his dog. A Korean guard was strolling the camp. Lights were off in the various huts and the evening check had long since been made. Yet the camp was alive with the sleepless. It was always thus.

'C'mon Peter,' the King whispered and led the way deeper into the foliage.

The planning had been good. So far. When he had arrived at the hut, the King was already prepared. 'Got to have tools to do a job right,' he had said, showing him a well-oiled pair of Jap boots—crepe soles and soft noiseless leather—and the 'outfit', a pair of black Chinese pants and short blouse.

Only Dino was in the know about the trip. He had bundled up the two kits and dumped them secretly in the jumping-off point. Then he had returned, and when all was clear Peter Marlowe and the King had walked out casually, saying that they were playing bridge with Larkin and another Aussie. They

175

had had to wait a nerve-wracking half hour before the way was clear for them to run into the storm drain beside the wire and change into their outfits and mud their faces and hands. Another quarter hour before they could run to the fence unobserved. Once they were through and in position, Dino had collected their discarded clothes.

Jungle at night. Eerie. But Peter Marlowe felt at home. It was just like Java, just like the surrounds of his own village, so his nervousness subsided a little.

The King led the way unerringly. He had made the trip five times before. He walked along, every sense alert. There was one guard to pass. This guard had no fixed beat, just a wandering patrol. But the King knew that most times the guard found a clearing somewhere and went to sleep.

After an anxious time, a time when every rotten stick or leaf seemed to shout their passing, and every living branch seemed to want to hold them back, they came to the path. They were past the guard. The path led to the sea. And then the village.

They crossed the path and began to circle. Above the heavy ceiling of foliage, a half-moon stuck in the cloudless sky. Just the right amount of light for safety.

Freedom. No circling wire and no people. Privacy at last. And it was a sudden nightmare to Peter Marlowe.

'What's up, Peter?' the King whispered, feeling something wrong.

'Nothing . . . it's just—well, being outside is such a shock.'

'You'll get used to it.' The King glanced at his watch. 'Got about a mile to go. We're ahead of schedule, so we'd better wait.'

He found an overgrowth of twisted vine and fallen trees and leaned against it. 'We can take it easy here.'

They waited and listened to the jungle. Crickets, frogs, sudden twitters. Sudden silences. The rustle of an unknown beast.

'I could use a smoke.'

'Me too.'

'Not here though.' The King's mind was alive. Half was listening to the jungle. The other was racing and rehashing the pattern of the deal to be. Yes, he told himself, it's a good plan.

He checked the time. The minute hand went slowly. But it

176

gave him more time to plan. The more time you plan before a deal, the better it is. No. slip-ups and bigger profit. Thank God for profit! The guy who thought of business was the real genius. Buy for a little and sell for more. Use your mind. Take a chance and money pours in. And with money all things are possible. Most of all, power.

When I get out, the King thought, I'm going to be a millionaire. I'm going to make so much money that it's going to make Fort Knox look like a piggy-bank. I'll build an organization. The organization'll be fitted with guys, loyal but sheep. Brains you can always buy. And once you know a guy's price you can use him or abuse him at will. That's what makes the world go round. There are the élite, and the rest. I'm the élite. I'm going to stay that way.

No more being kicked around or shoved from town to town. That's past. I was a kid then. Tied to Pa—tied to a man who waited tables or jerked gas or delivered phone books or trucked junk or whined handouts to get a bottle. Then cleaning up the mess. Never again. Now others are going to clear up my mess.

All I need is the dough.

'All men are created equal . . . certain inalienable rights.'

Thank God for America, the King told himself for the billionth time. Thank God I was born American.

'It's God's country,' he said, half to himself.

'What?'

'The States.'

'Why?'

'Only place in the world where you can buy anything, where you got a chance to make it. That's important if you're not born into it, Peter, and only a goddam few are. But if you're not—and you want to work—why, there's so many goddam opportunities, they make your hair curl. An' if a guy doesn't work and help himself, then he's no goddam good, and no goddam American, and—'

'Listen!' Peter Marlowe warned, suddenly on guard.

From the distance came the faint tread of approaching footsteps.

'It's a man,' whispered Peter Marlowe, sliding deeper into the protection of the foliage. 'A native.'

'How the hell d'you know?'

'Wearing native clogs. I'd say he was old. He's shuffling. Listen, you can hear his breath now.'

Moments later the native appeared from the gloaming and walked the path unconcerned. He was an old man and on his shoulders was a dead wild pig. They watched him pass and disappear.

'He noticed us,' said Peter Marlowe, concerned.

'The hell he did.'

'No. I'm sure he did. Maybe he thought it was a Jap guard, but I was watching his feet. You can always tell if you're spotted that way. He missed a beat in his stride.'

'Maybe it was a crack in the path or a stick.'

Peter Marlowe shook his head.

Friend or enemy? thought the King feverishly. If he's from the village then we're okay. The whole village knew when the King was coming, for they got their share from Cheng San, his contact. I didn't recognize him, but that's not surprising, for a lot of natives were out night-fishing when I went before. What to do?

'We'll wait, then make a quick reccy. If he's hostile, he'll go to the village, then report to the elder. The elder'll give us a sign to get the hell out.'

'You think you can trust them?'

'*I* can, Peter.' He started off again. 'Keep twenty yards in back of me.'

The found the village easily. Almost too easily, Peter Marlowe thought to himself suspiciously. From their position, on the rise, they surveyed it. A few Malays were squatting smoking on a veranda. A pig grunted here and there. Surrounding the village were coconut palm trees, and beyond it, the phosphorescent surf. A few boats, sails curled, fishing nets hanging still. No feel of danger.

'Seems all right to me,' Peter Marlowe whispered.

The King nudged him abruptly. On the veranda of the headman's hut was the headman and the man they had seen. The two Malays were deep in conversation, then a distant laugh broke the stillness and the man came down the steps.

They heard him call out. In a moment a woman came running. She took the pig from his shoulders, carried it to the fire-coals and put it on the spit. In a moment there were other Malays, joking, laughing, grouped around.

'There he is!' exclaimed the King.

Walking up the shore was a tall Chinese. Behind him a native furled the sails of the small fishing craft. He joined the headman and they made their soft salutations and they squatted down to wait.

'Okay,' grinned the King, 'here we go.'

He got up and, keeping to the shadows, circled carefully. On the back of the headman's hut a ladder soared to the veranda. high off the ground. The King was up it, Peter Marlowe close behind. Almost immediately they heard the ladder scrape away.

'Tabe,' smiled the King as Cheng San and Sutra, the headman, entered.

'Good you see, tuan,' said the headman, groping for English words. 'You makan-eat yes?' His smiled showed betel-nut stained teeth.

'Trima kassih-thanks.' The King put out his hand to Cheng San. 'How you been, Cheng San?'

'Me good or' time. You see I—' Cheng San sought the word and then it came. 'Here, good time maybe or' same.'

The King indicated Peter Marlowe. 'Ichi-bon friend. Peter, say something to them, you know, greetings and all that jazz. Get to work, boy.' He smiled and pulled out a pack of Kooas, offering them around.

'My friend and I thank thee for thy welcome,' Peter Marlowe began. 'We appreciate thy kindness to ask if we will eat with thee, knowing that in these times there is a lack. Surely only a snake in the jungle would refuse to accept the kindness of thy offer.'

Both Cheng San and the headman broke into huge smiles.

'Wah-lah,' Cheng Sang said. 'It will be good to be able to talk through thee to my friend Rajah all the words that are in my miserable mouth. Many times I have wanted to say that which neither I nor my good friend Sutra here could find the words to say. Tell the Rajah that he is a wise and clever man to find such a fluent interpreter.'

'He says I make a good mouthpiece,' said Peter Marlowe

179

happily, now calm and safe. 'And he's glad he can now give you the straight stuff.'

'For the love of God stick to your well-bred Limey talk. That mouthpiece mishmash makes you look like a bum yet.'

'Oh, and I've been studying Max assiduously,' Peter Marlowe said, crestfallen.

'Well, don't.'

'He also called you Rajah! That's your nickname from here on. I mean "here on in".'

'Crap off, Peter!'

'Up yours, brother!'

'C'mon, Peter, we haven't much time. Tell Cheng San this. About this deal I'm gonna—'

'You can't talk business yet, old man,' said Peter Marlowe, shocked. 'You'll hurt everything. First we'll have to have some coffee and something to eat, then we can start.'

'Tell 'em now.'

'If I do, they'll be very offended. Very. You can take my word for it.'

The King thought for a moment. Well, he told himself, if you buy brains, it's bad business not to use them—unless you've got a hunch. That's where the smart businessman makes or breaks—when he plays a hunch over the so-called brains. But in this case he didn't have a hunch, so he just nodded. 'Okay, have it your way.'

He puffed his cigarette, listening to Peter Marlowe speak to them. He studied Cheng San obliquely. His clothes were better than the last time. He wore a new ring that looked like a sapphire, maybe five carats. His neat, clean, hairless face was honey-toned and his hair well-groomed. Yep, Cheng San was doing all right for himself. Now old Sutra, he's not doing so good. His sarong's old and tattered at the hem. No jewellery. Last time he had a gold ring. Now he hasn't, and the crease mark where his ring had been worn was almost unnoticeable. That meant he hadn't just taken it off for tonight's show.

He heard the women off in the other part of the hut chattering softly, and outside, the quietness of the village by night. Through the glassless window came the smell of roasting pig. That meant the village was really in need of Cheng San—their black-market outlet for the fish the village was supposed to sell directly to the Japs—and were making him a gift of the pig. Or perhaps the old man who had just trapped a wild pig was having a party for his friends. But the crowd around the fire was waiting anxiously, just as anxiously as us. Sure, they're hungry too. That means that things must be tough in Singapore. The village should be well stocked with food and drink and everything. Cheng San couldn't be doing too well smuggling their fish to markets. Maybe the Japs had their eye on him. Maybe he's not long for this earth!'

So maybe he needs the village more than the village needs him. And is putting on a show for them—clothes and jewellery. Maybe Sutra's getting pissed off with lack of business and is ready to dump him for another black-marketeer.

'Hey, Peter,' he said. 'Ask Cheng San how's the fish biz in Singapore.' Peter Marlowe translated the question.

'He says that business is fine. Food shortages are such that he is able to obtain the best prices on the island. But he says the Japs are clamping down heavily. It's becoming harder to trade every day. And to break the market laws is becoming more and more expensive.'

Aha! Got you. The King exulted. So Cheng hasn't come *just* for my deal! It *is* fish and the village. Now how can I turn this to my advantage? Betcha Cheng San's having trouble delivering the merchandise. Maybe the Japs intercepted some boats and got tough. Old Sutra's no fool. No money, no deal, and Cheng San knows it. No makee tradee, no makee business and old Sutra'll sell to another. Yes, sir. So the King knew he could trade tough and mentally upped his asking price.

Then food arrived. Baked sweet potatoes, fried eggplant, coconut milk, thick slices of roasted pork, heavy with oil. Bananas. Papayas. The King marked that there was no millionaire's cabbage or lamb or saté of beef and no sweetmeats the Malays loved so much. Yeah, things were tough all right.

The food was served by the headman's chief wife, a wrinkled old woman. Helping her was Sulina, one of his daughters. Beautiful, soft, curved, honeyed skin. Sweet-smelling. Fresh sarong in their honour.

'Tabe, Sam,' winked the King at Sulina.

The girl bubbled with laughter and shyly tried to cover her embarrassment.

181

'Sam?' winced Peter Marlowe.

'Sure,' answered the King dryly. 'She reminds me of my brother.'

'Brother?' Peter Marlowe stared at him astonished.

'Joke. I haven't got a brother.'

'Oh!' Peter Marlowe thought a moment, then asked. 'Why Sam?'

'The old guy wouldn't introduce me,' said the King, not looking at the girl, 'so I just gave her the name. I think it suits her.'

Sutra knew that what they said had something to do with his daughter. He knew he had made a mistake to let her in here. Perhaps, in other times, he would have liked one of the tuan-tuan to notice her and take her back to his bungalow to be his mistress for a year or two. Then she would come back to the village well versed in the ways of men, with a nice dowry in her hands, and it would be easy for him to find the right husband for her. That's how it would have been in the past. But now romance led only to a haphazarded time in the bushes, and Sutra did not want that for his daughter even though it was time she became a woman.

He leaned forward and offered Peter Marlowe a choice piece of pig. 'Perhaps this would tempt thy appetite?'

'I thank thee.'

'You may leave, Sulina.'

Peter Marlowe detected the note of finality in the old man's voice and noticed the shadow of dismay that painted the girl's face. But she bowed low and took her leave. The old wife remained to serve the men.

Sulina, thought Peter Marlowe, feeling a long-forgotten urge. She's not as pretty as N'ai, who was without blemish, but she is the same age and pretty. Fourteen perhaps and ripe. My God, how ripe!

'The food is not to thy taste?' Cheng San asked, amused by Peter Marlowe's obvious attraction to the girl. Perhaps this could be used to advantage.

'On the contrary. It is perhaps too good, for my palate is not used to fine food, eating as we do.' Peter Marlowe remembered that for the protection of good taste, the Javanese spoke only in parables about women. He turned to Sutra. 'Once upon a time a

182

wise guru said that there are many kind of food. Some for the stomach, some for the eye and some for the spirit. Tonight, I have had food for the stomach. And the sayings of thee and Tuan Cheng San have been food for the spirit. I am replete. Even so, I have also—we have also—been offered food for the eye. How can I thank thee for thy hospitality?'

Sutra's face wrinkled. Well put. So he bowed to the compliment and said simply, 'It was a wise saying. Perhaps, in time, the eye may be hungry again. We must discuss the wisdom of the ancient another time.'

'What're you looking so smug about, Peter?'

'I'm not looking smug, just pleased with myself. I was just telling him we thought his girl was pretty.'

'Yes! She's a doll! How about asking her to join us for coffee?'

'For the love of God.' Peter tried to keep his voice calm. 'You don't come out and make a date just like that. You've got to take time, build up to it.'

'Hell, that's not the American way. You meet a broad, you like her and she likes you, you hit the sack.'

'You've no finesse.'

'Maybe. But I've got a lot of broads.'

They laughed and Cheng San asked what the joke was and Peter Marlowe told them that the King had said, 'We should set up shop in the village and not bother to go back to camp.'

After they had drunk their coffee, Cheng San made the first overture.

'I would have thought it risky to come from the camp by night. Riskier than my coming here to the village.'

First round to us, thought Peter Marlowe. Now, Oriental style, Cheng Sang was at a disadvantage, for he had lost face by making the opening. He turned to the King. 'All right, Rajah. You can start. We've made a point so far.'

'We have?'

'Yes. What do you want me to tell him?'

'Tell him I've a big deal. A diamond. Four carats. Set in platinum. Flawless, blue-white. I want thirty-five thousand dollars for it. Five thousand British Malay Straits dollars, the rest in Jap counterfeit money.'

Peter Marlowes eyes widened. He was facing the King, so his surprise was hidden from the Chinese. But Sutra marked it.

Since he was no part of the deal, but merely collected a percentage as a go-between, he settled back to enjoy the parry and thrust. No need to worry about Cheng San—Sutra knew to his cost that the Chinese could handle himself as well as anyone.

Peter Marlowe translated. The enormousness of the deal would cover any lapse of manners. And he wanted to rock the Chinese.

Cheng San brightened palpably, caught off his guard. He asked to see the diamond.

'Tell him I haven't got it with me. Tell him I'll make delivery in ten days. Tell him I have to have the money three days before I make delivery because the owner won't let it out of his possession until he has the money.'

Cheng San knew that the King was an honest trader. If he said he had the ring and would hand it over, then he would. He always had. But to get such an amount of money and pass it into the camp, where he could never keep track of the King—well, that was quite a risk.

'When can I see the ring?' he asked.

'Tell him if he likes he can come into the camp, in seven days.'

So I must hand over the money before I even *see* the diamond! thought Cheng San. Impossible, and Tuan Rajah knows it. Very bad business. If it really is four carats, I can get fifty—a hundred thousand dollars for it. After all, I know the Chinese who owns the machine that prints the money. But the five thousand in Malay Straits dollars—that is another thing. This he would have to buy black-market. And what a rate? Six to one would be expensive, twenty to one cheap.

'Tell my friend the Rajah,' he said, 'that this is a strange business arrangement. Consequently I must think, longer than a man of business should need to think.'

He wandered over to the window and gazed out.

Cheng San was tired of the war and tired of the undercover machinations that a businessman had to endure to make a profit. He thought of the night and the stars and the stupidity of man, fighting and dying for things which would have no lasting value. At the same time, he knew that the strong survive and the weak perish. He thought of his wife and his children, three sons and a daughter, and the things he would like to buy them to make them comfortable. He thought also of the second wife he would like to buy. Somehow or another he must make this deal. And it was worth the risk to trust the King.

The price is fair, he reasoned. But how to safeguard the money. Find a go-between whom he could trust. It would have to be one of the guards. The guard could see the ring. He could hand over the money if the ring was real and the weight right. Then the Tuan Rajah could make delivery, here at the village. No need to trust the guard to take the ring and turn it over. How to trust a guard?

Perhaps we could concoct a story—that the money was a loan to the camp from Chinese in Singapore—no, that would be no good, for the guard would have to see the ring. So the guard would have to be completely in the know. And would expect a substantial fee.

Cheng San turned back to the King. He noticed how the King was sweating. Ah, he thought, you want to sell badly! But perhaps you know I want to buy badly. You and I are the only ones who can handle such a deal. No one has the honest name for trading like you—and no one but I, of all the Chinese who deal with the camp, is capable of delivering so much money.

'So, Tuan Marlowe. I have a plan which perhaps would cover both my friend the Rajah and myself. First, we agree to a price. The price mentioned is too high, but unimportant at the moment. Second, we agree to a go-between, a guard whom we both can trust. In ten days I will give half the money to the guard. The guard can examine the ring. If it is truly as the owner claims, he can pass over the money to my friend the Rajah. The Rajah will make delivery here to me. I will bring an expert to weigh the stone. Then I will pay the other half of the money and take the stone.'

The King listened intently as Peter Marlowe translated.

'Tell him it's okay. But I've got to have the full price. The guy won't turn it over without the dough in his hands.'

'Then tell my friend the Rajah I will give the guard three-quarters of the agreed price to help him negotiate with the owner.'

Cheng San felt that seventy-five per cent would certainly cover the amount of money paid to the owner. The King would merely be gambling his profit, for surely he was a good enough

185

businessman to obtain a twenty-five per cent. fee!

The King had figured on three-quarters. That gave him plenty to manoeuvre with. Maybe he could knock a few bucks off the owner's asking price, nineteen-five. Yep, so far so good. Now we get down to the meat.

'Tell him okay. Who does he suggest as the go-between?'

'Torusumi.'

The King shook his head. He thought a moment, then said direct to Cheng San, 'How 'bout Immuri?'

'Tell my friend that I would prefer another. Perhaps Kimina?'

The King whistled. A corporal yet! He had never done business with him. Too dangerous. Got to be someone I know. 'Shagatasan?'

Cheng Sang nodded in agreement. This was the man he wanted, but he did not want to suggest it. He wanted to see who the King wanted—a last check on the King's honesty. Yes, Shagata was a good choice. Not too bright, but bright enough. He had dealt with him before. Good.

'Now, about the price,' said Cheng Sang. 'I suggest we discuss this. Per carat four thousand counterfeit dollars. Total sixteen thousand. Four thousand in Malay dollars at the rate of fifteen to one.'

The King shook his head blandly, then said to Peter Marlowe, 'Tell him I'm not going to crap around bargaining. The price is thirty-thousand, five in Straits dollars at eight to one, all in small notes. My final price.'

'You'll have to bargain a bit more,' said Peter Marlowe. 'How about saying thirty-three, then—'

The King shook his head. 'No. And when you translate use a word like "crap"!'

Reluctantly Peter Marlowe turned back to Cheng San. 'My friend says this: He is not going to mess around with the niceties of bargaining. His final price is thirty thousand—five thousand in Straits dollars at a rate of eight to one. All in small denomination notes.'

To his astonishment Cheng San said immediately, 'I agree!' for he too didn't want to fool with bargaining. The price was fair and he had sensed that the King was adamant. There comes a time in all good deals when a man must decide, yea or nay. The Rajah was a good trader.

They shook hands. Sutra smiled and brought forth a bottle of sake. They drank each other's health until the bottle was gone. Then they fixed the details.

In ten days Shagata would come to the American hut at the time of the night guard change. He would have the money and would see the ring before he handed over the money. Three days after, the King and Peter Marlowe would meet Cheng San at the village. If for some reason Shagata could not make the date, he would arrive the next day, or the next. Similarly, if the King couldn't make their appointment at the village, they were to come the next day.

After paying and receiving the usual compliments, Cheng San said that he had to catch the tide. He bowed courteously and Sutra went out with him, escorting him to the shore. Beside the boat they began their polite quarrel about the fish business.

The King was triumphant. 'Great, Peter. We're in!'

'You're terrific! When you said to give it to him in the teeth like that, well, old man, I thought you'd lost him. They just don't do those things.'

'Had a hunch,' was all the King said. Then he added, chewing on a piece of meat, 'You're in for ten per cent.—of the profit, of course. But you'll have to work for it, you son of a bitch.'

'Like a horse! God! Just think of all that money. Thirty thousand dollars would be a stack of notes perhaps a foot high.'

'More,' the King said, infected by the excitement.

'My God, you've got a nerve. How on earth did you arrive at the price? He agreed, boom, just like that. One moment's talk, then boom, you're rich!'

'Got a lot of worrying to do before it *is* a deal. Lot of things could go wrong. It ain't a deal till the cash is delivered and in the bank.'

'Oh, I never thought of that.'

'Business axiom. You can't bank talk. Only greenbacks!'

'I still can't get over it. We're outside the camp, we've more food inside us than we've had in weeks. And prospects look great. You're a bloody genius.'

'We'll wait and see, Peter.'

The King stood up. 'You wait here. I'll be back in an hour or so. Got another bit of business to attend to. So long as we're out of here in a couple of hours, we'll be okay. Then we'll hit the camp just before dawn. Best time. That's when the guards'll be at their lowest mark. See you,' and disappeared down the steps.

In spite of himself, Peter Marlowe felt alone, and quite a little afraid.

Christ, what's he up to? Where's he going? What if he's late? What if he doesn't come back? What if a Jap comes into the village? What if I'm left on my own? Shall I go looking for him? If we don't make it back by dawn, Christ, we'll be reported missing and we'll have to run. Where? Maybe Cheng San'll help? Too dangerous! Where does he live? Could we make the docks and get a boat? Maybe contact the guerrillas who're supposed to be operating?

Get hold of yourself Marlowe, you damn coward! You're acting like a three-year-old!

Curbing his anxiety, he settled down to wait. Then suddenly he remembered the coupling condenser—three hundred microfarads.

'Tabe, Tuan,' Kesseh smiled as the King entered her hut.

'Tabe, Kasseh!'

'You like food, yes?'

He shook his head and held her close, his hands moving over her body. She stood on tiptoe to put her arms around his neck, her hair a plume of black gold falling to her waist.

'Long time,' she said, warmed by his touch.

'Long time,' he replied. 'You miss me?'

'Uh-huh,' she laughed, aping his accent.

'He arrived yet?'

She shook her head. 'No like this thing, tuan. Has danger.'

'Everything has danger.'

They heard footsteps, and soon a shadow splashed the door. It opened and a small dark Chinese walked in. He wore a sarong and Indian chappals on his feet. He smiled, showing broken mildewed teeth. On his back was a war parang in a scabbard. The King noticed that the scabbard was well oiled. Easy to jerk that parang out and cut a man's head off—just like that. Tucked into the man's belt was a revolver.

The King had asked Kasseh to get in touch with the guerrillas operating in Johore and this man was the result. Like most, they were converted bandits now fighting the Japanese under the banner of the Communists, who supplied them with arms.

'Tabe. You speak English?' the King asked, forcing a smile. He didn't like the look of this Chinese.

'Why you want talk with us?'

'Thought we might be able to make a deal.'

The Chinese leered at Kasseh. She flinched.

'Beat it Kasseh,' the King said.

Noiselessly she left, going through the bead curtain into the rear of the house.

The Chinese watched her go. 'You lucky,' he said to the King. 'Too lucky. I bet woman give good time two, three men one night. No?'

'You want to talk a deal? Yes or no?'

'You watch, white man. Maybe I tell Japs you here. Maybe I tell them village safe for white prisoners. Then they kill village.'

'You'll end up dead, fast, that way.'

The Chinese grunted, then squatted down. He shifted the parang, slightly, menacingly. 'Maybe I take woman now.'

Jesus, thought the King, maybe I made a mistake.

'I got a proposal for you guys. If the war ends suddenly—or the Japs take it into their heads to start chopping us POW's up, I want you to be around for protection. I'll pay you two thousand American dollars when I'm safe.'

'How we know if Jap kill prisoners?'

'You'll know. You know most things that go on.'

'How we know you pay?'

'The American government will pay. Everyone knows there's a reward.'

'Two thousand!' Mahlu! We get two thousand any day. Kill bank. Easy.'

The King made his gambit. 'I'm empowered by our commanding officer to guarantee you two thousand a head for every American that is saved. If the shoot blows up.'

'I no understan'.'

'If the Japs start trying to knock us off—kill us. If the Allies land here, the Japs're going to get mean. Or if the Allies land on Japan, then the Japs here will take reprisals. If they do, you'll know and I want you to help us get away.'

'How many men?'

189

'Thirty.'

'Too many.'

'How many will you guarantee?'

'Ten. But the price will be five thousand per man.'

'Too much.'

The Chinese shrugged.

'All right. It's a deal. You know the camp?'

The Chinese showed his teeth in a twisted grin. 'We know.'

'Our hut's to the east. A small one. If we have to make a break, we'll break through the wire there. If you're in the jungle, you can cover us. How will we know if you're in position?'

Again the Chinese shrugged. 'If not, you die anyway.'

'Could you give us a signal?'

'No signal.'

This is crazy, the King told himself. We won't know when we're going to have to make a break, and if it's going to be sudden there'll be no way of getting a message to the guerrillas in time. Maybe they'll be there, maybe not. But if they figure there's five grand apiece for any of us they get out, then maybe they'll keep a good lookout from here on in.

'Will you keep an eye on the camp?'

'Maybe leader says yes, maybe no.'

'Who's your leader?'

The Chinese shrugged and picked his teeth.

'It's a deal then?'

'Maybe.' The eyes were hostile. 'You finish?'

'Yes.' The King stuck out his hand. 'Thanks.'

The Chinese looked down at the hand, sneered and went to the door. 'Remember. Ten only. Rest kill!' He left.

Well, it's worth a try, the King assured himself. Those bastards could sure as hell use the money. And Uncle Sam would pay. Why the hell not! What the hell do we pay taxes for?

'Tuan,' said Kasseh gravely as she stood at the door. 'I not like this thing.'

'Got to take a chance. If there's a sudden killing maybe we can get out.' He winked at her. 'Worth a try. We'd be dead anyway. So, what the hell. Maybe we got a line of retreat.'

'Why you not make deal for you alone? Why you not go with him now and escape camp?'

190

'Easy. First, it's safer at the camp than with the guerrillas. No point in trusting them unless there's an emergency. Second, one man's not worth their trouble. That's why I asked him to save thirty. But he could only handle ten.'

'How you choose ten?'

'It'll be every man for himself, as long as I'm okay.'

'Maybe your command officer no like only ten.'

'He'll like it if he's one of the lucky ones.'

'You think Japanese kill prisoners?'

'Maybe. But let's forget it, huh?'

She smiled. 'Forget. You hot. Take shower, yes?'

'Yes.'

In the shower section of the hut the King bailed water over himself from the concrete well. The water was cold, and it made him gasp and his flesh sting.

'Kasseh!'

She came through the curtains with a towel. She stood looking at him. Yes, her tuan was a fine man. Strong and fine and the colour of his skin pleasing. Wah-lah, she thought, I am lucky to have such a man. But he is so big and I am so small. He towers over me by two heads.

Even so, she knew that she pleased him. It is easy to please a man. If you are a woman. And not ashamed of being woman.

'What're you smiling at?' he asked her as he saw the smile.

'Ah, tuan, I just think, you are so big and I so small. And yet, when we lie down, there is not so much difference, no?'

He chuckled and slapped her fondly on the buttocks and took the towel. 'How 'bout a drink?'

'It is ready, tuan.'

'What else is ready?'

She laughed with her mouth and her eyes. Her teeth were stark white and her eyes deep brown and her skin was smooth and sweet-smelling. 'Who knows, tuan?' Then she left the room.

Now there's one helluva dame, the King thought, looking after her, drying himself vigorously. I'm a lucky guy.

Kasseh had been arranged by Sutra when the King had come to the village the first time. The details had been fixed neatly. When the war was over, he was to pay Kasseh twenty American dollars for every time he stayed with her. He had knocked a few bucks off the first asking price—business was business—but at twenty bucks she was a great buy.

'How do you know I'll pay?' he had asked her.

'I do not. But if you do not, you do not, and then I gained only pleasure. If you pay me, then I have money and pleasure too.' She had smiled.

He slipped on the native slippers she had left him, then walked through the bead curtains. She was waiting for him.

Peter Marlowe was still watching Sutra and Cheng San down by the shore. Cheng San bowed and got into the boat and Sutra helped shove the boat into the phosphorescent sea. Then Sutra returned to the hut.

'Tabe-lah!' Peter Marlowe said.

'Would thou eat more?'

'No thank you, Tuan Sutra.'

My word, thought Peter Marlowe, it's a change to be able to turn down food. But he had eaten his fill, and to eat more would have been impolite. It was obvious that the village was poor and the food would not be wasted.

'I have heard,' he said tentatively, 'that the news, the war news, is good.'

'Thus too I have heard, but nothing that a man could repeat. Vague rumours.'

'It is a pity that times are not like those in former years. When a man could have a wireless and hear news or read a newspaper.'

'True. It is a pity.'

Sutra made no sign of understanding. He squatted down on his mat and rolled a cigarette, funnel-like, and began to smoke through his fist, sucking the smoke deep within him.

'We hear bad tales from the camp,' he said at last.

'It is not so bad, Tuan Sutra. We manage, somehow. But not to know how the world is, that is surely bad.'

'I have heard it told that there was a wireless in the camp and the men who owned the wireless were caught. And that they are now in Outram Road Jail.'

'Hast thou news of them? One was a friend of mine.'

'No. We only heard that they had been taken there.'

'I would dearly love to know how they are.'

192

'Thou knowest the place, and the manner of all men taken there, so thou already knowest that which is done.'

'True. But one hopes that some may be lucky.'

'We are in the hands of Allah, said the Prophet.'

'On whose name be praise.'

Sutra glanced at him again; then, calmly puffing his cigarette, he asked, 'Where didst thou learn the Malay?'

Peter Marlowe told him of his life in the village. How he had worked the paddy fields and lived as a Javanese, which is almost the same as living as a Malay. The customs are the same and the language the same, except for the common Western words—wireless in Malaya, radio in Java, motor in Malaya, auto in Java. But the rest was the same. Love, hate, sickness and the words that a man will speak to a man or a man to a woman were the same. The important things were always the same.

'What was the name of thy woman in the village, my son?' Sutra asked. It would have been impolite to ask before, but now, when they had talked of things of the spirit and the world and philosophy and Allah and certain of the sayings of the Prophet, on whose name be praise, now it was not rude to ask.

'Her name was N'ai Jahan.'

The old man sighed contentedly, remembering his youth. 'And she loved thee much and long.'

'Yes.' Peter Marlowe could see her clearly.

She had come to his hut one night when he was preparing for bed. Her sarong was red and gold, and tiny sandals peeped from beneath its hem. There was a thin necklace of flowers around her neck and the fragrance of the flowers filled the hut and all his universe.

She had laid her bed roll beside her feet and bowed low before him.

'My name is N'ai Jahan,' she had said. 'Tuan Abu, my father, has chosen me to share thy life, for it is not good for a man to be alone. And thou has been alone for three months now.'

N'ai was perhaps fourteen, but in the sun-rain lands a girl of fourteen is already a woman with the desires of a woman and should be married, or at least with the man of her father's choice.

The darkness of her skin had a milk sheen to it and her eyes were jewels of topaz and her hands were petals of the fire

193

orchid and her feet slim and her child-woman body was satin and held within it the happiness of a hummingbird. She was a child of the sun and a child of the rain. Her nose was slender and fine and the nostrils delicate.

N'ai was all satin, liquid satin. Firm where it should be firm. Soft where it should be soft. Strong where it should be strong. And weak where it should be weak.

Her hair was raven. Long. A gossamer net to cover her.

Peter Marlowe had smiled at her. He had tried to hide his embarrassment and be like her, free and happy and without shame. She had taken off her sarong and stood proudly before him, and she had said, 'I pray that I shall be worthy to make thee happy and make thee soft-sleep. And I beg thee to teach me all the things that thy woman should know to make thee "close to God."'

Close to God, how wonderful, Peter Marlowe thought; how wonderful to describe love as being close to God.

He looked up at Sutra. 'Yes. We loved much and long. I thank Allah that I have lived and loved unto eternity. How glorious are the ways of Allah.'

A cloud reached out and grappled with the moon for possession of the night.

'It is good to be a man,' Peter Marlowe said.

'Does thy lack trouble thee tonight?'

'No. In truth. Not tonight.' Peter Marlowe studied the old Malay, liking him for the offer, smoothed by his gentleness.

'Listen, Tuan Sutra. I will open my mind to thee, for I believe that in time we could be friends. Thou couldst in time have time to weigh my friendship and the "I" of me. But war is an assassin of time. Therefore I would speak to thee as a friend of thine, which I am not yet.'

The old man did not reply. He puffed his cigarette and waited for him to continue.

'I have need of a little part of a wireless. Is there a wireless in the village, an old one? Perhaps if it is broken, I could take one such little piece from it.'

'Thou knowest that wirelesses are forbidden by the Japanese.'

'True, but sometimes there are secret places to hide that which is forbidden.'

Sutra pondered. A wireless lay in his hut. Perhaps Allah had sent Tuan Marlowe to remove it. He felt he could trust him because Tuan Abu had trusted him before. But if Tuan Marlowe was caught outside camp with the wireless, inevitably the village would be involved.

To leave the wireless in the village was also dangerous. Certainly a man could bury it deep in the jungle, but that had not been done. It should have been done but had not been done, for the temptation to listen was always too great. The temptation of the women to hear the "sway-music" was too great. The temptation to *know* when others did not know was great. Truly it is written, Vanity, all is vanity.

Better, he decided, to let the things that are the pink man's remain with the pink man.

He got up and beckoned Peter Marlowe and led the way through the bead curtains into the dark recesses of the hut. He stopped at the doorway to Sulina's bedroom. She was lying on the bed, her sarong loose and full around her, her eyes liquid.

'Sulina,' Sutra said, 'go onto the veranda and watch.'

'Yes, Father.' Sulina slipped off the bed and retied the sarong and adjusted her little baju jacket. Adjusted it, thought Sutra, perhaps a little too much, so the promise of her breasts showed clearly. Yes, it is surely time that the girl married. But whom? There are no eligible men.

He stood aside as the girl brushed past, her eyes low and demure. But there was nothing demure in the sway of her hips, and Peter Marlowe noticed them too. I should take a stick to her, Sutra thought. But he knew that he should not be angry. She was but a girl on the threshold of womanhood. To tempt is but a woman's way—to be desired is but a woman's need.

Perhaps I should give thee to the Englishman. Maybe that would lessen thy appetite. He looks more than man enough! Sutra sighed. Ah to be so young again.

From under the bed he brought out the small radio.

'I will trust thee. This wireless is good. It works well. You may take it.'

Peter Marlowe almost dropped it in his excitement. 'But what about thee? Surely this is beyond price.'

'It has no price. Take it with thee.'

Peter Marlowe turned the radio over. It was a mains set. In

195

good condition. The back was off and the tubes glinted in the oil light. There were many condensers. Many. He held the set nearer the light and carefully examined the guts of it, inch by inch.

The sweat began dripping off his face. Then he found the one, three hundred microfarads.

Now what do I do? he asked himself. Do I just take the condenser? Mac had said he was *almost* sure. Better to take the whole thing, then if the condenser doesn't fit ours, we've got another. We can cache it somewhere. Yes. It will be good to have a spare.

'I thank thee, Tuan Sutra. It is a gift that I cannot thank thee enough for. I and the thousands of Changi.'

'I beg thee protect us here. If a guard sees thee, bury it in the jungle. My village is in thy hands.'

'Do not fear. I will guard it with my life.'

'I believe thee. But perhaps this is a foolish thing to do.'

'There are times, Tuan Sutra, when I truly believe men are only fools.'

'Thou art wise beyond thy years.'

Sutra gave him a piece of material to cover it, then they returned to the main room. Sulina was in the shadows on the veranda. As they entered she got up.

'May I get thee food or drink, Father?'

'Wah-lah,' thought Sutra grumpily, she asks me but she means him. 'No. Get thee to bed.'

Sulina tossed her head prettily but obeyed.

'My daughter deserves a whipping, I think.'

'It would be a pity to blemish such a delicate thing,' Peter Marlowe said. 'Tuan Abu used to say, "Beat a woman at least once a week and thou wilt have peace in thy house. But do not beat her too hard, lest thou anger her, for then she will surely beat thee back and hurt thee greatly!"'

'I know the saying. It is surely true. Women are beyond comprehension.'

They talked about many things, squatting on the veranda looking at the sea. The surf was very slight, and Peter Marlowe asked permission to swim.

'There are no currents,' the old Malay told him, 'but sometimes there are sharks.'

'I will take care.'

'Swim only in the shadows near the boats. There have been times when Japanese walk along the shore. There is a gun emplacement three miles down the beach. Keep thy eyes open.'

'I will take care.'

Peter Marlowe kept to the shadows as he made for the boats. The moon was lowering in the sky. Not too much time, he thought.

By the boats some men and women were preparing and repairing nets, chatting and laughing one to another. They paid no attention to Peter Marlowe as he undressed and walked into the sea.

The water was warm, but there were cold pockets, as in all the Eastern seas, and he found one and tried to stay in it. The feeling of freedom was glorious, and it was almost as though he was a small boy again taking a midnight swim in the Southsea with his father nearby shouting, 'Don't go out too far, Peter! Remember the currents!'

He swam underwater and his skin drank the salt-chemic. When he surfaced, he spouted water like a whale and swam lazily for the shallows, where he lay on his back, washed by the surf, and exalted in his freedom.

As he kicked his legs at the surf half swirling his loins, it suddenly struck him that he was quite naked and there were men and women within twenty yards of him. But he felt no embarrassment.

Nakedness had become a way of life in the camp. And the months that he had spent in the village in Java had taught him that there was no shame in being a human being with wants and needs.

The sensual warmth of the sea playing on him, and the rich warmth of the food within him, fired his loins into sudden heat. He turned over abruptly on his belly and pushed himself back into the sea, hiding.

He stood on the sandy bottom, the water up to his neck, and looked back at the shore and the village. The men and women were still busy repairing their nets. He could see Sutra on the veranda of his hut, smoking in the shadows. Then, to one side, he saw Sulina, caught in the light from the oil lamp, leaning on the window frame. Her sarong was half held against her and she was looking out to sea.

He knew she was looking at him and he wondered, shamed, if she had seen. He watched her and she watched him. Then he saw her take away the sarong and lay it down and pick up a clean white towel to dry the sweat that sheened her body.

She was a child of the sun and a child of the rain. Her long dark hair hid most of her, but she moved it until it caressed her back and she began to braid it. And all the time she watched him, smiling.

Then, suddenly, every flicker of current was a caress, every touch of breeze, a caress, every thread of seaweed a caress— fingers of courtesans, crafty with centuries of learning.

'I'm going to take you, Sulina.

I'm going to take you, whatever the cost.

He tried to will Sutra to leave the veranda. Sulina watched. And waited. Impatient as he.

I'm going to take her, Sutra. Don't get in my way. Don't. Or by God . . .

He did not see the King approaching the shadows or notice him stop with surprise when he say him lying on his belly in the shallows.

'Hey, Peter. Peter!'

Hearing the voice through the fog, Peter Marlowe turned his head slowly and saw the King beckoning to him.

'Peter, c'mon. It's time to beat it.'

Seeing the King, he remembered the camp and the wire and the radio and the diamond and the camp and the war and the camp and the radio and the guard they had to pass and would they get back in time and what was the news and how happy Mac would be with the three hundred microfarads and the spare radio that worked. The man-heat vanished. But the pain remained.

He stood up and walked for his clothes.

'You got a nerve,' the King said.

'Why?'

'Walking about like that. Can't you see Sutra's girl looking at you?'

'She's seen plenty of men without clothes and there's

198

nothing wrong with that.' Without the heat there was no nakedness.

'Sometimes I don't understand you. Where's your modesty?'

'Lost that a long time ago.' He dressed quickly and joined the King in the shadows. His loins ached violently. 'I'm glad you came along when you did. Thanks.'

'Why?'

'Oh, nothing.'

'You scared I'd forgotten you?'

Peter Marlowe shook his head. 'No. Forget it. But thanks.'

The King studied him, then shrugged. 'C'mon. We can make it easy now.' He led the way past Sutra's hut and waved. 'Salamat.'

'Wait, Rajah. Won't be a second!'

Peter Marlowe ran up the stairs and into the hut. The radio was still there. Holding it under his arm, wrapped in the cloth, he bowed to Sutra.

'I thank thee. It is in good hands.'

'Go with God.' Sutra hesitated, then smiled. 'Guard they eyes, my son. Lest when there is food for them, thou canst not eat.'

'I will remember.' Peter Marlowe felt suddenly hot. I wonder if the stories are true, that the ancients can read thoughts from time to time. 'I thank thee. Peace be upon thee.'

'Peace be upon thee until our next meeting.'

Peter Marlowe turned and left. Sulina was at her window as they passed underneath it. Her sarong covered her now. Their eyes met and caught and a compact was given and received and returned. She watched as they shadowed up the rise towards the jungle and she sent her safe wishes on them until they disappeared.

Sutra sighed, then noiselessly went into Sullina's room. She was standing at the window dreamily, her sarong around her shoulders. Sutra had a thin bamboo in his hands and he cut her neatly and hard, but not too hard, across her bare buttocks.

'That is for tempting the Englishman when I had not told thee to tempt him,' he said, trying to sound very angry.

'Yes, Father,' she whimpered, and each sob was a knife in his heart. But when she was alone, she curled luxuriously on the mattress and let the tears roll a little, enjoying them. And the heat spread through her, helped by the sting of the blow.

When they were about a mile from the camp, the King and Peter Marlowe stopped for a breather. It was then that the King noticed for the first time the small bundle wrapped in cloth.

He had been leading the way, and so concentrated had he been on the success of the night's work, and so watchful of the darkness against possible danger, that he had not noticed it before.

'What you got? Extra chow?'

He watched while Peter Marlowe grinned and proudly unwrapped the cloth. 'Surprise!'

The King's heart missed six beats.

'Why, you goddam son of a bitch! Are you out of your skull?'

'What's the matter?' Peter Marlowe asked, flabbergasted.

'Are you crazy? That'll land us in more trouble than hell knows what. You got no right to risk our necks over a goddam radio. You got no right to use *my* contacts for your own goddam business.'

Peter Marlowe felt the night close in on him as he stared unbelievingly. Then he said, 'I didn't mean any harm—'

'Why, you goddam son of a bitch!' the King raged. 'Radios are poison.'

'But there isn't one in the camp—'

'Tough. You get rid of that goddam thing right now. And I'll tell you something else. We're finished. You and me. You got no right to get me mixed in something without telling me. I ought to kick the shit outta you!'

'Try it.' Now Peter Marlowe was angry and raw, as raw as the King. 'You seem to forget there's a war on and there's no wireless in the camp. One reason I came was because I hoped I might be able to get a condenser. But now I've a whole wireless and it works.'

'Get rid of it!'

'No.'

The two men faced each other, taut and inflexible. For a split second the King readied to cut Peter Marlowe to pieces.

But the King knew anger was of no value when an important decision had to be made, and now that he had gotten over the

200

first nauseating shock, he could be critical and analyse the situation.

First, he had to admit that although it had been bad business to risk so much, the risk had been successful. If Sutra hadn't been good and ready to give Peter the radio he'd've ducked the issue and said, 'Hell, there's no radio hereabouts.' So no harm was done. And it had been a private deal between Pete and Sutra 'cause Cheng San had already left.

Second, a radio that he knew about and one that wasn't in his hut would be more than useful. He could keep tabs on the situation and he'd know exactly when to make the break. So, all in all, there was no harm done—except that Peter had exceeded his authority. Now take that. If you trust a guy and hire him, you hire his brains. No point in having a guy around just to take orders and sit on his can. And Peter had sure been great during the negotiations. If and when the break came, well, Peter would be on the team. Got to have a guy to talk the lingo. Yeah, and Pete wasn't scared. So all in all, the King knew he'd be crazy to rip into him before his mind told him to use the new situation in a businesslike way. Yep, *he* had blown his stack like a two-year-old.

'Pete.' He saw the challenging set to Peter Marlowe's jaw. Wonder if I could take the son of a bitch. Sure. Got him by fifty—maybe eighty pounds.

'Yes?'

'I'm sorry I blew my stack. The radio's a good idea.'

'What?'

'I just said I was sorry. It's a great idea.'

'I don't understand you,' Peter Marlowe said helplessly. 'One moment you're a crazy man and the next you're saying that it's a good idea.'

The King liked this son of a bitch. Got guts. 'Eh, radios give me the creeps, no future in them.' Then he laughed softly. 'No resale value!'

'You're not really fed up with me any more?'

'Hell no. We're buddies.' he punched him playfully. 'I was just put out that you didn't tell me. That wasn't good.'

'I'm sorry. You're right. I apologize. It was ridiculous and unfair. Christ, I wouldn't want to jeopardize you in any way. Truly I'm sorry.'

201

'Shake. I'm sorry I blew my stack. But next time, tell me *before* you do anything.'

Peter Marlowe shook his hand. 'My word on it.'

'Good enough.' Well, thank God there was no sweat now. 'So what the hell do you mean by condenser?'

Peter Marlowe told him about the three water bottles.

'So all Mac needs is the one condenser, right?'

'He said he *thinks* so.'

'You know what I think? I think it'd be better just to take out the condenser and dump the radio. Bury it here. It'd be safe. Then if yours doesn't work we could always come back and get it. Mac could easily put the condenser back. To hide this radio in the camp'd be real tough, and it'd be a helluva temptation just to plug the goddam thing in, wouldn't it?'

'Yes.' Peter Marlowe looked at the King searchingly. 'You'll come back with me to get it?'

'Sure.'

'If—for any reason—I can't come back, would you come for it? If Mac or Larkin asked you to?'

The King thought a moment. 'Sure.'

'Your word?'

'Yes.' The King smiled faintly. 'You put quite a store by the "word" jazz, don't you, Peter.'

'How else can you judge a *man*?'

It took Peter Marlowe only a moment to snap the two wires joining the condenser to the innards of the radio. Another minute and the radio was wrapped in its protective cloth and a small hole scraped away in the jungle earth. They put a flat stone on the bottom of the hole, then covered the radio with a good thickness of leaves and smoothed the earth back and pulled a tree trunk over the spot. A couple of weeks in the dampness of its tomb would destroy its usefulness, but two weeks would be enough time to come back and pick it up if the bottles still didn't work.

Peter Marlowe wiped the sweat away, for a sudden layer of heat had settled on them and the sweat smell frenzied the increasing waves of insects clouding them. 'These blasted bugs!' He looked up at the night sky, judging the time a little nervously. 'Do you think we'd better go on now?'

'Not yet. It's only four-fifteen. Our best time is just before dawn. We'd better wait another ten minutes, then we'll be in position in plenty of time.' He grinned. 'First time I went through the wire I was scared and anxious too. Coming back I had to wait at the wire. I had to wait half an hour or more before the coast was clear. Jesus! I sweated.' He waved his hands at the insects. 'Goddam bugs.'

They sat awhile listening to the constant movement of the jungle. Swaths of fireflies cut patches of brilliance in the small rain ditches beside the path.

'Just like Broadway at night,' said the King.

'I saw a film once called *Times Square*. It was a newspaper yarn. Let me see. I think it was Cagney.'

'Don't remember that one. But Broadway, you got to see it for real. It's just like a day in the middle of the night. Huge neon signs and lights all over the place.'

'Is that your home? New York?'

'No. I've been there a couple of times. Been all over.'

'Where's your home?'

The King shrugged. 'My pa moves around.'

'What's his work?'

'That's a good question. Little of this, little of that. He's drunk most of the time.'

'Oh! That must be pretty rough.'

'Tough on a kid.'

'Do you have any family?'

'My ma's dead. She died when I was three. Got no brothers or sisters. My pa brought me up. He's a bum, but he taught me a lot about life. Number one, poverty's a sickness. Number two, money's everything. Number three, it doesn't matter how you get it as long as you get it.'

'You know, I've never thought much about money. I suppose in the service—well, there's always a monthly pay check, there's always a certain standard of living, so money doesn't mean much.'

'How much does your father make?'

'I don't know exactly. I suppose around six hundred pounds a year.'

'Jesus. That's only twenty-four hundred bucks. Why, I make thirteen hundred as a corporal myself. I sure as hell wouldn't work for that nothing dough.'

'Perhaps it's different in the States. But in England you can get by quite well. Of course our car is quite old, but that doesn't matter, and at the end of your service you get a pension.'

'How much?'

'Half your pay approximately.'

'That seems to me to be nothing. Can't understand why people go in the service. Guess because they're failures as people.'

The King saw Peter Marlowe stiffen slightly. 'Of course,' he added quickly, 'that doesn't apply in England. I was talking about the States.'

'The service is a good life—for a man. Enough money—an exciting life in all parts of the world. Social life's good. Then, well, an officer always has a great deal of prestige.' Peter Marlowe added almost apologetically, 'You know, tradition and all that.'

'You going to stay in after the war?'

'Of course.'

'Seems to me,' the King said, picking at his teeth with a little thread of bark, 'that it's too easy. There's no excitement or future in taking orders from guys who are mostly bums. That's the way it looks to me. And hell, you don't get paid nothing. Why Pete, you should take a look at the States. There's nothing like it in the world. No place. Every man for himself and every man's as good as the next guy. And all you have to do is figure an angle and be better than the next guy. Now that's excitement.'

'I don't think I'd fit in. Somehow I know I'm not a money-maker. I'm better off doing what I was born to do.'

'That's nonsense. Just because your old man's in the service—'

Goes back to 1720. Father to son. That's a lot of tradition to try to fight.'

The King grunted. 'That's quite a time!' Then he added, 'I only know about my dad and his dad. Before that—nothing. Least, my folks were supposed to have come over from the old country in the '80's.'

'From England?'

'Hell no. I think Germany. Or maybe Middle Europe. Who the hell cares? I'm an American and that's all that counts.'

'Marlowes are in the service and that's that!'

'Hell no. It's up to you. Look. Take you now. You're in the chips 'cause you're using your brains. You'd be a great businessman if you wanted to. You can talk like a Wog, right? I need your brains. I'm paying for the brains—now don't get on your goddam high horse. That's American style. You pay for brains. It's got nothing to do with us being buddies. Nothing. If I didn't pay, then I'd be a bum.'

'That's wrong. You don't have to be paid to help a bit.'

'You sure as hell need an education. I'd like to get you in the States and put you on the road. With your phoney Limey accent you'd knock the broads dead. You'd clean up. We'll put you in ladies' underwear.'

'Holy God.' Peter smiled with him, but the smile was tinged with horror. 'I could no more try to sell something than fly.'

'You can fly.'

'I meant without a plane.'

'Sure. I was making a joke.'

The King glanced at his watch. 'Time goes slow when you're waiting.'

'I sometimes think we'll never get out of this stinking hole.'

'Eh, Uncle Sam's got the Nips on the run. Won't take long. Even if it does, what the hell? We've got it made, buddy. That's all that counts.'

The King looked at his watch. 'We'd better take a powder.'

'What?'

'Get going.'

'Oh!' Peter Marlowe got up. 'Lead on, Macduff!' he said happily.

'Huh?'

'Just a saying. It means "Let's take a powder".'

Happy now that they were friends once more, they started into the jungle. Crossing the road was easy. Now that they had passed the area patrolled by the roving guard, they followed a short path and were within quarter of a mile of the wire. The King led, calm and confident. Only the clouds of fireflies and mosquitoes made their progress unpleasant.

'Jesus. The bugs are bad.'

'Yes. If I had my way I'd fry them all,' Peter Marlowe whispered back.

205

Then they saw the bayonet pointing at them, and stopped dead in their tracks.

The Japanese was sitting leaning against a tree, and his eyes were fixed on them, a frightening grin stretching his face, and the bayonet was held propped on his knees.

Their thoughts were the same. Christ! Outram Road! I'm dead. *Kill!*

The King was the first to react. He leaped at the guard and tore the bayoneted rifle away, rolled as he twisted aside, then got to his feet, the rifle butt high to smash it into the man's face. Peter Marlowe was diving for the guard's throat. A sixth sense warned him and his clutching hands avoided the throat and he slammed into the tree.

'Get away from him!' Peter Marlowe sprang to his feet and grabbed the King and pulled him out of the way.

The guard had not moved. The same wide-eyed malevolent grin was on his face.

'What the hell?' the King gasped, panicked, the rifle still held high above his head.

'Get away! For Christ's sake hurry!' Peter Marlowe jerked the rifle out of the King's hands and threw it beside the dead Japanese. Then the King saw the snake in the man's lap.

'Jesus,' he croaked as he went forward to take a closer look.

Peter Marlowe caught him frantically. 'Get away! Run, for God's sake!'

He took to his heels, away from the trees, carelessly crashing through the undergrowth. The King raced after him, and only when they had reached a clearing did they stop.

'You gone crazy?' The King winced, his breathing torturing him. 'It was only a goddam snake!'

'That was a flying snake,' Peter Marlowe wheezed. 'They live in trees. Instant death, old man. They climb the trees, then flatten their bodies and sort of spiral down to earth and fall or their victims. There was one in his lap and one under him. There was sure to be more 'cause they're always in nests.'

'Jesus!'

'Actually, old man, we ought to be grateful to those bloody things,' Peter Marlowe said, trying to slow his breathing. 'That Jap was still warm. He hadn't been dead more than a couple of minutes. He would've caught us if he hadn't been bitten. And

206

we should thank God for our quarrel. It gave the snakes time. We'll never be closer to pranging! To death! Never!'

'I don't ever want to see a goddam Jap with a goddam bayonet pointing at me in the middle of the goddam night again. C'mon. Better get away from here.'

When they were in position near the wire, they settled down to wait. They couldn't make their dash to the wire yet. Too many people about. Always people walking about, zombies walking the camp, the sleepless and the almost asleep.

It was good to rest, and both felt their knees shaking and were thankful to be alive again.

Jesus, this has been a night, the King thought. If it hadn't been for Pete I'd be a dead duck. I was going to put my foot down in the Jap's lap as I smashed down the rifle. My foot was six inches away, Snakes! Hate snakes. Sons of bitches!

And as the King calmed, his esteem for Peter Marlowe increased.

'That's the second time you saved my neck,' he whispered.

'You got to the rifle first. If the Jap hadn't been dead you'd've killed him. I was slow.'

'Eh, I was just in front.' The King stopped, then grinned. 'Hey Peter. We make a good team. With your looks and my brains, we do all right.'

Peter Marlowe began to laugh. He tried to hold it inside and rolled on the ground. The choked laughter and the tears streaming his face infected the King, and his laughter too began to contort him. At last Peter Marlowe gasped, 'For Christ sake, shut up.'

'You started it.'

'I did not.'

'Sure you did, you said, you said . . .' But the King couldn't continue. He wiped the tears away. 'You see that Jap? That son of a bitch was just sitting like an ape—'

'Look!'

Their laughter vanished.

On the other side of the wire Grey was walking the camp. They saw him stop outside the American hut. They saw him wait in the shadows, then look out across the wire, almost directly at them.

'You think he knows?' Peter Marlowe whispered.

'Don't know. But sure as hell we can't risk going in for a while. We'll wait.'

They waited. The sky began to lighten. Grey stood in the shadows looking at the American hut, then around the camp. The King knew from where Grey stood he could see his bed. He knew that Grey could see he wasn't in it. But the covers were turned back and he could be with the other sleepless, walking the camp. No law against being out of your bed. But hurry up, get to hell out of there, Grey.

'We'll have to go soon', the King said. 'Light's against us.'

'How about another spot?'

'He's got the whole fence covered, way up to the corner.'

'You think there's been a leak—someone sneaked?'

'Could be. Maybe just a coincidence.' The King bit his lip angrily.

'How about the latrine area?'

'Too risky.'

They waited. Then they saw Grey look once more over the fence towards them and walk away. They watched him until he rounded the jail wall.

'May be a phoney,' the King said. 'Give him a couple of minutes.'

The seconds were like hours as the sky lightened and the shadows began to dissolve. Now there was no one near the fence, no one in sight.

'Now or never, c'mon.'

They ran for the fence; in seconds they were under the wire and in the ditch.

'You go for the hut, Rajah. I'll wait.'

'Okay.'

For all his size the King was light on his feet and he swiftly covered the distance to his hut. Peter Marlowe got out of the ditch. Something told him to sit on the edge looking out of the camp over the wire. Then, from the corner of his eye, he saw Grey turn the corner and stop. He knew he had been seen immediately.

'Marlowe.'

'Oh hello, Grey. Can't you sleep either?' he said, stretching.

'How long have you been here?'

'Few minutes. I got tired of walking so I sat down.'

'Where's your pal?'

'Who?'

'The American,' Grey sneered.

'I don't know. Asleep I suppose.'

Grey looked at the Chinese type outfit. The tunic was torn across the shoulders and wet with sweat. Mud and shreds of leaves on his stomach and knees. A streak of mud on his face.

'How did you get so dirty? And why are you sweating so much? What're you up to?'

'I'm dirty because—there's no harm in a little honest dirt. In fact,' Peter Marlowe said as he got up and brushed off his knees and the seat of his pants, 'there is nothing like a little dirt to make a man feel clean when he washes it off. And I'm sweating because you're sweating. You know, the tropics—heat and all that!'

'What have you got in your pockets?'

'Just because you've a suspicious beetle brain doesn't mean that everyone is carrying contraband. There's no law against walking the camp if you can't sleep.'

'That's right,' Grey replied, 'but there is a law against walking outside the camp.'

Peter Marlowe studied him nonchalantly, not feeling nonchalant at all, trying to read what the hell Grey meant by that. Did he know? 'A man'd be a fool to try that.'

'That's right.' Grey looked at him long and hard. Then he wheeled around and walked away.

Peter Marlowe stared after him. Then he turned and walked in the other direction and did not look at the American hut. Today, Mac was due out of hospital. Peter Marlowe smiled, thinking of Mac's welcome home present.

From the safety of his bed, the King watched Peter Marlowe go. Then he focused on Grey, the enemy, erect and malevolent in the growing light.

Skeletal thin, ragged pair of pants, crude native clogs, no shirt, his armband, his threadbare Tank beret. A ray of sunlight burned the tank emblem in the beret, converting it from nothing into molten gold.'

How much do you know, Grey, you son of a bitch? The King asked himself.

BOOK THREE

XV

It was just after dawn.

Peter Marlowe lay on his bunk in half-sleep.

Was it a dream? he asked himself, suddenly awake. Then his cautious fingers touched the little piece of rag that held the condenser and he knew it was not a dream.

Ewart twisted in the top bunk and groaned awake.

''Mahlu on the night,' he said as he hung his legs over the bunk.

Peter Marlowe remembered that it was his unit's turn for the borehole detail. He walked out of the hut and prodded Larkin awake.

'Eh? Oh, Peter,' Larkin said, fighting out of sleep. 'What's up?'

It was hard for Peter Marlowe not to blurt out the news about the condenser, but he wanted to wait until Mac was there too, so he just said, 'Borehole detail, old man.'

'My bloody oath! What, again?' Larkin stretched his aching back, retied his sarong and slipped on his clogs.

They found the net and the five-gallon container and walked through the camp, which was just beginning to stir. When they reached the latrine area they paid no heed to the occupants and the occupants paid no heed to them.

Larkin lifted the cover off a borehole, Peter Marlowe quickly scooped the sides with the net. When he brought the net out of the hole it was full of cockroaches. He shook the net clean into the container and scraped again. Another fine haul.

Larkin replaced the cover and they moved to the next hole.

'Hold that thing still,' Peter Marlowe said. 'Now look what you did! I lost at least a hundred.'

'There's plenty more,' Larkin said with distaste, getting a better grip on the container.

The smell was very bad but the harvest rich. Soon the container was packed. The smallest of the cockroaches measured an inch and a half. Larkin clamped the lid on the container and they walked up to the hospital.

'Not my idea of a steady diet,' Peter Marlowe said.

'You really ate them, Peter in Java?'

'Of course. And so have you, by the way. In Changi.'

Larkin almost dropped the container. 'What?'

'You don't think I'd pass on a native delicacy and a source of protein to the doctors and not take advantage of it for us, do you?'

'But we had a pact!' Larkin shouted. 'We agreed, the three of us, that we'd not cook anything weird without telling the other first.'

'I told Mac and he agreed.'

'But I didn't, dammit!'

'Oh come on, Colonel! We've had to catch them and cook them secretly and listen to you say how good the cook-up was. We're just as squeamish as you.'

'Well, next time I want to know. That's a bloody order!'

'Yes, sir!' Peter Marlowe chuckled.

They delivered the container to the hospital cookhouse. To the special tiny cookhouse that fed the desperately sick.

When they got back to the bungalow Mac was waiting. His skin was grey-yellow and his eyes were bloodshot and his hands shaking, but he was over the fever. He could smile again.

'Good to have you back, cobber,' Larkin said, sitting down.

'Ay.'

Peter Marlowe absently took out the little piece of rag. 'Oh, by the way,' he said with studied negligence, 'this might come in handy sometime.'

Mac unwrapped the rag without interest.

'Oh my bloody word!' Larkin said.

'Dammit, Peter,' Mac said, his fingers shaking, 'are you trying to give me a heart attack?'

Peter Marlowe kept his voice as flat as his face, enjoying his

214

excitement hugely. 'No point in getting all upset about nothing.' Then he could contain his smile no longer. He beamed.

'You and your blasted Pommy underplay.' Larkin tried to be sour, but he was beaming too. 'Where'd you get it, cobber?'

Peter Marlowe shrugged.

'Stupid question. Sorry, Peter,' Larkin said apologetically.

Peter Marlowe knew he never would be asked again. It was far better they did not know about the village.

Now it was dusk.

Larkin was guarding. Peter Marlowe was guarding. Under cover of his mosquito net, Mac joined the condenser. Then, unable to wait any longer, with a prayer he fiddled the connecting wire into the electric source. Sweating, he listened into the single earphone.

An agony of waiting. It was suffocating under the net, and the concrete walls and concrete floor held the heat of the vanishing sun. A mosquito droned angrily. Mac cursed but did not try to find it and kill it, for suddenly there was static in the earphone.

His tense fingers, wet with the sweat that ran down his arms, slipped on the screwdriver. He dried them. Delicately he found the screw that turned the tuner and began to twist, gently, oh so gently. Static. Only static. Then suddenly he heard the music. It was a Glenn Miller recording.

The music stopped, and an announcer said, 'This is Calcutta. We continue the Glenn Miller recital with his recording "Moonlight Serenade."'

Through the doorway Mac could see Larkin squatting in the shadows, and beyond him men walking the corridor between the rows of cement bungalows. He wanted to rush out and shout, 'You laddies want to hear the news in a little while? I've got Calcutta tuned in!'

Mac listened for another minute, then disconnected the radio and carefully put the water bottles back into their sheaths and green-grey felt and left them carelessly on the beds. There would be a news broadcast from Calcutta at ten, so to save time Mac hid the wire and the earphone under the mattress instead of putting them into the third bottle.

He had been hunched under the net for so long that he had a

crick in his back, and he groaned when he stood up.

Larkin looked back from his station outside. 'What's the matter, cobber? Can't you sleep?'

'Nay, laddie,' said Mac, coming out to squat beside him.

'You should take it easy, first day out of hospital.' Larkin did not need to be told that it worked. Mac's eyes were lit with excitement. Larkin punched him playfully. 'You're all right, you old bastard.'

'Where's Peter?' Mac asked, knowing that he was guarding by the showers.

'Over there. Stupid bugger's just sitting. Look at him.'

'Hey, 'mahlu sana!' Mac called out.

Peter Marlowe already knew that Mac had finished, but he got up and walked back and said, ''Mahlu sendiris,' which means ''Mahlu yourself.' He, too, did not need to be told.

'How about a game of bridge?' Mac asked.

'Who's the fourth?'

'Hey, Gavin,' Larkin called out. 'You want to make a fourth?'

Major Gavin Ross dragged his legs out of the camp chair. Leaning on a crutch, he wormed himself from the next bungalow. He was glad for the offer of a game. Nights were always bad. So unnecessary, the paralysis. Once upon a time a man, and now a nothing. Useless legs. Wheelchaired for life.

He had been hit in the head by a tiny sliver of shrapnel just before Singapore surrendered. 'Nothing to worry about,' the doctors had told him. 'We can get it out soon as we can get you into a proper hospital with the proper equipment. We've plenty of time.' But there was never a proper hospital with the proper equipment and time had run out.

'Glad,' he said painfully as he settled himself on the cement floor. Mac found a cushion and tossed it over. 'Ta, old chap!' It took him a moment to settle while Peter Marlowe got the cards and Larkin arranged the space between them. Gavin lifted his left leg and bent it out of the way, disconnecting the wire spring that attached the toe of his shoe to the hand around his leg, just under the knee. Then he moved the other leg, equally paralysed, out of the way and leaned back on the cushion against the wall. 'That's better,' he said, stroking his Kaiser Wilhelm moustache with a quick nervous movement.

'How're the headaches?' Larkin asked automatically.

'Not too bad, old boy,' Gavin replied as automatically. 'You my partner?'

'No. You can play with Peter.'

'Oh Gad, the boy always trumps my ace.'

'That was only once,' Peter Marlowe said.

'Once an evening,' laughed Mac as he began to deal. ''Mahlu.'

'Two spades.' Larkin opened with a flourish.

The bidding continued furiously and vehemently.

Later that night Larkin knocked on the door of one of the bungalows.

'Yes?' Smedly-Taylor asked, peering into the night.

'Sorry to trouble you, sir.'

'Oh hello, Larkin. Trouble?' It was always trouble. He wondered what the Aussies had been up to this time as he got off his bed, aching.

'No, sir.' Larkin made sure there was no one in earshot. His words were quiet and deliberate. 'The Russians are forty miles from Berlin. Manila is liberated. The Yanks have landed on Corregidor and Iwo Jima.'

'Are you sure, man?'

'Yes, sir.'

'Who—' Smedly-Taylor stopped. 'No. I don't want to know anything. Sit down, Colonel,' he said quietly. 'Are you absolutely sure?'

'Yes, sir.'

'I can only say, Colonel,' the older man said tonelessly and solemnly, 'that I can do nothing to help anyone who is caught with—who is caught.' He did not even want to say the word wireless. 'I don't wish to know anything about it.' A shadow of a smile crossed the granite face and softened it. 'I only beg you guard it with your life and tell me immediately you hear anything.'

'Yes, sir. We propose—'

'I don't want to hear anything. Only the news.' Sadly Smedly-Taylor touched his shoulder. 'Sorry.'

'It's safer sir.' Larkin was glad the colonel did not want to know their plan. They had decided that they would tell only two persons each. Larkin would tell Smedly-Taylor and Gavin Ross; Mac would tell Major Tooley and Lieutenant Bosley—

both personal friends; and Peter would tell the King and Father Donovan, the Catholic chaplain. They were to pass the news on to two other persons they could trust, and so on. It was a good plan, Larkin thought. Correctly, Peter had not volunteered where the condenser came from. Good boy, that Peter.

Later that night, when Peter Marlowe returned to his hut from seeing the King, Ewart was wide awake. He poked his head out of the net and whispered excitedly, 'Peter. You heard the news?'

'What news?'

'The Russians are forty miles from Berlin. The Yanks have landed on Iwo Jima and Corregdor.'

Peter Marlowe felt the inner terror. Oh my God, so soon?

'Bloody rumours, Ewart. Bloody nonsense.'

'No, it isn't, Peter. There's a new wireless in the camp. It's the real stuff. No rumour. Isn't that great? Oh Christ, I forgot the best. The Yanks have liberated Manila. Won't be long now, eh?'

'I'll believe it when I see it.'

Maybe we should have just told Smedly-Taylor and no one else, Peter Marlowe thought as he lay down. If Ewart knows, there's no telling.

Nervously, he listened to the camp. You could almost feel the growing excitement of Changi. The camp knew that it was back in contact.

Yoshima was slimed with fear as he stood to attention in front of the raging General.

'You stupid, incompetent fool,' the General was saying.

Yoshima braced himself for the blow that was coming and it came, openhanded across the face.

'You find that radio or you'll be reduced to the ranks. Your transfer is cancelled. Dismiss!'

Yoshima saluted smartly, and his bow was the perfection of humility. He left the General's quarters, thankful that he had been let off so lightly. Damn these pestilential prisoners!

In the barracks he lined up his staff and raged at them, and slapped their faces until his hand hurt. In their turn, the sergeants slapped the corporals and they the privates and the privates the Koreans. The orders were clear. 'Get that radio or else.'

218

For five days nothing happened. Then the jailers fell on the camp and almost pulled it apart. But they found nothing. The traitor within the camp did not yet know the whereabouts of the radio. Nothing happened, except the promised return to standard rations was cancelled. The camp settled back to wait out the long days, made longer by the lack of food. But they knew that at least there would be news. Not rumours, but news. And the news was very good. The war in Europe was almost over.

Even so, there was a pall on the men. Few had reserve stocks of food. And the good news had a catch to it. If the war ended in Europe, more troops would be sent to the Pacific. Eventually there would be an attack on the home islands of Japan. And such an attack would drive the jailers berserk. They all knew there was only one end to Changi.

Peter Marlowe was walking towards the chicken area, his water bottle swinging at his hip. Mac, Larkin and he had agreed that perhaps it would be safer to carry the water bottles as much as possible. Just in case there was a sudden search.

He was in a good mood. Though the money he had earned was long since gone, the King had advanced food and tobacco against future earnings. God, what a man, he thought. But for him, Mac, Larkin and I would be as hungry as the rest of Changi.

The day was cooler. Rain the day before had settled the dust. It was almost time for lunch. As he neared the chicken coops his pace quickened. Maybe there'll be some eggs today. Then he stooped, perplexed.

Near the run that belonged to Peter Marlowe's unit was a small crowd, an angry, violent crowd. He saw to his surprise that Grey was there. In front of Grey was Colonel Foster, naked but for his filthy loincloth, jumping up and down like a maniac, incoherently screaming abuse at Johnny Hawkins, who was clasping his dog protectively to his chest.

'Hi, Max,' said Peter Marlowe as he came abreast of the King's chicken run. 'What's up?'

'Hi, Pete,' said Max easily, shifting the rake in his hands. He noticed Peter Marlowe's instinctive reaction to the 'Pete'. Officers! You try to treat an officer like a regular guy and call him by his name and then he gets mad. The hell with them. 'Yeah, Pete.' He repeated it just for good measure. 'All hell broke loose an hour aggo. Seems like Hawkins's dog got into the Greek's run and killed one of his hens.'

'Oh no!'

'They'll hand him his head, that's for sure.'

Foster was screaming. 'I want another hen and I want damages. The beast killed one of my children, I want a charge of murder sworn out.'

'But Colonel,' Grey said, at the end of his patience, 'it was a hen, not a child. You can't swear a—'

'My hens are my children, idiot! Hen, child, what's the difference? Hawkins is a dirty murderer. A murderer, you *hear*?'

'Look, Colonel,' Grey said angrily. 'Hawkins can't give you another hen. He's said he's sorry. The dog got off its leash—'

'I want a court-martial. Hawkins the murderer and his beast, a murderer.' Colonel Foster's mouth was flecked with foam. 'That bloody beast killed my hen and ate it. He ate it and there's only feathers to show for one of my children.'

Snarling, he suddenly darted at Hawkins, his hands outstretched, nails like talons, tearing at the dog in Hawkins's arms, screaming, 'I'll kill you and your bloody beast.'

Hawkins avoided Foster and shoved him away. The colonel fell to the ground and Rover whimpered with fear.

'I've said I'm sorry,' Hawkins choked out. 'If I had the money I'd gladly give you two, ten hens, but I can't! Grey—' Hawkins desperately turned to him—'for the love of God do something.'

'What the hell can I do?' Grey was tired and mad and had dysentery. 'You know I can't do anything. I'll have to report it. But you'd better get rid of that dog.'

'What do you mean?'

'Holy Christ,' Grey stormed at him, 'I mean get rid of it. Kill it. And if you won't, get someone else to do it. But, by God, see that it's not in the camp by nightfall.'

'It's my dog. You can't order—'

'The hell I can't!' Grey tried to control his stomach muscles. He liked Hawkins, always had, but that didn't mean anything now. 'You know the rules. You've been warned to keep it leashed and keep it out of this area. Rover killed and ate the hen. There are witnesses who saw him do it.'

Colonel Foster picked himself off the ground, his eyes black

220

and beady. 'I'm going to kill it,' he hissed. 'That dog's mine to kill. An eye for an eye.'

Grey stepped in front of Foster, who hunched ready for another attack. 'Colonel Foster. This matter will be reported. Captain Hawkins has been ordered to destroy the dog—'

Foster didn't seem to hear Grey. 'I want that beast. I'm going to kill it. Just like it killed my hen. It's mine. I'm going to kill it.' He began creeping forward, salivating. '*Just like it killed my child.*'

Grey held his hand out. 'No! Hawkins will destroy it.'

'Colonel Foster,' Hawkins said abjectly, 'I beg you, please, please, accept my apologies. Let me keep the dog, it won't happen again.'

'No it won't.' Colonel Foster laughed insanely. 'It's dead and it's mine.' He lunged forward, but Hawkins backed off and Grey caught the colonel's arm.

'Stop it,' Grey shouted, 'or I'll put you under arrest! This is no way for a senior officer to conduct himself. Get away from Hawkins. Get away.'

Foster tore his arm away from Grey. His voice was little more than a whisper as he talked directly to Hawkins. 'I'll get even with you, murderer. I'll get even with you.' He went back to his chicken coop and crawled inside, into his home, the place where he lived and slept and ate with his children, his hens.

Grey turned back to Hawkins. 'Sorry, Hawkins, but get rid of it.'

'Grey,' Hawkins pleaded, 'please take back the order. Please, I beg you, I'll do anything, anything.'

'I can't,' Grey had no alternative. 'You know I can't, Hawkins, old man. I can't. Get rid of it. But do it quickly.'

Then he turned on his heel and walked away.

Hawkins's cheeks were wet with tears, the dog cradled in his arms. Then he saw Peter Marlowe. 'Peter, for the love of God help me.'

'I can't, Johnny. I'm sorry, but there's nothing I can do or anyone can do.'

Grief-stricken, Hawkins looked around at the silent men. He was weeping openly now. The men turned away, for there was nothing that could be done. If a man had killed a hen, well, it would be almost the same, perhaps the same. A pitying mo-

221

ment, then Hawkins ran away sobbing, Rover still in his arms.

'Poor chap,' Peter Marlowe said to Max.

'Yeah, but thank God it wasn't one of the King's hens, Jesus, that'd be my lot.'

Max locked the coop and nodded to Peter Marlowe as he left.

Max liked looking after the hens. Nothing like an extra egg from time to time. And there's no risk when you suck the egg quick and pound the shell to dust and put it back in the hens' food. No clues left then. And the shells are good for the hens too. And hell, what's an egg here and there from the King? Just so long as there's at least one a day for the King, there's no sweat. Hell no! Max was indeed happy. For a whole week he'd be looking after the hens.

Later that day, after lunch, Peter Marlowe was lying on his bunk resting.

'Excuse me, sir.'

Peter Marlowe looked up and saw that Dino was standing beside the bunk. 'Yes?' He glanced around the hut and felt a twinge of embarrassment.

'Uh, can I speak to you, sir?' The 'sir' sounded impertinent as usual. Why is it Americans can't say 'sir' so that it sounds ordinary? Peter Marlowe thought. He got up and followed him out.

Dino led the way to the centre of the little clearing between the huts.

'Listen, Pete,' Dino said urgently. 'The King wants you. And you're to bring Larkin and Mac.'

'What's the matter?'

'He just said to bring them. You're to meet him inside the jail in Cell Fifty-four on the fourth floor in half an hour.'

Officers weren't allowed inside the jail. Japanese orders. Enforced by the camp police. God. Now that's risky.

'Is that all he said?'

'Yeah. That's all. Cell Fifty-four, fourth floor, in half an hour. See you around, Pete.'

Now what's up, Peter Marlowe asked himself. He hurried down to Larkin and Mac and told them.

'What do you think, Mac?'

'Well, laddie,' Mac said carefully, 'I dinna think that the

222

King'd lightly ask the three of us, without an explanation, unless it was important.'

'What about going into the jail?'

'If we get caught,' said Larkin, 'we better have a story. Grey'll hear about it sure enough and put a bad smell on it. Best thing to do is to go separately. I can always say I'm going to see some of the Aussies who're billeted in the jail. What about you, Mac?'

'Some of the Malayan Regiment are there. I could be visiting one of them. How about you, Peter?'

'There are some RAF types I could be seeing.' Peter Marlowe hesitated. 'Perhaps I should go and see what it's about and then come back and tell you.'

'No. If you're not seen going in, you might be caught coming out and stopped. Then they'd never let you back in. You couldn't disobey a direct order and go back a second time. No. I think we'd better go. But we'll go independently.' Larkin smiled. 'Mystery, eh? Wonder what's up?'

'I hope to God it isn't trouble.'

'Ah laddie,' said Mac. 'Living in these times is trouble. I wouldn't feel safe not going—the King got friends in high places. He might know something.'

'What about the bottles?'

They thought a moment, then Larkin broke the silence. 'We'll take them.'

'Isn't that dangerous? I mean, once inside the jail, if there's a snap search, we could never hide them.'

'If we're going to get caught, we're going to get caught.' Larkin was serious and hard-faced. 'It's either in the cards or it isn't.'

'Hey Peter,' Ewart called out as he saw Peter Marlowe leaving the hut. 'You forgot your armband.'

'Oh, thanks.' Peter Marlowe swore to himself as he went back to his bunk. 'Forgot the damned thing.'

'I'm always doing it. Can't be too careful.'

'That's right. Thanks again.'

Peter Marlowe joined the men walking the path beside the wall. He followed it north and turned the corner and before him was the gate. He slipped off his armband and felt suddenly naked and felt that the men who passed or approached were looking at him and wondering why this officer was not wearing an armband. Ahead, two hundred yards, was the end of the road west. The barricade was open now, for some of the work parties were returning from their day's work. Most of the labourers were exhausted, hauling the huge trailers with the stumps of trees that were dug with so much labour out of the swamps, destined for the camp cookhouses. Peter Marlowe remembered that the day after tomorrow he was going on such a party. He didn't mind the almost daily work parties to the airfield. That was easy work. But the wood detail was different. Hauling the logs was dangerous work. Many got ruptured from the lack of the tackle that would make the work easy. Many broke limbs and sprained ankles. They all had to go—the fit ones, once or twice a week, officers as well as men, for the cookhouse consumed much firewood—and it was fair that those who were fit collected for those who were not.

Beside the gate was the MP and on the opposite side of the gate the Korean guard leaned against the wall smoking, lethargically watching the men who passed. The MP was looking at the work party shuffling through the gate. There was one man lying on the trailer. One or two usually ended up that way, but they had to be very tired, or very sick, to be hauled back home to Changi.

Peter Marlowe slipped past the distracted guards and joined the men milling the huge concrete square.

He found his way into one of the cellblocks and began picking his way up the metal stairways and over the beds and bed rolls. There were men everywhere. On the stairways, in the corridors, and in the open cells—four or five to a cell designed for one man. He felt a growing horror of pressure from above, from below, from all around. The stench was nauseating. Stench from rotting bodies. Stench of unwashed human bodies. Stench from a generation of confined human bodies. Stench of walls, prison walls.

Peter Marlowe found Cell 54. The door was shut, so he opened it and went in. Mac and Larkin were already there.

'Christ, the smell of this place is killing me.'

'Me too, cobber,' said Larkin. He was sweating. Mac was sweating. The air was close and the concrete walls were moist

224

with their own wall-sweat and stained with the mould of years of wall-sweat.

The cell was about seven feet wide and eight feet long and ten feet high. In the centre of the cell, cemented to one wall, was a bed—a solid block of concrete three feet high and three feet wide and six feet long. Protruding from the bed was a concrete pillow. In one corner of the cell was a toilet—a hole in the floor which joined to the sewer. The sewers no longer worked. There was a tiny barred window nine feet up one wall, but the sky could not be seen because the wall was two feet thick.

'Mac. We'll give him a few minutes, then get out of this bloody place,' Larkin said.

'Ay, Laddie.'

'At least let's open the door,' Peter Marlowe said, the sweat pouring off him.

'Better keep it closed, Peter. Safer,' Larkin replied uneasily.

'I'd rather be dead than live here.'

'Ay. Thank God for the outside.'

'Hey, Larkin.' Mac indicated the blankets lying on the concrete bed. 'I don't understand where the men are who live in the cell. They can't all be on a work party.'

'I don't know either.' Larkin was getting nervous. 'Let's get out of here . . .'

The door opened and the King came in beaming with pleasure. 'Hi, you guys!' In his arms were some packages and he stood aside as Tex came in, also laden. 'Put 'em on the bed, Tex.'

Tex put down the electric hot plate and the large stewpan and kicked the door shut as they watched, astonished.

'Go get some water,' the King said to Tex.

'Sure.'

'What's going on? Why did you want to see us?' said Larkin.

The King laughed. 'We're going to have a cook-up.'

'For Christ sake! You mean to say you got us in here just for that? Why the hell couldn't we have done it in our billet?' Larkin was furious. The King merely looked at him and grinned. He turned his back and opened a package. Tex returned with the water and put the stewpan on the electric stove.

'Rajah, look, what—' Peter Marlowe stopped.

The King was emptying the best part of two pounds of

225

katchang idju beans into the water. Then he added salt and two heaping spoons of sugar. Then he turned around and opened another package wrapped in banana-leaf and held it up.

'Mother of God!'

There was sudden stunned silence in the cell.

The King was delighted with the effect of his surprise. 'Told you, Tex,' he grinned. 'You owe me a buck.'

Mac reached out and touched the meat. ''Mahlu. It's real.'

Larkin touched the meat. 'I'd forgotten what meat looked like,' he said in a voice hushed with awe. 'My bloody oath, you're a genius. Genius.'

'It's my birthday. So I figured we'd have a celebration. And I've got this,' the King said, holding up a bottle.

'What is it?'

'Sake!'

'I don't believe it,' Mac said. 'Why, there's the whole hind quarters of a pig here.' He bent forward and sniffed it. 'My God, it's real, real, real, and fresh as a day in May, hurray!'

They all laughed.

'Better lock the door, Tex.' The King turned to Peter Marlowe. 'Okay, partner?'

Peter Marlowe was still staring at the meat. 'Where the hell did you get it?'

'Long story!' The King took out a knife and scored the meat, then deftly broke the small hindquarters into two joints and put them into the stewpan. They all watched, fascinated, as he added a quantity of salt, adjusted the pan to the absolute centre of the hot plate, then sat back on the concrete bed and crossed his legs. 'Not bad, huh?'

For a long time no one spoke.

A sudden twist of the door handle broke the spell. The King nodded to Tex, who unlocked the door, opened it a fraction, then swung it wide. Brough entered.

He looked around astonished. Then noticed the stove. He went over and peered into the stewpot. 'I'll be goddamned!'

The King grinned. 'It's my birthday. Thought I'd invite you to dinner.'

'You got yourself a guest.' Brough stuck out his hand to Larkin. 'Don Brough, Colonel.'

'Grant's my Christian name! You know Mac and Peter?'

'Sure.' Brough grinned at them and turned to Tex. 'Hi, Tex!'

'Good to see you, Don.'

The King motioned to the bed. 'Take a seat, Don. Then we got to go to work!'

Peter Marlowe wondered why it was that American enlisted men and officers called themselves by Christian names so easily. It didn't sound cheap or unctuous—it seemed almost correct—and he had noticed that Brough was always obeyed as their leader even though they all called him Don—to his face. Remarkable.

'What's this work jazz?' asked Brough.

The King pulled out some strips of blankets. 'We're going to have to seal the door.'

'What?' Larkin said incredulously.

'Sure,' the King said. 'When this begins cooking, we're liable to have us a riot on our hands. The guys start smelling this, Crissake, figure for yourselves. We could get torn apart. This was the only place I could figure where we could cook in private. The smell will mostly go out the window. If we seal the door good, that is. We couldn't cook it outside, that's for sure.'

'Larkin was right,' said Mac solemnly. 'You're a genius. I'd never have thought of it. Believe me,' he added laughing, 'Americans, henceforth, are amongst my friends!'

'Thanks, Mac. Now we'd better do it.'

The King's guests took strips of blanket and stuffed them in the cracks around the door and covered the barred peephole in the door. When they had finished the King inspected their work.

'Good,' he said. 'Now, what about the window?'

They looked up at the little barred section of sky, and Brough said, 'Leave it open until the stew really begins to boil. Then we'll cover it and stand it as long as we can. Then we can open it up for a while.' He looked around. 'I figure it might be all right to let the perfume out sporadically. Like an Indian smoke signal.'

'Is there any wind?'

'Goddamned if I noticed. Anyone?'

'Hey Peter, give me a lift up, laddie,' said Mac.

Mac was the smallest of the men, so Peter Marlowe let him

227

stand on his shoulders. Mac peered through the bars, then licked his finger and held it out.

'Hurry up, Mac, for God's sake—you're no chicken, you know!' Peter Marlowe called out.

'Got to test for wind, you young bastard!' And again he licked his finger and held it out, and he looked so intent and so ridiculous that Peter Marlowe began laughing, and Larkin joined in, and they doubled up and Mac fell down six feet and grazed his leg on the concrete bed and began cursing.

'Look at my bloody leg, blast you,' Mac said, choking. It was only a little graze, but there was a trickle of blood. 'I bloody near scraped the skin off the whole bloody thing.'

'Look, Peter,' groaned Larkin, holding his stomach, 'Mac's got blood. I always thought he had only latex in his veins!'

'Go to hell, you bastards, 'mahlu!' Mac said irascibly, then a fit of laughter caught him and he got up and grabbed Peter Marlowe and Larkin and began to sing 'Ring around the roses, pocket full of posies . . .'

And Peter Marlowe grabbed Brough's arm, and Brough took Tex's, and the chain of men, hysterical with the song, wove around the stewpot and the King, seated crosslegged behind it.

Mac broke the chain. 'Hail, Caesar. We who are about to eat salute thee.'

As one, they threw him the salute and collapsed in a heap.

'Get off my blasted arm, Peter!'

'You've got your foot in my balls, you bastard,' Larkin swore at Brough.

'Sorry, Grant. Oh Jesus! I haven't laughed so much in years.'

'Hey, Rajah,' said Peter Marlowe, 'I think we all ought to stir it once for luck.'

'Be my guest,' the King said. It did his heart good to see these guys so happy.

Solemnly they lined up and Peter Marlowe stirred the brew, which was growing hot now. Mac took the spoon and stirred and bestowed an obscene blessing upon it. Larkin, not to be outdone, began to stir, saying, 'Boil, boil, boil and bubble . . .'

'You out of your mind?' said Brough. 'Quoting *Macbeth* for Chrissake!'

'What's the matter?'

'It's unluckly. Quoting *Macbeth*. Like whistling in a theatre dressing room.'

'It is?'

'Any fool knows that!'

'I'll be damned. Never knew that before.' Larkin frowned.

'Anyway, you quoted it wrong,' said Brough. 'It's "Double, double toil and trouble; Fire burn, and cauldron bubble"!'

'Oh no it isn't, Yankee. I know my Shakespeare!'

'Betcha tomorrow's rice.'

'Watch it, Colonel,' said Mac suspiciously, knowing Larkin's propensity for gambling. 'No man'd bet that lightly.'

'I'm right, Mac,' Larkin said, but he didn't like the smug expression on the American's face. 'What makes you so sure you're right?'

'Is it a bet?' asked Brough.

Larkin thought a moment. He liked a gamble—but tomorrow's rice was too high stakes. 'No. I'll lay my rice ration on the card table, but I'll be damned if I'll lay it on Shakespeare.'

'Pity,' Brough said. 'I could've used an extra ration. It's Act Four, Scene One, line ten.'

'How the hell can you be that exact?'

'Nothing to it,' Brough said. 'I was majoring in the arts at USC, with a big emphasis on journalism and playwriting. I'm going to be a writer when I get out.'

Mac leaned forward and peered into the pot. 'I envy you, laddie. Writing can be just about the most important job in the whole world. *If* it's any good.'

'That's a lot of nonsense, Mac,' said Peter Marlowe. 'There are a million things more important.'

'That just goes to show how little you know.'

'Business is much more important,' interjected the King. 'Without business, the world'd stop—and without money and a stable economy there'd be no one to buy any books.'

'To hell with business and economy,' Brough said. 'They're just material things. It's just like Mac says.'

'Mac,' said Peter Marlowe. 'What makes it so important?'

'Well, laddie, first it's something I've always wanted to do and can't. I tried many times, but I could never finish anything. That's the hardest part—to finish. But the most important thing is that writers are the only people who can *do* something about this planet. A businessman can't do anything—'

'That's crap,' said the King. 'What about Rockefeller? And Morgan and Ford and du Pont? And all the others? It's their philanthropy that finances a helluva lot of research and libraries and hospitals and art. Why, without their dough—'

'But they made their money at someone's expense,' Brough said crisply. 'They could easily plough some of their billions back to the men who made it for them. Those bloodsuckers—'

'I suppose you're a Democrat?' said the King heatedly.

'You betcha sweet life I am. Look at Roosevelt. Look what he's doing for the country. He dragged it up by its bootstrings when the goddam Republicans—'

'That's crap and you know it. Nothing to do with Republicans. It was an economic cycle—'

'Crapdoodle on economic cycles. The Republicans—'

'Hey, you fellows,' said Larkin mildly. 'No politics until we've eaten, what do you say?'

'Well, all right,' Brough said grimly, 'but this guy's from Christmas.'

'Mac, why is it so important? I still don't see.'

'Well. A writer can put down on a piece of paper an idea—or a point of view. If he's any good he can sway people, even if it's written on toilet people. And he's the only one in our modern economy who can do it—who can *change* the world. A businessman can't—without substantial money. A politician can't—without substantial position or power. A planter can't, certainly. An accountant can't, right, Larkin?'

'Sure.'

'But you're talking about propaganda,' Brough said. 'I don't want to write propaganda.'

'You ever written for movies, Don?' asked the King.

'I've never sold anything to anyone. Guy's not a writer until he sells something. But movies are goddam important. You know that Lenin said the movies were the most important propaganda medium ever invented?' He saw the King readying to assault. 'And I'm not a Commie, you son of a bitch, just because I'm a Democrat.' He turned to Mac. 'Jesus, if you read Lenin or Stalin or Trotsky you're called a Commie.'

'Well, you gotta admit, Don', said the King, 'a lotta Democrats are pinks.'

'Since when has being pro-Russian meant that a guy's a Communist? They are our allies, you know!'

'I'm sorry about that—in a historical way,' said Mac.

'Why?'

'We're going to have a lot of trouble afterwards. Particularly in the Orient. Those folk were stirring up a lot of trouble, even before the war.'

'Television's going to be the coming thing,' said Peter Marlowe, watching a thread of vapour dance the surface of the stew. 'You know, I saw a demonstration from Alexandra Palace in London. Baird is sending out a programme once a week.'

'I heard about television,' said Brough. Never seen any.'

The King nodded. 'I haven't either, but that could make one hell of a business.'

'Not in the States, that's for sure,' Brough grunted. 'Think of the distances! Hell, that might be all right for one of the little countries, like England, but not a real country like the States.'

'What do you mean by that?' asked Peter Marlowe, stiffening.

'I mean that if it wasn't for us, this war'd go on forever. Why, it's our money and our weapons and our power—'

'Listen, old man, we did all right alone—giving you buggers the time to get off your arse. It *is* your war just as much as ours.' Peter Marlowe glared at Brough, who glared back.

'Crap! Why the hell you Europeans can't go and kill yourselves off like you've been doing for centuries and let us alone, I don't know. We had to bail you out before—'

And in no time at all they were arguing and swearing and no one was listening and each had a very firm opinion and each opinion was right.

The King was angrily shaking his fist at Brough, who shook his fist back, and Peter Marlowe was shouting at Mac, when suddenly there was a crashing on the door.

Immediate silence.

'Wot's all the bleedin' row about?' a voice said.

'That you, Griffiths?'

'Who d'ja fink it was, Adolf bloody 'Itler? Yer want'a get us jailed or somefink?'

'No. Sorry.'

'Keep tha bleedin' noise down!'

231

'Who's that?' said Mac.

'Griffiths. He owns the cell.'

'What?'

'Sure. I hired it for five hours. Three bucks an hour. You don't get nothing for nothing.'

'You hired the cell?' repeated Larkin incredulously.

'That's right. This Griffiths is a smart businessman,' the King explained. 'There are thousands of men around, right? No peace and quiet, right? Well, this Limey hires the cell out to anyone who wants to be alone. Not my idea of a sanctuary, but Griffiths does quite a business.'

'I'll bet it wasn't his idea,' said Brough.

'Cap'n, I cannot tell a lie.' The King smiled. 'I must confess the idea was mine. But Griffiths makes enough to keep him and his unit going very well.'

'How much do you make on it?'

'Just ten per cent.'

'If it's only ten per cent., that's fair,' said Brough.

'It is,' the King said. The King would never lie to Brough, not that it was any of his business what the hell he did.

Brough leaned over and stirred the stew. 'Hey, you guys, it's boiling.'

They all crowded around. Yes, it was really boiling.

'We'd better fix the window. The stuff'll start smelling in a minute.'

They put a blanket over the barred outlet, and soon the cell was all perfume.

Mac, Larkin and Tex squatted against the wall, eyes on the stewpan. Peter Marlowe sat on the other side of the bed, and as he was nearest, from time to time he stirred the pot.

The water simmered gently, making the delicate little beans soar crescentlike to the surface, then cascade back into the depths of the liquid. A puff of steam effervesced, bringing with it the true richness of the meatbuds. The King leaned forward and threw in a handful of native herbs, turmeric, kajang, huan, taka and cloves and garlic, and this added to the perfume.

When the stew had been bubbling ten minutes, the King put the green papaya into the pot.

'Crazy,' he said. 'A feller could make a fortune after the war if

232

he could figure a way to dehydrate papaya. Now that'd tenderize a buffalo!'

'The Malays've always used it,' Mac answered, but no one was really listening to him and he wasn't listening to himself, really for the steamrichsweet surrounded them.

The sweat dribbled down their chests and chins and legs and arms. But they hardly noticed the sweat or the closeness. They only knew that this was not a dream, that meat was cooking— there before their eyes, and soon, very soon they would eat.

'Where'd you get it?' asked Peter Marlowe, not really caring. He just had to say something to break the suffocating spell.

'It's Hawkins' dog,' answered the King, not thinking about anything except my God does that smell or does that smell good!

'Hawkins' dog?'

'You mean Rover?'

'His dog?'

'I thought it was a small pig!'

'Hawkins' dog?'

'Oh my word!'

'You mean *that*'s the hind quarters of Rover?' said Peter Marlowe, appalled.

'Sure,' the King said. Now that the secret was out he didn't mind. 'I was going to tell you afterwards, but what the hell? Now you know.'

They looked at one another aghast.

Then Peter Marlowe, said, 'Mother of God. Hawkins' dog!'

'Now, look,' said the King reasonably. 'What's the difference? It was certainly the cleanest-eatingest dog I've seen. Much cleaner'n any pig. Or chicken for that matter. Meat's meat. Simple as that!'

Mac said testily, 'Quite right. Nothing wrong with eating dog. The Chinese eat them all the time. A delicacy. Yes. Certainly.'

'Yeah,' said Brough, half nauseated. 'But we're not Chinese and this's Hawkins' dog!'

'I feel like a cannibal,' said Peter Marlowe.

'Look,' the King said. 'It's just like Mac said. Nothing wrong with dog. Smell it, for Chrissake.'

'Smell it!' said Larkin for all of them. It was hard to talk, his

233

saliva almost choking him. 'I can't smell anything but that stew and it's the greatest smell I've ever smelled and I don't care whether it's Rover or not, I want to eat.' He rubbed his stomach, almost painfully. 'I don't know about you bastards, but I'm so hungry I've got cramps. The smell's doing something to my metabolism that's just not ordinary.'

'I feel sick, too. And it's got nothing to do with the fact that the meat's dog,' said Peter Marlowe. Then he added almost plaintively, 'I just don't want to eat Rover.' He glanced at Mac. 'How are we going to face Hawkins afterwards?'

'I don't know, laddie. I'll look the other way. Yes. I don't think I could face him.' Mac's nostrils quivered and he looked at the stew. 'That smell's so good.'

'Of course,' the King said blandly, 'anyone don't want to eat can leave.'

No one moved. Then they all leaned back, lost in their own thoughts. Listening to the bubble. Drinking in the fragrance. Magnificence.

'It's not shocking when you think of it,' said Larkin, more to persuade himself than the others. 'Look how affectionate we get with our hens. We don't mind eating them—or their eggs.'

'That's right, laddie. And do you remember that cat we caught and ate. We didn't mind that, did we, Peter?'

'No, but that was a stray. This is Rover!'

'It *was*! Now it's just meat.'

'Are you the guys that got the cat?' Brough asked, angry in spite of himself. 'The one about six months ago?'

'No. This was in Java.'

Brough said, 'Oh.' Then he happened to glance at the King. 'I might have guessed it,' he exploded. 'You, you bastard. And we scavenged for four hours.'

'You shouldn't get pissed off, Don. *We* got it. It was still an American victory.'

'My Aussies're losing their touch,' Larkin said.

The King lifted the spoon and his hand shook as he sampled the brew. 'Tastes good.' Then he prodded the meat. It was still tight to the bone. 'Be another hour yet.'

Another ten minutes and he tested again. 'Maybe a little more salt. What do you think, Peter?'

Peter Marlowe tasted. It was so good, so good. 'A dash, just a dash!'

They all tasted, in turn. A touch of salt, a fraction more huan, a little dab of sugar, a breath more turmeric. And they settled back to wait in the exquisite torture cell, almost asphyxiated.

From time to time they pulled the blanket from the window and let some of the perfume out and some new air in.

And outside of Changi, the perfume swam on the breeze. And inside the jail along the corridor, wisps of perfume leaked through the door and permeated the atmosphere.

'Christ, Smithy, can you smell it?'

''Course I can smell it. You think I've got no nose? Where's it coming from?'

'Wait a second! Somewhere up by the jail, somewhere up there!'

'Bet those yellow bastards are having a cook-up just outside the bleeding wire.'

'That's right. Bastards.'

'I don't think it's them. It seems to be coming from the jail.'

'Oh Christ, listen to Smithy. Look at him pointing, just like a bloody dog.'

'I tell you I can smell it coming from the jail.'

'It's just the wind. The wind's coming from that direction.'

'Winds never smelled like that before. It's meat cooking, I tell you. It's beef. I'd bet my life. Stewing beef.'

'New Jap torture. Bastards! What a dirty trick!'

'Maybe we're just imagining it. They say you can imagine a smell.'

'How in hell can we all imagine it? Look at all the men, they've all stopped.'

'Who says so?'

'What?'

'You said, "*They* say you can imagine a smell." Who's they?'

'Oh God, Smithy. It's just a saying.'

'But who're "they"?'

'How the hell do I know!'

'Then stop saying "they" said this or "they" said that. Enough to drive a man crazy.'

The men in the cell, the chosen of the King, watched him ladle a portion into a mess can and hand it to Larkin. Their eyes left Larkin's plate and went back to the ladle and then to Mac and back to the ladle and then to Brough and back to the ladle and then to Tex and back to the ladle and then to Peter Marlowe and back to the ladle and then to the King's portion. And when all were served, they fell to eating, and there was enough left over for at least two portions more per man.

It was agony to eat so well.

The katchang idju beans had broken down and were almost part of the thick soup now. The papaya had tenderized the meat and caused it to fall off the bones, and the meat came apart into chunks, dark brown from the herbs and the tenderizer and beans. The stew had the thickness of a real stew, an Irish stew, with flecks of honey oil globules staining the surface of their mess cans.

The King looked up from his bowl, dry and clean. He beckoned to Larkin.

Larkin just passed his mess can, and silently each one of them accepted another helping. This too disappeared. And then a last portion.

Finally the King put his plate away. 'Son of a bitch.'

'Perfection!' Larkin said.

'Superb,' said Peter Marlowe. 'I'd forgotten what it's like to chew. My jaws ache.'

Mac carefully scooped the last bean and belched. It was a wondrous belch. 'I'll tell ye laddies, I've had some meals in my time, from roast beef at Simpson's in Piccadilly to *rijsttafel* in the Hotel des Indes in Java, and nothing, not one meal, has ever approached this. Never.'

'I agree,' Larkin said, settling himself more comfortably. Even in the best place in Sydney—well, the steaks're great—but I've never enjoyed anything more.'

The King belched and passed around a pack of Kooas. Then he opened the bottle of sake and drank deeply. The wine was rough and strong, but it took away the over-rich taste in his mouth.

'Here,' he said, handing it to Peter Marlowe.

They all drank and they all smoked.

'Hey Tex, what about some Java?' yawned the King.

'Better give it a few more minutes before we open the door,' Brough said, not caring whether or not the door was opened just so long as he was left to relax. 'Oh God, I feel great!'

'I'm so full I think I'll bust,' Peter Marlowe said. 'That was without a doubt the finest—'

'For God's sake, Peter. We've all just said that. We all know it.'

'Well, I had to say it.'

'How'd you manage it?' Brough said to the King, stifling a yawn.

'Max told me about the dog killing the hen. I sent Dino to see Hawkins. He gave it to him. We got Kurt to butcher it. My share was the hindquarters.'

'Why should Hawkins give it to Dino?' asked Peter Marlowe.

'He's a veterinarian.'

'Oh, I see.'

'The hell he is,' Brough said. 'He's a merchant seaman.'

The King shrugged. 'So today he was a vet. Quit bitching!'

'I gotta hand it to you. Sure as hell I gotta hand it to you.'

'Thanks, Don.'

'How—how did Kurt kill it?' Brough asked.

'I didn't ask him.'

'Quite right, laddie,' said Mac. 'Now I think let's drop the subject, huh?'

'Good idea.'

Peter Marlowe got up and stretched. 'What about the bones?' he asked.

'We'll smuggle them out when we leave.'

'How about a little poker?' Larkin said.

'Good idea,' the King said crisply. 'Tex, you get the coffee going. Peter, you clean up a bit. Grant, you fix the door. Don, how about piling the dishes?'

Brough got up heavily. 'What the hell are you going to do?'

'Me?' The King raised his eyebrows. 'I'm just gonna sit.'

Brough looked at him. They all looked at him. Then Brough said, 'I've a good mind to make you an officer—just so as I can have the pleasure of busting you.'

'Two'll get you five of mine,' the King said, 'and that wouldn't do you any good.'

Brough looked at the others, then back at the King. You're

probably right. I'd find myself court-martialled.' He laughed. 'But there's no rule I can't take your dough.'

He pulled out a five-dollar note and nodded at the card deck in the King's hands. 'High card wins!'

The King spread the cards out. 'Pick one.'

Brough gloatingly showed the queen. The King looked at the deck, then picked a card—it was a jack.

Brough grinned. 'Double or nothing.'

'Don,' said the King mildly, 'quit while you're ahead.' He picked another card and turned it face up. An ace. 'I could just as easy pick another ace—they're my cards!'

'Why the hell didn't you beat me then?' said Brough.

'Now, Captain, sir.' The King's amusement was vast. 'It'd be impolite to take your dough. After all, you are our fearless leader.'

'Crap you!' Brough began stacking the plates and mess cans. 'If you can't beat 'em join 'em.'

That night, while most of the camp slept, Peter Marlowe lay under his mosquito net awake, not wishing to sleep. He got out of the bunk and picked his way through the maze of mosquito nets and went outside. Brough was also awake.

'Hi, Peter,' Brough called quietly. 'Come and sit down. Can't you sleep either?'

'Just didn't want to not just yet, feel too good.'

Above, the night was velvet.

'Gorgeous night.'

'Yes.'

'You married?'

'No,' Peter Marlowe replied.

'You're lucky. Don't think it'd be so bad if you're not married.' Brough was silent a minute. 'I go crazy wondering if she'll still be there. Or if she is, what about now? What's she up to now?'

'Nothing.' Peter Marlowe made the automatic response, N'ai vivid in his thoughts. 'Don't worry.' It was like saying, 'Stop breathing.'

'Not that I'd blame her, any woman. It's such a long time we've been away, such a long time. Not her fault.'

Brough shakily built a cigarette, using a little dried tea and the

238

butt of one of the Kooas. When it was alight he dragged deeply, then passed it over to Peter Marlowe.

'Thanks, Don.' He smoked, then passed it back.

They finished the cigarette in silence, racked by their longing. Then Brough got up. 'Guess I'll turn in now. See you around, Peter.'

'Good night, Don.'

Peter Marlowe looked back at the nightscape and let his eager mind drift again to N'ai. And he knew that tonight, like Brough, there was only one thing he could do or he would never sleep.

XVI

V-E Day came and the men of Changi were elated. But it was just another today and did not actually touch them. The food was the same, the sky the same, the heat the same, the sickness the same, the flies the same, the wasting away the same. Grey was still watching and waiting. His spy had notified him that soon the diamond would pass hands. Very soon now. Peter Marlowe and the King were waiting the day just as anxiously. Only four days to go.

B Day came and Eve delivered herself of twelve more young. The code for Birth Day had amused the King and his associates enormously; Grey had heard of B Day from his spy, and on that day he had surrounded that hut and searched all the men for watches or whatever was going to be sold on 'Barter' Day. Stupid cop! The King was not disturbed at the reminder that there was a spy in the hut. The third litter was launched.

Now there were seventy cages under the hut. Fourteen were already occupied. Soon twelve more would be filled.

The men had solved the problem of names in the simplest possible way. Males were given even numbers and females odd numbers.

'Listen,' said the King, 'we just got to get more cages prepared.'

They were in the hut having a board-meeting. The night was cool and pleasant. A waning moon was cloud-touched.

'We're about bushed,' Tex said. 'There just ain't no spare wire netting anywheres. The only thing we can do is to get the Aussies to help out.'

'We do that,' Max said slowly, 'we might just as well let the bastards take over the whole racket.'

The entire war effort of the American hut had been centred around the living gold that was rapidly exploding beneath them. Already a team of four men had extended the slit trenches into a network of passages. Now they had plenty of space for cages, but no wire with which to make them. Wire was desperately needed; B Day was looming again, and then soon after that another B Day and then another.

'If you could find a dozen or so fellows you could trust, you could give them a breeding pair and let them have their own farms,' said Peter Marlowe thoughtfully. 'We could just be the stock breeders.'

'No good Peter, we'd never be able to keep it quiet.'

The King rolled a cigarette and remembered that business had been bad recently and he had not had a tailor-made for a whole week. 'The only thing to do,' he said after a moment's reflection, 'is to bring Timsen into the deal.'

'That lousy Aussie's bad enough competition as it is,' said Max.

'We got no alternative,' the King said with finality. 'We got to get cages—and he's the only guy who'd have the knowhow—and the only one I'd trust to keep his mouth shut. If the farm goes according to plan, there's enough dough in it for everyone.' He looked up at Tex. 'Go get Timsen.'

Tex shrugged and went out.

'Come on, Peter,' the King said, 'we'd better check below.'

He led the way through the trapdoor. 'Holy cow,' he said as he saw the extent of the excavations. 'We dig any more and the whole goddam hut'll fall in, then where the hell'd we be!'

'Don't you worry, chief,' Miller said proudly. He was in charge of the excavation party. 'I got me a scheme so we can just go around the concrete pilings. We've enough room for fifteen hundred cages now, if we can get the wire. Oh yeah. And we could double the space if we could lay our hands on enough timber to shore up tunnels. Easy.'

The King walked along the main trench to inspect the animals. Adam saw him coming and viciously hurled himself at the wire as though ready to tear the King to pieces.

'Friendly, huh?'

241

Miller grinned. 'The bastard knows you from somewheres.'

'Perhaps we should call a halt to breeding,' Peter Marlowe said. 'Until the cages are ready.'

'Timsen's the answer,' the King said. 'If anyone can get us the supplies it's his bunch of thieves.'

They climbed back into the hut and wiped the dirt off. After a shower they felt better.

'Hi, cobber.' Timsen walked down the length of the hut and sat down. 'You Yanks frightened of getting your balls blown off or something?' He was tall and tough, with deepset eyes.

'What're you talking about?'

'The way you bastards are digging slit trenches you'd think the whole bloody Air Force's about to drop on Changi.'

'No harm in being careful.' The King wondered again whether they should chance taking Timsen in. 'Won't be long before they clobber Singapore. And when they do, we're going to be underground.'

'They'll never hit Changi. They know we're here. 'Least the Pommies do. 'Course when you Yanks're in the sky there's no telling where the hell the bombs drop.'

He was taken on a tour of inspection. And immediately he saw the immensity of the organization. And the enormousness of the scheme.

'My gawd, cobber,' Timsen said breathlessly, when they were back in the hut. 'I got to hand it to you. My Gawd. And to think we thought you were just scared. My Gawd, you must have room for five or six hundred—'

'Fifteen hundred,' the King interrupted nonchalantly, 'and this B Day there's going—'

'B Day?'

'Birth Day.'

Timsen laughed. 'So that's B Day. We been trying to figure that one out for weeks. Oh, my word.' His laughter boomed. 'You're bloody geniuses.'

'I'll admit it was my idea.' The King tried not to let the pride show, but it did. After all, it *was* his idea. 'This B Day we got at least ninety young due. The one after that something like three hundred.'

Timsen's eyebrows almost touched his hair line.

242

'Tell you what we're prepared to do.' The King paused, revising the offer. 'You supply us with the material to make a thousand more cages. We'll hold our complete stock to a thousand—only the best. You market the produce and we'll split fifty-fifty. On a deal this size, they'll be enough for everyone.'

'When do we start selling?' Timsen said at once. Even so, in spite of the huge possibilities, he felt seedy.

'We'll give you ten hind legs in a week. We'll use the males first and keep the females. We figure, the hind legs only. We'll step up the number as we get going.'

'Why only ten to start with?'

'If we put more on the market at first, the guys'll be suspicious. We'll have to take it easy.'

Timsen thought a moment. 'You sure the—er—meat'll be—okay?'

Now that he had made a commitment to supply, the King felt squeamish himself. But hell, meat's meat and business is business. 'We're just offering meat, *Rusa tikus*.'

Timsen shook his head, the lips pursed. 'I don't like the idea of selling it to my Aussies,' he said queasily. 'My word. That don't seem right. Oh my word no. Not that I'm—well—it don't seem right at all. Not to my Diggers.'

Peter Marlowe nodded, feeling as sick. 'Nor to our chaps either.'

The three of them looked at each other. Yes, the King told himself, it doesn't seem right at all. But *we* got to survive. And . . . suddenly his mind blew open.

He turned white and said tightly, 'Get—the – others. I've just had a brainstorm.'

The Americans were quickly assembled. Tense, they watched the King. He was calmer, but he had not yet spoken. He just smoked his cigarette, seemingly oblivious of them. Peter Marlowe and Timsen glanced at each other, perturbed.

The King got up and the electricity increased. He stubbed his cigarette. 'Men,' he began, and there was a thinness, a strange exhaustion to his voice. 'B Day's four days off. We expect—' he referred to the stock chart written on the atap wall—'Yeah, to increase our stock to a little over a hundred. I've made a deal with our friend and associate Timsen. He's going to supply material for a thousand cages, so by the time we wean the litters, the housing problem's solved. He and his group are going to market the produce. We're just going to concentrate on breeding the best strains.' He stopped, and looked steadily at each man. 'Men. A week from today the farm begins marketing.'

Now that the appalling day was fixed, their faces fell.

'You really think that we should?' asked Max apprehensively.

'Will you wait a minute, Max?'

'I don't know about marketing,' said Byron Jones III, fidgeting with his eye patch. 'The idea makes me . . .'

'Will you wait for Chrissake,' the King said impatiently. 'Men.' Everyone bent forward as, almost overcome, the King spoke in the barest whisper. 'We're only going to sell to officers! Brass! Majors and up!'

'Oh, my Gawd!' breathed Timsen.

'Jesus H. Christ!' said Max, inspired.

'What?' said Peter Marlowe thunderstruck.

The King felt like a god. 'Yeah, officers. They're the only bastards who can afford to buy. Instead of a mass business, we'll make it a luxury trade.'

'And the buggers who can afford to buy are the ones you'd want to feed the meat to!' said Peter Marlowe.

'You're a bloody toff,' said Timsen, awed. 'Genius. Why, I know three bastards I'd give my right arm to see eat rat meat and then tell 'em . . .'

'I know two,' said Peter Marlowe, 'that I'd give the meat to, let alone sell to. But if you gave it to the buggers—they're so cheap they'd smell a rat!'

Max got up and shouted above the laughter, 'Listen, you guys. Listen. Listen a minute.' He turned to the King. 'You know, I've, well, I've—' He was so moved that it was difficult for him to speak. 'I've—I haven't always been on your side. No harm in that. It's a free country. But this—this is such a huge—such a—that, well—' He stuck out his hand solemnly. 'I'd like to shake the hand of the man that thought of that idea! I think we should all shake the hand of true genius. On behalf of all the enlisted men in the world—I'm proud of you. The King!'

Max and the King shook hands.

Tex was swaying exuberantly from side to side. 'Sellars and Prouty and Grey—he's on the list . . .'

'He's got no money,' the King said.

'Hell, we'll give him some,' Max said.

'We can't do that. Grey's no fool. He'd be suspicious,' Peter Marlowe said.

'What about Thorsen—that bastard—'

'None of the Yank officers. Well,' said the King delicately, 'maybe one or two.'

The cheer was quickly squashed.

'How about the Aussies?'

'Leave that to me, mate,' said Timsen. 'I've already got three dozen customers in mind.'

'What about the Limeys?' Max said.

'We can all think of some of them.' The King felt huge and powerful and ecstatic. 'It's lucky the bastards who've the dough, or the means to get the dough, are the ones you want to feed and then tell what it is they've eaten,' he said.

Just before lights-out, Max hurried through the doorless doorway and whispered to the King, 'A guard's heading this way.'

'Who?'

'Shagata.'

'Okay,' said the King, trying to keep his voice level. 'Check that all our guards are in position.'

'Okay.' Max hurried away.

The King bent close to Peter Marlowe. 'Maybe there's a slip-up,' he said nervously. 'Come on, we'd better get ready.'

He slipped out of the window and made sure the canvas overhang was in position. Then he and Peter Marlowe sat under it and waited.

Shagata poked his head under the canvas, and when he recognized the King, he quietly slipped into the overhang and sat down. He propped his rifle against the wall and offered a pack of Kooas.

'Tabe,' he said.

'Tabe,' Peter Marlowe replied.

'Hi,' said the King. His hand was shaking as he took the cigarette.

'Thou has something to sell me tonight?' Shagata asked sibilantly.

'He asks if you've anything to sell him tonight.'

'Tell him no!'

'My friend is overwhelmed that he has nothing to tempt a man of taste this evening.'

'Would your friend have such an article in say three days?'

The King sighed with relief when Peter Marlowe translated this. 'Tell him yes. And tell him he's wise to check.'

'My friend says that it is probable that on that day he would have something to tempt a man of taste. And my friend adds that he feels that to do business with such a careful man is a good portent for the satisfactory conclusion of said transaction.'

'It is always wise when matters must be arranged in the bleakness of night.' Shagata-san sucked in his breath. 'If I do not arrive in three nights, wait each night for me. A mutual friend has indicated that he may not be able to do his part with complete accuracy. But I am assured that it will be three nights from tonight.'

Shagata got up and gave the pack of cigarettes to the King. A slight bow and the darkness took him once more.

Peter Marlowe told the King what Shagata had said, and the King grinned. 'Great. Just great. You want to come by tomorrow morning? We can discuss plans.'

'I'm on the airfield work party.'

'You want me to get a sub for you?'

Peter Marlowe laughed and shook his head.

'You'd better go anyway,' said the King. 'In case Cheng San wants to make contact.'

'Do you think there's anything wrong?'

'No. Shagata was wise to check. I would have. Everything's going according to plan. Another week and the whole deal'll be fixed.'

'I hope so.' Peter Marlowe thought about the village, and prayed that the deal would go through. He desperately wanted to go there again, and if he did, he knew that he would have to have Sulina or he would lose his sanity.

'What's the matter?' The King had felt more than seen Peter Marlowe's shudder.

'I was just thinking I'd like to be in Sulina's arms right now,' Peter Marlowe replied uneasily.

'Yeah.' The King wondered if he might foul up over the broad.

Peter Marlowe caught the look and smiled faintly. 'You've nothing to worry about, old chum. I wouldn't do anything foolish, if that's what you were thinking.'

'Sure.' The King smiled. 'We got a lot to look forward to—and tomorrow's the show. You heard what it's about?'

'Only that it's called *Triangle*. And it stars Sean.' Peter Marlowe's voice was suddenly flat.

'How did you nearly kill Sean?' The King had never asked bluntly before, knowing that with a man like Peter Marlowe it was always dangerous to ask direct questions about private matters. But now he had felt instinctively that the time was correct.

'There's not much to tell,' Peter Marlowe said immediately, glad that the King had asked him. 'Sean and I were in the same squadron in Java. The day before the war ended there, Sean didn't come back from a mission. I thought he'd had it.

'About a year ago—the day after we came here from Jave—I went to one of the camp shows. When I finally recognized Sean on the stage, you can imagine what a shock it was. He was playing a girl, but I didn't think anything of that—someone always has to take the girl's parts—and I just sat back and enjoyed the show. I couldn't get over finding him alive and fit, and I couldn't get over what a sensational girl he made—the way he walked and talked and sat—his clothes and his wig were perfect. I was very impressed with his performance—and yet I knew he'd never had anything to do with theatricals before.

'After the show I went backstage to see him. There were some others waiting too, and after a while I got the weirdest feeling that these fellows were like the characters you meet at any stage door anywhere—you know, chaps with their tongues hanging out waiting for their girl friends.

'Finally the dressing room door opened and everyone surged in. I tagged along last and stood in the doorway. It was only then that it hit me that the men were all queers! Sean was sitting on a chair and they seemed to pour all over him, fawning on him and calling him "darling", hugging him and then telling him how "marvellous" he was—treating him like the beautiful star of the show. And Sean—Sean was enjoying it! Christ, he was actually enjoying their pawing! Like a bitch in heat.

'Then he suddenly saw me, and of course he was shocked too.

'He said "Hello, Peter" but I couldn't say anything. I stood staring at one of the bloody queers who had his hand on Sean's knee. Sean was wearing a sort of flowing negligée and silk stockings and panties, and I got the feeling that he'd even arranged the folds of the negligée to show off his leg above the stocking—and it looked as if he had breasts under the negligée. Then I suddenly realized he wasn't wearing a wig—all that hair was his own, and just as long and wavy as a girl's.

'Then Sean asked everybody to leave. "Peter's an old friend I thought was dead," he said. "I have to talk to him. Go on, please."

'When they'd gone I asked Sean, "What in God's name has happened to you? You were actually enjoying those scum pawing you."

'"What in God's name has happened to all of us?" Sean answered. Then he said with that wonderful smile of his, "I'm so glad to see you, Peter. I thought you were very dead. Sit down a moment while I clean my face off. We've a lot to talk about. Did you come on the Java work party?"

'I nodded, still in a state of shock, and Sean turned back to the mirror and began to wipe the makeup off with face cream. "What happened to you, Peter?" he asked. "Did you get shot down?"

'When he started to take off the makeup I began to relax—everything seemed more normal. I told myself that I'd been stupid—that this was all part of the show—you know, keeping up the legend—and I was sure he'd only been pretending to enjoy it. So I apologized and said, "Sorry, Sean—you must think me a bloody fool! My God, it's good to know you're all right. I thought you'd had it too." I told him what had happened to me and then asked about him.

'Sean told me he'd been pranged by four Zeroes and had to parachute. When he finally got back to the airfield and found my plane, it was just a shambles. I told him how I'd set fire to it before I left——I hadn't wanted the bloody Japs to repair the wing.

'"Oh," he said, "well, I just presumed you'd pranged yourself landing—that you'd had it. I stayed in Bandung at Headquarters with the rest of the bods and then we were all put into a camp. Shortly afterwards we were sent to Batavia and from there to here."

'Sean was looking at himself in the mirror all the time, and his face was as smooth and fine as any girl's. Suddenly I got the strangest feeling that he had forgotten all about me. I didn't know what to do. Then he turned away from the mirror and looked right at me, and he was frowning in a funny way. All at once I sensed how unhappy he was, so I asked him if he wanted me to go.

'"No," he said. "No, Peter, I want you to stay."

'And then he picked up a girl's purse that was on the dressing table, dug out a lipstick and began making up his lips.

'I was stunned. "What're you doing?" I said.

'"Putting on lipstick, Peter."

'"Come off it, Sean," I said. "A joke's a joke. The show was over half an hour ago."

'But he went right on, and when his lips were perfect he powdered his nose and brushed his hair, and by God he was the beautiful girl again. I couldn't believe it. I still thought in some weird way he was playing a joke on me.

'He patted a curl here and there and then sat back and examined himself in the mirror, and he seemed absolutely satisfied with what he saw. Then he saw me in the mirror staring at him and he laughed. "What's the matter, Peter?" he said. "Haven't you been in a dressing room before?"

'"Yes," I said, "I have—a girl's dressing room."

'He looked at me a long time. Then he straightened his negligée and crossed his legs. "This is a girl's dressing room," he said.

'"Come off it, Sean," I said, getting irritated, "it's me, Peter Marlowe. We're in Changi remember? The show's over and now everything's normal again."

'"Yes," he said perfectly calmly, "everything's normal."

'It took me a long time to say anything. "Well," I managed to get out at last, "aren't you going to get out of those clothes and clean that muck off your face?"

'"I like these clothes, Peter," he said, "and I always wear makeup now." He got up and opened a cupboard and by God it was full of sarongs and dresses and panties and bras and so on. He turned around and he was perfectly calm. "These are the only clothes I wear nowadays," he said. "I *am* a woman."

'"You must be out of your mind," I said.

'Sean walked over and stared up at me, and I couldn't get it out of my head that somehow this was a girl—he looked like one and acted like one and talked like one and smelled like one. "Look, Peter," he said, "I know it's difficult for you to understand, but I've changed. I'm no longer a man, I'm a woman."

'"You're no more a bloody woman than I am!" I yelled. But it didn't seem to touch him at all. He just stood there smiling like a madonna, and then he said, "I'm a woman, Peter." He touched my arm just the way a girl would, and he said, "Please treat me as a woman."

'Something in my head seemed to snap. I grabbed his arm and ripped the negligée off his shoulder and tore off the padded bra and shoved him in front of the mirror.

'"You call yourself a woman?" I shouted. "Look at yourself! Where are your bloody breasts?"

'But Sean didn't look up. He just stood in front of the mirror with his head down and his hair falling over his face. The negligée was hanging off him and he was naked to the waist. I grabbed him by the hair and jerked his head up. "Look at yourself, you bloody deviate!" I yelled. "You're a man, by God, and you always will be."

'He just stood there saying nothing at all, and finally I realized he was crying. Then Rodrick and Frank Parrish rushed in and shoved me out of the way, and Parrish pulled the negligée around Sean and took him in his arms, and all the time Sean just went on crying.

'Frank kept hugging him and saying, "It's all right, Sean, it's all right." Then he looked at me, and I knew he wanted to kill me. "Get out of here, you bloody bastard," he said.

'I don't even know how I got out of there—when I finally came to I was wandering around the camp, and I was beginning

250

to realize that I'd had no right, no right at all, to do what I'd done. It was insane.'

Peter Marlowe's face was naked with anguish. 'I went back to the theatre. I had to try to make my peace with Sean. His door was locked but I thought I heard him inside. I knocked and knocked, but he wouldn't answer and he wouldn't open the door, so I got angry again and I shoved the door open. I wanted to apologize to his face, not through a door.

'He was lying on the bed. There was a big cut on his left wrist and there was blood all over the place. I put a tourniquet on him and somehow got hold of old Doc Kennedy and Rodrick and Frank. Sean looked like a corpse, and he didn't make a sound all the time Kennedy was sewing up the scissor slash. When Kennedy finished, Frank said to me, "Are you satisfied now, you rotten bastard?"

'I couldn't say anything. I just stood there hating myself.

'"Get out and stay out," Rodrick said.

'I started off, but then I heard Sean calling me, in a kind of weak, faint whisper. I turned around and saw that he was looking at me not angrily, but as if he pitied me. "I'm sorry, Peter," he said. "It wasn't your fault."

'"Christ, Sean," I managed to say. "I didn't mean you any harm."

'"I know," he said. "Please be my friend, Peter."

'Then he looked at Parrish and Rodrick and said, "I wanted to go away, but now," and he smiled his wonderful smile, "I'm so happy to be home again."'

Peter Marlowe's face was drained. The sweat was running down his neck and chest. The King lit a Kooa.

Peter Marlowe half shrugged, helplessly, then got up and walked away, deep in his remorse.

XVII

'Come on, hurry up,' Peter Marlowe said to the yawning men lined up bleakly outside the hut. It was just after dawn and breakfast was already memory and the deficiency of it served only to increase the men's irritability. And, too, the long sun-hot day at the airfield was ahead of them. Unless they had the luck.

It was rumoured that today one detail was going to the far west side of the airfield where the coconut trees grew. It was rumoured that three trees were going to be cut down. And the heart of a coconut tree was not only edible but very nutritious and a great delicacy, it was called "millionaire's cabbage", for a whole coconut tree had to die to provide it. Along with the millionaire's cabbage there would be coconuts as well. More than enough for a thirty-man detail. So officers and enlisted men alike were tense.

The sergeant in charge of the hut came up to Peter Marlowe and saluted. 'That's the lot, sir. Twenty men including me.'

'We're supposed to have thirty.'

'Well, twenty's all we have. The rest're sick or on wood detail. Nothin' I can do about it.'

'All right. Let's get up to the gate.'

The sergeant got the men under way and they began streaming loosely along the jail wall to join the rest of the airfield detail near the barricade-gate west. Peter Marlowe beckoned to the sergeant and got the men herded together in the best position—near the end of the line, where they were likelier to be chosen for the tree detail. When the men noticed that their officer had

252

manoeuvred them just right they began to pay attention and sorted themselves out quickly.

They all had their rag shirts tucked into grub-bags. Grub-bags were an institution, and took many forms. Sometimes they were regulation haversacks, sometimes suitcases, sometimes rattan baskets, sometimes bags, sometimes a cloth and a stick, sometimes a piece of material. But all the men carried some container for the plunder to be. On a work party there was always plunder, and if it wasn't millionaire's cabbage, or coconut, it could be driftwood, firewood, coconut husks, bananas, oil palm nuts, edible roots, leaves of many types, or even sometimes papaya.

Most of the men wore clogs of wood or tyre rubber. Some wore shoes with the toes cut out. And some had boots. Peter Marlowe was wearing Mac's boots. They were tight, but for a three mile march and a work party they were better than clogs.

The snake of men began marching through the gate west, an officer in charge of each company. At the head was a group of Koreans and at the tail was a single Korean guard.

Peter Marlowe's group waited near the rear for space to join the march. He was looking forward to the trek and the prospect of the trees. He shifted his shirt more comfortably in the rucksack strap and adjusted his water bottle—not *the* bottle, for to take that would have been dangerous on a work party. You could never tell when a guard or someone else might want to take a drink.

Finally it was time to move, and he and his men began to walk towards the gate. As they passed the guardhouse they saluted, and the squat little Japanese sergeant stood on the verandah and returned their salute stiffly. Peter Marlowe gave the number of his men to the other guard, who checked them against the total already tallied.

Then they were outside the camp and walking the tarmac road. It curled easily, with gentle hills and dales, then sped through a rubber plantation. The rubber trees were unkempt and untapped. Now that's strange, thought Peter Marlowe, for rubber was at a premium and a vital food for war.

'Hello, Duncan,' he said as Captain Duncan and his group began to pass. He fell into step beside Duncan, keeping his eyes on his own group, the next ahead.

'Isn't it great to have news again?' Duncan said.

'Yes,' he replied automatically, 'If it's true.'

'Must say it sounds too good to be true.'

Peter Marlowe liked Duncan. He was a little Scot, red-haired and middle-aged. Nothing seemed to faze him. He always had a smile and a good word. Peter Marlowe had the feeling that something was different about him today. Now what was it?

Duncan noted his curiosity and grimaced to show his new false teeth.

'Oh that's it,' said Peter Marlowe. 'I was wondering what was different.'

'How do they look?'

'Oh, better than none at all.'

'Now that's a fine remark. I thought they looked pretty good.'

'I can't get used to aluminium teeth. They look all wrong.'

'Went through bloody hell to have mine taken out. Bloody hell!'

'Thank God my teeth are all right. Had to have them filled last year. Rotten business. You're probably wise to have had all yours taken out. How many did—'

'Eighteen,' said Duncan angrily. 'Makes you want to spit blood. But they were completely rotten. Doc said something about the water and lack of chewable material and rice diet and lack of calcium. But my God, these false ones feel great.' He chomped once or twice reflectively, then continued, 'The dental chaps are very clever the way they make them. Lot of ingenuity. Of course, I have to admit it's a bit of a shock—not having white teeth. But for comfort, why, lad, I haven't felt so good in years, white or aluminium makes no difference. Always had trouble with my teeth. To hell with teeth anyway.'

Up ahead, the column of men moved into the side of the road as a bus began to pass. It was ancient and puffing and steaming and had seats for twenty-five passengers. But inside were nearly sixty men, women and children, and outside another ten were hanging on with fingers and toes. The top of the bus was piled with cages of chickens and baggage and mat-rolls. As the asthmatic bus passed the natives looked curiously at the men and the men eyed the crates of half-dead chickens and hoped the bloody bus would break down or go into a ditch and then they could help push it out of the ditch and liberate a dozen or so chickens. But today the bus passed, and there were many curses.

Peter Marlowe walked alongside Duncan, who kept on chattering about his teeth and showing them in the broadness of his smile. But the smile was all wrong. It looked grotesque.

Behind them a Korean guard, slouching lethargically, shouted at a man who fell out of the line to the side of the road, but the man merely dropped his pants and quickly relieved himself and called out 'Sakit marah'—dysentery—so the guard shrugged and took out a cigarette and lit it while he waited, and quickly the man was back in line once more.

'Peter,' said Duncan quietly, 'cover for me.'

Peter Marlowe looked ahead. About twenty yards from the road, on a little path beside the storm ditch were Duncan's wife and child. Ming Duncan was Singapore Chinese. Since she was Oriental, she was not put into a camp along with the wives and children of the other prisoners, but lived freely in the outskirts of the city. The child, a girl, was beautiful like her mother, and tall for her age, and she had a face that would never wear a sigh upon it. Once a week they 'happened' to pass by so that Duncan could see them. He always said that as long as he could see them Changi was not so bad.

Peter Marlowe moved between Duncan and the guard, shielding him, and let Duncan fall back to the side of his men.

As the column passed by, the mother and child made no sign. When Duncan passed, their eyes met his, briefly, and they saw him drop the little piece of paper to the side of the road, but they kept on walking, and then Duncan had passed and was lost in the mass of men. But he knew they had seen the paper, and knew that they would keep on walking until all the men and all the guards were gone; then they would return and find the paper and they would read it and the thought made Duncan happy. *I love you and miss you and you are both my life*, he had written. The message was always the same, but it was always new, both to him and to them, for the words were written afresh, and the words were worth saying, over and over and over. Forever.

'Don't you think she's looking well?' Duncan said as he rejoined Peter Marlowe.

'Wonderful, you're very lucky. And Mordeen's growing up to be a beauty.'

'Ay, a real beauty that one. She'll be six this September.'

The happiness faded, and Duncan fell silent. 'How I wish this war was over,' he said.

'Won't be long now.'

'When you get married, Peter, marry a Chinese girl. They make the best wives in the world.' Duncan had said the same thing many times. 'I know that it's hard to be ostracized, and hard on the children—but I'll die content if I die in her arms.' He sighed. 'But you won't listen. You'll marry some English girl and you'll think you're living. What a waste! I know, I've tried both.'

'I'll have to wait and see, won't I, Duncan?' Peter Marlowe laughed. Then he quickened his pace to get into position ahead of his men. 'I'll see you later.'

'Thanks, Peter,' Duncan called after him.

They were almost up to the airfield now. Ahead was a group of guards waiting to take their parties to work areas. Beside the guards were mattocks and spades and shovels. Already many of the men were streaming under guard across the airfield.

Peter Marlowe looked west. There was one party heading for the trees already. Bloody hell!

He stopped his men and saluted the guards, noticing that one of them was Torusumi.

Torusumi recognized Peter Marlowe, and smiled, 'Tabe!'

'Tabe,' replied Peter Marlowe, embarrassed by Torusumi's obvious friendliness.

'I will take thee and thy men,' said Torusumi and nodded to the implements.

'I thank thee,' said Peter Marlowe and nodded at the sergeant. 'We're to go with him.'

'That bleeder works the east end,' said the sergeant irritably. 'Just our bloody luck.'

'I know that,' said Peter Marlowe just as irritably, and as the men moved forward to get the tools he said to Torusumi, 'I hope today thou wilt be taking us to the west end. It is cooler there.'

'We are to go to the east end. I know it is cooler on the west side, and I always get the east.'

Peter Marlowe decided to gamble. 'Perhaps thou shouldst ask for better treatment.' It was dangerous to make a suggestion to a Korean or a Japanese. Torusumi observed him coldly, then turned abruptly and went over to Azumi, a Japanese corporal, who stood grimly to one side. Azumi was known for his bad temper.

Apprehensively, Peter Marlowe watched Torusumi bow and start to speak rapidly and harshly in Japanese. And he felt Azumi's stare on him.

Beside Peter Marlowe the sergeant was also watching the exchange anxiously. 'What'd you say, sir?'

'I said it'd be a good idea if we went to the west end for a change.'

The sergeant winced. If the officer got a slap the sergeant got one automatically. 'You're taking a chance—' He stopped abruptly as Azumi began walking towards them, followed by Torusumi, deferentially two paces behind.

Azumi, a small bowlegged man, halted five paces from Peter Marlowe, then stared up into his face for perhaps ten seconds. Peter Marlowe readied himself for the slap that was to come. But it didn't. Instead Azumi suddenly smiled and showed his gold teeth and sucked in air and took out a pack of cigarettes. He offered Peter Marlowe one and said something in Japanese which Peter Marlowe didn't understand, but he caught 'Shoko-san' and was even more astonished, since he hadn't been called Shoko-san before. 'Shoko' is 'officer' and 'san' means 'mister', and to be called Mr Officer by a fiendish little bastard like Azumi was praise indeed.

'Arignato,' Peter Marlowe said, accepting the light. 'Thank you' was the only Japanese he knew, apart from 'Stand easy' and 'Attention' and 'Quick march' and 'Salute' and 'Come here, you white bastard.' He ordered the sergeant, who was obviously nonplussed, to get the men lined up.

'Yes, sir,' said the sergeant, glad of an excuse to get out of range.

Then Azumi snapped in Japanese at Torusumi and Torusumi moved up too and said, 'Hotchatore,' which means 'Quick March'. When they were halfway across the airfield and well out of Azumi's hearing distance, Torusumi smiled at Peter

Marlowe. 'We're going to the west end today. And we're going to cut down the trees.'

'We are? I don't understand.'

'It is simple. I told Azumi-san that thou art the King's interpreter, and that I felt he should know this, since he takes ten per cent of our profits. So,' Torusumi shrugged, 'of course we must look after each other. And maybe we can discuss some business during the day.'

Peter Marlowe weakly ordered the men to halt.

'What's the matter, sir?' asked the sergeant.

'Nothing, Sergeant, Listen, all of you! Now no noise. We've got the trees.'

'Oh bloody hell how great.'

There was the beginning of a cheer, quickly stifled.

When they got to the three trees, Spence and his working party were already there with their guard. Torusumi went up to the guard and they had a slanging match in Korean. But Spence and his angry men were lined up and marched away by the furious guard. 'Why the hell have you got the trees, you bastard? We were here first!' Spence called out.

'Yes,' said Peter Marlowe sympathetically. He knew how Spence felt.

Torusumi beckoned to Peter Marlowe and sat down in the shade and propped his rifle against a tree. 'Post a guard,' he yawned. 'I hold thee responsible if I am caught asleep by any pestilential Japanese or Korean.'

'Thou mayest sleep soft in my trust,' Peter Marlowe replied.

'Wake me at the hour of food.'

'It will be done.'

Peter Marlowe posted guards in vantage points, then led the furious assault on the trees. He wanted the trees down and carved up before anyone changed their orders.

By noon the three trees were down and the millionaire's cabbage out of the trees. The men were all exhausted and antbitten, but that didn't matter, for today's booty was huge. There were two coconuts per man to take home and another fifteen left over. Peter Marlowe said that they would save five for Torusumi and share the other ten for lunch. He divided two millionaire's cabbage and said that the other should be kept for

Torusumi and Azumi, just in case they wanted it. If they didn't, then it too would be divided.

Peter Marlowe was propped against a tree, panting from the exertion, when a sudden danger whistle rocked him to his feet and he was quickly beside Torusumi, shaking him awake.

'A guard, Torusumi-san, hurry.'

Torusumi scrambled to his feet and brushed down his uniform. 'Good. Go back to the trees and look busy,' he said softly.

Then Torusumi wandered nonchalantly into the clearing. When he recognized the guard, he relaxed and motioned the man into the shade and they both propped their rifles and lay back and began to smoke. 'Shoko-san,' Torusumi called out. 'Rest easy, it is only my friend.'

Peter Marlowe smiled, then called out, 'Hey, Sergeant. Cut open a couple of the best young coconuts and take them to the guards.' He couldn't take them himself, for he would have lost much face.

The sergeant chose the two carefully and sliced the tops off. The outside husks were green-brown and two inches thick and pithy on the deep imbedded nut. The white meat that lined the interior of the nut was just soft enough and easy to eat with a spoon if you'd a mind, and the juice cool and sweet-tasting.

'Smith,' he called out.

'Yes, Sarn't.'

'Take these over to the bloody Nips.'

'Why me? I'm bloody well always having to do more than the—'

'Get your arse over here.'

Smith, a spare little Cockney, grumbled to his feet and did as he was ordered.

Torusumi and the other guard drank deeply. Then Torusumi called out to Peter Marlowe, 'We thank thee.'

'Peace be with thee,' replied Peter Marlowe.

Torusumi jerked out a crumpled pack of Kooas and handed them to Peter Marlowe.

'I thank thee,' said Peter Marlowe.

'Peace be with thee,' Torusumi replied politely.

There were seven cigarettes. The men insisted that Peter Marlowe take two. The other five were split up, one to four men, and by general consent the cigarettes were to be smoked after lunch.

Lunch was rice and fish water and weak tea. Peter Marlowe took only rice and mixed in a touch of blachang. For desert he enjoyed his share of coconut. Then he settled tiredly against the stump of one of the trees and looked over the airfield, waiting for the lunch hour to end.

To the south there was a hill, and surrounding the hill were thousands of Chinese coolies. They all carried two bamboo baskets on a bamboo pole over their shoulders, and they walked up the hill and collected two baskets of earth and walked down the hill and emptied the two baskets. Their movement was perpetual and you could almost see the hill disappear. Under the burning sun.

Peter Marlowe had been coming to the airfield four, five times a week for almost two years now. When he and Larkin had first seen the site, with its hills and swamps and sand, they had laughed and thought that it would never be turned into an airfield. After all, the Chinese had no tractors or bulldozers. But now, two years later, there was already one operative strip, and the big one, the bomber strip, was nearly finished.

Peter Marlowe marvelled at the patience of all those worker-ants and wondered what their hands could not do if they were set in motion with modern equipment.

His eyes closed and he was asleep.

'Ewart! Where's Marlowe?' Grey asked curtly.

'On a work party at the airfield. Why?'

'Just tell him to report to me immediately he gets back.'

'Where'll you be?'

'How the hell do I know! Just tell him to find me.' As Grey left the hut he felt a spasm building, and he began to hurry to the latrines. Before he got halfway the spasm climaxed and a little of the bloody mucus oozed out of him, soaking even more the grass pad he wore in his pants. Tormented and very weak, he leaned against a hut to gather strength.

Grey knew that it was time to change the pad once more, the fourth time today, but he didn't mind. At least the pad was hygienic and it saved his pants, the only pair he possessed. And without the pad he could not walk around. Disgusting, he told himself, just like a sanitary napkin. What a bloody mess! But at least it was efficient.

He should have reported sick today, but he couldn't not when he had Marlowe nailed. Oh no, this was too good to miss, and he wanted to see Marlowe's face when he told him. It was worth the pain to know he had him. The cheap, no-good bastard. And through Marlowe the King'd sweat a little. In a couple of days he could have them both. For he knew about the diamond and knew that contact was to be made within the next week. He didn't know yet exactly when, but he would be told. You're clever, he told himself, clever to have such an efficient system.

He went up to his jail hut and told the MP to wait outside. He changed the pad and scrubbed his hands, hoping to wash the stain away, the invisible stain.

Feeling better, Grey forced himself off the veranda steps and headed for the supply hut. Today he was to make his weekly inspection of the supplies of rice and food. The supplies always checked, for Lieutenant-Colonel Jones was efficient and dedicated and always weighed the day's rice himself, personally, in public. So there was never any chance of skulduggery.

Grey admired Lieutenant-Colonel Jones and liked the way he did everything himself—then there were no slips. He envied him too, for he was very young to be a lieutenant-colonel. Just thirty-three. Makes you sick, he told himself, he's a lieutenant-colonel and you're a lieutenant—and the only difference is being in the right job at the right time. Still, you're doing all right, and making friends who will stand up for you when the war's over. Of course, Jones was a civilian soldier, so he wouldn't stay in the service afterwards. But Jones was a pal of Samson and also of Smedly-Taylor, Grey's boss, and he played bridge with the camp Commandant. Lucky bastard, I can play bridge as good as you can, but I don't get invited, and I work harder than anyone.

When Grey got to the supply hut, the day's issue of rice was still in progress.

'Morning, Grey,' Jones said. 'I'll be right with you.' He was a tall man, handsome, well-educated, quiet. He had a boyish face and was nicknamed the Boy Colonel.

'Thank you, sir.'

Grey stood and watched as the cookhouse representatives—a sergeant and an enlisted man—came up to the scales. Each cookhouse supplied two men to pick up the allotment—one to keep an eye on the other. The tally of men submitted by the representative was checked and the rice weighed out. Then the tally sheet was initialled.

When the last cookhouse had been served, the remains of the sack of rice was lifted by Quartermaster Sergeant Blakely and carried into the hut. Grey followed Lieutenant-Colonel Jones inside and listened absently as Jones wearily gave him the figures: 'Nine thousand four hundred and eighty-three officers and men. Two thousand three hundred and seventy and three-quarters pounds of rice issued today, four ounces per man. Twelve bags approx.' He nodded to the empty jute bags. Grey watched him count them, knowing that there would be twelve. Then Jones continued, 'One bag was short ten pounds,'—this was not unusual—'and the residue is twenty and a quarter pounds.'

The lieutenant-colonel went over and picked up the almost empty sack and put it on the scales that Quartermaster Sergeant Blakely had pulled inside the hut. He carefully placed the weights on the platform and built them up to twenty and one quarter pounds. The sack lifted and balanced. 'It checks,' he smiled, satisfied, looking at Grey.

Everything else—a side of beef, sixteen tubs of dried fish, forty pounds of gula malacca, five dozen eggs, fifty pounds of salt and bags of peppercorns and dried chillis—checked out perfectly also.

Grey signed the store chart, and winced as another spasm racked him.

'Dysentery?' asked Jones, concerned.

'Just a touch, sir.' Grey looked around the semidarkness, then saluted. 'Thank you, sir. See you next week.'

'Thank you, Lieutenant.'

On the way out, Grey was hit by another spasm and stumbled against the scale, knocking it over and scattering the weights across the dirt floor.

'Sorry,' Grey cursed, 'bloody careless of me.' He lifted the machine and groped on the floor for the weights, but Jones and Blakely were already on their knees picking them up.

262

'Don't bother, Grey,' Jones said, then he barked at Blakely, 'I've told you before to put the scale in the corner.'

But Grey had already picked up a two-pound weight. He couldn't believe what he saw, and he carried the weight to the door and inspected it in the light to make certain his eyes weren't deceiving him. They weren't. In the bottom of the iron weight was a small hole packed hard with clay. He picked out the clay with a fingernail, his face chalky.

'What is it, Grey?' said Jones.

'This weight's been tampered with.' The words were an accusation.

'What? Impossible!' Jones went up to Grey. 'Let me see that.' For an eternity he studied it, then smiled.

'It's not been tampered with. This is merely a corrective hole. The particular weight was probably a fraction heavier than it was supposed to be.' He laughed weakly. 'My God, you had me worried for a moment.'

Grey walked rapidly over to the rest of the weights and picked up another one. It too had a hole in it.

'Christ! They've all been tampered with!'

'That's absurd,' Jones said. 'They're just corrective—'

'I know enough about weights and measures,' Grey said, 'to know holes aren't allowed. Not corrective holes. If the weight's wrong, it's never issued.'

He whirled on Blakely, who cringed against the door. 'What do you know about it?'

'Nothing, sir,' Blakely said, terrified.

'You'd better tell me!'

'I don't know anything, sir, honest—'

'All right, Blakely. You know what I'm going to do? I'm going to go out of the hut and I'm going to tell everyone I meet about you, everyone—and I'm going to show them this weight, and before I can report it to Colonel Smedly-Taylor you'll be torn apart.'

Grey started for the door.

'Wait, sir,' Blakely choked out. 'I'll tell you. It wasn't me, sir, it was the colonel. He made me do it. He caught me pinching a little rice and he swore he'd turn me in if I didn't help him—'

'Shut up, you fool,' Jones said. Then, in a calmer voice, he

263

said to Grey, 'The fool's trying to implicate me. I never knew anything—'

'Don't listen to him, sir,' Blakely interrupted, babbling. 'He always weighs the rice himself. Always. And he has the key to the safe that he keeps the weights in. You know yourself how he does it all. And anyone who handles weights has to look at the bottom sometimes. However well the holes're camouflaged, you've got to notice them. And it's been going on for a year or more.'

'*Shut up, Blakely*!' Jones screamed. 'Shut up.'

Silence.

Then Grey said, 'Colonel, how long have these weights been used?'

'I don't know,'

'A year? Two years?'

'How the hell do I know? If the weights are fixed it's nothing to do with me.'

'But you have the key and you keep them locked up?'

'Yes, but that doesn't mean—'

'Have you ever looked at the bottom of the weights?'

'No, but—'

'That's somewhat strange, isn't it?' said Grey relentlessly.

'No, it isn't, and I won't be cross-examined by—'

'You'd better be telling the truth, for your own sake.'

'Are you threatening me, Lieutenant? I'll have you court-martialled—'

'I don't know about that, Colonel. I'm here legally and the weights have been tampered with, haven't they?'

'Now look here, Grey—'

'Haven't they?' Grey held the weight up to Jones's drained face, which was no longer boyish.

'I—suppose—so,' said Jones, 'but that doesn't mean—'

'It means that either Blakely or you is responsible. Perhaps both of you. You're the only two allowed here. The weights are short, and one or both of you has been taking the extra ration.'

'It wasn't me, sir,' Blakely whined. 'I only got a pound in every ten—'

'Liar!' shouted Jones.

'Oh no I'm not. I've told you a thousand times we'd be for it.'

264

He turned to Grey, wringing his hands. 'Please, sir, please, don't say anything. The men'd tear us to pieces.'

'You bastard, I hope they do.' Grey was glad that he had found the false weights. Oh yes, he was glad.

Jones took out his cigarette box and began to roll a cigarette. 'Would you like one?' he said, the boy face jowled and strangely sick and tentatively smiling.

'No thank you.' Grey hadn't had a smoke for four days and he needed one.

'We can sort this out,' Jones said, his boyishness and good breeding returning. 'Perhaps someone *has* tampered with the weights. But the amount is insignificant. I can easily get the other weights, correct ones—'

'So, you admit that they're crooked?'

'I'm only saying, Grey—' Jones stopped. 'Get out, Blakely. Wait outside.'

Immediately Blakely turned for the door.

'Stay where you are, Blakely,' Grey said. Then he glanced back at Jones, his manner deferential. 'There's no need for Blakely to go, is there, sir?'

Jones studied him through the smoke, then said, 'No. Walls don't have ears. All right. You'll get a pound of rice a week.'

'Is that all?'

'We'll make it two pounds per week, and half a pound of dried fish. Once a week.'

'No sugar? Or eggs?'

'They both go to the hospital, you know that.'

Jones waited and Grey waited and Blakely sobbed in the background. Then Grey began to leave, pocketing the weight.

'Grey, just a minute.' Jones took two eggs and offered them to him. 'Here, you'll get one a week, along with the rest of the supplies. And some sugar.'

'I'll tell you what I'm going to do, Colonel. I'm going to go down to Colonel Smedly-Taylor and tell him what you said and I'm going to show him the weights—and if there's a borehole party, and I pray there will be one, I'm going to be there and I'm going to shove you down, but not too fast, because I want to see you die. I want to hear you scream and see you die, for a long time. Both of you.'

Then he went out of the hut into the sun, and the heat of the day hit him and the pain ripped through his insides. But he willed himself to walk and started slowly down the hill.

Jones and Blakely at the door of the supply hut watched him go. And both were terrified.

'Oh Christ, sir, what's going to happen?' Blakely whimpered. 'They'll string us up—'

Jones jerked him back into the hut, slammed the door and backhanded him viciously. 'Shut up!

Blakely was babbling on the floor and tears were streaming down his face, so Jones jerked him up and smashed him again.

'Don't hit me, you've no right to hit—'

'Shut up and listen.' Jones shook him again. 'Listen, damn you to hell. I've told you a thousand times to use the real weights on Grey's inspection day, you bloody incompetent fool. Stop snivelling and listen. First, you're to deny that anything was said. You understand? I made no offer to Grey, you understand?'

'But sir—'

'You're to deny it, you understand?'

'Yes, sir.'

'Good. We'll both deny it and if you stick to the story I'll get us out of this mess.'

'Can you? Can you, sir?'

'I can if you deny it. Next. You know nothing about the weights and neither do I. You understand?'

'But we're the only ones—'

'You understand?'

'Yes, sir.'

'Next. Nothing took place here except that Grey discovered the false weights and you and I were just as astonished. You understand?'

'But—'

'Now tell me what happened. God damn you, tell me!' Jones bellowed, towering over him.

'We—we were finishing the check, and then—then Grey fell against the weighing machine, and the weights got knocked over, and—and then we discovered the weights were false. Is that all right, sir?'

'What happened next?'

'Well, sir.' Blakely thought a moment, then his face lit up.

266

'Grey asked us about the weights, and I'd never seen that they were false, and you were just as surprised. Then Grey left.'

Jones offered him some tobacco. 'You've forgotten what Grey said. Don't you remember? He said, "If you give me some extra rice, a pound a week, and an egg or two, I won't report this." And then I told him to go to hell, that I would report the weights myself and would report him too, and I was beside myself with worry about the false weights. How did they get there? Who was the swine?'

Blakely's little eyes filled with admiration. 'Yes, sir, I remember distinctly. He asked for a pound of rice and an egg or two. Just like you said.'

'Then remember it, you stupid fool! If you'd used the right weights and held your tongue we wouldn't be in this mess. Don't you fail me again or I'll put the blame on you. It'll be your word against mine.'

'I won't fail, sir, I promise—'

'It's our word against Grey's anyway. So don't worry. *If* you keep your head and remember!'

'I won't forget, sir, I won't.'

'Good.' Jones locked the safe and the front door of the hut and left the area.

Jones is a sharp man, Blakely persuaded himself, he'll get us out of this. Now that the shock of being discovered had worn off he was feeling safer. Yes, and Jones'll have to save his own neck to save yours. Yes, Blakely my man, you're smart yourself, smart to make sure you've got the goods on him, just in case of a double-cross.

Colonel Smedly-Taylor scrutinized the weight ponderously.

'Astonishing!' he said. 'I just can't believe it.' He looked up keenly. 'You seriously mean to tell me that Lieutenant-Colonel Jones offered to *bribe* you? With camp provisions?'

'Yes, sir. It was exactly like I told you.'

Smedly-Taylor sat down on his bed in the little bungalow and wiped off the sweat, for it was hot and sultry. 'I don't believe it,' he repeated, shaking his head.

'They were the only ones who had access to the weights—'

'I know that. It's not that I dispute your word, Grey, it's just so, well, incredible.'

267

Smedly-Taylor was quiet for a long time and Grey waited patiently.

'Grey.' The colonel still examined the weight and the tiny hole as he continued. 'I'll think what to do about this. The whole—affair—is fraught with danger. You must not mention this to anyone, *anyone*, you understand?'

'Yes, sir.'

'My God, if it's as you say, well. those men would be massacred.' Again Smedly-Taylor shook his head. 'That two men—that Lieutenant-Colonel Jones could—the camp rations! And every weight is false?'

'Yes, sir.'

'How much do you think they are light, all in all?'

'I don't know, but perhaps a pound in every four hundred pounds. I suppose they were getting away with three or four pounds of rice per day. Not counting the dried fish or the eggs. Perhaps there are others mixed up in this—there would have to be. They couldn't cook rice and not have it noticed. Probably a cookhouse's mixed up in it too.'

'My God!' Smedly-Taylor got up and began pacing. 'Thank you, Grey, you've done a fine job. I'll see that it goes into your official report.' He put out his hand. 'A good job, Grey.'

Grey shook his hand firmly. 'Thank you, sir. I'm only sorry I didn't discover it before.'

'Now, not a word to anyone. That's an order!'

'I understand.' He saluted and left, his feet hardly touching the ground.

That Smedly-Taylor should say, 'I'll see that it goes into your official report!' Maybe they'd promote him, Grey thought with sudden hope. There had been a few camp promotions and he could certainly use the upped rank. Captain Grey—it had a nice ring to it. Captain Grey!

The afternoon was dragging now. Without work, it was difficult for Peter Marlowe to keep the men on their feet, so he organized foraging parties and kept the guards changing, for Torusumi was sleeping again. The heat was vicious and the air parched and everyone cursed the sun and prayed for night.

Finally Torusumi woke up and relieved himself in the undergrowth and picked up his rifle and began to walk up and down to take the sleep away. He screamed at some of the men who were dozing, and he shouted to Peter Marlowe, 'I beg thee get these sons of pigs up and about and make them work, or at least make them look as though they are working.'

Peter Marlowe came over. 'I'm sorry that thou are troubled.' Then he turned to the sergeant: 'For Christ sake, you know you were supposed to keep an eye on him. Get these bloody idiots up and dig a hole or chop that bloody tree or cut some palm fronds, you bloody idiot!'

The sergeant was suitably apologetic and in no time he had the men hurrying about, pretending to be busy. They had it down to a fine art.

A few husks of coconut were removed, and a few fronds were piled, and a few first saw cuts made in the trees. If they worked at the same speed, day after day, well, soon the whole area would be clean and level.

The sergeant tiredly reported back to Peter Marlowe. 'They're all as busy as they'll ever be, sir.'

'Good. Won't be long now.'

'Look, sir, would you—would you do something—for me?'

'What?'

'Well, it's like this. Seeing as how—as you—well . . .' He wiped his mouth on his sweatrag, embarrassed. But it was too good an opportunity to miss. 'Look at this.' He brought out a fountain pen. 'Would you see if the Nip'll buy it?'

'You mean you want me to sell it for you?' Peter Marlowe gaped at him.

'Yes, sir. It's—well—I thought, you being a friend of the King like, you'd know—maybe you'd know how to go about it.'

'It's against orders to sell to the guards, both our orders and theirs.'

'Aw, come on, sir, you can trust me. Why, you and the King—'

'What about me and the King?'

'Nothing, sir,' said the sergeant cautiously. What's the matter with this bugger? Who's he trying to fool? 'I just thought you might help me. And my unit, of course.'

Peter Marlowe looked at the sergeant and at the pen and wondered why he had got so angry. After all, he *had* sold for the

King—or at least, tried to sell for the King—and truthfully he was a friend of the King. And there was nothing wrong in that. If it wasn't for the King they would have never got the tree area. More likely he would be nursing a busted jaw, or at least a slapped face. So he should really uphold the reputation of the King. He did get you the coconuts.

'What do you want for it?'

The sergeant grinned. 'Well, it isn't a Parker, but it's got a gold nib,' and he unscrewed the top and showed it, 'so it should be worth something. Maybe you could see what he'd give.'

'He'll want to know what you want for it. I'll ask him, but you set a price.'

'If you could get me—sixty-five dollars, I'd be happy.'

'Is it worth that much?'

'I think so.'

The pen did have a gold nib and a fourteen carat mark, and as near as Peter Marlowe could judge it was genuine. Not like the other pen.

'Where'd you get it?'

'It's mine, sir. I've been keeping it against a rainy day. Been raining a lot recently.'

Peter Marlowe nodded briefly. He believed the man. 'All right. I'll see what I can do. You keep an eye on the men, and make sure there's a guard out.'

'Don't you worry, sir. The buggers won't bat a bleeding eyelid.'

Peter Marlowe found Torusumi leaning against a squat tree, heavy with a grasping vine. 'Tabe,' he said.

'Tabe.' Torusumi glanced at his watch, and yawned. 'In an hour we can go. It's not time yet.' He took off his cap and wiped the sweat off his face and neck. 'This stinking heat and stinking island!'

'Yes.' Peter Marlowe tried to make the words sound important, as though it were the King speaking and not he: 'One of the men has a pen he wishes to sell. It occurred to me that thee, as a friend, might wish to buy it.'

'Astaghfaru'llah! Is it a Parka?'

'No.' Peter Marlowe brought out the pen and unscrewed the top and held the nib so it caught the sunlight. 'But it has a gold nib.'

Torusumi examined it. He was disappointed that it wasn't a Parker, but that would have been too much to expect. Certainly not on the airfield. A Parker would be handled by the King personally.

'It's not worth much,' he said.

'Of course. If thou dost not wish to consider it . . .' Peter Marlowe put the pen back in his pocket.

'I can consider it. Perhaps we can pass the hour, considering such a worthless item.' He shrugged. 'It would only be worth seventy-five dollars.'

Peter Marlowe was amazed that the first bid was so high. The sergeant can't have any idea of its value. God, I wish I knew how much it was really worth.

So they sat and haggled. Torusumi got angry and Peter Marlowe was firm and they settled on a hundred and twenty dollars and a pack of Kooas.

Torusumi got up and yawned again. 'It is time to go.' He smiled. 'The King is a good teacher. The next time I see him I will tell him how thou hast taken advantage of my friendship by driving such a hard bargain.' He shook his head with feigned self-pity. 'Such a price for such a miserable pen! The King will surely laugh at me. Tell him, I beg thee, that I will be on guard in seven days from today. Perhaps he can find me a watch. A good one—this time.'

Peter Marlowe was content that he had safely made his first real transaction for what seemed to be a fair price. But he was in a quandary. If he gave all the money to the sergeant, the King would be very upset. That would ruin the price structure that the King had so carefully built. And Torusumi would certainly mention the pen and the amount to the King. However, if he gave the sergeant only what he had asked and kept the rest, well that was cheating, wasn't it? Or was it good 'business'? In truth, the sergeant had asked for sixty-five, and that's what he should get. And Peter Marlowe did owe the King a lot of money.

He wished he'd never started the stupid business. Now he was caught in the trap of his own making. Trouble with you, Peter, is you've too big an idea of your own importance. If you'd said no to the sergeant you wouldn't be up the creek now. What are you going to do? Whatever you do is going to be wrong!

271

He strolled back slowly, pondering. The sergeant had already lined the men up, and took Peter aside expectantly. 'They're all ready, sir. An' I've checked the tools.' He lowered his voice. 'Did he buy it?'

'Yes.' Then Peter Marlowe made the decision. He put his hand in his pocket and gave the sergeant the bundle of notes. 'Here you are. Sixty-five dollars.'

'Sir, you're a bloody toff! He peeled off a five-dollar bill and offered it to him. 'I owe you a dollar-fifty.'

'You don't owe me anything.'

'Ten per cent's yours. That's legal, an' I'm happy to pay it. I'll give you the dollar an' a half soon as I get change.'

Peter Marlowe shoved the note back. 'No,' he said, feeling suddenly guilty. 'Keep it.'

'I insist,' the sergeant said, pushing the note back into his hand.

'Look, Sergeant—'

'Well, at least take the five. I'd feel terrible, sir, if you didn't Terrible. I can't thank you enough.'

All the way back to the airfield Peter Marlowe was silent. He felt unclean with the monstrous bundle of notes in his pocket, but at the same time he knew that he owed the money to the King and was pleased to have it, for it would buy extras for the unit. The only reason the sergeant had asked him was because he knew the King, and the King, not the sergeant was his friend. The whole miserable business was still going round and round in his mind when he got back to his hut.

'Grey wants to see you, Peter,' Ewart said.

'What for?'

'I don't know, Peter boy. But he seemed peed off about something.'

Peter Marlowe's tired mind adjusted to the new danger. It had to be something to do with the King. Grey meant trouble. Now, think, think, Peter. The village? The watch? The diamond? Oh my God—the pen? No, that's being foolish. He can't know about that yet. Shall I go to the King? Maybe he'd know what it's about. Dangerous. Perhaps that's why Grey told Ewart, to force me to make a mistake. He must have known I was on a work party.

No point in going like a lamb to the slaughter when you're

hot and dirty. A shower, then I'll stroll up to the jail hut. Take my time.

So he went to the shower. Johnny Hawkins was under one of the spouts.

'Hello, Peter,' Hawkins said.

Suddenly guilt flushed Peter Marlowe's face. 'Hello, Johnny.' Hawkins looked ill. 'Say, Johnny, I—I was so sorry—'

'Don't want to talk about it,' Hawkins said. 'I'd be glad if you never mentioned it.'

Does he know, Peter Marlowe asked himself, appalled, that I'm one of the ones who—ate?—even now—was it only yesterday?—the sudden thought was revolting: cannibalism. He can't, surely, for then he would have tried to kill me. I know if I were in his shoes, *I* would. Or would I?

My God, what a state we've come to. Everything that seems wrong is right, and vice versa. It's too much to understand. Much too much. Stupid screwed-up world. And the sixty dollars and the pack of Kooas I've earned, and at the same time stolen—or made—which is it? Should I give them back? That would be quite wrong.

'Marlow!'

He turned and saw Grey standing malevolently at the side of the shower.

'You were told to report to me when you got back!'

'I was told you wanted to see me. As soon as I'd showered I was going to—'

'I left orders that you were to report to me immediately.' There was a thin smile on Grey's face. 'But it doesn't matter. You're under hut arrest.'

There was a quiet in the showers and all the officers were watching and listening.

'What for?'

Grey rejoiced in the flash of concern he saw. 'For disobeying orders.'

'What orders?'

'You know as well as I do. That's right, sweat! Your guilty conscience will trouble you a little—if you've got a conscience, which I doubt. You're to report to Colonel Smedly-Taylor after supper. And be dressed like an officer, not a bloody tart!'

Peter Marlowe snapped off the shower and slipped into his

273

sarong and made the knot with a deft twist, conscious of the curious stares of the other officers. His mind was in a turmoil wondering what the trouble was, but he tried to hide his anxiety. Why give Grey the satisfaction?

'You're really so ill-bred, Grey. Such a bore,' he said.

'I've learned a lot about breeding today, you bloody sod,' Grey said. 'I'm glad I don't belong to your stinking class, you rotten bugger. All shysters, cheats, thieves—'

'For the last time, Grey, button your mouth, or by God I'll button it for you.'

Grey tried to control himself. He wanted to pit himself against this man, here and now. He could beat him, he knew he could. Any time. Dysentery or no. 'If we ever get out of this mess alive, I'll look for you. The first thing. The very first thing.'

'It would be a pleasure. But until that time, if you ever insult me again I'll whip you.' Peter Marlowe turned to the other officers. 'You all heard me. I'm giving him warning. I'm not going to be sworn at by this lower-class ape.' He whipped around on Grey. Now stay away from me.'

'How can I when you're a lawbreaker?'

'What law?'

'Be at Colonel Smedly-Taylor's after supper. And one more thing—you're under hut arrest until time to report.'

Grey walked away. Most of his exultation had been drained from him. It was stupid to call Marlowe names. Stupid, when there was no need.

XVIII

When Peter Marlowe arrived outside Colonel Smedly-Taylor's bungalow, Grey was already there.

'I'll tell the colonel you arrived,' Grey said.

'You're so kind.' Peter Marlowe felt uncomfortable. The peaked Air Force cap he had borrowed irritated. The ragged but clean shirt he wore irritated. Sarongs are so much more comfortable, he told himself, so much more sensible. And thinking of sarongs he thought of tomorrow. Tomorrow was the money exchange day. For the diamond. Tomorrow Shagata was to bring the money and then in three days the village once more. Maybe Sulina . . .

You're a fool to think about her. Get your wits with you, you're going to need them.

'All right, Marlowe. 'Tenshun', Grey ordered.

Peter Marlowe came to attention and began to march, militarily correct, into the colonel's room. As he passed Grey he whispered, 'Up you, Jack,' and felt a little better, and then he was in front of the colonel. He saluted smartly and fixed his eyes through the colonel.

Seated behind a crude desk, cap on, swagger cane on the table, Smedly-Taylor looked at Peter Marlowe bleakly and returned the salute punctiliously. He prided himself on the way he handled camp discipline. Everything he did was Army. By the book.

He sized up the young man in front of him—standing erect. Good, he told himself, that's at least in his favour. He remained

275

silent for a while, as was his custom. Always unsettle the accused. At last he spoke.

'Well, Flight Lieutenant Marlowe? What have you got to say for yourself?'

'Nothing, sir. I don't know what I'm charged with.'

Colonel Smedly-Taylor glanced at Grey, surprised, then frowned back at Peter Marlowe. 'Perhaps you break so many rules that you have difficulty remembering them. You went into the jail yesterday. That's against orders. You were not wearing an arm-band. That's against orders.'

Peter Marlowe was relieved. It was only the jail. But wait a minute—what about the food?

'Well,' the colonel said curtly, 'did you, or didn't you?'

'Yes, sir.'

'You knew you were breaking two orders?'

'Yes, sir.'

'Why did you go into the jail?'

'I was just visiting some men.'

'Oh?' The colonel waited, then said caustically, ' "Just visiting some men"?'

Peter Marlowe said nothing, only waited. Then it came.

'The American was also in the jail. Were you with him?'

'For part of the time. There is no law against that, sir. But I did break—the two orders.'

'What mischief were you two cooking up?'

'Nothing, sir.'

'So you admit that the two of you are connected with mischief from time to time?'

Peter Marlowe was furious with himself for not thinking before he answered, knowing that with this man, a fine man, he was out of his league. 'No, sir.' His eyes focused on the colonel. But he said nothing. One rule. When you're up before authority, you just say 'No, sir,' 'Yes, sir' and tell the truth. It was an inviolate rule that officers always told the truth, and here he was, against all his heritage, against everything he knew to be correct, telling lies and partial truths. That was quite wrong. Or was it?

Colonel Smedly-Taylor now began to play the game he had played so many times before. It was easy for him to toy with a man and then slaughter him, if he felt like it. 'Look, Marlowe,' he said, his manner becoming fatherly, 'it has been reported that you are involving yourself with undesirable elements. You would be wise to consider your position as an officer and a gentleman. Now this association—with this American. He *is* a black-marketeer. He hasn't been caught yet, but we know, and so you must know. I would advise you to cease this association. I can't order it, of course, but I advise it.'

Peter Marlowe said nothing, bleeding inside. What the colonel said was true, and yet the King was his friend and his friend was feeding and helping both him and his unit. And he was a fine man, fine.

Peter Marlowe wanted to say, 'You're wrong, and I don't care. I like him and he's a good man and we've had fun together and laughed a lot,' and at the same time he wanted to admit the sales, and admit the village, and admit the diamond, and admit the sale today. But Peter Marlowe could see the King behind bars—robbed of his stature. So he steeled himself to keep from confessing.

Smedly-Taylor could easily detect the tumult in the youth in front of him. It would be so simple for him to say. 'Wait outside, Grey,' and then, 'Listen, my boy, I understand your problem. My God, I've had to father a regiment for almost as long as I can remember. I know the problem—you don't want to rat on your friend. That's commendable. But you're a career officer, an hereditary officer—think of your family and the generations of officers who have served the country. Think of them. Your honour's at stake. You have to tell the truth, that's the law.' And then his little sigh, practised over a generation, and 'Let's forget this nonsense of the infraction of rules by going into the jail I've done it myself, several times. But if you want to confide in me . . .' and he'd let the words hang with just the right amount of gravity and out would come the secrets of the King and the King would be in the camp jail—but what purpose would that serve?

For the moment, the colonel had a greater worry—the weights. That could be a catastrophe of infinite proportions.

Colonel Smedly-Taylor knew that he could always get whatever information he wanted from this child at his whim—he knew the men so very well. He knew he was a clever commander—by God, he should be after all this time—and the first rule was keep the respect of your officers, treat them leniently until they really stepped out of line, then devour one of them ruthlessly as a lesson to the others. But you had to pick the right time, and the right crime, and the right officer.

'All right, Marlowe,' he said firmly. 'I'll fine you a month's pay. I'll keep it off your record and we'll say no more about it. But don't break any more rules.'

'Thank you, sir.' Peter Marlowe saluted and left, glad to be away from the interview. He had been on the threshold of telling everything. The colonel was a good and kind man, and his reputation for fairness was vast.

'Your conscience bothering you?' Grey asked outside the bungalow, noticing the sweat.

Peter Marlowe didn't answer. He was still upset and enormously relieved to have escaped.

The Colonel called out, 'Grey! Could I see you for a moment?'

'Yes, sir.' Grey looked a last time at Peter Marlowe. One month's pay! Not very much, considering that the colonel had him. Grey was surprised and not a little angry that Marlowe had got off so lightly. But, at the same time, he had seen Smedly-Taylor operate before. And he knew that the colonel was tenacious as a bulldog, that he played men like fish. He must have a plan, to let Marlowe go so easily.

Grey stepped around Peter Marlowe and went inside once more.

'Er, close the door, Grey.'

'Yes, sir.'

When they were alone, Colonel Smedly-Taylor said, 'I've seen Lieutenant-Colonel Jones and Quartermaster-Sergeant Blakely.'

'Yes, sir?' Now we're getting somewhere!

'I have relieved them of their duties as from today,' the colonel said, playing with the weight.

Grey's smile was broad. 'Yes, sir.' Now, when would the court-martial be, and how would it be arranged, and would it be in camera and would they be reduced to the ranks? Soon everyone in camp would know that he, Grey, had caught them at their treachery; he, Grey, was a guardian angel, and my God, how wonderful that would be.

'And we'll forget the matter,' the colonel said.

Grey's smile vanished. 'What?'

'Yes. I have decided to forget the matter. And so will you. In fact I repeat my order. You are not to mention this to anyone and you are to forget it.'

Grey was so astounded that he sank to the bed and stared at the colonel. 'But we can't do that, sir!' he burst out. 'We caught them redhanded. Stealing the camp food. That's your food and my food. And they tried to bribe me. To bribe me!' His voice became hysterical. 'Holy Christ, I caught them, they're thieves, they deserve to be hanged and quartered.'

'True.' Colonel Smedly-Taylor nodded gravely. 'But I think, under the circumstances, that this is the wisest decision.'

Grey leaped to his feet. 'You can't do that!' he shouted. 'You can't let them off scot-free! You can't—'

'Don't tell me what I can or cannot do!'

'I'm sorry,' Grey said, fighting for control. 'But, sir, those men are thieves. I caught them. You've got the weight.'

'I've decided that this is the end of the matter.' His voice was calm. 'The matter is closed.'

Grey's temper snapped. '*By God*, it's not closed. I won't let it be closed! Those bastards've been eating when we've been hungry! They deserve to get chopped! And I insist—'

Smedly-Taylor's voice overrode the hysteria. 'Shut up, Grey! You can't *insist* on anything. The matter is closed.'

Smedly-Taylor sighed heavily and picked up a piece of paper and said, 'This is your official report. I've added something today. I'll read it to you. "I strongly recommend Lieutenant Grey for his work as Provost Marshal of the Camp Police. His performance of duty is, beyond question, excellent. I would like to recommend that he be given the acting rank of Captain".' He looked up from the paper. 'I propose sending this to the Camp Commandant today and recommending that your promotion be effective from today's date.' He smiled. 'You know of course that he has the authority to promote you. Congratulations, Captain Grey. You deserve it.' He offered Grey his hand.

But Grey didn't accept it. He merely looked at it and at the paper, and he knew. 'Why, you rotten bastard! You're buying me off. You're as bad—maybe you've been eating the rice too. Why, you shit, you dirty rotten shit—'

'You hold your tongue, you jumped-up subaltern! Stand to attention! *I said stand to attention!*'

'You're in with them, and I'm not going to let any of you get away with it.' Grey shouted and snatched the weight off the table and backed away. 'I can't prove anything about you yet, but I've got proof against them. This weight—'

'What about the weight, Grey?'

It took Grey an age to look down at the weight. The bottom was unmarred.

'I said, "What about the weight?"' Stupid fool, Smedly-Taylor thought contemptuously as he watched Grey search for the hole. What a fool! I could eat him for breakfast and not notice it.

'It's not the one I gave you,' Grey choked. 'It's not the same. It's not the same.'

'You're quite wrong. It's the same one.' The colonel was quite calm.

He continued, his voice benign and solicitous. 'Now, Grey, you're a young man. I understand that you want to stay in the Army when the war's over. That's good. We can use intelligent, hard-working officers. Regular Army's a wonderful life. Certainly. And Colonel Samson was telling me how highly he thinks of you. As you know, he's a friend of mine. I'm sure I could prevail upon him to add to my recommendation that you should be granted a permanent commission. You're just over-wrought, understandably so. These are terrible times. I think it's wise to let this matter drop. It would be ill-advised to involve the camp in a scandal. Very ill-advised. I'm sure you understand the wisdom of this.'

He waited, despising Grey. At just the correct time—for he was an expert—he said, 'Do you want me to send your recommendation for captaincy to the Camp Commandant?'

Grey slowly turned to the paper, eyeing it with horror. He knew that the colonel could give or withhold, and where he could give or withhold, he could also slaughter. Grey knew he was beaten. Beaten. He tried to speak, but so vast was his misery that he could not speak. He nodded and he heard Smedly-Taylor say, 'Good, you can take it as read that your captaincy is confirmed. I feel sure my recommendation and Colonel Samson's will add tremendous weight to your being granted a permanent commission after the war,' and he felt himself go out of the room and up to the jail hut and dismiss the MP and he didn't care that the man looked at him as though he were mad. Then he was alone inside the jail hut. He shut the door and sat on the edge of the bed within the cell and his misery erupted and he wept.

Broken.

Ripped apart.

Tears wet his hands and face. His spirit whirled in terror, teetering on the brink of the unknown, then fell into eternity . . .

When Grey came to, he was lying on a stretcher being carried by two MP's. Dr Kennedy was clomping ahead. Grey knew that he was dying but he did not care. Then he saw the King standing beside the path, looking down at him.

Grey noticed the neat polished shoes, the trousers' crease, the tailor-made Kooa, the well-fed countenance. And he remembered that he had a job to do. He could not die yet. Not yet. Not while the King was well-creased and polished and well fed. Not with the diamond in the offing. By God, no!

'We'd better make this the last game,' Colonel Smedly-Taylor was saying. 'Musn't miss the show.'

'Can't wait to get an eyeful of Sean,' Jones said, sorting his cards. 'Two diamonds.' He opened smugly.

'You've the luck of the devil,' Sellars said sharply. 'Two spades.'

'Pass.'

'Not always the luck of the devil, partner,' Smedly-Taylor said with a thin smile. His granite eyes looked at Jones. 'You were pretty stupid today.'

'It was just bad luck.'

'There's no excuse for bad luck,' Smedly-Taylor said, studying his cards. 'You should have checked. You were incompetent not to check.'

'I've said I'm sorry. You think I don't realize that it was stupid? I'll never do that again. Never. I never knew what it was like to be panicked.'

'Two no trumps.' Smedly-Taylor smiled at Sellars. 'This'll make it rubber, partner.' Then he turned to Jones again. 'I've

281

recommended that Samson take over from you—you need a "rest". That'll take Grey off the scent—oh yes, and Sergeant Donovan'll be Samson's Quartermaster-Sergeant.' He laughed shortly. 'It's a pity we have to change the system, but it doesn't matter. We'll just have to make sure that Grey's busy on the days the false weights are used.' He looked back at Sellars. 'That'll be your job.'

'Very good.'

'Oh, by the way, I fined Marlowe a month's pay. He's in one of your huts, isn't he?'

'Yes,' Sellars said.

'I was soft on him, but he's a good man, comes from a good family—not like that lower-class sod Grey. My God, what a bloody nerve—to think I'd recommend him for a permanent commission. That's just the sort of guttersnipe we don't need in the Regular Army. My God, no! If he gets a permanent commission it'll be over my dead body.'

'I quite agree,' Sellars said with distaste. 'But with Marlowe you should have made it three months' pay. He can afford it. That damned American's got the whole camp tied up.'

'He has for the time being,' Smedly-Taylor grunted and re-examined his cards once more, trying to cover his slip.

'You've something on him?' Jones asked tentatively. Then he added, 'Three diamonds.'

'Blast you,' Sellars said. 'Four spades.'

'Pass.'

'Six spades,' Smedly-Taylor said.

'Do you really have something on the American?' Jones asked again.

Colonel Smedly-Taylor kept his face blank. He knew about the diamond ring and he'd heard that a deal had been made, that the ring would change hands soon. And when the money was in the camp, well, a plan had been thought of—a good plan, a safe plan, a private plan—to get the money. So he just grunted and smiled his thin smile and said offhand, 'If I have, I'm certainly not going to tell you about it. You're not to be trusted.'

When Smedly-Taylor smiled, they all smiled, relieved.

Peter Marlowe and Larkin joined the stream of men going into the open-air theatre.

The stage lights were already on and the moon beamed down. At capacity the theatre could hold two thousand. The seats, which fanned out from the stage, were planks set on coconut stumps. Each show was repeated for five nights, so that everyone in camp could see it at least once. Seats were allocated by lot and were always at a premium.

Most of the rows were already crammed. Except the front rows where the officers always sat in front of the enlisted men and came later. Only the Americans did not follow the custom.

'Hey, you two,' the King called out. 'You want to sit with us?' He had the favoured seat on the aisle.

'Well, I'd like to, but you know—' Peter Marlowe said uncomfortably.

'Yeah. Well, see you later.'

Peter Marlowe glanced at Larkin and knew he was thinking too that it was wrong not to sit with your friends if you wanted—and at the same time it was wrong to sit there.

'You, er, want to sit here, Colonel?' he asked, passing the buck and hating himself for passing the buck.

'Why not?' Larkin said.

They sat down, acutely embarrassed, aware of their defection and aware of the atonished eyes.

'Hey, Colonel!' Brough leaned over, a smile creasing his face. 'You'll get handed your head. Bad for discipline and all that jazz.'

'If I want to sit here, I'll sit here.' But Larkin wished he hadn't agreed so readily.

'How're things, Peter?' the King asked.

'Fine thanks.' Peter Marlowe tried to overcome his discomfort. He felt everyone was looking at him. He had not yet told the King about the sale of the pen, what with being on the carpet in front of Smedly-Taylor, and the brawl he had almost had with Grey . . .

'Evening, Marlowe.'

He glanced up and winced as he saw Smedly-Taylor passing. Flint eyes.

'Evening, sir,' he replied weakly. Oh my God, he thought, that's torn it.

There was a sudden quickening of excitement as the Camp Commandant walked down the aisle and sat down at the very front row. The lights dimmed. The curtain parted. On the stage was the five-piece camp band, and standing in the centre of the stage was Phil, the band leader.

Applause.

'Good evening,' Phil began. 'Tonight we're presenting a new play by Frank Parrish called *Triangle*, which takes place in London before the war. It stars Frank Parrish, Brod Rodrick, and the one and only Sean Jennison . . .'

Tumultuous cheers. Catcalls. Whistles. Shouts of 'Where's Sean?' and 'What war?' and 'Good old Blighty' and 'Get on with it' and 'We want Sean!'

Phil gave the downbeat with a flourish and the overture began.

Now that the show was on, Peter Marlowe relaxed a little.

Then it happened.

Dino was abruptly at the King's side and whispering urgently in his ear. 'Where?' Peter Marlowe heard the King say. Then, 'Okay, Dino. You beat it back to the hut.'

The King leaned across. 'We gotta go, Peter.' His face was taut, his voice barely a whisper. 'A certain guy wants to see us.'

Oh my God! Shagata! Now what? 'We can't just get up and leave now,' Peter Marlowe said uneasily.

'The hell we can't. We both got a touch of dysentery. C'mon.' The King was already walking up the aisle.

Nakedly aware of the astonished eyes, Peter Marlowe hurried after him.

They found Shagata in the shadows behind the stage. He was nervous too. 'I beg thee forgive my bad manners in sending for thee suddenly, but there is trouble. One of the junks of our mutual friend was intercepted and he is presently being questioned for smuggling by the pestilential police.' Shagata felt lost without his rifle and knew that if he was caught in the camp off duty he would be put in the windowless box for three weeks. 'It occurred to me that if our friend is questioned brutally, he may implicate us.'

'Jesus,' the King said.

Unsteadily he accepted a Kooa and the three of them went deeper into the shadows.

'I thought that, thou being a man of experience,' Shagata continued with a rush, 'thou might have a plan whereby we could extricate ourselves.'

'He's got a hope!' the King said.

His mind raced back and forth and it always gave him the same answer. Wait and sweat.

'Peter. Ask him if Cheng San was on the junk when it was stopped.'

'He says no.'

The King sighed. 'Then maybe Cheng San can squeeze out of it.' He thought again, then said, 'The only goddam thing we can do is wait. Tell him not to panic. He's got to keep tabs on Cheng San somehow and find out if he talks. He's got to send us word if the goddam shoot blows.'

Peter Marlowe translated.

Shagata sucked air between his teeth. 'I am impressed that the two of thee are so calm while I am fluttering with fear, for if I am caught I shall be lucky if they shoot me first. I will do as thou sayest. If thou art caught, I beg thee try not to implicate me. I will try to do likewise.' His head jerked around as there was a soft warning whistle. 'I must leave thee. If all goes well we will keep to the plan.' He hurriedly thrust the pack of Kooas into Peter Marlowe's hand. 'I do not know about thee and thy gods, but I certainly talk to mine, long and hard, on our mutual behalf.'

Then he was gone.

'What if Cheng San lets the cat out?' Peter Marlowe asked, his stomach an aching knot. 'What can we do?'

'Make a break.' The King shakily lit another cigarette and leaned back against the side of the theatre, hugging the shadows. 'Better that than Outram Road.'

Behind them the overture ended to applause and cheers and laughter. But they did not hear the applause and cheers and laughter.

Rodrick was standing in the wings glowering at the stage hands setting the stage for the play, chasing them, hurrying them.

'Major!' Mike rushed up to him. 'Sean's throwing a fit. He's crying his bloody eyes out!'

'Oh for the love of Heaven! What happened? He was all right a minute ago,' Rodrick exploded.

'I don't know for certain,' Mike said sullenly.

Rodrick cursed again and hurried away. Anxiously he knocked on the dressing room door. 'Sean, it's me. Can I come in?'

There were muffled sobs coming through the door. 'No. Go away. I'm not going on. I just can't.'

'Sean. Everything's all right. You're just overtired, that's all. Look—'

'Go away and leave me alone,' Sean shouted hysterically through the door. 'I'm not going on!'

Rodrick tried the door but it was locked. He rushed back to the stage. 'Frank!'

'What do you want?' Frank, covered with sweat, was irritably perched on a ladder fixing a light that refused to work.

'Come down here! I've got to talk—'

'For the love of God, can't you see I'm busy? Do it yourself, whatever it is,' he flared. 'Do I have to do everything? I've still got to get changed and still haven't got my makeup on!' He looked up at the catwalk again. 'Try the other banks of switches, Duncan. Come on, man, hurry.'

Beyond the curtain Rodrick could hear the growing chorus of impatient whistles. Now what do I do? he asked himself frantically. He began to go back to the dressing room.

Then he saw Peter Marlowe and the King near the side door. He ran down the steps.

'Marlowe. You've got to help me!'

'What's up?'

'It's Sean, he's throwing a tantrum,' Rodrick began breathlessly, 'refuses to go on. Would you talk to him? Please. I can't do a thing with him. Please. Talk to him. Will you?'

'But—'

'Won't take you a second,' Rodrick interrupted. 'You're my last chance. Please. I've been worried about Sean for weeks. His part would be hard enough for a woman to play, let alone . . .' He stopped, then went on weakly, 'Please, Marlowe, I'm afraid of him. You'd do us all a great service.'

Peter Marlowe hesitated. 'All right.'

'Can't thank you enough, old boy.' Rodrick mopped his brow and led the way through the pandemonium to the back of the theatre, Peter Marlowe reluctantly in tow. The King followed absently, his mind still concentrating on how and where and when to make the break.

They stood in the little corridor. Uneasily Peter Marlowe knocked. 'It's me, Peter. Can I come in, Sean?'

Sean heard him through the fog of terror, slumped on his arms in front of the dressing table.

'It's me, Peter. Can I come in?'

Sean got up, the tears streaking his makeup, and unbolted the door. Peter Marlowe hesitantly came into the dressing room. Sean shut the door.

'Oh Peter, I can't go on. I've had it. I'm at the end,' Sean said helplessly. 'I can't pretend any more, not any more. I'm lost, lost, God help me!' He hid his face in his hands. 'What am I going to do? I can't face it any more. I'm nothing. Nothing!'

'It's all right, Sean old chum,' Peter Marlowe said, deep with pity. 'No need to worry. You're very important. Most important person in the whole camp, if the truth be known.'

'I wish I were dead.'

'That's too easy.'

Sean turned and faced him. 'Look at me, for the love of God! What am I? What in God's name am I?'

In spite of himself, Peter Marlowe could only see a girl, a girl in pathetic torment. And the girl was wearing a white skirt and high heels and her long legs were silk-stockinged and her blouse showed the swell of breasts beneath.

'You're a woman, Sean,' he said as helplessly. 'God knows how—or why—but you are.'

And then the terror and the self-hatred and the torment left Sean.

'Thank you, Peter,' Sean said. 'Thank you with all my heart.'

There was a tentative knock on the door. 'On in two minutes,' Frank called anxiously through the door. 'Can I come in?'

'Just a second.' Sean went to the dressing table and brushed away the tear stains and repaired the makeup and stared at the reflection.

'Come in, Frank.'

The sight of Sean took Frank's breath away, as it always had. 'You look wonderful!' he said. 'You all right?'

287

'Yes. Afraid I made a bit of a fool of myself. Sorry.'

'Just overwork,' Frank said, hiding his concern. He glanced at Peter Marlowe. 'Hello, good to see you.'

'Thanks.'

'You'd better get ready, Frank,' Sean said. 'I'm all right now.'

Frank felt the girl's smile, deep within him, and automatically fell into the pattern that he and Rodrick had begun three years before and bitterly regretted ever since. 'You're going to be marvellous, Betty,' he said, hugging Sean. 'I'm proud of you.'

But now, unlike all the countless other times, suddenly they were man and woman, and Sean relaxed against him, needing him with every molecule of being. And Frank knew it.

'We'll—we're on in a minute,' he said unsteadily, rocked by the suddenness of his own need. 'I've—I've got to get ready.' He left.

'I'd, er, better be getting back to my seat,' Peter Marlowe said, deeply troubled. He had felt more than seen the spark between them.

'Yes.' But Sean hardly noticed Peter Marlowe.

A final check of the makeup and then Sean was waiting for a cue in the wings. The usual terrored ecstasy. Then Sean walked on and *became*. The cheers and wonder and lust poured over *her*—eyes following as *she* sat and crossed *her* legs, as *she* walked and talked—eyes reaching out, touching *her*, feeding on *her*. Together *she* and the eyes became one.

'Major,' Peter Marlowe said as he and the King and Rodrick stood in the wings watching, 'what's this Betty business?'

'Oh, part of the whole mess,' Rodrick replied miserably. 'That's the name of Sean's part this week. We've—Frank and I—we always call Sean by the part he's playing.'

'Why?' the King asked.

'To help him. Help him get into the part.' Rodrick looked back to the stage waiting for his cue. 'It started as a game,' he said bitterly, 'now it's an unholy joke. We created that—that woman—God help us. We're responsible.'

'Why?' Peter Marlowe said slowly.

'Well, you remember how tough it was in Java.' Rodrick glanced at the King. 'Because I was an actor before the war, I was assigned the job of starting the camp theatricals.' He let his eyes stray back to the stage, to Frank and Sean. Something strange about those two tonight, he thought. Critically he studied their performances and knew them to be inspired. 'Frank was the only other professional in the camp so we started to work getting shows together. When we got to the job of casting, of course, someone had to play the female roles. No one would volunteer, so the authorities detailed two or three. One of them was Sean. He was bitterly opposed to doing it, but you know how stubborn senior officers are. "Someone's got to play a girl, for God's sake," they said to him. "You're young enough to look like one. You don't shave more than once a week. And it's only putting on clothes for an hour or so. Think of what it'll do for everyone's morale." And however much Sean raved and cursed and begged, it did no good.

'Sean asked me not to accept him. Well, there's no future in working with unco-operative talent, so I tried to have him dropped from the company. "Look," I said to the authorities, "acting's a great psychological strain . . ."

'"Poppycock!"' they said. '"What harm can come of it?"'

'"The fact that he's playing a female might warp him. If he were the slightest way inclined . . ."'

'"Stuff and nonsense,"' they said. '"You damned theatrical people've pervert on the brain. Sergeant Jennison? Impossible! Nothing wrong with him! Damn fine fighter pilot! Now look here, Major. This is the end of it. You're ordered to take him and he's ordered to do it!"'

'So Frank and I tried to smooth Sean down, but he swore he was going to be the worst actress in the world, that he was going to make sure that he was sacked after the first disastrous performance. We told him that we couldn't care less. His first performance was terrible. But after that he didn't seem to hate it so much. To his surprise, he even seemed to like it. So we really started to work. It was good having something to do—it took your mind off the stinking food and stinking camp. We taught him how a woman talks and walks and sits and smokes and drinks and dresses and even thinks. Then, to keep him in the mood, we began to play make-believe. Whenever we were in the theatre, we'd get up when he came in, help him into a chair, you know, treat him like a real woman. It was exciting at first, trying to keep up the illusion, making sure Sean was never seen dressing or undressing, making sure his costumes were always concealing but just suggestive enough. We even got special permission for him to have a room of his own. With his own shower.

'Then, suddenly, he didn't need coaching any more. He was as complete a woman on the stage as it was possible to be.

'But little by little, the woman began to dominate him off stage too, only we didn't notice it. By this time, Sean had grown his hair quite long—the wigs we had were no damn good. Then Sean started to wear a woman's clothes all the time. One night someone tried to rape him.

'After that Sean nearly went out of his mind. He tried to crush the woman in him but he couldn't. Then he tried to commit suicide. Of course it was hushed up. But that didn't help Sean, it made things worse and he cursed us for saving him.

'A few months later there was another rape attempt. After that Sean buried his male self completely. "I'm not fighting it any more," he said. "You wanted me to be a woman, now they believe I am one. All right. I'll be one. Inside I feel I *am* one, so there's no need to pretend any more. I *am* a woman, and I'm going to be treated like one."

'Frank and I tried to reason with him, but he was quite beyond us. So we told ourselves that it was only temporary, that Sean'd be all right later. Sean *was* great for morale and we knew we could never get anyone a tenth as good as Sean to play the girl. So we shrugged and continued the game.

'Poor Sean. He's such a wonderful person. If it wasn't for him, Frank and I would have given up the ghost long ago.'

There was a roar of applause as Sean made another entrance from the other side of the stage. 'You've no idea what applause'll do to you,' Rodrick said, half to himself, 'applause and adoration. Not unless, you've experienced it yourself. Out there, on the stage. No idea. It's fantastically exciting, a frightening, terrifying, beautiful drug. And it's always poured into Sean. Always. That and the lust—yours, mine, all of us.'

Rodrick wiped the sweat off his face and hands. 'We're responsible all right, God forgive us.'

His cue came and he walked onto the stage.

'Do you want to go back to our seats?' Peter Marlowe asked the King.

'No. Let's watch from here. I've never been backstage before.

Something I always wanted to do.' Is Cheng San spilling his guts right now, the King asked himself.

But the King knew there was no value in worrying. They were committed and he was ready—whatever card came up. He looked back at the stage. His eyes watched Rodrick and Frank and Sean. Inexorably, his eyes followed Sean. Every movement, every gesture.

Everyone was watching Sean. Intoxicated.

And Sean and Frank and the eyes became one, and together the brooding passion on the stage soared into the players and into the watchers, ripping them bare.

When the curtain descended on the last act, there was utter silence. The watchers were spellbound.

'My God,' Rodrick said, awed. 'That's the greatest compliment they could ever pay us. And you deserve it, you two, you were inspired. Truly inspired.'

The curtain began to rise, and when it was completely up the awful silence shattered and there were cheers and ten curtain calls and more cheers and then Sean stood alone drinking the life-giving adoration.

In the continuing ovation, Rodrick and Frank came out a last time to share the triumph, two creators and a creation, the beautiful girl who was their pride and their nemesis.

The audience filed quietly out of the auditorium. Each man was thinking of home, thinking of *her*, locked in his own brooding hurt. What's *she* doing, right now?

Larkin was the most hit. Why in God's name call the girl Betty? Why? And my Betty—is she—would she—is she now, is she now in someone else's arms?

And Mac. He was swept with fear for Mem. Did the ship get sunk? Is she alive? Is my son alive? And Mem—would she—is she now—is she? It's been so long, my God, how long?

And Peter Marlowe. What of N'ai, the peerless? My love, my love.

And all of them.

Even the King. He was wondering who she was with—the vision of loveliness he had seen when he was still in his teens, still on the bum—the girl who'd said with a perfumed handkerchief to her nose that white trash smell worse than niggers.

The King smiled sardonically. Now that was one hell of a

broad, he told himself as he turned his mind to more important things.

The lights went out now in the theatre. It was empty but for the two in the landlocked dressing room.

BOOK FOUR

XIX

The King and Peter Marlowe waited with growing impatience. Shagata was long overdue.

'What a stinking night,' the King said irritably. 'I'm sweating like a pig.'

They were sitting in the King's corner and Peter Marlowe was watching the King play solitaire. There was a tension in the sultry air settling the camp from the moonless sky. Even the constant scratchings from beneath the hut were hushed.

'I wish he'd get here if he's coming,' Peter Marlowe said.

'I wish we knew what the hell happened with Cheng San. Least the son of a bitch could've done was to send us word.' The King glanced out of his window towards the wire for the thousandth time. He was seeking a sign from the guerrillas that should be there—must be there! But there was no movement, no sign. The jungle, like the camp, drooped and was still.

Peter Marlowe winced as he flexed the fingers of his left hand and moved his aching arm into a more comfortable position.

The King looked back. 'How's it feel?'

'Hurts like hell, old chum.'

'You should get it looked at.'

'I'm on sick call tomorrow.'

'Lousy piece of luck.'

'Accidents happen. Nothing you can do about it.'

It had happened two days previously. On the wood detail. One moment Peter Marlowe had been straining in the swamp against the weight of the fanged tree stump, hauling it with twenty other sweating pairs of hands into the trailer, and the next moment the hands had slipped and his arm had been caught between the stump and the trailer. He had felt the ironhard barbs of wood rip deep into his arm muscle, the weight of the tree stump almost crushing his bones, and he had screamed in agony.

It had taken minutes for the others to lift the stump and pull his numbed arm free and lay him on the earth, his blood weeping into swamp-ooze—the flies and bugs and insects swarming, frantic with the bloodsweet smell. The wound was six inches long and two wide and deep in parts. They had pulled out most of the root daggers from the wound and poured water over it and cleaned it as best they could. They had put on a tourniquet, then fought the tree stump onto the trailer and laboured it home to Changi. He had walked beside the trailer, faint with nausea.

Dr Kennedy had looked at the wound and doused it with iodine while Steven held his good hand and he was starched with pain. Next the doctor had put a little zinc ointment on part of the wound, and grease on the rest to stop the clotting blood from melding with the dressing. Then the doctor had bandaged the arm.

'You're bloody lucky, Marlowe,' he said. 'No bones broken and the muscles are undamaged. More or less just a flesh wound. Come back in a couple of days and we'll take another look at it.'

The King looked up sharply from the cards as Max hurried into the hut.

'Trouble,' Max said, his voice low and strained. 'Grey's just left the hospital, heading this way.'

'Keep him tailed, Max. Better send Dino.'

'Okay.' Max hurried out.

'What do you think, Peter?'

'If Grey's out of the hospital, he must know, something's up.'

'He knows, all right.'

'What?'

'Sure. He has a stoolie in the hut.'

'My God. Are you sure?'

'Yes. And I know who.'

The King put a black four on a red five and the red five on a black six and cleared another ace.

296

'Who is it?'

'I'm not telling you, Peter.' The King smiled hard. 'Better you don't know. But Grey has a man here.'

'What are you going to do about it?'

'Nothing. Yet. Maybe later I'll feed him to the rats.' Then the King smiled and changed the subject. 'Now the Farm was one helluva'n idea, wasn't it?'

Peter Marlowe wondered what he would do if he knew who it was. He knew that Yoshima had a plant too, somewhere in the camp, the one who gave old Daven away, the one who had not been caught yet, who was still unknown—the one who was looking for the bottled radio right now. He thought the King was wise to conceal the knowledge, then there would be no slip-up, and he did not resent that the King did not tell him who it was. But even so, he examined possibilities.

'Do you really think,' he asked, that the—meat'll be all right?'

'Hell, I don't know,' the King said. 'Whole idea's sickening when you think about it. But—and it's a big but—business is business. With the twist we got, it's a genius idea!'

Peter Marlowe smiled and forgot the hurt of his arm. 'Don't forget. I get the first leg.'

'Anyone I know?'

'No.'

The King laughed: 'You wouldn't hold out on your buddy?'

'I'll tell you when delivery's made.'

'When it comes right down to it, meat's meat and food's food. Take the dog, for instance.'

'I saw Hawkins a day or so ago.'

'What happened?'

'Nothing. I certainly didn't want to say anything and he didn't want to talk about it.'

'He's on the ball, that guy. What's over's over.' Then the King said uneasily, tossing the cards on the table, 'I wish Shagata'd get here.'

Tex peered through the window. 'Hey!'

'Yeah?'

'Timsen says the owner's getting panicky. How long you going to wait?'

'I'll go see him.' The King slipped out of the window and whispered. 'You watch the shop, Peter. I won't be far away.'

297

'All right,' Peter Marlowe said. He picked up the cards and began to shuffle them, shuddering as the ache rose and fell and rose again.

The King kept to the shadows, feeling many eyes on him. Some were the eyes of his guards and the rest were alien and hostile. When he found Timsen, the Aussie was in a sweat.

'Hey, cobber. I can't keep him here forever.'

'Where is he?'

'When your contact arrives, I produce him. That's the deal. He ain't far away.'

'You better keep your eye on him. You don't want him knocked off, do you?'

'You stick to your end, I'll stick to mine. He's well guarded.' Timsen sucked on his Kooa, then passed it over to the King, who took a drag.

'Thanks.' The King nodded up towards the jail wall, east. 'You know about them?'

''Course.' The Aussie laughed. 'Tell you another thing. Grey's on his way down here right now. Whole area's lousy with cops and bushwackers. I know of one Aussie gang, and I hear there's another that's got wind of the deal. But my cobbers've got the area taped. Soon as we get the money, you get the diamond.'

'We'll give the guard another ten minutes. If he doesn't arrive then we'll plan again. Same plan, different details.'

'Right, mate. I'll see you after grub tomorrow.'

'Let's hope it's tonight.'

But it was not that night. They waited, and still Shagata did not arrive, so the King called off the operation.

The next day Peter Marlowe joined the swarm of men waiting outside the hospital. It was after lunch and the sun tormented the air and the earth and the creatures of the earth. Even the flies were somnambulant. He found a patch of shade and squatted heavily in the dust and began to wait. The throb of his arm had worsened.

It was after dusk when his turn came.

Dr Kennedy nodded briefly to Peter Marlowe and indicated for him to sit. 'How're you today?' he said absently.

'Not too bad, thank you.'

Dr Kennedy leaned forward and touched the bandage. Peter Marlowe screamed.

'What the devil's the matter?' Dr Kennedy said angrily. 'I hardly touched you, for God's sake!'

'I don't know. The slightest touch hurts like bloody hell.'

Dr Kennedy stuck a thermometer in Peter Marlowe's mouth and then set the metronome clicking and took his pulse. Abnormal, pulse rate ninety. Bad. Temperature normal, and that was also bad. He lifted the arm and sniffed the bandage. It had a distinct mousy odour. Bad.

'All right,' he said, 'I'm going to take the bandage off. Here.' He gave Peter Marlowe a small piece of tyre rubber which he picked out of the sterilizing fluid with a pair of surgical tongs. 'Bite on this. I can't help hurting you.'

He waited until Peter Marlowe had put the rubber between his teeth, then as gently as he could, he began unwinding the bandage. But it was clotted to the wound and now part of the wound and the only thing to do was rip, and he was not as deft as he should be and once was.

Peter Marlowe had known a lot of pain. And when you know a thing, intimately, you know its limitations and its colour and its moods. With practice—and courage—you can let yourself slip into pain and then the pain is not bad, only a welling, controllable. Sometimes it is even good.

But this pain was beyond agony.

'Oh God,' Peter Marlowe whimpered through the rubber bite-piece, tears streaming, his breathing sporadic.

'It's over now,' Dr Kennedy said, knowing that it was not. But there was nothing more he could do, nothing. Not here. Certainly the patient should have morphine, any fool knows that, but I can't afford a shot. 'Now let's have a look.'

He studied the open wound carefully. It was puffy and swollen and there were shades of yellow hue with purple patches. Mucoused.

'Hum,' he said speculatively and leaned back and played with his fingers, making a steeple and looking away from the wound to the steeple. 'Well,' he said at length, 'we have three alternatives.' He got up and began pacing, stoop-shouldered, and then said monotonously, as though delivering a lecture, 'The wound has now taken on other attributes. Clostridial myositis. Or, to put it more simply, the wound is gangrenous. Gas gangrenous. I can lay open the wound and excise the infected tissue, but I don't think that will do, for the infection is deep. So I would have to take out part of the forearm muscles and then the hand won't be of use anyway. The best solution would be to amputate—'

'What!'

'Assuredly.' Dr Kennedy was not talking to a patient, he was only giving a lecture in the sterile classroom of his mind. 'I propose a high guillotine amputation. Immediately. Then perhaps we can save the eblow joint—'

Peter Marlowe burst out desperately, 'It's just a flesh wound. There's nothing wrong with it, it's just a flesh wound!'

The fear of his voice brought Dr Kennedy back, and he looked at the white face a moment. 'It *is* a flesh wound, but very deep. And you've got toxaemia. Look, my boy, it's quite simple. If I had a serum I could give it to you, but I haven't got any. If I had sulphonamides I could put them on the wound, but I haven't got any. The only thing I can do is amputate—'

'You must be out of your mind!' Peter Marlowe shouted at him. 'You talk about amputating my arm when I've only got a flesh wound.'

The doctor's hand snaked out and Peter Marlowe shrieked as the fingers held his arm far above the wound.

'There you see! That's not *just* a flesh wound. You've got toxaemia and it'll spread up your arm and into your system. If you want to live we'll have to cut it off. At least it'll save your life!'

'You're not cutting off my arm!'

'Please yourself. It's that or—' The doctor stopped and sat down wearily. 'I suppose it is your privilege if you want to die. Can't say I blame you. But my God, boy, don't you realize what I'm trying to tell you! You *will* die if we *don't* amputate.'

'You're not going to touch me!' Peter Marlowe's lips were drawn from his teeth and he knew he'd kill the doctor if he touched him again. 'You're out of your mind!' he shouted. 'It's a flesh wound.'

'All right. Don't believe me. We'll ask another doctor.'

Kennedy called another doctor and he confirmed the diagnosis and Peter Marlowe knew that the nightmare was not a dream. He did have gangrene. Oh my God! The fear washed his strength away. He listened, terrified. They explained that the gangrene was caused by bacilli multiplying deep down in his arm, breeding death, right now. His arm was a cancerous thing. It had to be cut off. Cut off to the elbow. It had to be cut off soon or the entire arm would have to be removed. But he wasn't to worry. It wouldn't hurt. They had plenty of ether now—not like the old days.

And then Peter Marlowe was outside the hospital, his arm still on him—bacilli breeding—tied with a clean bandage, and he was groping his way down the hill, for he had told them, the doctors, that he would have to think this over . . . Think what over? What was there to think? He found himself outside the American hut and he saw that the King was alone in the hut and all was prepared for Shagata's coming—if he came that night.

'Jesus, what's with you, Peter?'

The King listened, his dismay growing as the story spilled out.

'Christ!' He stared at the arm, which rested on the table.

'I swear to God I'd rather die than live a cripple. I swear to God!' Peter Marlowe looked up at the King, pathetic, unguarded, and out of his eyes came a scream: *Help, help, for the love of God, help*!

And the King thought, Holy cow, what would I do if I was Peter and that was my arm, and what about the diamond—got to have Peter to help there, got to . . .

'Hey,' whispered Max urgently from the doorway. 'Shagata's on his way.'

'All right, Max. What about Grey?'

'He's down by the wall under cover. Timsen knows about him. His Aussies're covering.'

'Good, beat it and get ready. Spread the word.'

'Okay,' Max hurried away.

'Come on, Peter, we got to get ready,' the King said.

But Peter Marlowe was in shock. Useless.

'Peter!' The King shook him roughly 'Get up and get with it!' he grated. 'Come on. You've got to help. *Get up*!'

He jerked Peter Marlowe to his feet.

'Christ, what—'

'Shagata's coming. We've got to finish the deal.'

301

'To hell with your deal!' Peter Marlowe screamed, brinked on insanity. 'To hell with the diamond! They're going to cut off my arm.'

'No, they're not!'

'You're goddam right they're not. I'm going to die first—'

The King back handed him hard, then slapped him viciously.

The raving stopped abruptly and Peter Marlowe shook his head. 'What the hell—'

'Shagata's coming. We got to get ready.'

'He's coming?' Peter Marlowe asked blankly, his face burning from the blows.

'Yes.' The King saw that Peter Marlowe's eyes were once more guarded and he knew that the Englishman was back in the world. 'Jesus,' he said, weak with relief. 'I had to do something, Peter, you were shouting your head off.'

'Was I? Oh, sorry, what a fool.'

'You all right now? You got to keep your wits about you.'

'I'm all right now.'

Peter Marlowe slipped through the window after the King. And he was glad of the shaft of pain that soared up his arm as his feet hit the ground. You panicked, you fool, he told himself. You, Marlowe, you panicked like a child. Fool. So you have to lose your arm. You're lucky it's not a leg, then you'd really be crippled. What's an arm? Nothing. You can get an artificial one. Sure. With a hook. Nothing wrong with a false arm. Nothing. Could be quite a good idea. Certainly.

'Tabe,' Shagato greeted them as he ducked under the flap of canvas which shielded the overhang.

'Tabe,' said the King and Peter Marlowe.

Shagata was very nervous. The more he had thought about this deal the less he liked it. Too much money, too much risk. And he sniffed the air like a dog pointing. 'I smell danger,' he said.

'He says, "I can smell danger."'

'Tell him not to worry, Peter. I know about the danger and it's taken care of. But what about Cheng San?'

'I tell thee,' Shagata whispered hurriedly, 'that the gods smile upon thee and me and our friend. He is a fox, that one, for the pestilential police let him out of their trap.' The sweat was running down his face and soaking him. 'I have the money.'

302

The King's stomach turned over. 'Tell him we'd better dispense with the yak and get with it. I'll be right back with the goods.'

The King found Timsen in the shadows.

'Ready?'

'Ready.' Timsen whistled a bird call in the dark. Almost at once it was answered. 'Do it fast, mate. I can't guarantee to hold you safe for long.'

'Okay.' The King waited and out of the darkness came a lean Aussie corporal.

'Hi, cobber. Name's Townsend. Bill Townsend.'

'Come on.'

The King hurried back to the overhang while Timsen kept guard and his Aussies fanned out ready for the escape route.

Down by the corner of the jail, Grey was waiting impatiently, Dino had just whispered in his ear that Shagata had arrived, but Grey knew that the preliminaries would take a while. A while, and then he could move.

Smedly-Taylor's phalanx was ready too, waiting for the transfer to take place. Once Grey was in motion, they too would move.

The King was under the flap with Townsend nervously beside him.

'Show him the diamond,' the King ordered.

Townsend opened his ragged shirt and pulled out a cord and on the end of the cord was the diamond ring. Townsend was trembling as he showed it to Shagata, who focused his portable lamp on the stone. Shagata examined it carefully, a bead of ice-light on the end of a piece of string. Then he took it and scratched the glass surface of the lamp. It screetched and left its mark.

Shagata nodded, sweating. 'Very well.' He turned to Peter Marlowe. 'Truly it is a diamond,' he said and took out calipers and carefully measured the extent of the stone. Again he nodded. 'Truly it is four carats.'

The King jerked his head. 'All right. Peter, you wait with Townsend.'

Peter Marlowe got up and beckoned to Townsend and together they went outside the flap and waited in the darkness. And around them they could feel eyes. Hundreds of eyes.

'Bloody hell,' Townsend winced, 'wish I'd never got the stone. The strain's killing me, my bloody oath.' His palsied fingers played with the string and the jewel, making sure for the millionth time that it was around his neck. 'Thank God this's the last night.'

The King watched with increasing excitement as Shagata opened his ammunition pouch and planked down three inches of notes, and opened his shirt and brought out a two-inch bundle, and from his side pockets more bundles until there were two piles of notes, each six inches high. Rapidly the King started counting the notes, and Shagata made a quick nervous bow and left. He pushed past the flap, and when he was once more on the path he felt safer. He adjusted his rifle and began to walk the camp and almost knocked down Grey, who was coming up fast.

Grey cursed and hurried past, ignoring the torrent of abuse from Shagata. This time Shagata did not run after the bastard stinking POW as he should and beat some courtesy into him, for he was thankful to be away and anxious to get back to his post.

'Cops,' Max whispered urgently outside the flap.

The King scooped up the notes and tore out of the overhang, whispering to Townsend as he ran, 'Get lost. Tell Timsen I've the money now and we'll pay off tonight when the heat's off.'

Townsend vanished.

'Come on, Peter.'

The King led the way under the hut as Grey rounded the corner.

'Stay where you are, you two!' Grey shouted.

'Yes, sir!' Max called grandly from the shadows and moved in the way, Tex beside him, covering the King and Peter Marlowe.

'Not you two.' Grey tried to push past.

'But you wanted us to stop—' began Max easily, moving back in Grey's way.

Grey shoved past furiously and darted under the hut in pursuit.

The King and Peter Marlowe had already jumped into the slit trench and were up the other side. Another group ran interferences as Grey ran after them.

Grey spotted them tearing down the jail wall and blew his

whistle, alerting the MP's already stationed. The MP's moved out into the open and guarded the area from jail wall to jail wall, and from jail wall to barbed fence.

'This way,' the King said as he jumped through the window of Timsen's hut. No one in the hut paid any attention to them, but many saw the bulge in the King's shirt.

They raced through the hut and out the door. Another group of Aussies appeared and covered their retreat just as Grey panted up to the window and caught a fleeting glimpse of them. He rushed around the hut. The Aussies had covered their exit.

Grey called out abruptly, 'Which way did they go? Come on! *Which way?*'

A chorus of 'Who?' 'Who, sir?'

Grey pushed his way through them and hurried into the open.

'Everyone's in position, sir,' an MP said, running up to him.

'Good. They can't get far. And they won't dare dump the money. We'll start moving in on them. Tell the others.'

The King and Peter Marlowe ran towards the north end of the jail and stopped.

'Goddam it to hell!' the King said.

Where there should have been a phalanx of Aussies to run interference for them, now there were only MPs. Five of them.

'What next?' Peter Marlowe said.

'We'll have to backtrack, C'mon!'

Moving quickly, the King asked himself, What the hell's gone wrong? Then suddenly he found it. Four men blocked their run. They had handkerchiefs over their faces and heavy sticks in their hands.

'Better hand over the money, mate, if you don't want to get hurt.'

The King feinted, then charged, with Peter Marlowe at his side. The King ploughed into one man and kicked another in the groin. Peter Marlowe blocked a blow, biting back a scream as it glanced off his arm, and tore the stick out of the man's grasp. The other bushwhacker took to his heels and was swallowed by the darkness.

'Chrissake,' the King panted, 'let's get out of here.'

Again they were off. They could feel eyes following them and any moment they expected another attack. The King skidded to a stop.

'Look out! Grey!'

They turned back, and keeping to the side of a hut, ducked underneath it. They lay for a moment, their chests heaving. Feet ran past and they heard snatches of angry whispers—

'They went that way. Got t' get 'em before the stinking cops.'

'The whole goddam camp's after us,' the King said.

'Let's stick the money here,' Peter Marlowe said helplessly. 'We can bury it.'

'Too risky. They'd find it in a minute. Goddammit, everything was going fine. Except that bastard Timsen let us down.' The King wiped the dirt and sweat off his face. 'Ready?'

Which way?'

The King did not answer. He just crawled silently from under the hut and ran with the shadows, Peter Marlowe following close behind. He headed sure-footed across the path and jumped into the deep storm ditch beside the wire. He squirmed his way down it until they were almost opposite the American hut and stopped and leaned against the wall of the ditch, his breath fluttering. Around them was a whispered uproar and over them was a whispered uproar.

'What's up?'

'The King's on the run with Marlowe—they've got thousands of dollars with them.'

'The hell they have! Quick, maybe we can catch them.'

'Come on!'

'We'll get the money.'

And Grey was getting reports and so was Smedly-Taylor and so was Timsen and the reports were confusing and Timsen was cursing and hissing at his men to find them before Grey or Smedly-Taylor's men found them.

'Get that money!'

Smedley-Taylor's men were waiting, watching Timsen's Aussies, and they were confused too. Which way did they go? Where to look?

And Grey was waiting. He knew that both escapes were blocked, north and south. It was only a question of time. And now the search was closing. Grey knew he had them, and when he caught them they would have the money. They wouldn't dare let go of it, not now. It was too much money. But Grey didn't know about Smedly-Taylor's men or Timsen's Aussies.

'Look,' Peter Marlowe said as he carefully lifted his head and peered around into the darkness.

The King's eyes narrowed, searching. Then he saw the MP's fifty yards away. He spun around. there were many other ghosts, hurrying, looking, searching. 'We've had it,' he said frantically.

Then the King looked out, over the wire. The jungle was dark. And there was a guard plodding along the other side of the wire. Okay, he told himself. The last plan. The shit-or-bust plan.

'Here,' he said urgently, and he took out all the money and stuffed it into Peter Marlowe's pockets. 'I'll cover for you. Go through the wire. It's our only chance.'

'Christ, I'll never make it. The guard'll spot me—'

'Go on, it's our only chance!'

'I'll never make it. Never.'

'When you get through, bury it and come back the same way. I'll cover for you. Goddammit, you've got to go.'

'For God's sake, I'll get killed. He's not fifty feet away,' Peter Marlowe said. 'We'll have to give up!'

He looked around, wildly seeking another escape route, and the sudden careless movement slammed his forgotten arm against the wall of the drain and he groaned, agonized.

'You save the money, Peter!' the King said desperately, 'and I'll save your arm.'

'You'll what?'

'You heard me! Beat it!'

'But how can you—'

'Beat it,' the King interrupted harshly. '*If* you save the dough.'

Peter Marlowe stared for an instant into the eyes of the King, then he slipped out of the trench and ran for the wire and slid under it, every moment expecting a bullet in his head. At the second of his dash, the King jumped out of the trench and whirled towards the path. He tripped deliberately and slammed down into the dust with a shout of rage. The guard glanced abruptly through the wire and laughed loudly, and when he

307

turned back to his post, he saw only a shadow which might have been anything. Certainly not a man.

Peter Marlowe was hugging the earth and he crawled like a thing of the jungle into the dank vegetation and held his breath and froze. The guard came closer and closer and then his foot was an inch away from Peter Marlowe's hand and then the other foot straddled it a pace away, and when the guard was five paces away, Peter Marlowe slithered deeper into the brush, into the darkness, five, ten, twenty, thirty, and when he was forty paces away and safe, his heart seemed to begin again and he had to stop, stop for breath, stop for his heart, stop for the hurt of his arm, the arm that was going to be his once more. If the King said—it *was*.

So he lay on the earth and prayed for breath and prayed for life and prayed for strength and prayed for the King.

The King breathed now that Peter Marlowe had made it to the jungle. He got up and began to brush himself down, and Grey with an MP, was beside him.

'Stand where you are.'

'Who, me?' The King pretended to peer into the darkness and recognize Grey. 'Oh, it's you. Good evening, Captain Grey.' He shoved the MP's restraining arm away. 'Take your hands off me!'

'You're under arrest,' said Grey, sweating and dirt-covered from the chase.

'For what? Captain.'

'Search him, Sergeant.'

The King submitted calmly. Now that the money wasn't on him there was nothing that Grey could do. Nothing.

'Nothing on him, sir,' the MP said.

'Search the ditch.' Then, to the King: 'Where's Marlowe?'

'Who?' asked the King blandly.

'Marlowe!' Grey shouted. No money on this swine and no Marlowe!

'Probably taking a walk, Sir.' The King was polite, and his mind was centred only on Grey and the present danger, for he could sense that the danger was not completely past and that beside the jail wall were a group of malevolent ghosts, watching him for an instant before they disappeared.

'Where did you put the money?' Grey was saying.

'What money?'

'The money from the sale of the diamond.'

'What diamond? Sir!'

Grey knew he was beaten for the moment. He was beaten unless he could find Marlowe with the money on him. All right, you bastard, Grey thought, beside himself with rage, all right, I'll let you go, but I'll watch you and you'll lead me to Marlowe.

'That's all for the moment,' Grey said. 'You've beaten us this time. But there'll be another.'

The King walked back to his hut, chuckling to himself. You think I'm going to lead you to Peter, don't you, Grey? But you're so goddam smart you're naïve.

Inside the hut, he found Max and Tex. They too were sweating.

'What happened?' said Max.

'Nothing. Max, go find Timsen. Tell him to wait under the window. I'll talk to him there. Tell him not to come into the hut. Grey's still watching us.'

'Okay.'

The King put the coffee on. His mind was working now. How to make the exchange? Where to make it? What to do about Timsen? How to draw Grey off from Peter?

'You wanted me, mate?'

The King didn't turn to the window. He simply looked down the hut. The Americans got the message and left him alone. He watched Dino leave and returned Dino's twisted smile.

'Timsen?' he said, busying himself with the coffee.

'Yes, mate?'

'I ought to cut your goddam throat.'

'It wasn't my fault, cobber. Something went wrong—'

'Yeah. You wanted the money and the diamond.'

'No harm in trying, cobber.' Timsen chuckled. 'It won't happen again.'

'You're goddamned right.' The King liked Timsen. Lot on the ball. And no harm in trying, not when the stakes are so high. And he needed Timsen. 'We'll make the transfer during the day. Then there won't be any "slip-ups". I'll send you word when.'

'Right, cobber. Where's the Pommy?'

'What Pommy?'

Timsen laughed. 'See yer tomorrow!'

The King drank his coffee and called Max to guard the fort. Then he jumped cautiously out of the window, darted into the shadows and made his way carefully to the jail wall. He was careful not to be observed, but not too careful, and he laughed to himself as he felt Grey following. He pretended well, back-tracking through the huts and dodging this way and that. Grey relentlessly dogged his footsteps, and the King led him up to the jail gate and through the gate into the cellblocks. Finally the King headed for the cell on the fourth floor and pretended to increase his concern as he went into the cell and left the door half ajar. Every quarter hour or so he'd open the door and peer anxiously around, and this went on until Tex arrived.

'All clear,' Tex said.

'Good.'

Peter was back and safe and there was no need to keep up the pretence, so he returned to his hut and winked at Peter Marlowe. 'Where you been?'

'Thought I'd see how you were getting on.'

'Like some Java?'

'Thanks.'

Grey stood in the doorway. He said nothing, just looked. Peter Marlowe was wearing only his sarong. No pockets in a sarong. His armband was on his shoulder.

Peter Marlowe lifted the cup to his lips and drank the coffee and his eyes were locked on Grey and then Grey disappeared into the night.

Peter Marlowe got up exhaustedly. 'Think I'll turn in now.'

'I'm proud of you, Peter.'

'You meant what you said, didn't you?'

'Sure.'

'Thanks.'

That night the King was worrying about a new problem. How in the hell could he do what he had said he would do?

310

XX

Larkin was deeply troubled as he strode up the path towards the Aussie hut. He was worried about Peter Marlowe—his arm seemed to be troubling him more than somewhat, hurting too much to be brushed off as just a flesh wound. He was worried too about old Mac. Last night Mac'd been talking and screaming in his sleep. And he was worried about Betty. Had bad dreams himself the last few nights, all twisted up, Betty and him, with other men in bed with her, and him watching and her laughing at him.

Larkin entered the hut and went over to Townsend, who was lying in his bunk.

Townsend's eyes were puffed and closed and his face was scratched and his arms and chest were bruised and scratched. When he opened his mouth to answer, Larkin saw the bloody gap where teeth should have been.

'Who did it, Townsend?'

'Don't know,' Townsend whimpered. 'I wuz bushwhacked.'

'Why?'

Tears welled and dirtied the bruises. 'I'd—I'd a—nothing—nothing. I don't—know.'

'We're alone, Townsend. Who did it?'

'I don't know.' A sobbing moan burst from Townsend's lips. 'Oh Christ, they hurt me, hurt me.'

'Why were you bushwhacked?'

'I—I—' Townsend wanted to shout, 'The diamond, I had the diamond,' and he wanted the colonel's help to get the bastards who'd stolen it from him. But he couldn't tell about the dia-

311

mond, for then the colonel'd want to know where he'd got it and then he'd have to say from Gurble. An' then there'd be questions about Gurble, where had *he* got it from—Gurble? The suicide? Then maybe they'd say that it wasn't suicide, it were murder, but it weren't, least, he, Townsend, didn't think so, but who knows, maybe someone did Gurble in for the diamond. But that particular night Gurble was away from his bunk and I'd felt the outline of the diamond ring in his mattress and slipped it out and took off into the night and who could prove anythin'—and Gurble happened to suicide that night so there weren't no harm. Except that maybe I murdered Gurble, murdered him by stealing the stone, maybe that was the final straw for Gurble, being kicked out of the unit for stealing rations and then having the diamond stole. Maybe that'd put him off his head, poor bastard, an' make him jump into the borehole! But stealing rations didn't make sense, not when a man's a diamond to sell. No sense. No sense at all. Except that maybe I was the cause of Gurble's death and I curse myself, again and again, for stealing the diamond. Since I become a thief I got no peace, no peace, no peace. An' now, now I'm glad, glad that it's gone from me, stolen from me.

'I don't know,' Townsend sobbed.

Larkin saw that it was no use and left Townsend to his pain.

'Oh, sorry, Father,' Larkin said, as he almost bumped Father Donovan down the hut steps.

'Hello, old friend.' Father Donovan was wraithlike, impossibly emaciated, his eyes deepset and strangely peaceful. 'How are you? And Mac? And young Peter?'

'Fine, thanks.' Larkin nodded back towards Townsend. 'Do you know anything about this?'

Donovan looked at Townsend and replied gently, 'I see a man in pain.'

'Sorry, I shouldn't have asked.' Larkin thought a moment, smiled. 'Would you like a game of bridge? Tonight? After supper?'

'Yes. Thank you. I'd like that.'

'Good. After supper.'

Father Donovan watched Larkin walk away and then went over to Townsend's bed. Townsend was not a Catholic. But Father Donovan gave of himself to all, for he knew that all men

312

are children of God. But are they, all of them? he asked himself in wonder. Could children of God do such things?

At noon the wind and the rain came together. Soon everything and everyone was drenched. Then the rain stopped and the wind continued. Pieces of thatch ripped away and whirled across the camp, mixing with loose fronds and rags and coolie hats. Then the wind stopped and the camp was normal with sun and heat and flies. Water in the storm channels gushed for half an hour, then began to sink into the earth and stagnate. More flies gathered.

Peter Marlowe wandered up the hill listlessly. His feet were mud-stained like his legs, for he had let the tempest surround him, hoping that the wind and the rain would take away the brooding hurt. But they had not touched him.

He stood outside the King's window and peered in.

'How do you feel, Peter, buddy?' the King asked as he got up from his bed and found a pack of Kooas.

'Awful.' Peter Marlowe sat on the bench under the overhang, nauseated from the pain. 'My arm's killing me.' His laugh was brittle. 'Joke!'

The King jumped down and forced a smile. 'Forget it—'

'How the hell can I forget it?' Immediately Peter Marlowe regretted the outburst. 'Sorry. I'm jumpy. Don't know what I'm saying half the time.'

'Have a cigarette.' The King lit it for him. Yep, the King told himself, you're in a spot. The Limey learns fast, very fast. At least I think so. Let's see. 'We'll complete the deal tomorrow. You can get the money tonight. I'll cover for you.'

But Peter Marlowe didn't hear him. His arm was burning a word into his brain. Amputate! And he could hear the saw shrieking and feel it cutting, grinding bone-dust, *his* bone-dust. A shudder racked him. 'What—about this?' he muttered and looked up from his arm. 'Can you really do something?'

The King nodded and told himself, There, you see. You were right. Only Pete knows where the money is, but Pete won't get the money until you've set up the cure. No cure, no dough. No dough, no sale. No sale, no loot. So he sighed and said to himself, Yes, you're pretty smart cookie to know men so well. But when you figure it right, like you did last night, it wasn't a

313

bad trade. If Pete hadn't taken the chance we'd both be in jail with no money and no nothing. And Pete had brought them luck. The deal was better than ever. And apart from that, Pete's all right. A good guy. And hell, who wants to lose an arm anyway. Pete's got a right to put the pressure on. I'm glad he's learned.

'Leave it to Uncle Sam!'

'Who?'

'Uncle Sam?' The King stared at him blankly. 'The American symbol. You know,' he said exasperatedly, 'like John Bull.'

'Oh, sorry. I'm just—today—I'm just—' A wave of nausea surged over Peter Marlowe.

'You beat it back to your bunk and relax. I'll take care of it.'

Peter Marlowe got up unsteadily. He wanted to smile and thank the King and shake his hand and bless him, but he remembered the word, and he felt only the saw, so he half nodded and walked out of the hut.

For Chrissake, the King told himself bitterly. He thinks I'd let him down, that I wouldn't do nothin', unless he had the screws on me. Chrissake, Peter, I would help. Sure. Even though you didn't have me by the shorts. Hell. You're my friend.

'Hey, Max.'

'Yeah.'

'Get Timsen here on the double.'

'Sure,' Max said and left.

The King unlocked the black box and took out three eggs. 'Tex. You like to cook yourself an egg? Along with these two?'

'Hell no,' Tex said, grinning, and he took the eggs. 'Hey, I took a look at Eve. Swear to God she's fatter today.'

'Impossible. She was only mated yesterday.'

Tex danced a little jig. 'Twenty days an' we're all daddies again.' He accepted the oil and headed outside for the cooking area.

The King lay back on his bunk, scratching a mosquito bite thoughtfully and watching the lizards on the rafters hunt and fornicate. He closed his eyes and began to drowse contentedly. Here it was only twelve o'clock, and already he'd done a hard day's work. Hell, everything'd been sewn up by six o'clock this morning.

He chuckled to himself as he remembered. Yes sir, it pays to have a good reputation and it pays to advertise . . .

It had happened just before dawn. He had been soft asleep. Then a cautious, muted voice had interrupted his dreams.

He awoke at once and looked out of the window and had seen a little weasel of a man staring at him in the shadowed contrails of the dawn. A man he had never seen before.

'Yeah?'

'I got somethin' yer wanter buy.' The man's voice had been expressionless and hoarse.

'Who're you?'

In answer the little man had opened his grimy fist with its broken, dirt-flecked finger nails. The diamond ring was in his palm. 'Price's ten thousand. For a quick sale,' he added sardonically. Then the fingers had snapped tight as the King moved to pick the ring up, and the fist was withdrawn. 'Tonight.' The man had smiled toothlessly. 'It's the right one, never fear.'

'Are you the owner?'

'It's in me 'and, ain't it?'

'It's a deal. What time?'

'You wait in. I'll see yer when there ain't no narks abart.'

And the man had gone as suddenly as he had appeared.

The King settled more comfortably, gloating. Poor Timsen, he told himself, that poor son of a bitch's got egg on his face! I get the ring for half price.

'Morning, cobber,' Timsen said. 'You wanted me?'

The King opened his eyes and covered a yawn with his hand as Tiny Timsen walked up the hut.

'Hi.' The King swung his legs off the bed and stretched luxuriously. 'Tired today. Too much excitement. You want an egg? Got a couple cooking.'

'Too right I'd like an egg.'

'Make yourself at home.' The King could afford to be hospitable. 'Now let's get down to business. We'll close the deal this afternoon.'

'Na.' Timsen shook his head. 'Not t'day. Tomorrer.'

The King was hard put not to beam.

'The heat'll be off by then,' Timsen was saying. 'Hear that Grey's got himself out've hospital. He'll be eyeing this place.' Timsen seemed gravely concerned. 'We got to watch out. You

315

an' me. Don't want anything to go wrong. I got to watch out for you, too. Don't forget we're cobbers.'

'To hell with tomorrow,' the King said, feigning disappointment. 'Let's do it this afternoon.'

And he listened, shouting with laugher inside, listened while Timsen said how important it was to be careful: the owner's scared, why he even got beat up last night, and why, it wuz only me and my men what saved the poor bastard. So the King knew for sure then that Timsen was bleeding, that the diamond had slipped through his slimy mitts, that he was playing for time. Why, I'll bet, the King told himself ecstatically, that the Aussies are going out of their skulls trying to find the hijacker. I wouldn't like to be him—if they find him. So he allowed himself to be persuaded. Just in case Timsen did find the guy and the original deal stood.

'Well, okay,' the King said grudgingly. 'I suppose you got a point. We'll make it tomorrow.' He lit another cigarette and took a drag and passed it over and said sweetly, still playing the game: 'On these hot nights few of my boys sleep. At least four of them are up. All night.'

Timsen understood the threat. But he had other things on his mind. Who, for the love uv God, who bushwhacked Townsend? He prayed that his men would find the buggers quick. He knew he had to find the bushwhackers before they got to the King with the diamond, for then he'd be out of luck. 'I know how it is. Just the same with my boys—lucky they're so close to my poor old pal Townsend.' Stupid bastard. How in the hell could a bugger be so weak as to allow himself to be jumped and not holler afore it was too late? 'Man can't be too careful these days, either.'

Tex brought in the eggs and the three men ate them with lunch-rice, and washed it all down with strong coffee. By the time Tex took out the dishes, the King had the conversation just where he wanted it.

'I know a guy who's in the market for some drugs.'

Timsen shook his head. 'He's got an 'ope, poor bastard. Ain't possible! Too right.' Ah, he thought. Drugs! Who'd that be for? Not the King, certainly. He looks healthy enough, an' not for resale either. The King never deals in drugs, which is all right, for that leaves the market in my hands. Must be for someone

316

close to the King, though. Otherwise he'd never get involved. Drug trade's not his meat. Old McCoy! Of course. I heard he wasn't so well these days. Maybe the colonel. He ain't been lookin' too well either. 'I heard of a limey who's some quinine. But Jesus wept, he wants a bloody fortune for it.'

'I want some antitoxin. A bottle. And sulphonamide powder.'

Timsen let out a whistle. 'Not an 'ope!' he said. Antitoxin and sulpha! Gangrene! The Pommy. Christ, gangrene! And the whole pattern fell neatly into place. Got to be the Pommy! Not through cunning alone had Timsen cornered the drug market. He knew enough about drugs from civvy street, where he had worked as an assistant druggist, which no bastard but him knew, because then the bastards would've put him in the Medical Corps, and that would've meant no fighting and no killing, and no self-respecting Aussie'd let his country down and dear old Blighty down by being just a stinking noncombatant medical orderly.

'Not an 'ope,' he said again, shaking his head.

'Listen,' the King said. 'I'll level with you.' Timsen was the only man who could get it in the whole world, so he had to get his help. 'It's for Peter.'

'Tough.' Timsen said. But inside he sympathized. Poor bugger. Gangrene. Good man, lots of guts. He still felt the smash the Pommy'd given him last night. When the four of them had fallen on the King and the Pommy.

Timsen had found out about Peter Marlowe when he had been taken up by the King. A man can't be too careful and information's always important. And Timsen knew about the four German planes and about the three Nips, and he knew about the village and how the Pommy'd tried to escape from Java, not like a lot who'd meekly sat and taken it. And yet, when you thought about it, it was pretty stupid to try. So far to go. Yes. Too far. Yes, this Pommy's a beaut.

Timsen wondered if he could risk sending a man into the Japanese doctor's quarters to get drugs. It was risky, but the quarters and the route had been pegged. Poor bugger Marlowe, he must be sick with worry. Of course I'll get the drugs—and it'll be done for free, or just for expenses.

Timsen hated selling drugs, but someone had to, better him

than someone else, for the cost was always reasonable, as reasonable as possible, and he knew he could make a fortune selling to the Japanese, but he never did, only to the camp and really only for a slight profit, when you thought of the risks involved.

'It makes you sick,' Timsen said 'when you think of all those Red Cross medical supplies in the go-down on Kedah Street.'

'Hell, that's a rumour.'

'Oh, no it ain't. I've seen it, mate. On a work party I was. Stashed full of Red Cross stuff—plasma, quinine, sulpha— everything from floor to ceiling and still in their cases. Why, the go-down must be a good hundred yards long and thirty wide. An' it's all going to those bugger Nips.They let the stuff in all right. Comes through Chungking, I'm told. The Red Cross give it to the Siamese—they turn it over to the Nips—all consigned for POW's, Changi. Christ, I've even seen the labels, but the Nips just use it for their own monkeys.'

'Anyone else know about this?'

'I tol' the colonel and he tol' the Camp Commandant, who told that Nip bastard—what's 'is name, oh yus, Yoshima—and the Camp Commandant, see, well, he demanded the supplies. But the Nips just laughed at him and said it was a rumour and that was the last of it. No work parties 'ave ever gone again. Lousy fuggers. Ain't fair, not when we need the drugs so bad. They could give us a little. My cobber died six months back for want of a little insulin—and I saw crates of it. Crates.' Timsen rolled a cigarette and coughed and spat and was so incensed he kicked the wall.

He knew there was no future in getting upset about it. And there was no way to get at *that* go down. But he could get antitoxin and sulpha for the Pommy. Oh, my word, yes—and he'd give it to him for nothing.

But Timsen was much too clever to allow the King to see through him. That would be childish, to let the King know he'd a soft spot, for sure as God's country was Down Under, the King'd use that as a lever sometime later on. Yus, an' he had to have the King for the deal of the diamond. Oh bugger! I'd forgotten about that dirty bushwhacker.

So Timsen named an extortionate figure and allowed himself to be beaten down. But he made the price steep, for he knew the

King could afford it, and if he said he'd get the goods for a low price, the King'd be very suspicious.

'All right,' the King said glumly. 'You got a deal.' Inside he wasn't glum. Not too glum. He'd expected Timsen to soak him, but although the price was higher than he wanted to pay, it was fair.

'It'll take three days,' Timsen said, knowing that three days would be too late.

'I've got to have it tonight.'

'Then it'll cost you another five hundred.'

'I'm a friend of yours!' the King said, feeling real pain. 'We're buddies and you stick me for another five C's.'

'All right, cobber.' Timsen said sad, doglike. 'But you know how it is. Three days is the best I can do.'

'Goddammit. All right.'

'An' the nurse'll be an extra five hundred.'

'For Chrissake! What the hell's the nurse for?'

Timsen enjoyed seeing the King squirm. 'Well,' he said agreeably, 'what're you going to do with the stuff when you've got it? How you going to treat the patient?'

'How the hell do I know?'

'That's what the five hundred's for. I suppose you're going to give the stuff to the Pommy and he's going to take it up to the 'ospital and say to the nearest sawbones, "I got hantitoxin and sulpha, fix my bleedin' arm up," and then the doc's going to say, "We ain't got no hantitoxin so where the 'ell did you get this from?", and when the Pommy won't tell, the bastards'll steal it off him and give it to some stinking Limey colonel who's a slight case of piles.'

He deftly took the packet of cigarettes out of the King's pocket and helped himself. 'And,' he said, but now completely serious, 'you have to find a place where you can treat him private-like. Where he can lie down. These hantitoxins're tough on some men. An' part of the deal's that I accept no responsibility if the treatment turns sour.'

'If you've got antitoxin and sulpha, what can go sour?'

'Some folks can't take it. Nausea. Tough. And it mayn't work. Depends how much of the toxin's already in his system.'

Timsen got up. 'Sometime tonight. Oh yes, an' the equipment'll cost another five hundred.'

The King exploded. 'What equipment, for Chrissake?'

'Hypodermics and bandages and soap. Jesus!' Timsen was almost disgusted. 'You think hantitoxin's a pill you stick up 'is arse?'

The King stared after Timsen sourly, kicking himself. Thought you were so clever, didn't you, finding out what cured gangrene for a cigarette and then, nut-head, you forget to ask what the hell you did with the stuff once you got it.

Well, the hell with it. The dough's committed. And Pete's got his arm back. And the cost's all right too.

Then the King remembered the foxy little hijacker and he beamed. Yes, he felt very pleased with the day's work.

XXI

That evening Peter Marlowe gave his food away. He did not give it to Mac or Larkin as he should, but to Ewart. He knew that if he had given it to his unit they would have forced him to reveal what was the matter. And there was no point in telling them.

That afternoon, sick with pain and worry, he had gone to see Dr Kennedy. Again he had been crazed with agony while the bandage was ripped away. Then the doctor had said simply. 'The poison's above the elbow. I can amputate below, but it's a waste of time. Might as well do the operation in one time. You'll have a nice stump—at least five inches from the shoulder. Enough, for an artificial arm to be strapped to. Quite enough.' Kennedy had templed his fingers calmly. 'Don't waste any more time, Marlowe,' and he had laughed dryly and quipped, 'Domani é troppo tardi,' and when Peter Marlowe had looked at him blankly without understanding, he said flatly, 'Tomorrow may be too late.'

Peter Marlowe had stumbled back to his bunk and had lain in a pool of fear. Then dinner had come and he had given it away.

'You got fever?' Ewart said happily, filled by the extra food.

'No.'

'Can I get you anything?'

'For Christ's sake leave me alone!' Peter Marlowe turned away from Ewart. After a time he got up and left the hut, regretting that he had agreed to play bridge with Mac and Larkin and Father Donovan for an hour or two. You're a fool, he told himself bitterly, you should have stayed in your bunk until it was time to go through the wire to get the money.

321

But he knew that he could not have lain on his bunk, hour after hour, until it was safe to go. Better to have something to do.

'Hi, cobber!' Larkin's face crinkled with his smile.

Peter Marlowe did not return the smile. He just sat grimly in the doorway. Mac glanced at Larkin, who shrugged imperceptibly.

'Peter,' Mac said, forcing good humour, 'the news is better every day, isn't it? Won't be long before we're out of here.'

'Too right!' Larkin said.

'You're living in a fools' paradise. We'll never get out of Changi.' Peter Marlowe did not wish to be harsh, but he could not restrain himself. He knew Mac and Larkin were hurt, but he would do nothing to ease the hurt. He was obsessed with the five-inch stump. A chill dissolved his spine and pierced his testicles. How the hell could the King really help? How? Be realistic. If it was the King's arm—what could I do, however much I'm his friend? Nothing. I don't think there's anything he can do—in time. Nothing. You'd better face it, Peter. It's amputate or die. Simple. And when it comes down to it, you can't die. Not yet. Once you're born, you are obligated to survive. At all costs.

Yes, Peter Marlowe told himself, you'd better be realistic. There's nothing the King can do, nothing. And you shouldn't have put him on the spot. It's your worry, not his. Just get the money and give it to him and go up to the hospital and lie on the table and let them cut your arm off.

So the three of them—he, Mac and Larkin—sat in the fetid night. Silent. When Father Donovan joined them they forced him to eat a little rice and blachang. They made him eat it then, for if they had not, he would have given it away, as he gave away most of his rations.

'You're very kind to me,' Donovan said. His eyes twinkled as he added, 'Now, if you three would see the error of your ways and come over to the right side of the fence, you'd complete my evening.'

Mac and Larkin laughed with him. Peter Marlowe did not laugh.

'What's the matter, Peter?' Larkin said, an edge to his voice. 'You've been like a dingo with a sore arse all evening.'

'No harm in being a little out of sorts,' Donovan said quickly, healing the ragged silence. 'My word, the news is very good, isn't it?'

Only Peter Marlowe was outside the friendship that was in the little room. He knew his presence was suffocating, but there was nothing he could do. Nothing.

The game started, and Father Donovan opened with two spades.

'Pass,' Mac said grumpily.

'Three diamonds,' Peter Marlowe said, and as soon as he had said it he wished he hadn't, for he had stupidly overbid his hand and had said diamonds when he should have said hearts.

'Pass,' Larkin said testily. He was sorry now that he had suggested the game. There was no fun in it. No fun.

'Three spades,' Father Donovan said.

'Pass.'

'Pass,' Peter Marlowe said, and they all looked at him surprised.

Father Donovan smiled. 'You should have more faith—'

'I'm tired of faith.' The words were sudden-raw and very angry.

'Sorry, Peter, I was only—'

'Now look here, Peter,' Larkin interrupted sharply, 'just because you're in a bad humour—'

'I'm entitled to an opinion and I think it was a bad joke,' Peter Marlowe flared. Then he whirled back on Donovan. 'Just because you martyr yourself by giving your food away and sleeping in the men's barracks, I suppose that gives you the right to be *the* authority. Faith's a lot of nothing! Faith's for children—and so is God. What the hell can He do about anything? Really do? Eh? *Eh*?'

Mac and Larkin stared at Peter Marlowe without recognition.

'He can heal,' Father Donovan said, knowing about the gangrene. He knew many things he did not want to know.

Peter Marlowe slammed his cards down on the table. 'Shit!' he shouted, berserk. 'That's shit and you know it. And another thing while we're on the subject. God! You know, *I* think God's a maniac, a sadistic, evil maniac, a bloodsucker—'

'Are you out of your mind, Peter?' Larkin exploded.

'No, I'm not. Look at God,' Peter Marlowe raved, his face

contorted. 'God's nothing but evil—if He really is God. Look at all the bloodshed that's been committed in the name of God.' He shoved his face nearer Donovan's. 'The Inquisition. Remember? All the thousands that were burned and tortured to death in *His* Name? By the Catholic saidsts? And we won't even think about the Aztecs and Incas and the poor bloody Indian millions. And the Protestants burning and killing the Catholics; and the Catholics, the Jews and the Mohammedans; and the Jews, more Jews—and the Mormons and Quakers and the whole stinking mess. Kill, torture, burn! Just so long as it's in the name of God, you're all right. What a lot of hypocrisy! Don't give me faith! It's nothing!'

'And yet you have faith in the King,' Father Donovan said quietly.

'I suppose you're going to say he's an instrument of God?'

'Perhaps he is. I don't know.'

'I must tell him that.' Peter Marlowe laughed hysterically. 'He'd laugh to high heaven.'

'Listen, Marlowe!' Larkin got up, shaking with rage. 'You'd better apologize or get out!'

'Don't worry, *Colonel*,' Peter Marlowe slammed back, 'I'm leaving.' He got up and glared at them, hating them, hating himself. 'Listen, priest. You're a joke. Your skirts're a joke. You're an unholy joke, you and God. You don't serve God because God's the devil. You're the servant of the devil.' And then he scooped up some of the cards off the table and threw them into Father Donovan's face and stormed out into the darkness.

'What in God's name has happened to Peter?' Mac said, shattering the appalled silence.

'In God's name,' Father Donovan said compassionately. 'Peter has gangrene. He has to have his arm amputated or he will die. You could see the scarlet streaks clearly, above his elbow.'

'What?' Larkin stared at Mac, petrified. Then simultaneously they both got up and began hurrying out. But Father Donovan called them back.

'Wait, there's nothing you can do.'

'Dammit, there must be something.' Larkin stood in the doorway. 'The poor lad—and I thought—the poor lad—'

'There's nothing to do, except wait. Except have faith, and pray. Perhaps the King will help, can help.' Then Father Donovan added tiredly, 'The King *is* the only man who can.'

Peter Marlowe stumbled into the American hut. 'I'll get the money now,' he muttered to the King.

'Are you crazy? There's too many people around.'

'To hell with the people,' Peter Marlowe said angrily. Do you want the money or not?'

'Sit down. *Sit down!*' The King forced Peter to sit and gave him a cigarette and forced him to drink coffee and thought, Jesus, what I have to do for a little loot. Patiently he told Peter Marlowe to keep his wits about him, that everything was going to be all right, for the cure was already arranged, and after an hour Peter Marlowe was calmer and at least coherent. But the King knew he was not getting through to him. He saw that he was nodding from time to time but he knew, deep down, that Peter Marlowe was quite beyond him, and if he was beyond him, the King, he was beyond anyone.

'Is it time now?' Peter Marlowe asked, almost blinded with pain, knowing if he did not go now he would never go.

The King knew that it was too early for safety, but he knew too that he could not keep him in the hut any longer. So he sent guards in all directions. The whole area was covered. Max was watching Grey, who was on his bunk. Byron Jones III was watching Timsen. And Timsen was north, by the gate, waiting for the drug shipment, and Timsen's boys, another source of danger, were still desperately combing the area for the hijacker.

The King and Tex watched Peter Marlowe walk, zombi-like out of the hut and across the path and up to the storm ditch. He wavered on the brink, then stepped across it and began to stagger towards the fence.

'Jesus,' Tex said. 'I can't watch!'

'I can't either,' the King said.

Peter Marlowe was trying to focus his eyes on the fence, through the pain and delirium that was engulfing him. He was praying for a bullet. He could stand the agony no longer. But no bullet came, so he walked on, grimly erect, then reeled against the fence. He grabbed a wire to steady himself for a moment.

Then he bent down to step through the wires and gave a little moan as he fell into the dregs of hell.

The King and Tex ran to the fence and picked him up and dragged him away from the fence.

'What's the matter with him?' someone asked from the darkness.

'Guess he's just gone stir-crazy,' the King said. 'Come on, Tex, let's get him in the hut.'

They carried him into the hut and laid him on the King's bed. Then Tex hurried away to recall their guards and the hut returned to normal. Just one guard out.

Peter Marlowe lay on the bed, moaning and mumbling deliriously. After a while, he came out of the faint. 'Oh Christ,' he gasped and tried to get off the bed, but his body defeated him.

'Here,' the King said anxiously, giving him four aspirins. 'Take it easy, you'll be all right.' His hand was shaking as he helped him to drink some water. Son of a bitch, he thought bitterly, if Timsen doesn't bring the stuff tonight Peter won't make it, and if he doesn't then how the hell am I going to get the dough? Son of a bitch!

When Timsen finally arrived the King was a wreck.

'Hi, cobber.' Timsen was nervous too. He had to cover for his best cobber up by the main gate while the man had gone through the wire and into the Japanese doctor's quarters, which were fifty yards away and not so very far from the Yoshima house and too near the guardhouse for any man's nerves. But the Aussie had sneaked in and sneaked out, and while Timsen knew there ain't no thief in the world like a Digger on the make for a piece of merchandise, no thief in the world, even so, he had sweated, waiting until the man got back safely.

'Where we going to fix him?' he asked.

'Here.'

'All right. Better post some guards.'

'Where's the nurse?'

'I'm the first one,' Timsen said queasily. 'Steven can't get down 'ere now. He'll take on from me.'

'You sure you know what the hell you're doing?'

'Strike a bleedin' light,' Timsen said. ''Course I know. You got some water boiling?'

'No.'

'Well get some! Don't you Yanks know anything?'

'Keep your shirt on!'

The King nodded to Tex and Tex got the water going. Timsen undid the surgical haversack and laid out a little towel.

'I'll be goddamned,' Tex said. 'I ain't never seen something so clean before. Why, it's almost blue it's so white.'

Timsen spat and washed his hands carefully with a new cake of soap and started to boil the hypodermic and forceps. Then he bent over Peter Marlowe and slapped his face a little.

'Hey, cobber!'

'Yes,' Peter Marlowe said, weakly.

'I'm going to clean the wound, right?'

Peter Marlowe had to concentrate. 'What?'

'I'm going to give you the hantitoxin—'

'I've got to get up to the hospital,' he said drunkenly. 'It's time now—cut it—I'm telling you—' His spirit left him once more.

'Just as well,' Timsen said.

When the hypodermic was sterilized, Timsen gave an injection of morphine. 'You help,' he said brusquely to the King. 'Keep the bloody sweat out of me eyes.' Obediently the King got a towel.

Timsen waited until the injection reacted, then he ripped off the old bandage and laid the wound bare. 'Jesus! The whole wound area was puffy and purple and green. 'I think it's too late.'

'My God,' the King said. 'No wonder the poor son of a bitch was crazy.'

Gritting his teeth, Timsen carefully cut away the worst of the rotted, putrid skin and probed deep and washed the wound as clean as he could. Then he sprinkled sulpha powder over it and neatly rebandaged it. When this was done, he straightened and sighed. 'My bleeding back!' He looked at the purity of the bandage, then turned to the King. 'Got a piece of shirt?'

The King grabbed a shirt from the wall and gave it to him. Timsen ripped the arm out and tore it into a rough bandage and wrapped it on top of the bandage.

'What the hell's that for?' the King asked blearily.

'Camouflage,' Timsen said. 'I suppose you think he can walk

327

around the camp with nice new bandage on him and not get stopped by curious docs and MP's asking him where the hell he got it?'

'Oh, I see.'

'Well now, that's something!

The King let the crack pass. He was too qualmish with the memory of Peter Marlowe's arm and the smell of it and the blood and the clotted mucoused bandage that lay on the floor. 'Hey, Tex, get rid of that stinking thing.'

'Who, me? Why—'

'Get rid of it.'

Tex reluctantly picked up the bandage and went outside. He kicked the soft earth away and buried it, and was sick. When he came back he said, 'Thank God I don't have to do this every day.'

Timsen shakily filled the hypodermic and bent over Peter Marlowe's arm. 'You got to watch. Watch for Christ's sake,' he growled as he saw the King turn away. 'If Steven doesn't come, maybe you'll have to do it. The injection's got to be intravenous, right? You find the vein. Then you just stick the needle in and inch out a little until you can pull some blood into the syringe. See? Then you're sure the needle's in the vein. Once you're sure, you just squirt the hantitoxin in. But not fast. Take about three minutes for the cc.'

The King watched, revolted, until the needle was jerked out and Timsen pressed a little piece of cotton wool over the puncture.

'Goddammit,' the King said. 'I'll never be able to do that.'

'You want to let him die, okay.' Timsen was sweating and nauseated too. 'An' my old man wanted me to be a doctor!' He pushed the King out of the way and put his head out of the window and was violently sick. 'Get some coffee for God's sake.'

Peter Marlowe stirred and became half awake.

'You're going to be all right, cobber. You understand me?' Timsen bent over him, gentle.

Peter Marlowe nodded myopically and lifted his arm. For a moment he stared at it unbelievingly, then he muttered, 'What happened? It's—still on—it's still on!'

'Of course it's on,' the King said proudly. 'We just fixed you up. Antitoxin, the lot. Me and Timsen!'

But Peter Marlowe only looked at him, his mouth working and no words coming out. Then at length, he said in a whisper, 'It's still—on.' He used his right hand to feel the arm that should not be there but was. And when he was sure he was not dreaming, he lay back in a pool of sweat and closed his eyes and began to cry. A few minutes later he was asleep.

'Poor bugger,' Timsen said. 'He must've thought he was on the op table.'

'How long's he going to be out?'

'About another couple of hours. Listen,' Timsen said, 'he's got to have an injection every six hours until the toxin's out of him. For, say about forty-eight hours. And new dressings every day. And more sulpha. But you got to remember. He *must* keep up the injections. And don't be surprised if he vomits all over the place. There's bound to be a reaction. A bad one. I made the first dose heavy.'

'You think he'll be all right?'

'I'll answer that in ten days.' Timsen got the haversack together and made a neat little parcel of the towel, soap, hypodermic, antitoxin and sulpa powder. 'Now let's settle up, right?'

The King took out the pack that Shagata had given him. 'Smoke?'

'Ta.'

When the cigarettes were lit the King said, matter of fact, 'We can settle up when the diamond deal goes through.'

'Oh no, mate. I delivers, I get paid. That's nothing to do with this,' Timsen said sharply.

'No harm in waiting a day or so.'

'You got enough money and then some from the profit—' He stopped suddenly as he hit upon the answer. 'Oho! he said with a broad smile, jerking his thumb at Peter Marlowe. 'No money until your cobber goes an' gets it, right?'

The King slipped off his wrist watch. 'You want to hold this as security?'

'Oh no, matey, I trust you.' He looked at Peter Marlowe. 'Well, seems like a lot depends on you, old son.' When he turned back to the King his eyes were crinkled merrily. 'Gives me time, too, don't it?'

329

'Huh?' the King said innocently.

'Come off it, mate. You know the ring's been bushwhacked. There's only you in the camp what can handle it. If I could've, you think I'd let you in on it?' Timsen's beam was seraphic. 'So that gives me time to find the bushwhacker, right? If he comes to you first, you won't have the money to pay, right? Without the money he won't let go of it, right? No money, no deal.' Timsen waited and then said benignly. ''Course you could tell me when the bastard offers it, couldn't you? After all, it's my property, right?'

'Right,' the King said agreeably.

'But you won't,' Timsen sighed. 'Wot a lot of ruddy thieves.'

He bent over Peter Marlowe and checked his pulse, 'Hum,' he said reflectively. 'Pulse's up.'

'Thanks for the help, Tim.'

'Think nothing of it, mate. I got a vested interest in the bastard, right? And I'm going t'watch him like a ruddy 'awk. Right?'

He laughed again and went out.

The King was exhausted. After he had made himself some coffee he felt better, and he lay back in the chair and drifted into sleep.

He awoke with a start and looked at the bed. Peter Marlowe was staring at him.

'Hello,' Peter Marlowe said weakly.

'How you feel?' The King stretched and got up.

'Like hell. I'm going to be sick any moment. You know, there's nothing—nothing I can say—'

The King lit the last of the Kooas and stuck it between Peter Marlowe's lips. 'You earned it, buddy.'

While Peter Marlowe lay gathering strength, the King told him about the treatment and what had to be done.

'The only place I can think of,' Peter Marlowe said, 'is the colonel's place. Mac can wake me and help me down from the hut, I can lie on my own bunk most of the time.'

The King gingerly held one of his mess cans as Peter Marlowe vomited.

'Better keep it handy. Sorry. My God,' Peter Marlowe said aghast as he remembered. 'The money! Did I get it?'

'No. You passed out this side of the wire.'

330

'Oh God, I don't think I could make it tonight.'

'No sweat, Peter. Soon as you feel better. No point in taking chances.'

'It won't harm the deal?'

'No. Don't worry about that.'

Peter Marlowe was sick again, and when he had recovered he looked terrible. 'Funny,' he said, holding back a retch. 'Had a weird dream. Dreamed I had a terrific row with Mac and the colonel and old Father Donovan. My God, I'm glad it was a dream.' He forced himself up on his good arm, wavered and lay back. 'Help me up, will you?'

'Take your time. It's only just after lights-out.'

'Mate!'

The King leaped to the window and stared out into the darkness. He saw the faint outline of the little weasel man crouching against the wall.

''Urry,' the man whispered. 'I got the stone 'ere.'

'You'll have to wait,' the King said. 'I can't give you the money for two days.'

'Why you rotten bastard—'

'Listen, you son of a bitch,' the King said. 'If you want to wait for two days, great! If you don't, go to hell!'

'All right, two days.' The man swore obscenely and disappeared.

The King heard his feet patter away, and in a moment he heard other feet hot in pursuit. Then silence, broken only by the hum of the crickets.

'What was that all about?' Peter Marlowe said.

'Nothing,' replied the King, wondering if the man had escaped. But he knew that whatever happened, he would get the diamond. So long as he got the money.

XXII

For two days Peter Marlowe battled with death. But he had the will to live. And he lived.

'Peter!' Mac gently shook him awake.

'Yes, Mac?'

'It's time.'

Mac helped Peter Marlowe off the bunk and together they manoeuvred down the steps, youth leaning on age, and made their way in the darkness to the bungalow.

Steven was already there and waiting. Peter Marlowe lay on Larkin's bunk and submitted again to the needle stab. He had to bite hard not to shout; Steven was gentle, but the needle was blunt.

'There,' Steven said. 'Now let's take your temperature.' He put the thermometer in Peter Marlowe's mouth, then took off the bandages and looked at the wound. The swelling was down and the green and purple hue was gone and hard clean scabs covered the wound. Steven spread more sulpha powder on the wound.

'Very good.' Steven was pleased with the success of the treatment, but not pleased with today at all. That dirty Sergeant Flaherty, he thought, nasty man. He knows I hate doing it, but he picks me every time. 'Rotten,' he said out loud.

'What?' Mac and Larkin and Peter Marlowe were concerned.

'Isn't it all right?' Peter Marlowe asked.

'Oh yes, dear. I was talking about something else. Now let's see the temperature.' Steven took the thermometer out and smiled at Peter Marlowe, reading the measure. 'Normal. At least, just a point over normal but that doesn't matter. You're lucky, very lucky.' He held up the empty antitoxin bottle. 'I just gave you the last of it.'

Steven took his pulse. 'Very good.' He looked up at Mac. 'Do you have a towel?'

Mac gave it to him and Steven put cold water on it and put a compress on Peter Marlowe's head. 'I found these,' he said, giving him two aspirins. 'They'll help a little, dear. Now rest for a while.' He turned to Mac and got up and sighed and smoothed his sarong around his hips. 'There's nothing more for me to do. He's very weak. You'll have to give him some broth. And all the eggs you can get. And take care of him.' He turned back and looked at the gauntness of Peter Marlowe. He must have lost fifteen pounds in the last two days and that's dangerous at his weight, poor boy. He can't weigh more than eight stone, which isn't much for his size.'

'Er, we'd like to thank you, Steven,' Larkin said gruffly. 'We er, appreciate all your work. You know.'

'Always glad to help,' said Steven brightly, fixing a lock of hair that curled on his forehead.

Mac glanced at Larkin. 'If there's anything, er, Steven, we can do—just say the word.'

'That's very kind. You're both so—kind,' he said delicately, admiring the colonel, increasing their embarrassment, playing with the Saint Christopher locket that he wore around his neck. 'If you could just do my borehole detail for me tomorrow, well, I'd do anything. Just anything. I can't stand those smelly cockroaches. Disgusting,' he gushed. 'Would you?'

'All right, Steven,' Larkin said sourly.

'We'll see you at dawn then,' Mac grunted and moved back a little, out of the way of Steven's attempted caress. Larkin was not quick enough and Steven put his hand on the colonel's waist and patted it affectionately. 'Night, dears. Oh, you're both so kind to Steven.'

When he'd gone, Larkin glared at Mac. 'You say anything and I'll pin your ears back.'

Mac chuckled. 'Eh, mon, dinna fash yoursel'. But you certainly gave the impression you enjoyed it.' He bent down to Peter Marlowe, who had been watching. 'Eh, Peter?'

'I think you're both ready for a piece,' said Peter Marlowe, smiling faintly. 'He's well paid, but you two go offering your

333

services, tempting him. But what he could see in you two old farts, damned if I know.

Mac grinned at Larkin. 'Ah, the wee laddie's better than somewhat. Now he can pull his weight for a change. And not, how is it the King puts it—ah yes—and not "goof off".'

'Is it two or three days since the first injection?' Peter Marlowe said.

'Two days.'

Two days? Feels more like two years, Peter Marlowe thought. But tomorrow I'll be strong enough to get the money.

That night, after the last roll call, Father Donovan came to play bridge with them. When Peter Marlowe told them about the nightmare quarrel he had had with them, they all laughed.

'Eh, laddie,' Mac said, 'your mind can play strange tricks with you when there's fever on you.'

'Yes,' Father Donovan said. Then he smiled at Peter. 'I'm glad your arm is healed, Peter.'

Peter Marlowe smiled back. 'There's not much that goes on that you don't get to know about, is there?'

'There's not much that goes on that He doesn't know about.' Donovan was very sure and completely peaceful. 'We're in good hands.' Then he chuckled and added, 'Even you three!'

'Well, that's something,' Mac said, 'though I think the colonel is far beyond the pale!'

After the game, and after Donovan had left, Mac nodded to Larkin. 'You keep a lookout. We'll hear the news, then call it a night.'

Larkin watched the road and Peter Marlowe sat on the veranda and tried to keep his eyes alert. Two days. Needles in his arm and now he was cured and had his arm back. Strange days, dream days, and now it was all right.

The news was enormously good, and they all went back to their beds. Their sleep was dreamless and contented.

At dawn, Mac went to the chicken run and found three eggs. He brought them back and made an omelet and filled it with a little rice he had saved from yesterday and perfumed it with a sliver of garlic.

Then he carried it up to Peter Marlowe's hut, and woke him and watched while he ate it all.

Suddenly Spence rushed into the hut.

'Hey, chaps!' he shouted. 'There's some mail in the camp!'

Mac's stomach turned over. Oh God, let there be one for me!

But there was no letter for Mac.

In all there were forty-three letters among the ten thousand. The Japanese had given mail to the camp twice in three years. A few letters. And on three occasions the men had been allowed to write a post card of twenty-five words. But whether these cards were ever delivered they did not know.

Larkin was one who got a letter. The first he had ever received.

His letter was dated April 21, 1945. Four months old. The age of the other letters varied from three weeks to more than two years.

Larkin read and reread the letter. Then he read it to Mac, Peter Marlowe and the King, sitting on the veranda of the bungalow.

Darling, This letter is number 205, it began. I am well and Jeannie is well and Mother is staying with us and we live just where we've always lived. We have had no news of you since your letter dated February 1, 1942, posted from Singapore. But even so we know you're well and happy, and we're praying for your safe return.

I've started each letter off the same, so if you've read the above before, forgive me. But it's difficult, not knowing if this one will reach you, if any of them have. I love you. I need you. And I miss you more than I can bear at times.

Today I feel sad. I don't know why, but I am. I don't want to be depressed and I wanted to tell you all manner of wonderful things.

Perhaps I'm sad because of Mrs Gurble. She got a post card yesterday and I didn't. I'm just selfish I suppose. But that's me. Anyway, be sure to tell Vic Gurble that his wife, Sarah, got a post card dated January 6, 1943. She is well and his son is bonny. Sarah is so happy that she is back in contact again. Oh yes, and the Regiment girls are all right. Timsen's mother is just grand. And don't forget to remember me to Tom Masters. I saw his wife last night. She's well too and making a lot of money for him. She's in a new business. Oh yes and I saw Elizabeth Ford, Mary Vickers . . .

Larkin looked up from the letter. 'She mentions maybe a dozen wives. But the men're dead. All of 'em. The only man who's alive is Timsen.'

'Read on, laddie,' said Mac quickly, achingly aware of the agony that was written in Larkin's eyes.

Today's hot, Larkin continued, *and I'm sitting on the veranda and Jeannie's playing in the garden and I think this weekend I'll go up to the cottage in the Blue Mountains.*

I'd write about the news, but that's not allowed.

Oh God, how do you write into a vacuum? How do I know? Where are you, my love, for the love of Christ, where are you? I won't write any more. I'll just finish the letter here and won't send it . . . oh my love, I pray for you—pray for me. Please pray for me, pray for me—

After a pause, Larkin said, 'There's no signature and it's—the address is in my mother's handwriting. Well, what do you think of that?'

'You know how it is with a lass,' Mac said. She probably just put it in a drawer and then your mother found it and airposted it off, without reading it, without asking her. You know how mothers are. More than likely Betty forgot all about it and the next day she wrote another letter when she felt better.'

'What does she mean by "Pray for me"?' Larkin asked. 'She knows I do, every day. What's going on? For Christ's sake, is she sick or something?'

'There's no need to worry, Colonel,' Peter Marlowe said.

'What the hell do you know about these things?' Larkin flared abruptly. 'How the hell can't I worry!'

'Well, at least you know she's all right, and your daughter's all right,' Mac slammed back, beside himself with longing. 'Bless your luck that far! We've not had a letter! None of us! You're lucky!' And he stamped out furiously.

'I'm sorry, Mac.' Larkin ran after him and pulled him back. 'I'm sorry, it's just that, after such a time—'

'Eh, laddie, it wasn't anything you said. It was just me. It's me who should apologize. I was sick with jealousy. I think I hate these letters.'

'You can say that again,' the King said. ''Nough to drive you crazy. Guys that get 'em go crazy, guys that don't go crazy. Nothing but trouble.

It was dusk. Just after chow. The whole American hut was assembled.

Kurt spat on the floor and put the tray down.

'Here's nine. I kept one. My ten per cent.' He spat again and left.

They all looked at the tray.

'I think I'm going to be sick again,' Peter Marlowe said.

'Don't blame you,' the King agreed.

'I don't know about that.' Max cleared his throat. 'They look just like rabbit legs. Small, sure, but still rabbit legs.'

'You want to try one?' the King asked.

'Hell no. I just said they looked like them. I can have an opinion, can't I?'

'My ruddy oath,' Timsen said. 'Never thought we'd really sell any.'

'If I didn't know—' Tex stopped. 'I'm so hungry. An' I ain't see that much meat since we got that dog—'

'What dog?' Max asked suspiciously.

'Oh hell, it was, er, years ago,' Tex said. 'Back in, er, '43.'

'Oh.'

'Goddam!' said the King, still fascinated by the tray. 'It looks all right.' He bent forward and sniffed the meat, but did not put his nose too close. 'It smells all right . . .'

'But it ain't,' Byron Jones III interrupted acidly. 'It's rat meat.'

The King pulled his head back. 'What the hell you say that for, you son of a bitch! he said through the laughter.

'Well, it is rat, for Chrissake. The way you were going on, it was enough to make a guy hungry!'

Peter Marlowe carefully picked up a leg and laid it on a banana leaf. 'This I've got to have,' he said, and returned to his hut. He went to his bunk and whispered to Ewart, 'Maybe we'll eat very well tonight.'

'What?'

'Never mind. Something special.' Peter Marlowe knew that Drinkwater was overhearing them; furtively he put the banana leaf on his shelf and said to Ewart, 'I'll be back in a mo'.' Half an hour later he came back and the banana leaf was gone and so was Drinkwater. 'Did you go out?' Peter Marlowe asked Ewart.

'Only for a moment. Drinkwater wanted me to get some water for him. Said he was feeling proper poorly.' And then Peter Marlowe had hysterics and everyone in the hut thought he had gone off his head. Only when Mike shook him could he stop laughing. 'Sorry, just a private joke.'

When Drinkwater came back Peter Marlowe pretended to be mortally concerned about the loss of some food, and Drinkwater was concerned too and said, licking his chops, 'What a dirty trick,' and Peter Marlowe's hysterics began again.

At length Peter Marlowe groped into his bunk and lay back, exhausted by the laughter. And quickly this exhaustion added to the exhaustion of the last two days. He fell asleep, and in his dreams Drinkwater was eating mountains of little haunches and he, Peter Marlowe, was there watching all the time, and Drinkwater kept saying, 'What's the matter? They're delicious, delicious . . .'

Ewart shook him awake. 'There's an American outside, Peter. Wants to talk to you.'

Peter Marlowe still felt weak and nauseated, but he got off the bed. 'Where's Drinkwater?'

'I don't know. He took off after you had the fit.'

'Oh,' Peter Marlowe laughed again. 'I was afraid it might have been a dream.'

'What?' Ewart studied him.

'Nothing.'

'Don't know what's getting into you, Peter. You've been acting very strange lately.'

Tex was waiting for Peter Marlowe in the lee of the hut. 'Pete,' he whispered. 'The King sent me. You've overdue.'

'Oh blast! Sorry, I dropped off.'

'Yeah, that's what he figured. "Better get with it," he told me to tell you.' Tex frowned. 'You all right?'

'Yes. Still a bit weak. I'll be all right.'

Tex nodded, then hurried away. Peter Marlowe rubbed his face and then walked down the steps to the asphalt road and stood under the shower, his body drinking strength from the cold. Then he filled his bottle and walked heavily to the latrines. He chose a hole at the bottom of the slope as near as possible to the wire.

There was only a thread of a moon. He waited until the latrine area was momentarily empty, then he slipped across the naked ground and under the wire and into the jungle. He kept low as he skirted the wire, avoiding the sentry that he knew was meandering the path between jungle and fence. It took him an

338

hour to find the spot where he had hidden the money. He sat down and took the inches of notes and tied them around his thighs, and doubled his sarong around his waist. Now, instead of reaching the ground, the sarong was knee length, and the bulk of it helped to hide the untoward thickness of his legs.

He had to wait another hour just outside the latrine area before he could slip under the wire. He squatted down on the borehole in the darkness to catch his breath and wait until his heart was calmer. At length he picked up his bottle and left the latrine area.

'Hello, cobber,' Timsen said with a grin, coming out of the shadows. 'Gorgeous night, ain't it?'

'Yes,' Peter Marlowe said.

'Beaut of a night for a walk, right?'

'Oh?'

'Mind if I walk along with you?'

'No. Come along, Tim, I'm happy to have you. Then there won't be any bloody hijackers. Right?'

'Right, mate. You're a toff.'

'You're not bad yourself, you old bastard.' Peter Marlowe slapped him on the back. 'I never did thank you.'

'Think nothing of it, mate. My bloody oath,' Timsen chuckled, 'you nearly had me fooled. I thought you was only going to take a pong.'

The King was grim when he saw Timsen, but at the same time he was not too grim, for the money was once more in his possession. He counted it and put it in the black box.

'Now all we need's the ice.'

'Yus, mate.' Timsen cleared his throat. 'If we catch the bushwhacker, before he comes 'ere or after he comes 'ere, then I gets the price we agreed, right? If you buy the ring from him and we don't catch him—then you're the winner, right? Fair enough?'

'Sure,' the King said, 'It's a deal.'

'Good-oh! God help him if we catch him.' Timsen nodded to Peter Marlowe and walked out.

'Peter, take the bed,' the King said. sitting on the black box. 'You look wrung out.'

'I thought I'd go on back.'

'Stick around. Might need someone I can trust.' The King was sweating, and the heat of the money from the black box seemed to be burning through the wood.

So Peter Marlowe lay on the bed, his heart still aching from the strain. He slept, but his mind was alert.

'Mate!'

The King jumped to the window. 'Now?'

''Urry.' The little man was vastly afraid and the white of his eyes caught the light as they darted back and forth. 'c'mon 'urry.'

The King slammed the key into the lock and threw back the lid and took out the pile of ten thousand he had already counted and rushed back to the window. 'Here. Ten grand. I've counted it. Where's the diamond?'

'When I gets the money.'

'When I've got the diamond,' the King said, still holding tight to the notes.

The little man stared up belligerently and then opened his fist. The King stared at the diamond ring, examining it, not making a move to take it. Got to make sure, he told himself urgently. Got to make sure. Yes, it's the one. I think it's the one.

'Go on, mate,' grated the little man. 'Take it!'

The King let go of the notes only when he had a firm grip on the ring, and the little man darted away. The King held his breath and bent down beside the light and examined the ring carefully.

'We've done it, Peter buddy,' he whispered, elated. 'We've done it. We got the diamond and we've got the money.'

The stress of the last few days closing in on him, the King opened a little sack of coffee beans and made as though to bury the diamond deep within. Instead, he palmed the ring neatly. Even Peter Marlowe, the closest man to him, was fooled. As soon as he had locked the box he was overcome with a fit of coughing. No one saw him transfer the ring to his mouth. He felt around for the cup of cold coffee and drank it down, swallowing the stone. Now the diamond was safe. Very safe.

He sat on a chair waiting for the tension to pass. Oh yes, he told himself exultantly. You've done it.

A danger whistle cut the stillness.

Max slipped through the doorway. 'Cops,' he said, and quickly joined the game of poker.

'Goddam!' The King forced his legs to move and he grabbed the stacks of money. He threw an inch at Peter Marlowe, stuffed an inch into his own pockets, and raced down the room to the poker table and gave each man a stack which they stuffed in their pockets. Then he dealt out the rest on the table and grabbed another seat and joined the game.

'Come on, for Chrissake, deal,' the King said.

'All right. All right,' Max said, 'Five card.' He pushed out a hundred dollars. 'Hundred to play.'

'Make it two,' Tex said, beaming.'

'I'm in!'

They were all in and gloating and happy and Max dealt the first two cards and dealt himself an ace up. 'I bet four hundred!'

'Your four and up four,' said Tex, who had a deuce face up and nothing in the hole.

'I'm in,' said the King, and then he looked up and Grey was standing at the door. Between Brough and Yoshima. And behind Yoshima were Shagata and another guard.

XXIII

'Stand by your beds,' Brough ordered, his face stark and drawn.

The King shot a murderous glance at Max, who was the night's lookout. Max had failed in his job. He had said 'Cops' and not noticed the Japanese. If he had said 'Japs' a different plan would have been used.

Peter Marlowe tried to get to his feet. Standing made his nausea worse, so he stumbled to the King's table and leaned against it.

Yoshima was looking down at the money on the table. Brough had already seen it and winced. Grey had noticed it and his pulse had quickened.

'Where did this money come from?' Yoshima said.

There was a vast silence.

Then Yoshima shouted, 'Where did this money come from?'

The King was dying inside. He had seen Shagata, and knew Shagata was nervous, and the King knew he was within an ace of Outram Road. 'It's gambling money, sir.'

Yoshima walked the length of the hut until he was in front of the King. 'None from black market?' he asked.

'No sir,' he said, forcing a smile.

Peter Marlowe felt the vomit rising. He reeled heavily and almost fell, and could not keep his eyes focused. 'Can I sit— please?' he said.

Yoshima looked down the room and noticed the armband.

'What is an English officer doing here?' He was surprised, for his informants had told him there was very little fraternization with the Americans.

'I—was—just visiting . . .' But Peter Marlowe could not continue. 'Excuse—' he lurched to the window and vomited.

'What's the matter with him?' Yoshima asked.

'I think—it's fever, sir.'

'You,' Yoshima said to Tex, 'sit him on that chair.'

'Yes, sir,' Tex said.

Yoshima looked back at the King. 'How is there so much money without black market?' he said silkily.

The King was conscious of the eyes upon him, the conscious of the appalling silence and conscious of the diamond inside him, and conscious of Shagata in the doorway. He cleared his throat. 'Just, we've—saved our dough for gambling!'

Yoshima's hand cracked against the King's face, rocking him backward. 'Liar!'

The blow did not hurt, really, but at the same time it seemed to be a death smash. My God, the King told himself, I'm dead. My luck's run out.

'Captain Yoshima.' Brough began to walk up the length of the hut. He knew there was no use in trying to interfere—perhaps he would make it worse—but he had to try.

'*Shut up!*' Yoshima said. 'The man lies. Everyone knows. Stinking Yank!'

Yoshima turned his back on Brough and looked up at the King. 'Give me your water bottle!'

In a dream, the King got his bottle off the shelf and handed it to Yoshima. The Japanese poured the water out, shook the bottle and peered into it. Then he tossed it on the floor and moved to Tex. 'Give me your water bottle.'

Peter Marlowe's stomach heaved again. What about the water bottles? His brain screamed. Are Mac and Larkin being searched? And what happens if Yoshima asks for mine? He gagged and staggered to the window.

Yoshima worked his way around the hut, examining every bottle. At last he stood in front of Peter Marlowe.

'Your water bottle.'

'I—' began Peter Marlowe, and again nausea overwhelmed him and buckled his knees and he was beyond speech.

Yoshima turned to Shagata and said something furiously in Japanese at him.

Shagata said, 'Hai.'

'You!' Yoshima pointed at Grey. 'Go with this man and the guard and get the water bottle.'

'Very well.'

'Excuse me, sir,' the King said quickly. 'His water bottle's here.'

The King reached under his bed and pulled out a bottle, his spare, kept in secret against a rainy day.

Yoshima took it. It was very heavy. Heavy enough to contain a radio or part of a radio. He pulled out the cork and upended it. A stream of dry rice grains poured out. And kept pouring until it was empty and light. No radio inside.

Yoshima hurled the bottle away. 'Where is the radio?' he shouted.

'There isn't one—' began Brough, hoping to God Yoshima wouldn't ask him why the Englishman, who was visiting, should put his water bottle under a bed.

'Shut up.'

Yoshima and the guards searched the hut, making sure that there were no more water bottles, and then Yoshima went through the water bottles again.

'Where is the water bottle radio?' he shouted. 'I know it is here. That one of you has it! Where is it?'

'There's no radio here,' Brough repeated. 'If you like we'll strip the whole hut for you.'

Yoshima knew that somehow his information was wrong. This time he had not been told the hiding place, only that it was contained in a water bottle, or water bottles, and tonight one of the men who owned it was, at this moment, in the American hut. His eyes looked at each man. Who? Oh, he could certainly march them all up to the guardhouse, but that wouldn't help—not without the radio. The General didn't like failures. And without the radio—

So this time he had failed. He turned to Grey. 'You will inform the Camp Commandant that all water bottles are confiscated. They are to be taken up to the guardhouse tonight!'

'Yes, sir,' Grey said. His whole face seemed eyes.

Yoshima realized that by the time the water bottles were

taken to the guardhouse the one or ones containing the radio would be buried or hidden. But that didn't matter—it would make the search easier, for the hiding place would have to be changed, and in the changing eyes would be watching. Who would have thought a radio could be put inside a water bottle?

'Yankee pigs,' he snarled. 'You think you're so clever. So strong. So big. Well, remember. If this war lasts a hundred years we will beat you. Even if you beat the Germans. We can fight on alone. You will never beat us, never. You may kill many of us, but we will kill many more of you. You will never conquer us. Because we are patient and not afraid to die. Even if it takes two hundred years—eventually we will destroy you.'

Then he stormed out.

Brough turned on the King. 'You're supposed to be on the ball and you let the Jap bastard and guards walk into the hut, with all that loot spread around. You need your head examined.'

'Yes, sir. I sure as hell do.'

'And another thing. Where's the diamond?'

'What diamond, sir?'

Brough sat down. 'Colonel Smedly-Taylor called me in and said that Captain Grey had information that you've got a diamond ring you're not supposed to have. You—and Flight Lieutenant Marlowe. Of course, any searching to be done, I've got to be present. And *I've* no objection to Captain Grey looking—so long as I'm here. We were just about to high-tail it over here when Yoshima busted in with his guards and started yakking about he was going to search this hut—one of you was supposed to have a radio in a water bottle—how crazy can you get? Grey and I were told to go with him.' Now that the search was over, he thanked God there was no water-bottle radio here, and he knew also that Peter Marlowe and the King were part of the radio detail. Why else would the King pretend that an American water bottle belonged to the Englishman?

'All right,' Brough said to the King, 'take your clothes off. You're going to be searched. And your bunk and your black box.' He turned around. 'The rest of you guys keep it quiet and get on with your game.' He glanced back at the King. 'Unless you want to hand over the diamond.'

'What diamond, sir?'

As the King began undressing, Brough went over to Peter Marlowe. 'Anything I can get you, Pete?' he asked.

'Just some water.'

'Tex,' Brough ordered, 'get some water.' Then to Peter Marlowe: 'You look terrible, what is it?'

'Just—fever—feel rough.' Peter Marlowe lay back on Tex's bed and forced a weak smile. 'That bloody Jap frightened me to death.'

'Me too.'

Grey went through the King's clothes and the black box and his shelves and the sack of beans, and the men were astonished when the search failed to uncover the diamond.

'Marlowe!' Grey stood in front of him.

Peter Marlowe's eyes were bloodshot, and he could hardly see. 'Yes?'

'I want to search you.'

'Listen, Grey,' Brough said. 'You're within your rights to search here if I'm here. But you got no authority—'

'It's all right,' Peter Marlowe said. 'I don't mind. If I don't—he'll only—think . . . Give me a hand, will you?'

Peter Marlowe took off his sarong and threw it and the inch of money onto a bed.

Grey went through the hems carefully. Angrily, he threw the sarong back. 'Where did you get this money?'

'Gambling,' Peter Marlowe said, retrieving his sarong.

'You,' Grey barked at the King. 'What about this?' He held up another inch of notes.

'Gambling, sir,' the King said innocently, as he dressed, and Brough hid a smile.

'Where's the diamond?'

'What diamond? Sir.'

Brough got up and moved down to the poker table. 'Looks as though there's no diamond.'

'Then where did all this money come from?'

'The man says that it's gambling money. There's no law against gambling. Of course I don't approve of gambling either,' he added with a thin smile, his eyes on the King.

'You know that's not possible!' Grey said.

'It's not probable, if that's what you mean,' interrupted Brough. He was sorry for Grey—with his death-bright eyes, his mouth twitching and his hands palsied—sorry for him. 'You wanted to search here, and you've searched, and there's no diamond.'

He stopped as Peter Marlowe began to reel towards the door. The King caught him just before he fell.

'Here, I'll help you,' the King said. 'I'd better take him to his hut.'

'You stay here,' said Brough. 'Grey, maybe you'd give him a hand.'

'He can drop dead as far as I'm concerned.' Grey's eyes went to the King. 'You too! But not before I've caught you. And I will.'

'When you do, I'll throw the book at him.' Brough glanced at the King. 'Right?'

'Yes. Sir.'

Brough glanced back at Grey. 'But until you do—or he disobeys *my* orders—there's nothing to be done.'

'Then order him to stop black-marketing,' Grey said.

Brough kept his temper. 'Anything for a peaceful life,' he said, and felt his men's contempt and smiled inside. Sons of bitches. 'You,' he said to the King. 'You're ordered to stop black-marketing. As I understand black-marketing it means to sell food and goods, anything, to your own people—for profit. You're not to sell anything for profit.'

'Dealing in contraband, that's black-marketing.'

'Captain Grey, selling for profit or even stealing from the enemy is not black-marketing. There's no harm in a little trading.'

'But it's against orders!'

'Jap orders! And I don't acknowledge enemy orders. And they *are* the enemy.' Brough wanted to end this nonsense. 'No black-marketing. It's ordered.'

'You Americans stick together—I'll say that for you.'

'Now don't you start. I've had enough for one night from Yoshima. No one's black-marketing here or breaking any laws that are laws—so far as I know. Now that's the end of it. I catch anyone stealing anything or selling food for profit or drugs for profit I'll break his arm off myself and stuff it down his throat. And I'm senior American officer and these are my men and that's what I say. Understand?'

Grey stared at Brough and promised himself that he would watch him too. Rotten people, rotten officers. He turned and stalked out of the hut.

'Help Peter back to his bunk, Tex,' said Brough.

'Sure, Don.'

Tex lifted him in his arms and grinned at Brough. 'Like a baby, sir,' he said and went out.

Brough stared at the money on the poker table. 'Yep,' he said, nodding, as though to himself, 'gambling's no good. No goddam good at all.' He looked up at the King and said sweetly, 'I don't approve of gambling, do you?'

Watch yourself, the King told himself, Brough's got that mean officer look about him. Why is it only son of bitch officers get that look and why is it you always know it—and can always smell the danger twenty feet away?'

'Well,' the King said, offering Brough a cigarette and holding the light for him, 'I guess it depends on how you look at it.'

'Thanks. Nothing like a tailor-made.' Once more Brough's eyes locked on the King's. 'And how do you look at it, Corporal?'

'If I'm winning, it looks good. If I'm losing, not so good,' and added under his breath, You son of a bitch, what the hell's on your mind?

Brough grunted and looked at the stack of notes in front of the place where the King had been seated. Nodding thoughtfully, he thumbed through the notes and held them in his hand. All of them. His eyes saw the large piles in front on every place. 'Looks like everybody's winning in this school,' he said reflectively to no one in particular.

The King didn't answer.

'Looks like you could afford a contribution.'

'Huh?'

'Yes, "huh", goddammit!' Brough held up the notes. 'About this much. To go into the goddam pool. Officers and enlisted men alike.'

The King moaned. Best part of four hundred dollars. 'Jesus, Don . . .'

'Gambling's a bad habit. Like swearing, goddammit. You play cards, you might just lose the money, then where'd you be? A contribution'd save your soul for better things.'

Barter, you fool, the King told himself. Settle for half.

'Gee, I'd be happy to—'

'Good.' Brough turned to Max. 'You too, Max.'

'But sir—' the King began heatedly.

'You've had your say.'

Max tried not to look at the King, and Brough said, 'That's right Max. You look at him. Good man. He's made a contribution, why the hell can't you?'

Brough took three-fourths of the notes from each stack and counted the money quickly. In front of them. The King had to sit and watch.

'That makes ten bucks a man for a week for six weeks,' said Brough. 'Thursday's payday. Oh yeah. Max! Collect all water bottles and take them up to the guardhouse. Right now!' He stuffed the money into his pocket, then walked to the door. At the door he had a sudden thought. He took the notes out once more and peeled off a single five-dollar bill. Looking at the King, he tossed it into the centre of the table.

'Burying money.' His smile was angelic. 'Night, you guys.'

Throughout the camp, the collection of water bottles was under way.

Mac and Larkin and Peter Marlowe were in the bungalow. On the bed, beside Peter Marlowe, were their water bottles.

'We could take the wireless out of them and drop the cases down the borehole,' Mac said. 'Those bloody bottles are going to be difficult to hide now.'

'We could drop 'em as they are down a borehole,' Larkin said.

'You don't really mean that, do you, Colonel?' asked Peter Marlowe.

'No cobber. But I said it, an' we should all decide what to do.'

Mac picked up one of the bottles. 'Perhaps they'll return the other ones in a day or so. We canna hide the guts of the bottles any better than they're hid now.' He looked up and said venomously, 'But who's the bastard who knows?'

They stared at the water bottles.

'Isn't it about time to listen for the news?' Peter Marlowe said.

'Ay laddie,' Mac said and looked at Larkin.

'I agree,' he said.

The King was still awake when Timsen peered through the window. 'Cobber?'

'Yeah?'

Timsen held up a bundle of notes. 'We got the ten you paid.'

The King sighed and he opened his black box and paid Timsen what was owed.

'Thanks, cobber.' Timsen chuckled. 'Hear you had a set-to with Grey and Yoshima.'

'So?'

'Nothin'—just a pity Grey didn't find the stone. I wouldn't be in your shoes—or Pete's for that. Oh dear, no. Very dangerous, right?'

'Go to hell, Timsen.'

Timsen laughed. 'Just a friendly warning, right? Oh, yus. The first shipment of netting's under the hut, enough for a hundred or so cages.' He peeled off one hundred and twenty dollars. 'I sold the first shipment at thirty a leg. Here's your cut—fifty-fifty.'

'Who got 'em?'

Timsen winked. 'Just friends of mine. 'Night, cobber.'

The King relaxed on his bed and rechecked to see that the net was once more tight under his mattress. He was alert for danger. He knew that he could not go to the village for two days, and between then and now, many eyes would be watching and waiting. That night his sleep was fitful, and the next day he stayed in the hut surrounded by guards.

After lunch there was a sudden search of the bungalow area. Three times the guards went through the little rooms before the search was called off.

At nightfall Mac groped his way to the latrine area and pulled up the three water bottles that were dangling on a string in one of the boreholes. He cleaned them and brought them back to the room and connected them. He, Larkin and Peter Marlowe listened to the news, memorizing it. Afterwards, he did not take the bottles back to their cache, for though he had been cautious, he knew he had been observed.

The three of them decided not to hide the bottles any more. They knew, without despair, that very soon they would be caught.

XXIV

The King hurried through the jungle. As he approached the camp he became more careful until he was in a position just opposite the American hut. He lay on the ground and yawned contentedly, waiting for the moment to slip across the path and under the wire and back to the safety of the hut. The balance of the money bulked his pocket.

He had gone alone to the village. Peter Marlowe was not fit enough to go with him. He had met Cheng San and given him the diamond. Then they had had a feast and he had gone to Kasseh and she had welcomed him.

Dawn was painting the new day as the King sneaked under the wire and into the hut. It was only when he got in bed that he noticed that his black box was missing.

'Why, you stupid sons of bitches!' he screamed. 'Can't you be trusted to do a goddam thing!'

'Goddammit to hell,' Max said. 'It was there a few hours ago. I got to go to the latrine.'

'Where the hell is it now?'

But none of the men had seen or heard anything.

'Get Samson and Brant,' the King said to Max.

'Jesus,' Max said, 'it's a little early—'

'I said get 'em!'

In half an hour Colonel Samson arrived, wet with fear. 'What's the matter? You know I mustn't be seen here.'

'Some son of a bitch has stolen my box. You can help find out who did it.'

'How can I—?'

351

'I don't care how,' the King interrupted. 'Just keep your ears open around the officers. There's no more dough for you until I know who's done it.'

'But Corporal, I had nothing to do with it.'

'As soon as I know, the weekly pay-off'll start again. Now beat it.'

A few minutes later Major Brant arrived and got the same treatment. As soon as he left, the King fixed himself some breakfast whil the others in the hut were scouring the camp. He had just finished eating when Peter Marlowe came in. The King told him about the theft of the black box.

'That's a bad bit of luck,' Peter Marlowe said.

The King nodded, then winked. 'It doesn't matter. I got the rest of the dough from Cheng San—so we've plenty. I just thought it was about time to bear down a little. The guys got careless—and it's a matter of principle.' He handed him a small pile of notes. 'Here's your cut from the diamond.'

Peter Marlowe wanted the money badly. But he shook his head. 'You keep it. I owe you much more than I can ever pay you. And there's the money you put out for the medicine.'

'All right, Peter. But we're still partners.'

Peter Marlowe smiled. 'Good.'

The trapdoor opened and Kurt climbed up into the room.

'Seventy so far,' he said.

'Huh?' the King said.

'It's B Day.'

'Goddam,' the King said. 'I'd forgotten all about it.'

'Just as well I didn't aint it? I'll butcher another ten in a few days. No need in feeding the males. There's five or six that're big enough!'

The King felt sick, but he said, 'All right. I'll tell Timsen.'

When Kurt had gone Peter Marlowe said, 'I don't think I'll come around for a day or so.'

'Huh?'

'I think it's better. We can't hide the wireless any more. We've decided the three of us to stay around the room.'

'You want to commit suicide? Get rid of the goddam thing if you figure you're spotted. Then if you're questioned—deny it.'

'We thought about that, but ours is the only wireless left—so

352

we want to keep it going as long as we can. With a little luck we won't be caught.'

'You better look after number one, buddy.'

Peter Marlowe smiled. 'Yes, I know. That's why I'm not coming here for a while. Don't want to drag you into anything.'

'What're you going to do if Yoshima starts heading your way?'

'Make a run for it.'

'Run where, for God's sake?'

'Better that than just sit.'

Dino, the guard of the moment, stuck his head through the doorway. 'Excuse me, but Timsen's heading this way.'

'Okay,' the King said. 'I'll see him.' He turned back to Peter Marlowe. 'It's your neck, Peter. My advice is dump it.'

'Wish we could, but we can't.'

The King knew that there was nothing he could do.

'Hi, cobber,' Timsen said as he came in, his face taut with anger. 'Heard you had a bad bit of luck, right?'

'I need a new set of watchdogs, that's for sure.'

'You and me both,' Timsen said furiously. 'The bush-whackers dumped your black box under my bloody hut. *My hut*!

'What?'

'That's right. It's there, under my hut, clean as a whistle. Bloody bastards, that's the truth. No Aussie'd steal it and dump it under my hut. No sir. Got to be a Pommy or a Yank.'

'Like who?'

'I don't know. All I know is they weren't none of mine. You got my ruddy oath on that.'

'I'll believe you. But you can spread the word—there's a thousand bucks reward for the proof as to who hijacked my box.' The King reached under his pillow and deliberately pulled out the pile of notes that Cheng San had given him for the completion of the sale. He peeled off three hundred dollars and offered them to Timsen, who was staring wide-eyed at the vastness of the pile. 'I need some sugar and coffee and oil—maybe a coconut or two. You fix it?'

Timsen took the money, unable to tear his eyes from the remaining pile of notes. 'You completed the sale, right? My ruddy oath, never thought you'd do it. But you have, right?'

'Sure,' the King said nonchalantly. 'I got enough to last a month or two.'

'A bloody year, mate,' Timsen said, overwhelmed. He turned and walked slowly to the door, then looked back with a sudden laugh. 'A thousand, eh? I'd say that'd produce results, right?'

'Yeah,' the King said. 'Just a question of time.'

Within the hour the news of the reward had spread the camp. Eyes began to watch with renewed interest. Ears were tuned to catch the whispers on the wind. Memories were searched and researched. It was only a question of time before the thousand would be claimed.

That night when the King walked the camp he felt, as never before, the hate and the envy and the strength of the eyes. It made him feel good and better than good, for he knew that they all knew he had a vast pile of notes where they had none—that he, of all of them, truly had it made.

Samson sought him out, and Brant—and many others—and though he sickened at their fawning, it pleased him enormously that for the first time they did it in public. He passed the MP hut, and even Grey, standing outside, merely returned his neat salute and did not call him in to be searched. The King smiled to himself, knowing that even Grey was thinking about the stack of notes and the reward.

Nothing could touch the King now. The stack of notes were safety and life and power. And they were his alone.

XXV

When Yoshima came this time, he came stealthily but with great speed. He did not come as usual, through the camp along the road, but he came with many guards through the wire, and when Peter Marlowe saw the first of the guards the bungalow was already surrounded and there was nowhere to run. Mac was still under his mosquito net, listening through the earphone, when Yoshima swooped into the bungalow.

Peter Marlowe and Larkin and Mac were herded into one corner. Then Yoshima picked up the earphone and listened. The radio was still connected and he heard the tail end of the news broadcast.

'Very ingenious,' he said, putting the earphone down. 'Your names, please?'

'I'm Colonel Larkin, this is Major McCoy and this is Flight Lieutenant Marlowe.'

Yoshima smiled. 'Would you like a cigarette?' he asked.

They each took a cigarette and accepted a light from Yoshima, who also lit one for himself. They all smoked in silence. Then Yoshima spoke.

'Disconnect the radio and come with me.'

Mac's fingers trembled as he bent down. He looked around nervously as another Japanese officer appeared abruptly out of the night. The officer whispered urgently in Yoshima's ear. For a moment Yoshima stared at him speechless, then he snapped at a guard, who posted himself in the doorway, and hurried away with the officer and all the other guards.

'What's up?' said Larkin, his eyes on the guard, who covered them with a bayoneted rifle.

Mac stood near his bed, above the radio, his knees shaking, hardly breathing. When at length he could talk he said hoarsely, 'I think I know. It's the news. I didn't have time to tell you. We've—we've a new type of bomb. An atom bomb. Yesterday at nine-fifteen in the monring *one* was dropped on Hiroshima. The whole city disappeared. They say the casualties'll be in the hundreds of thousands—men, women and children!'

'Oh my God!'

Larkin sat suddenly, and the nervous guard cocked his rifle and half pressed the trigger as Mac shouted in Malay, 'Wait, he's just sitting!

'All of you sit!' the guard shouted back in Malay, cursing them. When they had obeyed him, he said, 'Thou art fools! Be more careful as thou move—for I am responsible that thou do not escape. Sit where thou art. And stay where thou art! I will shoot thee without question.'

So they sat and did not talk. In time they fell asleep, dozing restlessly under the harsh light of the electric lamp, slapping at the mosquitoes until dawn took away the mosquitoes.

At dawn the guard was changed. Still the three friends sat. Outside the bungalow nervous men walked the path, but they looked the other way until they were well clear of the condemned room.

The day was bleak under the scorching sky. It dragged long, longer than any day had ever dragged.

In the middle of the afternoon the three looked up as Grey approached the guard and saluted. In his hands were two mess cans.

'Can I give them this? Makan?' He opened the mess cans and showed the guard the food.

The guard shrugged and nodded.

Grey walked across the veranda and put the food down at the doorway, his eyes red-rimmed and piercing.

'Sorry it's cold,' he said.

'Come to gloat, Grey, old man?' Peter Marlowe said with a mirthless smile.

'It's no bloody satisfaction to me that *they* are going to put you

356

away. I wanted to catch you breaking the laws—not see you caught for risking your life for the good of us all. Just your bloody luck you'll go in a blaze of glory.'

'Peter,' Mac whispered, 'distract the guard!'

Peter Marlowe got up and quickly moved into the doorway. He saluted the guard and asked permission to go to the latrine. The guard pointed to the ground just outside the bungalow. Peter Marlowe squatted in the dirt and relieved himself, hating to do it there in the open, but thankful that they were not going to be made to do it in the little room. As the guard watched Peter Marlowe, Mac whispered the news to Grey, who blanched. Grey got up and nodded to Peter Marlowe, who nodded back, and saluted the guard once more. The guard pointed at the fly-covered mess and told Grey to return with a bucket and clean it away.

Grey passed the news on to Smedly-Taylor, who whispered it to the others, and soon the whole of Changi knew—long before Grey had found a bucket and had cleaned away the mess and set another bucket on the ground for them to use.

The first of the great fears permeated the camp. The fear of reprisal.

At sundown the guard was changed again and the new guard was Shagata. Peter Marlowe tried to talk to him, but Shagata just motioned him back into the little room with his bayonet. 'I cannot talk with thee. Thou has been caught with a radio, which is forbidden. I will shoot even thee if any of thee attempt to escape. I do not wish to shoot thee.' And he moved back to the door.

'My bloody oath,' Larkin said. 'I wish they'd just finish us off.'

Mac looked at Shagata. 'Sir,' he said, motioning towards his bed, 'I beg thee a favour. May I rest there, please? I slept little in the night.'

'Assuredly. Rest while thou hast time, old man.'

'I thank thee. Peace be upon thee.'

'And upon thee.'

Mac went over to his bed and lay down. He let his head rest on the pillow. 'It's still connected,' he said, keeping his voice level with difficulty. 'There's a music recital. I can hear it clearly.'

Larkin saw the earphone near Mac's head and suddenly laughed. Then they were all laughing. Shagata jerked his rifle towards the men. 'Stop it,' he shouted, frightened by the laughter.

'We beg thy pardon,' Peter Marlowe said. 'It is just that we who are so near eternity find small things amusing.'

'Truly thou art near death—and also a fool to be caught breaking the law. But I hope that I may have the courage of laughter when my time arrives.' He threw a pack of cigarettes into the room. 'Here,' he said. 'I'm sorry that thou hast been caught.'

'No sorrier than I,' Peter Marlowe said.

He divided the cigarettes and glanced across at Mac. 'What's the recital?'

'Bach, laddie,' Mac said, hard put not to break out into hysterical laughter again. He moved his head nearer the earphone. 'Shut up, will you, now. I'd like to enjoy the music.'

'Maybe we can take turns,' Larkin said. 'Though anyone who can enjoy Bach is a bit of a wet.'

Peter Marlowe smoked his cigarette and said pleasantly to Shagata, 'Thank thee for thy cigarettes.'

Flies were swarming the bucket and its rough lid on top. The afternoon rains came early and settled the stench, and then the sun came out and began to dry the wetness of Changi.

The King walked down the line of bungalows, conscious of the eyes on him. He stopped cautiously outside the condemned bungalow. 'Tabe, Shagata-san,' he said. 'Ichi-bon day, no? Can I talk to my ichi-bon friend?'

Shagata stared at him uncomprehendingly.

'He begs thy permission to talk to me,' Peter Marlowe said.

Shagata thought a moment, then nodded. 'Because of the money I made from the sale, I will let thee talk.' He turned to Peter Marlowe.' 'If I have thy word that thou wilt not try to escape.'

'Thou hast our words.'

'Be quick. I will watch.' Shagata moved so that he could keep an eye on the road.

'There's a rumour that guards are pouring into the guardhouse,' the King began nervously. 'Goddamned if I'm going to sleep tonight. They're just the sort of bastards who'd do it at night.' His lips felt dry and he had been watching the wire all day hoping for a sign from the guerrillas that would trigger the decision to make a break. But there had been none. 'Listen.' He dropped his voice and told them about the plan. 'When the killing starts, rush the guard and break out near our hut. I'll try and cover for the three of you, but don't hope for much.'

Then he got up and nodded to Shagata and walked away. Once in the American hut he called a council of war. He told them of his plan, but he didn't tell them that only ten could go. They all discussed the plan and then decided to wait. 'Can't do more,' Brough said, echoing their fears. 'If we tried now, we'd be shot to pieces.'

Only the very sick slept that night. Or those—the infinite few—who could commit themselves peacefully into the hands of God—or Fate. Dave Daven was sleeping.

'They brought Dave back from Outram Road this afternoon,' Grey had whispered as he brought them their evening meal.

'How is he?' Peter Marlowe asked.

'He only weighs seventy pounds.'

Daven slept that night and the next awesome day, and he died in his coma as Mac was listening to the news commentator: 'The second atom bomb has destroyed Nagasaki. President Truman has issued a last ultimatum to Japan—surrender unconditionally or face total destruction.'

The next day the work parties went out and, unbelievably, returned. Rations continued to come into the camp and Samson weighed the rations in public and took extra down to the men who had put him in charge of supplies. There were still two days' rations in the store hut and cookhouses, and there was cooked food, and the flies swarmed and nothing changed.

The bedbugs bit and the mosquitoes bit and rats suckled their young. A few men died. Ward Six had three new patients.

Another day and another night and another day. Then Mac heard the holy words: 'This is Calcutta calling. The Tokyo radio has just announced that the Japanese Government has surrendered unconditionally. Three years, two hundred and fifty days since the Japanese attacked Pearl Harbor—the war is over. God save the King!'

Soon all of Changi knew. And the words became part of the earth and sky and walls and cells of Changi.

Still, for two more days and two more nights nothing changed. On the third day the Camp Commandant walked along the line of bungalows with Awata, the Japanese sergeant.

Peter Marlowe and Mac and Larkin saw the two men approaching, and they died a thousand times for each pace the men took. They knew at once that their time had come.

XXVI

'Pity,' Mac said.

'Yes,' replied Larkin.

Peter Marlowe simply stared at Awata, frozen.

The Camp Commandant's face was etched deep with fatigue, but even so, his shoulders were squared and he walked firmly. He was dressed neatly as always, the left arm of his shirt tucked neatly into his belt. On his feet were wooden slippers, and he wore his peaked cap, grey-green with years of tropic sweat. He walked up the steps of the veranda and hesitated in the doorway.

'Good morning,' he said hoarsely as they got up.

'Awata snapped gutturally at the guard. The guard bowed and fell into place beside Awata. Another curt order and the two men shouldered their rifles and walked away.

'It's over,' the Camp Commandant said throatily. 'Bring the wireless and follow me.'

Numbly they did as he ordered, and they walked out of the room into the sun. And the sun and the air felt good. They followed the Camp Commandant up the street watched by the stunned eyes of Changi.

The six senior colonels were waiting in the Camp Commandant's quarters. Brough was also there. They all saluted.

'Stand easy, please,' the Camp Commandant said, returning the salute. Then he turned to the three. 'Sit down. We owe you a debt of gratitude.'

Eventually Larkin said, 'It's really over?'

'Yes. I've just seen the General.' The Camp Commandant

looked around the speechless faces, collecting his thoughts. 'At least I think it's over,' he said. 'Yoshima was with the General. I said—I said, "The war's over", The General just stared at me when Yoshima translated. I waited, but he said nothing, so I said again. "The war's over. I—I—I demand your surrender."' The Camp Commandant rubbed his bald head. 'I didn't know what else to say. For a long time the General just looked at me. Yoshima said nothing, nothing at all.

'Then the General said and Yoshima interpreted, "Yes. The war is over. You will return to your post in the camp. I have ordered my guards to turn their backs on the camp and guard you against anyone who tries to force an entrance into the camp to hurt you. They are *your* guards now—for your protection— until I have further orders. You are still responsible for the camp's discipline."

'I didn't know what to say, so I asked him to double the rations and give us medicines and he said, "Tomorrow the rations will be doubled. You will receive medical supplies. Unfortunately, we do not have much. But you are responsible for discipline. My guards will protect you against those who wish to kill you." "Who are they?" I asked. The General shrugged and said, "Your enemies. This interview is over."'

'Goddam,' Brough said. 'Maybe they want us to go out—to give them an excuse to shoot us.'

'We can't let the men out,' Smedly-Taylor said, appalled, 'they'd riot. But we must do something. Perhaps we should tell them to hand over their weapons—'

The Camp Commandant held up his hand. 'I think all we can do is wait. I'm—I think someone will arrive. And until they do, I think it's best we carry on as usual. Oh yes. We are allowed to send a bathing party to the sea. Five men from each hut. In rotation. Oh my God,' he said, and it was a prayer, 'I hope no one goes off half-cocked. There's still no guarantee that the Japs here will obey the surrender. They may even go on fighting. All we can do is hope for the best—and prepare for the worst.'

He paused and looked at Larkin. 'I think that the wireless should be left here.' He nodded at Smedly-Taylor. 'You'll arrange for permanent guards.'

'Yes, sir.'

362

'Of course,' the Camp Commandant said to Larkin, including Peter Marlowe and Mac, 'you are still to operate it.'

'If you don't mind, sir,' Mac said. 'Let someone else do that. I'll repair it if anything goes wrong, but, well, I suppose you'll want to have it connected twenty-four hours a day. We couldna do that—and somehow—well, speaking for myself, now that it's in the open, let people share in the listening.'

'Take care of it, Colonel!' The Camp Commandant said.

'Yes, sir,' Smedly-Taylor said.

'Now we'd better discuss operations.'

Outside the Camp Commandant's quarters a group of curious bystanders—including Max—began to collect, impatient to learn what was being said, and what had happened, and why the Japanese guard had been taken off the radio.

When Max could stand the strain no longer, he ran back to the American hut.

'Hey, you guys!' he managed to shout.

'The Japs're coming?' The King was ready to jump through the window and head for the fence.

'No! Jesus,' Max said, out of breath, unable to go on.

'Well, what the hell's up?' the King said.

'They've taken the Jap guards off Pete and the radio!' Max said getting his breath. 'Then the Camp Commandant took Pete, Larkin and the Scot—*and* the radio—up to his quarters. There's a big pow-wow going on there right now. All the senior colonels are there—even Brough's there!'

'You sure?' the King asked.

'I tell you I saw it with my own eyes, but I don't believe it either.'

In the violent silence, the King pulled out a cigarette and then Tex said what he had already realized.

'It's over then. It's really over. That's what it's gotta mean— if they've taken the guard off the radio!' Tex looked around. 'Doesn't it?'

Max sank heavily onto his bunk and wiped the sweat off his face. 'That's what I figure. If they've taken the guard away, that means that they're gonna give up here—not go on fighting.' He peered at Tex helplessly. 'Doesn't it?'

But Tex was lost in his own private bewilderment. At length he said impassively, 'It's over.'

The King soberly puffed his cigarette. 'I'll believe it when I see it.' Then, suddenly, in the eerie silence, he was afraid.

Dino was automatically maiming flies. Byron Jones III absently moved a bishop. Miller took it and left his queen unguarded. Max was staring at his feet. Tex scratched.

'Well, I don't feel different.' Dino said and stood up. 'I gotta go take a piss,' and he went out.

'Don't know whether I'm gonna laugh or cry,' Max said. 'Just feel like I'm gonna throw up.'

'Don't make sense,' Tex said aloud, but he was talking to himself and did not know that he had spoken. 'Just don't make sense.'

'Hey, Max,' the King said. 'You want to fix some coffee?'

Automatically Max went out and filled the saucepan with water. When he came back he plugged in the hot plate and set the saucepan on it. He began to go back to his bunk, but he stopped in his tracks, turned around and stared at the King.

'What's the matter, Max?' the King said uneasily.

Max just looked at him, his lips moving spastically and soundlessly.

'What the hell're you staring at?'

Suddenly Max grabbed the saucepan and hurled it through the window.

'You out of your goddam mind?' the King exploded. 'You got me all wet!'

'That's tough,' Max shouted, his eyes bulging.

'I ought to beat the bejesus outta you! You gone crazy?'

'The war's over. Get your own goddam coffee,' Max screamed, a touch of foam in the corners of his lips.

The King was on his feet and towering over Max, his face mottled with rage. 'You get outta here before I put my foot through your face!'

'You do that, just do that, but don't forget I'm a top sergeant! I'll have you court-martialled!'

Max began to laugh hysterically, then abruptly the laughter turned to tears, shattering tears, and Max fled the hut, leaving a horrified silence in his wake.

'Crazy son of a bitch,' the King muttered. 'Fix some water, will you, Tex,' and he sat down in his corner.

Tex was at the doorway, staring after Max. He looked around slowly. 'I'm busy,' he said after an agony of indecision.

The King's stomach turned over. He forced back his nausea and set his face.

'Yeah,' the King said with a grim smile. 'So I notice.' He could feel the depths of the stillness. He took out his wallet and selected a note. 'Here's a ten-spot. Get unbusy and go get some water, will you.' He hid the ache in his bowels and watched Tex.

But Tex said nothing, just shuddered nervously and looked away.

'You still got to eat—till it's really over,' the King said disdainfully, then looked around the hut. 'Who wants some coffee?'

'I'd like some coffee,' Dino spoke up, unapologetically. He fetched the saucepan and filled it and set it to cook.

The King dropped the ten-dollar note on the table. Dino stared at it.

'No thanks,' he said throatily, shaking his head, 'just the coffee.' He walked unsteadily back down the length of the hut.

Self consciously the men turned away from the King's smouldering contempt. 'I hope for your sakes, you sons of bitches, the war's over for real,' the King said.

Peter Marlowe walked out of the Camp Commandant's quarters and hurried towards the American hut. He replied automatically to the greetings of the men he knew and he could sense the constant eyes—incredulous eyes—that watched him. Yes, he thought, I don't believe it either. Soon to be home, soon to fly again, soon to see my old man again, drink with him, laugh with him. And all the family. God, it'll be strange. I'm alive. I'm alive. I made it!

'Hello, you fellows!' He beamed as he entered the hut.

'Hi, Peter,' Tex said as he jumped to his feet and shook his hand warmly. 'Boy, were we glad to hear about the guard, old buddy!'

'That's a masterpiece of understatement,' Peter Marlowe said and laughed. As they surrounded him, he basked in the warmth of their greetings.

'What happened with the Brass?' Dino asked.

Peter Marlowe told them, and they became even more

apprehensive. All except Tex. 'Hell, there's no need to prepare for the worst. It's over!' he said confidently.

'It's over for sure,' Max said gruffly as he walked into the hut.

'Hello, Max, I—' Peter Marlowe did not continue. He was shocked by the frightening look in Max's eyes.

'You all right?' he asked, perturbed.

''Course I'm all right!' Max flared. He shoved past and fell on his bunk. 'What the hell're you staring at? Can't a guy lose his temper once in a while without all you bastards staring?'

'Take it easy,' Tex said.

'Thank Christ, I'll be outta this lousy dump soon.' Max's face was grey-brown and his mouth twitched. 'And that goes for you lousy bastards!'

'Shut up, Max!'

'Go to hell!' Max wiped the spittle from his chin; he reached into his pocket and pulled out a wad of ten-dollar notes, then savagely ripped them and scattered them like confetti.

'What the hell's gotten into you, Max?' Tex asked.

'Nothin', you son of a bitch! The bills're no goddam good.'

'Huh?'

'I just been to the store. Yeah. Thought I'd get me a coconut. But that goddam Chinee wouldn't take my dough. Wouldn't take it. Said he'd sold his whole stock to the goddam Camp Commandant. On a note. 'The English Government promises to pay! Strait Dollars!' you can wipe your goddam ass on the Jap bucks—that's all they're good for!'

'Wow,' Tex said. 'That's the clincher. If the Chinese won't take the dough, then we've really got it made, eh, Peter?'

'We have indeed.' Peter Marlowe felt warmed by their friendship. Even Max's malevolent stare could not destroy his happiness. 'Can't tell you how much you fellows have helped me, you know, kidding around and all that.'

'Hell,' Dino said. 'You're one of us.' He punched him playfully. 'You're not bad for a goddam Limey!'

'You better get your ass State-side when you get out. We might even let you become an American!' Byron Jones III said.

'You gotta see Texas, Peter boy. You ever get to the States, you gotta come to *the* State!'

'Not much chance of that,' Peter Marlowe said amid the

366

catcalls. 'But if I ever do, you can depend on it.' He glanced towards the King's corner. 'Where's our fearless leader?'

'He's dead!' Max roared with obscene laughter.

'What!' Peter Marlowe said, frightened in spite of himself.

'He's still alive,' Tex said. 'But he's dead all the same.'

Peter Marlowe looked searchingly at Tex. Then he saw the expressions on all their faces. Suddenly he felt very sad. 'Don't you think that's a little abrupt?'

'Abrupt nothin'.' Max spat. 'He's dead. We worked our asses off for the son of a bitch, and now he's dead.'

Peter Marlowe pounced on Max, loathing him. 'But when things were bad, he gave you food and money and—'

'We worked for it!' Max screamed, the tendons in his neck stretching. 'I took enough crap from that bastard!' His eyes saw the rank insignia on Peter Marlowe's arm. 'And from you, you Limey bastard! You wanna kiss my ass like you kissed his?'

'Shut up, Max,' Tex said warningly.

'Drop dead, you Lone Star pimp!' Max spat at Tex and the spittle streaked the rough wood floor.

Tex flushed. He hurled himself at Max and smashed him against the wall with a backhanded blow across the face. Max reeled and fell off his bunk, but he whirled to his feet, grabbed a knife off his shelf and lunged at Peter Marlowe. Tex just managed to catch Max's arm, and the knife only scored Peter Marlowe's stomach. Dino grabbed Max around the throat and shoved him back on the bunk.

'You outta your skull?' Dino gasped.

Max stared up, his face twitching, his eyes fixed on Peter Marlowe. Suddenly he began screaming, and he hurled himself off the bunk fighting insanely, his arms flailing, lips stretched from his teeth, nails clawing. Peter Marlowe grabbed an arm and they all fell on Max and hauled him back to the bunk. It took three men to hold him down as he kicked and screamed and fought and bit.

'He's flipped!' Tex shouted. 'Clobber him, someone!'

'Get some rope!' Peter Marlowe yelled frantically as he held on to Max, his forearm jammed under Max's chin, away from the grinding teeth.

Dino shifted his grip, worked one arm free, and smashed Max on the jaw, knocking him unconscious. 'Jesus,' he said to

Peter Marlowe as they stood up. 'He goddam near murdered you!'

'Quick,' Peter Marlowe said urgently. 'Put something between his teeth, he'll bite his bloody tongue off.'

Dino found a piece of wood and they tied it between Max's teeth. Then they tied his hands.

When Max was secure, Peter Marlowe relaxed, weak with relief. 'Thanks, Tex. If you hadn't stopped that knife, I would have had it.'

'Think nothing of it. Reflex action. What we going to do about him?'

'Get a doctor. He just had a fit, that's all. There wasn't any knife.' Peter Marlowe rubbed the score on his stomach as he watched Max jerking spastically. 'Poor bugger!'

'Thank God you stopped him, Tex,' Dino said. 'Gives me a sweat to think about it.'

Peter Marlowe looked at the King's corner. It seemed very lonely. Unconsciously he flexed his hand and arm and gloried in its strength.

'How is it, Peter?' Tex asked.

It took Peter Marlowe a long time to find the right words. 'Alive, Tex, alive—not dead.' Then he turned and walked out of the hut into the sun.

When he found the King eventually, it was already dusk. The King was sitting on a broken coconut stump in the north vegetable garden, half hidden by vines. He was staring moodily out of the camp and made no sign that he heard Peter Marlowe approaching.

'Hello, old chap,' Peter Marlowe said cheerfully, but the welcome in him died when he saw the King's eyes.

'What do you want? Sir?' The King asked insultingly.

'I wanted to see you. Just wanted to see you.' Oh my God, he thought with pity, as he saw through his friend.

'Well, you've seen me. So now what?' The King turned his back. 'Get lost!'

'I'm your friend, remember?'

'I got no friends. Get lost!'

Peter Marlowe squatted down beside the coconut stump and found the two tailor-made cigarettes in his pocket. 'Have a smoke. I got them off Shagata!'

'Smoke 'em yourself. Sir!'

For a moment Peter Marlowe wished that he had not found the King. But he did not leave. He carefully lit the two cigarettes and offered one to the King. The King made no move to take it.

'Go on, please.'

The King smashed the cigarette out of his hands. 'Screw you and your goddam cigarette. You want to stay here? All right!' He got up and began to stride away.

Peter Marlowe caught his arm. 'Wait! This is the greatest day in our lives. Don't spoil it because your cellmates got a little thoughtless.'

'You take your hand away,' the King said through his teeth, 'or I'll stomp it off!'

'Don't worry about them,' Peter Marlowe said, the words beginning to pour out of him. 'The war's over, that's the important thing. It's over and we've survived. Remember what you used to drum into me? About looking after number one? Well you're all right! You've made it! What does it matter what they say?'

'I don't give a good goddam about them! They've got nothing to do with it. And I don't give a good goddam about you!' The King ripped his arm away.

Peter Marlowe stared at the King helplessly. 'I'm your friend, dammit. Let me help you!'

'I don't need your help!'

'I know. But I'd like to stay friends. Look,' he continued with difficulty. 'You'll be home soon—'

'The hell I will,' the King said, his blood roaring in his ears. 'I got no home!'

The wind rustled the leaves. Crickets grated monotonously. Mosquitoes swarmed around them. Hut lights began to cast harsh shadows and the moon sailed in a velvet sky.

'Don't worry, old chum,' Peter Marlowe said compassionately. 'Everything's going to be all right.' He did not flinch from the fear he saw in the King's eyes.

'Is it?' the King said in torment.

'Yes.' Peter Marlowe hesitated. 'You're sorry it's over, aren't you?'

'Leave me alone. Goddammit, leave me alone!' the King shouted and turned away and sat on the coconut stump.

'You'll be all right,' Peter Marlowe said. 'And I'm your friend. Never forget it.' He reached out with his left hand and touched the King's shoulder, and he felt the shoulder jerk away under his touch.

''Night, old chum,' he said quietly. 'See you tomorrow.' And miserably he walked away. Tomorrow, he promised himself, tomorrow I'll be able to help him.

The King shifted on the coconut stump, glad to be alone, terrified by his loneliness.

Colonel Smedly-Taylor and Jones and Sellars were cleaning their plates.

'Magnificent!' Sellars said, licking the juice off his fingers.

Smedly-Taylor sucked the bone, though it was already quite clean. 'Jones, my boy. I have to hand it to you.' He belched. 'What a superb way to end *the* day! Delicious! Just like rabbit! A little stringy and somewhat tough, but delicious!'

'Haven't enjoyed a meal so much in years,' Sellars chortled. 'The meat's a little greasy, but by Jove, just marvellous.' He glanced at Jones. 'Can you get any more? One leg each isn't very much!'

'Perhaps.' Jones picked up the last grain of rice delicately. His plate was dry and empty and he was feeling very full. 'It was a bit of luck, wasn't it?'

'Where did you get them?'

'Blakely told me about them. An Aussie was selling them.' Jones belched. 'I bought all he had.' He glanced at Smedly-Taylor. 'Lucky you had the money.'

Smedly-Taylor grunted. 'Yes.' He opened a wallet and tossed three hundred and sixty dollars on the table. 'There's enough for another six. No need to stint ourselves, eh, gentlemen?'

Sellars looked at the notes. 'If you had all this money hidden away, why didn't you use a little months ago?'

'Why indeed?' Smedly-Taylor got up and stretched. 'Because I was saving it for today! And that's the end of it,' he added. His granite eyes locked on Sellars.

'Oh, come off it, man, I don't want you to say anything. I just can't understand how you managed to do it, that's all.'

Jones smiled. 'Must have been an inside job. I hear the King nearly had a heart attack!'

'What's the King got to do with my money?' Smedly-Taylor asked.

'Nothing.' Jones began counting the money. There were, indeed, three hundred and sixty dollars, enough for twelve *Rusa tikus* haunches at thirty dollars each, which was their real price not sixty dollars as Smedly-Taylor believed. Jones smiled to himself thinking that Smedly-Taylor could well afford to pay double, now that he had so much money. He wondered how Smedly-Taylor had managed to effect the theft, but he knew Smedly-Taylor was right to keep a tight rein on his secrets. Like the other three *Rusa tikus*. The ones that he and Blakely had cooked and eaten in secret this afternoon. Blakely had eaten one, he had eaten the other two. And the two added to the one he had just devoured was the reason that he was satiated. 'My God,' he said, rubbing his stomach, 'don't think I could eat as much every day!'

'You'll get used to it,' Sellars said. 'I'm still hungry. Try and get some more, there's a good chap.'

Smedly-Taylor said, 'How about a rubber or two?'

'Admirable,' said Sellars. 'Who'll we get as a fourth?'

'Samson?'

Jones laughed. 'I'll bet he'd be very upset if he knew about the meat.'

'How long do you think it'll take our fellows to come to Singapore?' Sellars asked, trying to conceal his anxiety.

Smedly-Taylor looked at Jones. 'A few days. At the most a week. If the Japs here are really going to give in.'

'If they leave us the wireless, they mean to.'

'I hope so. My God, I hope so.'

They looked at one another, the goodness of the food forgotten, lost in the worry of the future.

'Nothing to worry about. It's—it's going to be all right.' Smedly-Taylor said, outwardly confident. But inside he was panicked, thinking of Maisie and his sons and daughter, wondering if they were alive.

Just before dawn a four-engined airplane roared over the camp. Whether it was Allied or Japanese no one knew, but at the first sound of the engines the men had been panic-stricken waiting for the expected bombs that would rain down. When the bombs did not fall and the airplane droned away, the panic built once more. Perhaps they've forgotten us—they'll never come.

Ewart groped his way into the hut and shook Peter Marlowe awake. 'Peter, there's a rumour that the plane circled the airfield—that a man parachuted out of it?'

'Did you see it?'

'No.'

'Did you talk to anyone who did?'

'No. It's just a rumour.' Ewart tried not to show his fear. 'I'm scared to death that as soon as the fleet comes into the harbour the Japs'll go crazy.'

'They won't!'

'I went up to the Camp Commandant's office. There's a whole group of chaps there, they keep giving out news bulletins. The last one said that—' for a moment Ewart couldn't speak, then he continued—'that the casualties in Hiroshima and Nagasaki are over three hundred thousand. They say people are still dying like flies there—that this hell-bomb does something to the air and keeps on killing. My God, if that happened to London and I was in charge of a camp like this—I'd—I'd slaughter everyone. I would, by God I would.'

Peter Marlowe calmed him, then left the hut and walked to the gate in the gathering light. Inside, he was still afraid. He knew that Ewart was right. Such a hell-bomb was too much. But he knew, of a sudden, a great truth, and he blessed the brains that had invented the bombs. Only the bombs had saved Changi from oblivion. Oh yes, he told himself, whatever happens because of the bombs, I will bless the first two and the men who made them. Only they have given me back my life when there was truly no hope of life. And though the first two have consumed a multitude, by their very vastness they have saved the lives of countless hundred thousand others. Ours. And *theirs*. By the Lord God, this is the truth.

He found himself beside the main gate. The guards were there as usual. Their backs were toward the camp, but they still had rifles in their hands. Peter Marlowe watched them curiously. He was sure that these men would blindly die in defence of men who only a day ago were their despised enemies.

My God, Peter Marlowe thought, how incredible some people are.

Then suddenly, out of the growing light of dawn, he saw an apparition. A strange man, a real man who had breadth and thickness, a man who looked like a *man*. A white man. He wore a strange green uniform and his parachute boots were polished and his beret decal flashed like fire and he had a revolver on his wide belt and there was a neat field pack on his back.

The man walked the centre of the road, his heels click-clicking until he was in front of the guardhouse.

The man—now Peter Marlowe could see that he wore the rank of a captain—the captain stopped and glared at the guards and then he said, 'Salute, you bloody bastards.'

When the guards stared at him stupidly, the captain went up to the nearest guard and ripped the bayoneted rifle out of his hands and stuck it viciously in the ground, and said again, 'Salute me, you bloody bastards.'

The guards stared at him nervously. Then the captain pulled out his revolver and fired a single round into the earth at the feet of the guards and said, 'Salute, you bloody bastards.'

Awata, the Japanese sergeant, Awata the Fearful, sweating and nervous, stepped forward and bowed. Then they all bowed.

'That's better, you bloody bastards,' the captain said. Then he tore the rifle out of each man's hands and threw it on the ground. 'Get back into the bloody guardhouse.'

Awata understood the movement of his hand. He ordered the guards to line up. Then, on his command, they bowed again.

The captain stood and looked at them. Then he returned the salute.

'Salute, you bloody bastards,' the captain said once more.

Again the guards bowed.

'Good,' the captain said. 'And next time I say salute, salute!'

Awata and all the men bowed and the captain turned and walked to the barricade.

Peter Marlowe felt the eyes of the captain on him and on the men near him, and he started with fear and backed away.

He saw first revulsion in the eyes of the captain, then compassion.

The captain shouted at the guards. 'Open this bloody gate, you bloody bastards.'

Awata understood the point of the hand and quickly ran out with three guards and pulled the barricade out of the way.

Then the captain walked through, and when they began to close it again he shouted, 'Leave that bloody thing alone.' And they left it alone and bowed in salute.

Peter Marlowe tried to concentrate. This was wrong. All wrong. This could not be happening. Then, suddenly, the captain was standing in front of him.

'Hello,' the captain said. 'I'm Captain Forsyth. Who's in charge here?' the words were soft and very gentle. But Peter Marlowe could only see the captain looking at him from head to toe.

What's the matter? What's wrong with me? Peter Marlowe desperately asked himself. What's the matter with me? Frightened, he backed another step.

'There's no need to be afraid of me.' The captain's voice was deep and sympathetic. 'The war's over. I've been sent to see that you're all looked after.'

The captain took a step forward. Peter Marlowe recoiled and the captain stopped. Slowly the captain took out a pack of Players. Good English Players.

'Would you like a cigarette?'

The captain stepped forward, and Peter Marlowe ran away, terrified.

'Wait a minute!' the captain shouted after him. Then he approached another man, but the man turned tail and fled too. And all the men fled from the captain.

The second great fear engulfed Changi.

Fear of myself. Am I all right? Am I, after all this time? I mean, am I all right in the head? It *is* three and a half years. And my God, remember what Vand der Zelt said about impotence? Will it work? Will I be able to make love? Will I be all right? I saw the horror in the eyes of the captain when he looked at me. Why? What was wrong? Do you think, dare I ask him, dare I . . . am I all right?

When the King first heard about the officer, he was lying on his bed, brooding. True, he still had the choice position under the window, but now he had the same space as the other men—six feet by four feet. When he had returned from the north garden he had found his bed and chairs moved, and other beds were now spread into the space that was his by right. He had said nothing and they had said nothing, but he had looked at them and they had all avoided his eyes.

And, too, no one had collected or saved his evening meal. It had just been consumed by others.

'Gee,' Tex had said absently, 'I guess we forgot about you. Better be here next time. Every man's responsible for his own chow.'

So he had cooked one of his hens. He had cleaned it and fried it and eaten it. At least he had eaten half of it and kept half of it for breakfast. Now he had only two hens left. The others had been consumed during the last days—and he had shared them with the men who had done the work.

Yesterday he had tried to buy the camp store, but the pile of money that the diamond had brought was worthless. In his wallet he still had eleven American dollars, and these were good currency. But he knew—chilled—he could not last forever on eleven dollars and two hens.

He had slept little the previous night. But in the bleak watches of the early morning he had faced himself and told himself that this was weak and foolish and not the pattern of a King—it did not matter that when he had walked the camp earlier people had looked through him—Brant and Prouty and Samson and all the others had passed by and not returned his salute. It had been the same with everyone. Tinker Bell and Timsen and the MP's and his informants and employees—men he had helped or known or sold for or given food or cigarettes or money. They had all looked at him as though he did not exist. Where always eyes had been watching him, and hate had been surrounding him when he walked the camp, now there was nothing. No eyes, no hate, no recognition.

It had been freezing to walk the camp a ghost. To return to his home a ghost. To lie in bed a ghost.

Nothingness.

Now he was listening as Tex poured out to the hut the incredible news of the captain's arrival, and he could sense the new fear gnawing at them.

'What's the matter?' he said. 'What're you all so goddam silent about? A guy's arrived from outside, that's all.'

No one said anything.

The King got up, galled by the silence, hating it. He put on his best shirt and his clean pants and wiped the dust off his polished shoes. He set his cap at a jaunty angle and stood for a moment in the doorway.

'Think I'm going to have me a cook-up today,' he said to no one in particular.

When he glanced around he could see the hunger in their faces and the barely concealed hope in their eyes. He felt warmed again and normal again, and looked at them selectively.

'You going to be busy today, Dino?' he said at length.

'Er, no. No,' Dino said.

'My bed needs fixing and there's some laundry.'

'You, er, want me to do them?' Dino asked uncomfortably.

'You want to?'

Dino swore under his breath, but the remembrance of the perfume of the chicken last night shattered his will. 'Sure,' he said.

'Thanks, pal,' said the King derisively, amused by Dino's obvious struggle with his conscience. He turned and started down the steps.

'Er, which hen d'you want to have?' Dino called out after him.

The King did not stop. 'I'll think about that,' he said. 'You just fix the bed and the laundry.'

Dino leaned against the doorway, watching the King walk in the sun along the jail wall and around the corner of the jail. 'Son of a bitch!'

'Go get the laundry,' Tex said.

'Crap off! I'm hungry.'

'He aced you into doing his work without any goddam chicken.'

'He'll eat one today,' Dino said stubbornly. 'And I'll help him eat it. He's never eaten one before without giving the helper some.'

'What about last night?'

'Hell, he was fit to be tied 'cause we took over his space.' Dino was thinking about the English captain and home and his girl friend and wondered if she was waiting or if she was married.

376

Sure, he told himself sullenly, she'll be married and no one'll be there. How the hell am I going to get me a job?

'That was before,' Byron Jones III was saying. 'I'll bet the son of a bitch cooks it and eats it in front of us.' But he was thinking about his home. Goddamned if I'm going to stay there any more. Got to get me my own apartment. Yeah. But where the hell's the dough coming from?

'So what if he does?' Tex asked. 'We got maybe two or three days to go.' Then home to Texas, he was thinking. Can I get my job back? Where the hell will I live? What am I going to use for dough? When I get in the hay, is it going to work?

'What about the Limey officer, Tex? You think we should go talk with him?'

'Yeah, we should. But hell, later today, or tomorrow. We gotta get used to the idea. Tex suppressed a shudder. 'When he looked at me—it was as though, just like he was looking at a—a geek! Holy cow, what's so goddam wrong with me? I look all right, don't I?'

They all studied Tex, trying to see what the officer had seen. But they saw only Tex, the Tex they had known for three and a half years.

'You look all right to me,' Dino said finally. 'If anyone's a freak it's him. Goddamned if I'd parachute into Singapore alone. Not with all the lousy Japs around. No sir! He's the real freak.'

The King was walking along the jail wall. You're a stupid son of a bitch, he told himself. What the hell're you so upset about? All's well in the world. Sure. And you're still the King. You're still the only guy who knows how to get with it.

He cocked his hat at a rakish angle and chuckled as he remembered Dino. Yeah, that bastard would be cursing, wondering if he'd really get the chicken, knowing he'd been aced into working. The hell with him, let him sweat, the King thought cheerfully.

He crossed the path between two of the huts. Around the huts were groups of men. They were all looking north, towards the gate, silently, motionless. He rounded another hut and saw the officer standing in a pool of emptiness, staring around bewildered, his back towards him. He saw the officer go towards some men and laughed sardonically as he saw them retreat.

Crazy, he thought cynically. Plain crazy. What's there to be scared of? The guy's only a captain. Yep, he's sure going to need a hand. But what the hell he's so scared about beats me!

He quickened his pace, but his footsteps made no noise.

''Morning sir,' he said crisply, saluting.

Captain Forsyth spun around, startled. 'Oh! Hello.' He returned the salute with a sigh of relief. 'Thank God someone here is normal.' Then he realized what he had said. 'Oh, sorry. I didn't mean—'

'That's all right,' the King said agreeably. 'This dump's enough to put anyone off kilter. Boy, are we pleased to see you. Welcome to Changi!'

Forsyth smiled. He was much shorter than the King but built like a tank. 'Thank you. I'm Captain Forsyth. I've been sent to look after the camp until the fleet arrives.'

'When's that?'

'Six days.'

'Can't they make it any sooner?'

'These things take time, I suppose.' Forsyth nodded towards the hut. 'What's the matter with everyone? It's as though I was a leper.'

The King shrugged. 'Guess they're in a state of shock. Don't believe their eyes yet. You know how some guys are. And it has been a long time.'

'Yes it has,' Forsyth said slowly.

'Crazy that they'd be scared of you.' The King shrugged again. 'But that's life, and their business.'

'You're an American?'

'Sure. There are twenty-five of us. Officers and enlisted men. Captain Brough's our senior officer. He got shot down flying the hump in '43. Maybe you'd like to meet him?'

'Of course.' Forsyth was dead-tired. He had been given this assignment in Burma four days ago. The waiting and the flight and the jump and the walk to the guardhouse and the worry of what he would meet and what the Japanese would do and how the hell he was going to carry out his orders, all these things had wrecked his sleep and terrored his dreams. Well, old chap, you asked for the job and you've got it and here you are. At least you passed the first test up at the main gate. Bloody fool, he told himself, you were so petrified all you could say was 'Salute, you bloody bastards.'

From where he stood, Forsyth could see clusters of men staring at him from the huts and the windows and the doorways and shadows. They were all silent.

He could see the bisecting street, and beyond the latrine area. He noticed the scores of huts and his nostrils were filled with the stench of sweat and mildew and urine. Zombies were everywhere—zombies in rags, zombies in loincloths, zombies in sarongs—boned and meatless.

'You feeling okay?' the King asked solicitously. 'You don't look so hot.'

'I'm all right. Who are those poor buggers?'

'Just some of the guys,' the King said. 'Officers.'

'What?'

'Sure. What's wrong with them?'

'You mean to tell me those are officers?'

'That's right. All these huts're officers' huts. Those rows of bungalows are where the Brass live, majors and colonels. There's about a thousand Aussies and Lim—English,' he said quickly, correcting himself, 'in huts south of the jail. Inside the jail are about seven or eight thousand English and Aussies. All enlisted men.'

'Are they all like that?'

'Sir?'

'Do they all look like that? Are they all dressed like that?'

'Sure.' The King laughed. 'Guess they do look like a bunch of bums at that. It sure never bothered me up to now.' Then he realized that Forsyth was studying him critically.

'What's the matter?' he asked, his smile fading.

Behind and all around men were watching, Peter Marlowe among them. But they all stayed out of range. They were all wondering if their eyes really saw a man, who looked like a man, with a revolver at his waist, talking to the King.

'Why're you so different from them?' Forsyth said.

'Sir?'

'Why're you properly dressed—and they're all in rags?'

The King's smile returned. 'I've been looking after my clothes. I guess they haven't.'

'You look quite fit.'

'Not as fit as I'd like to be, but I guess I'm in good shape. You like me to show you around? Thought you'd need a hand. I could rustle up some of the boys, get a detail together. There's no supplies in the camp worth talking about. But there's a truck up at the garage. We could drive into Singapore and liberate—'

'How is it that you are apparently unique here?' Forsyth interrupted, the words like bullets.

'Huh?'

Forsyth pointed a blunt finger at the camp. 'I can see perhaps two or three hundred men but you're the only one clothed. I can't see a man who's not as thin as a bamboo, but you,' he turned back and looked at the King, his eyes flinty, 'you are in good shape.'

'I'm just the same as them. I've been on the ball. And lucky.'

'There's no such thing as luck in a hellhole like this!'

'Sure there is,' the King said. 'And there's no harm in looking after your clothes, no harm in keeping fit as you can. Man's got to look after number one. No harm in that!'

'No harm at all,' Forsyth said, 'providing it's not at the expense of others!' Then he barked, 'Where's the Camp Commandant's quarters?'

'Over there.' The King pointed. 'The first row of bungalows. I don't know what's gotten into you. I thought I could help. Thought you'd need someone to put you in the picture—'

'I don't need *your* help, Corporal! What's your name?'

The King was sorry that he had taken the time out to try to help. Son of a bitch, he thought furiously, that's what comes of trying to help! 'King. Sir.'

'You're dismissed, Corporal. I won't forget you. And I'll certainly make sure I see Captain Brough at the earliest opportunity.'

'Now what the hell does that mean?'

'It means I find you entirely suspicious,' Forsyth rapped. 'I want to know why you're fit and others aren't. To stay fit in a place like this you've got to have money, and there would be very few ways to get money. Very few ways. Informing, for one! Selling drugs or food for another—'

'I'll be goddamned if I'll take that crap—'

'You're dismissed, Corporal! But don't forget I'll make it my business to look into you!'

It took a supreme effort for the King to keep from smashing his fist into the captain's face.

'You're dismissed,' Forsyth repeated, then added viciously, 'Get out of my sight!'

The King saluted and walked away, blood filming his eyes.

'Hello,' Peter Marlowe said, intercepting the King. 'My God, I wish I had your guts.'

The King's eyes cleared and he croaked. 'Hi, Sir.' He saluted and began to pass.

'My God, Rajah, what the hell's the matter?'

'Nothing. Just don't—feel like talking.'

'Why? If I've done something to hurt you, or get you fed up with me, tell me. Please.'

'Nothing to do with you.' The King forced a smile, but inside he was screaming, Jesus, what've I done that's so wrong? I fed the bastards and helped them, and now they look at me as though I'm not here any more.

He looked back at Forsyth and saw him walk between two huts and disappear. And him, he thought in agony, he thinks I'm a goddam informer.

'What did he say?' Peter Marlowe asked.

'Nothing. He—I've got to—do something for him.'

'I'm your friend. Let me help. Isn't it enough that I'm here?'

But the King only wanted to hide. Forsyth and the others had taken away his face. He knew that he was lost. And faceless, he was terrified.

'See you around,' he muttered and saluted and hurried away. Jesus God, he wept inside, give me back my face. Please give me back my face.

The next day a plane buzzed the camp. Out of its belly poured a supply drop. Some of the supplies fell into the camp. Those that fell outside the camp were not sought. No one left the safety of Changi. It still could be a trick. Flies swarmed, a few men died.

Another day. Then planes began to circle the airstrip. A full colonel strode into the camp. With him were doctors and orderlies. They brought medical supplies. Other planes circled and landed.

Suddenly there were jeeps screaming through the camp and huge men with cigars and four doctors. They were all Americans. They rushed into the camp and stabbed the Americans with needles and gave them gallons of fresh orange juice and food and cigarettes and embraced them—their boys, their hero boys. They helped them into the jeeps and drove them to Changi Gate, where a truck was waiting.

Peter Marlowe watched, astonished. They're not heroes, he thought, bewildered. Neither are we. We lost. We lost the war, our war. Didn't we? We're not heroes. We're not!

He saw the King through the fog of his mind. His friend. He had been waiting the days to talk with him, but each time he had found him the King had put him off. 'Later,' the King had always said, 'I'm busy now.' When the new Americans had arrived there still had been no time.

So Peter Marlowe stood at the gate, with many men, watching the departure of the Americans, waiting to say a last goodbye to his friend, waiting patiently to thank him for his arm and the laughter they had had together.

Among the watchers was Grey.

Forsyth was standing tiredly beside the lorry. He handed over the list. 'You keep the original, sir,' he said to the senior American officer. 'Your men are all listed by rank, service and serial number.'

'Thanks,' said the major, a squat, heavy jowled paratrooper. He signed the paper and handed back the other five copies. 'When're the rest of your folks arriving?'

'A couple of days.'

The major looked around and shuddered. 'Looks like you could use a hand.'

'Have you any excess drugs, by any chance?'

'Sure. We got a bird stacked with the stuff. Tell you what. Once I've got our boys on their way, I'll bring it all back in our jeep. I'll let you have a doc and two orderlies until yours get here.'

'Thanks.' Forsyth tried to rub the fatigue out of his face. 'We could use them. I'll sign for the drugs. SEAC will honour my signature.'

'No goddam paper. You want the drugs, you got 'em. That's what they're there for.'

He turned away. 'All right, Sergeant, get 'em in the truck.' He walked over to the jeep and watched as the stretcher was lashed securely. 'What you think, Doc?'

'He'll make it State-side.' The doctor glanced up from the unconscious figure neatly trussed in the straitjacket, 'but that's about it. His mind's gone for good.'

'Son of a bitch,' the major said wearily, and he made a check mark against Max's name on the list. 'Seems kinda unfair.' He dropped his voice. 'What about the rest of them?'

'Not good. Withdrawal symptoms generally. Anxiety about the future. There's only one that's in halfway decent shape physically.'

'I'll be goddamned if I know how any of 'em made it. You been in the jail?'

'Sure. Just a quick runaround. That was enough.'

Peter Marlowe was watching morosely. He knew his unhappiness was not due solely to the departure of his friend. It was more than that. He was sad because the Americans were leaving. Somehow he felt he belonged there with them, which was wrong, because they were foreigners. Yet he knew he did not feel like a foreigner when he was with them. Is it envy? he asked himself. Or jealousy? No, I don't think so. I don't know why, but I feel they're going home and I'm being left behind.

He moved a little closer to the truck as the orders began to sound and the men began to climb aboard. Brough and Tex and Dino and Byron Jones III and all the others resplendent in their new starched uniforms, looking unreal. They were talking and shouting and laughing. But not the King. He stood slightly to one side. Alone.

Peter Marlowe was glad that his friend was back once more with his own people, and he prayed that once the King was on his way all would be well with him.

'Get in the truck, you guys.'

'C'mon, get in the goddam truck.'

'Next stop State-side!'

Grey was unaware that he was standing beside Peter Marlowe. 'They say,' he said looking at the truck, 'that they've a plane to fly them all the way back to America. A special plane. Is that possible? Just a handful of men and some junior officers?'

Peter Marlowe had also been unaware of Grey. He studied

him, despising him. 'You're such a goddam snob, Grey, when it comes down to it.'

Grey's head whipped around. 'Oh, it's you.'

'Yes.' Peter Marlowe nodded at the truck. 'They think that one man's as good as another. So they get a plane, all to themselves. It's a great idea when you think of it.'

'Don't tell me the upper classes have at last realized—'

'Oh shut up!' Peter Marlowe moved away, his bile rising.

Beside the truck was a sergeant, a vast man with many stripes on his sleeve and an unlit cigar in his mouth. 'C'mon. Get in the truck,' he repeated patiently.

The King was the last on the ground.

'For Chrissake, get in the truck!' the sergeant growled. The King didn't move. Then, impatiently, the sergeant threw the cigar away, and stabbing the air with his finger shouted, 'You! Corporal! Get your goddam ass in the truck!'

The King came out of his trance. 'Yes, Sergeant. Sorry, Sergeant!'

Meekly he got into the back of the truck and stood while everyone else sat, and around him there were excited men talking one to another, but not to him. No one seemed to notice him. He held to the side of the truck as it roared into life and swept the Changi dust into the air.

Peter Marlowe frantically ran forward and held up his hand to wave at his friend. But the King did not look back. He never looked back.

Suddenly, Peter Marlowe felt very lonely, there by Changi Gate.

'That was worth watching,' Grey said, gloating.

Peter Marlowe turned on him. 'Go away before I do something about you.'

'It was good to see him go like that. "You, Corporal, get your goddam arse in the truck".' There was a vicious glint in Grey's eyes. 'Like the scum he was.'

But Peter Marlowe only remembered the King as he truly was. That wasn't the King who meekly said, 'Yes, Sergeant.' Not the King. This had been another man, torn from the womb of Changi, the man that Changi had nurtured so long.

'Like the thief he was,' Grey said deliberately.

384

Peter Marlowe bunched his good left fist. 'I told you before, a last time.'

Then he slammed his fist into Grey's face, knocking him backwards, but Grey stayed on his feet and threw himself at Peter Marlowe. The two men tore at each other and suddenly Forsyth was beside them.

'Stop it,' he ordered. 'What the hell are you two fighting about?'

'Nothing,' Peter Marlowe said.

'Take your hand off me,' Grey said and pulled his arm from Forsyth. 'Get out of the way!'

'Any more trouble out of either of you and I'll confine you to your quarters.' Appalled, Forsyth noticed that one man was a captain and the other a flight lieutenant. 'Ought to be ashamed of yourselves, brawling like common soldiers! Go on, both of you, get out of here. The war's over, for God's sake!'

'Is it?' Grey looked once at Peter Marlowe, then walked off.

'What's between you two?' Forsyth said.

Peter Marlowe stared into the distance. The truck was nowhere to be seen. 'You wouldn't understand,' he said and turned away. Forsyth watched him until he disappeared. You can say that a million times, he thought exhaustedly. I don't understand anything about any of you.

He turned back to Changi gate. There were, as always, groups of men silently staring out. The gate was, as always, guarded. But the guards were officers and no longer Japanese or Koreans. The day he had arrived, he had ordered them away and posted an officer guard to keep the camp safe and to keep the men in. But the guards were unnecessary, for no one had tried to break out. I don't understand, Forsyth told himself tiredly. It doesn't make sense. Nothing here makes sense.

It was only then that he remembered he had not reported the suspicious American—the corporal. He had had so much to worry about that the man had completely slipped his mind. Bloody fool, now it's too late! Then he recalled that the American major was coming back. Good, he thought, I'll tell him. He can deal with him.

Two days later more Americans arrived. And a real American General. He was swarmed like a queen bee by photographers and reporters and aides. The General was taken to the Camp Commandant's bungalow. Peter Marlowe and Mac and Larkin were ordered there. The General picked up the earphone of the radio and pretended to listen.

'Hold that, General!'

'Just one more, General!'

Peter Marlowe was shoved to the front and told to bend over the radio as though explaining it to the General.

'Not that way—let's see your face. Yeah, let's see your bones, Sam, in the light. That's better.'

That night the third and last and greatest fear crucified Changi.

Fear of tomorrow.

All Changi knew, now, that the war *was* over. The future had to be faced. The future outside of Changi. The future was *now*. Now.

And the men of Changi withdrew into themselves. There was nowhere else to go. Nowhere to hide. Nowhere but inside. And inside was terror.

The Allied Fleet arrived at Singapore. More outsiders converged on Changi.

It was then that the questions began.

—Name, rank, serial number, unit?

—Where did you fight?

—Who died?

—Who was killed?

—What about atrocities? How many times were you beaten? Who did you see bayoneted?

—No one? Impossible? Think, man. Use your head! Remember. How many died? On the boat? Three, four, five? Why? Who was there?

—Who's left in your unit? Ten? Out of a regiment? Good, that's better. Now, how did the others die? Yes, the details!

—Ah, you saw them bayoneted?

—Three Pagoda Pass? Ah, the railroad! Yes. We know about that. What can you add? How much food did you get? Anaesthetics? Sorry, of course, I forgot. Cholera?

—Yes, I know all about Camp Three. What about Fourteen?

The one on the Burma–Siam border? Thousands died there, didn't they?

With the questions, the outsiders brought opinions. The men of Changi heard them furtively whispered, one to another.

—Did you see that man? My God, it's impossible! He's walking around naked! In public!

—And look over there! There's a man doing it in public! And good God, he's not using paper! He's using water and his hands! My God—they all do!

—Look at that filthy bed! My God, the place is crawling with bugs!

—What degradation these poor swines have sunk to—worse than animals!

—Ought to be in an insane asylum! Certainly the Japs did it to them, but all the same it'd be safer to lock them up. They don't seem to know what's right and what's wrong!

—Look at them lap up that filth! My God, you give them bread and potatoes and they want rice!

—Got to get back to the ship. Can't wait to bring the fellows out. Chance of a lifetime, never see this again.

—My God, those nurses are taking a chance, walking around

—Rubbish, they're safe enough. Seen a lot of the girls coming up to have a look. By jove, that one's a corker!

—Disgusting the way the POWs are looking at them!

With the questions and the opinions the outsiders brought answers.

—Ah, Flight Lieutenant Marlowe? Yes we've had a cable answer from the Admiralty. Captain Marlowe RN is, er, I'm afraid your father's dead. Killed in action on the Murmansk run. September 10, '43. Sorry. Next!

—Captain Spence? Yes. We've a lot of mail for you. You can get it at the guardhouse. Oh yes. Your—your wife and child were killed in London in an air raid. January this year. Sorry. A V2. Terrible. Next!

—Lieutenant-Colonel Jones? Yes, sir. You'll be on the first party leaving tomorrow. All senior officers are going. Bon voyage! Next!

—Major McCoy? Oh yes, you were inquiring about your wife and son. Let me see, they were aboard the *Empress of Shropshire*, weren't they? The ship that sailed from Singapore on February 9, 1942? Sorry, we've no news, except that we know it was sunk somewhere off Borneo. There are rumours that there were survivors, but if there were or where they would be—no one knows. You'll have to be patient! We hear there are POW camps all over—the Celebes—Borneo—you'll have to be patient! Next!

—Ah, Colonel Smedly-Taylor? Sorry, bad news, sir. Your wife was killed in an air raid. Two years ago. Your youngest son, Squadron Leader P. R. Smedly-Taylor VC, was lost over Germany in '44. Your son John is presently in Berlin with the occupation forces. Here is his address. Rank? Lieutenant-Colonel. Next!

—Colonel Larkin? Oh, Australians are dealt with somewhere else. Next!

—Captain Grey? Ah, well, it's somewhat difficult. You see, you were reported lost in action in '42. I'm afraid your wife remarried. She's—er—well, here's her present address. I don't know, sir. You'll have to ask the Solicitor General's Office. Afraid legalities are out of my line. Next!

—Captain Ewart? Oh yes, the Malayan Regiment? Yes, I'm happy to tell you your wife and three children are safe and well. They're at Cha Song Camp in Singapore. Yes, we've transport for you this afternoon. I beg your pardon? Well I don't know. The memo says three—not two children. Perhaps it's an error. Next!

More men went swimming now. But the outside was still fearful and the men that went were glad to be back inside once more. Sean went swimming. He walked down to the shore with the men and in his hand was a bundle. When the party got to the beach, Sean turned away, and the men laughed and jeered, most of them, at the pervert who wouldn't take off his clothes like anyone else.

'Pansy!'
'Bugger!'
'Rotten fairy!'
'Homo!'

Sean walked up the beach, away from the jeers, until he found a private place. He slipped off his short pants and shirt and put on the evening sarong and padded bra and belt and stockings and combed his hair and put on makeup. Carefully, very carefuly. And then the girl stood up, confident and very happy. She put on her high-heeled shoes and walked into the sea.

The sea welcomed her and made her sleep easy, and then, in the course of time, devoured the clothes and body and the time of her.

A major was standing in the doorway of Peter Marlowe's hut. His tunic was crusted with medal ribbons and he seemed very young. He peered around the hut at the obscenities lying on their bunks or changing or preparing to take a shower. His eyes came to rest on Peter Marlowe.

'What the fugging hell are you staring at?' Peter Marlowe screamed.

'Don't talk to me like that! I'm a major and—'

'I don't give a goddam if you're Christ! Get out of here! *Get out!*'

'Stand to attention! I'll have you court-martialled!' the major snapped, eyes popping, sweat pouring. 'Ought to be ashamed of yourself, standing there in a skirt—'

'It's a sarong—'

'It's a skirt, standing in a skirt, half-naked! You POW's think you can get away with anything. Well, thank God you can't. And now you'll be taught respect for—'

Peter Marlowe caught up his hafted bayonet, rushed to the door and thrust the knife in the major's face. 'Get away from here or by Christ I'll cut your fugging throat . . .'

The Major evaporated.

'Take it easy, Peter,' Phil muttered. 'You'll get us all into trouble.'

'Why do they stare at us? Why? Goddammit why?' Peter Marlowe shouted. There was no answer.

A doctor walked into the hut, a doctor with a Red Cross on his arm, and he hurried—but pretended not to hurry—and smiled at Peter Marlowe. 'Don't pay any attention to him,' he said, indicating the major who was walking through the camp.

'Why the hell do all you people stare at us?'

'Have a cigarette and calm down.'

The doctor seemed nice enough and quiet enough, but he was an outsider—and not to be trusted.

'Have a cigarette and calm down! That's all you bastards can say,' Peter Marlowe raged. 'I said, why do you all stare at us?'

The doctor lit a cigarette himself and sat on one of the beds and then wished he hadn't, for he knew that all the beds were diseased. But he wanted to help. 'I'll try to tell you,' he said quietly. 'You, all of you, have suffered the unsufferable and endured the unendurable. You're walking skeletons. Your faces are all eyes, and in the eyes there's a look . . .' He stopped a moment, trying to find the words, for he knew that they needed help and care and gentleness. 'I don't quite know how to describe it. It's furtive—no, that's not the right word, and it's not fear. But there's the same look in all your eyes. And you're all alive, when by all the rules you should be dead. We don't know why you aren't dead or why *you've* survived—I mean each of you here, why you? We, from the outside, stare at you because you're fascinating . . .'

'Like freaks in a goddam side show, I suppose?'

'Yes,' said the doctor calmly. ''That would be one way of putting it, but—'

'I swear to Christ I'll kill the next bugger who looks at me as though I'm a monkey.'

'Here,' the doctor said, trying to appease him. 'Here are some pills. They'll calm you down—'

Peter Marlowe knocked the pills out of the doctor's hand and shouted. 'I don't want any goddam pills. I just want to be left alone!' And he fled the hut.

The American hut was deserted.

Peter Marlowe lay on the King's bed and wept.

''Bye, Peter,' Larkin said.

''Bye, Colonel.'

''Bye, Mac.'

'Good luck, laddie.'

'Keep in touch.'

Larkin shook their hands, and then he walked up to Changi Gate, where trucks were waiting to take the last of the Aussies to ships. To home.

'When are you off, Peter?' Mac asked after Larkin had disappeared.

'Tomorrow. What about you?'

'I'm leaving now, but I'm going to stay in Singapore. No point in getting a boat until I know which way.'

'Still no news?'

'No. They could be anywhere in the Indies. But if she and Angus were dead, I think I'd know. Inside.' Mac lifted his rucksack and unconsciously checked that the secret can of sardines was still safe. 'I heard a rumour there are some women in one of the camps in Singapore who were on the *Shropshire*. Perhaps one of them will know something or give me a clue. If I can find them.' He looked old and lined but very strong. He put out his hand. 'Salamat.'

'Salamat.'

'Puki 'mhalu!'

'Senderis,' said Peter Marlowe, conscious of his tears but not ashamed of them. Nor was Mac of his.

'You can always write me care of the Bank of Singapore, laddie.'

'I will. Good luck, Mac.'

'Salamat!'

Peter Marlowe stood in the street that bisected the camp and watched Mac walk the hill. At the top of the hill, Mac stopped and turned and waved once. Peter Marloe waved back, and then Mac was lost in the crowd.

And now, Peter Marlowe was quite alone.

Last dawn in Changi. A last man died. Some of the officers of Hut Sixteen had already left. The sickest ones.

Peter Marlowe lay under his mosquito net in his bunk in half-sleep. Around him men were waking, getting up, going to relieve themselves. Barstairs was standing on his head practising yoga, Phil Mint was already picking his nose with one hand and maiming flies with the other, the bridge game already started, Myner already doing scales on his wooden keyboard, and Thomas already cursing the lateness of breakfast.

'What do you think, Peter?' Mike asked.

Peter Marlowe opened his eyes and studied him. 'Well, you look different. I'll say that.'

Mike rubbed his shaven top lip with the back of his hand. 'I feel naked.' he looked back at himself in the mirror. Then he shrugged. 'Well, it's off and that's that.'

'Hey, grub's up,' Spence called out.

'What is it?'

'Porridge, toast, marmalade, scrambled eggs, bacon, tea.'

Some men complained about the smallness of their portions, some complained about the bigness.

Peter Marlowe took only scrambled eggs and tea. He mixed the eggs into some rice he had saved from yesterday and ate with vast enjoyment.

He looked up as Drinkwater bustled in. 'Oh, Drinkwater.' He stopped him. 'Have you got a minute?'

'Why, certainly.' Drinkwater was surprised at Peter Marlowe's sudden affability. But he kept his pale blue eyes down, for he was afraid that his consuming hatred for Peter Marlowe would spill out. Hold on, Theo, he told himself. You've stuck it for months. Don't let go now. Only a few more hours, then you can forget him and all the other awful men. Lyles and Blodger had no right to tempt you. No right at all. Well, they got what they deserved.

'You remember that rabbit leg you stole?'

Drinkwater's eyes flashed. 'What—what are you talking about?'

Across the aisle, Phil stopped scratching and looked up.

'Oh, come on, Drinkwater,' Peter Marlowe said. 'I don't care any more. Why the hell should I? The war's over and we're out of it. But do you remember the rabbit leg, don't you?'

Drinkwater was too clever to be caught as simply as that. 'No,' he said gruffly, 'no I don't.' But he was hard put not to say delicious, delicious!

'It wasn't rabbit, you know'

'Oh? Sorry, Marlowe—it wasn't me. And I don't know, to this day, who took it, whatever it was!'

'I'll tell you what it was,' Peter Marlowe said, glorying in the moment. 'It was rat meat. Rat meat.'

Drinkwater laughed. 'You're very amusing,' he said sarcastically.

'Oh but it was rat! Oh yes it was. I caught a rat. It was big and hairy and there were scabs all over it. And I think it had plague.'

Drinkwater's chin trembled, his jowls shaking.

Phil winked at Peter Marlowe, and nodded cheerfully,

'That's right, Reverend. It was all scabby. I saw Peter skin the leg . . .'

Then Drinkwater vomited all over his nice clean uniform and rushed out and vomited some more, Peter Marlowe began laughing and soon the entire hut was roaring.

'Oh God,' Phil said weakly. 'I've got to hand it to you, Peter. What a brilliant idea. To pretend it was a rat. Oh my God! That pays the bugger back!

'But it really was rat,' Peter Marlowe said, 'I planted it so he'd steal it.'

'Oh yes, of course,' Phil said sarcastically, automatically using his fly-swat. 'Don't try to cap such a wonderful story! Wonderful!'

Peter Marlowe knew they would not believe him. So he didn't say any more. No one would believe him unless he showed the Farm to them . . . My God! The Farm! And his stomach turned over.

He put on his new uniform. On the epaulets was his rank— flight lieutenant. On his left breast, his wings. He looked around at his possessions—bed, mosquito net, mattress, blanket, sarong, rag shirt, a ragged pair of shorts, two pairs of clogs, knife, spoon and three aluminium plates. He scooped everything off his bed and carried it outside and set fire to it.

'Hey you . . . oh excuse me, sir,' the sergeant said. 'Fires're dangerous.' The servant was an outsider, but Peter Marlowe wasn't afraid of outsiders. Not now.

'Beat it,' snapped Peter Marlowe.

'But sir . . .'

'I said beat it, goddammit!'

'Yes, sir.' The sergeant saluted and Peter Marlowe felt very pleased that he wasn't afraid of outsiders any more. He returned the salute and then wished he hadn't, for he didn't have his cap on. So he tried to cover his mistake with 'Oh, where the hell's my cap?' and walked back into the hut feeling the fear of outsiders returning. But he forced it away and swore to himself, by the Lord my God, I'll never be afraid again. Never.

He found his cap and the concealed can of sardines. He put the can in his pocket and walked down the stairs of the hut and up the road beside the wire. The camp was almost deserted now. The last of the English troops were going today, on the same convoy as his. Going away. Long after all the Aussies had left, and an age after the Yanks. But that was only to be expected. We're slow but very sure.

He stopped near the American hut. The canvas flap of the overhang waved miserably on a wind of the past. Then Peter Marlowe went inside the hut for the last time.

The hut was not empty. Grey was there, polished and uniformed.

'Come to look a last time at the place of your triumphs?' he asked venomously.

'That's one way of putting it.' Peter Marlowe rolled a cigarette and replaced the savings in his tobacco box. 'And now the war's over. Now we're equal, you and me.'

'That's right.' Grey's face was stretched, his eyes snakelike. 'I hate your guts.'

'Remember Dino?'

'What about him?'

'He was your informer, wasn't he?'

'I suppose there's no harm in admitting it now.'

'The King knew all about Dino.'

'I don't believe you.'

'Dino was giving you information on orders. On the King's orders!' Peter Marlowe laughed.

'You're a bloody liar!'

'Why should I lie?' Peter Marlowe's laugh died abruptly. 'The time for lying's over. Finished. But Dino *was* doing it on orders. Remember how you were always just too late? Always.'

Oh my God, thought Grey. Yes, yes. I can see that now.

Peter Marlowe drew on his cigarette. 'The King figured that if you didn't get real information, you'd really try to get an informer. So he gave you one.'

Suddenly Grey felt very tired. Very tired. A lot of things were hard to understand. Many things, strange things. Then he saw Peter Marlowe and the taunting smile and all his pent-up misery exploded. He slammed across the hut and kicked the King's bed over and scattered his possessions, then whipped on Peter Marlowe. 'Very clever! But I saw the King cut down to size, and I'll see it happen to you. And your stinking class!'

'Oh?'

'You can bet your bloody life! I'll fix you somehow, if I have to

394

spend the rest of my life doing it. I'll beat you in the end. Your luck's going to run out.'

'Luck's got nothing to do with it.'

Grey pointed a finger in Peter Marlowe's face. 'You were born lucky. You've ended Changi lucky. Why, you've even escaped with what precious little soul you ever had!'

'What're you talking about?' Peter Marlowe shoved the finger away.

'Corruption. Moral corruption. You were saved just in time. A few more months around the King's evil and you'd have been changed forever. You were beginning to be a great liar and a cheat—like him.'

'He wasn't evil and he cheated no one. All he did was adapt to circumstances.'

'The world'd be a sorry place if everyone hid behind that excuse. There's such a thing as morality.'

Peter Marlowe threw his cigarette on the floor and ground it to dust. 'Don't tell me you'd rather be dead with your goddam virtues than alive and know you've had to compromise a little.'

'A little?' Grey laughed harshly. 'You sold out everything. Honour—integrity—pride—all for a handout from the worst bastard in this stinkhole!'

'When you think about it, the King's sense of honour was pretty high. But you're right in one thing. He did change me. He showed me that a man's a man, irrespective of background. Against everything I've been taught. So I was wrong to sneer at you for something you had no hand in, and I'm sorry for that. But I don't apologize for despising you for the man you are.'

'At least I didn't sell my soul!' Grey's uniform was streaked with sweat and he stared malevolently at Peter Marlowe. But inside he was choked with self-hatred. What about Smedly-Taylor? He asked himself. That's right, I sold out too. I did. But at least *I* know what *I* did wrong. I know it. And I know why I did it. I was ashamed of my birth, and I wanted to belong to the gentry. To your bloody class, Marlowe. In the service. But now I couldn't care less. 'You buggers've got the world by the shorts,' he said aloud, 'but not for long, by God, not any more. We're going to get even, people like me. We didn't fight the war to be spat on. We're going to get even.'

'Jolly good luck!'

Grey tried to control his breathing. He unclenched his fists with an effort and wiped the sweat out of his eyes. 'But you, you're not worth fighting. You're dead!'

'The point is we're both very much alive.'

Grey turned away and walked to the doorway. On the top step he turned back. 'Actually, I should thank you and the King for one thing,' he said viciously. 'My hatred of you two kept me alive.' Then he strode away and never looked back.

Peter Marlowe gazed out at the camp, then back at the hut and the scattered possessions of the King. He picked up the plate that had served the eggs and noticed that it was already covered with dust. Absently he stood the table upright and put the plate on it, lost in thought. Thoughts of Grey and the King and Samson and Sean and Max and Tex and where was Mac's wife and was N'ai just a dream and the General and the outsiders and home and Changi.

I wonder, I wonder, he thought helplessly. Is it wrong to adapt. Wrong to survive? What would I have done had I been Grey? What would Grey have done if he'd been me? What is good and what is evil?

And Peter Marlowe knew, tormented, that the only man who could, perhaps, tell him had died in freezing seas on the Murmansk run.

His eyes looked at the things of the past—the table where his arm had rested, the bed where he had recovered, the bench he and the King had shared, the chairs they had laughed in—already ancient and moulding.

In the corner was a wad of Japanese dollars. He picked them up and stared at them. Then he let them drop, one by one. As the notes settled, flies clustered on them, swarmed and clustered back once more.

Peter Marlowe stood in the doorway. 'Good-bye,' he said with finality to all that had belonged to his friend. 'Good-bye and thanks.'

He walked out of the hut and along the jail wall until he reached the line of trucks that waited patiently at the gate of Changi.

Forsyth was standing beside the last truck, glad beyond gladness that his work was finished. He was exhausted and the

396

mark of Changi was in his eyes. He ordered the convoy to begin.

The first truck moved and the second and the third, and all the trucks left Changi, and only once did Peter Marlowe look back.

When he was far away.

When Changi looked like a pearl in an emerald oyster shell, blue-white under a bowl of tropical skies—when Changi stood on a slight rise and around was a belt of green, and farther off the green gave way to blue-green seas, and the seas to infinity of horizon.

And then, in *his* turn, he looked back no more.

That night Changi was deserted. By men. But the insects remained.
And the rats.

They were still there. Beneath the hut. And many had died, for they had been forgotten by their captors. But the strongest were still alive.

Adam was tearing at the wire to get at the food outside his cage, fighting the wire as he had been fighting it for as long as he had been within the cage. And his patience was rewarded. The side of the cage ripped apart and he fell on the food and devoured it. And then he rested and with renewed strength he tore at another cage, and in the course of time devoured the flesh within.

Eve joined him and he had his fill of her and she of him and then they foraged in consort. Later the whole side of a trench collapsed, and many cages were opened and the living fed on the dead, and the living-weak became food for the living-strong until the survivors were equally strong. And then they fought among themselves and foraged.

And Adam ruled, for he was the King. Until the day his will to be King deserted him. Then he died, food for a stronger. And the strongest was always the King, not by strength alone, but King by cunning and luck and strength together. Among the rats.

JAMES CLAVELL

TAI-PAN

Dirk Struan was the ruler – the Tai-pan – of the most powerful trading company in the Far East. He was also a pirate, an opium smuggler, a master manipulator of men, a ruthless intriguer and a mighty lover.

Set in the turbulent days of the founding of Hong Kong in the 1840's, Tai-pan is the exciting story of a man and an island. For Dirk Struan was determined to transform the barren island called Hong Kong into the brightest jewel of the British Empire. And the opium run was the surest and most dangerous way for him to achieve riches beyond imagination . . .

'Packed with action . . . gaudy and flamboyant with blood and sin, treachery and conspiracy, sex and murder . . . Grand entertainment'

New York Times

'Intensely readable and exciting'

Sunday Telegraph

'The most stirring and exciting historical novel I have ever read'

Robin Moore,
author of *The French Connection*

CORONET BOOKS

JAMES CLAVELL

SHŌGUN

Here from the world's master story teller is a magnificent saga of feudal Japan, a stunningly dramatic re-creation of an exotic and alien world.

JOHN BLACKTHORNE, whose dream is to be the first English-man to circumnavigate the globe, to wrest control of the trade between Japan and China from the Portuguese, and to return home a man of wealth and position.

TORANAGA, the most powerful feudal lord in Japan, who strives and schemes to seize ultimate power by becoming Shōgun – supreme military dictator – and to unite the warring samurai fiefdoms under his own masterful and farsighted leadership.

LADY MARIKO, a Catholic convert whose conflicting loyalties to the Church and her country are compounded when she falls in love with Blackthorne, the barbarian intruder.

'An extraordinary performance . . . one of the major works of fiction this year'

Publishers Weekly

'SHŌGUN does for Japan what *Gone With the Wind* did for the South'

Time

CORONET BOOKS

JAMES CLAVELL

KING RAT is the third novel in the Asian saga that so far consists of:

1600 A.D.	....	Shōgun
1841 A.D.	....	Tai-Pan
1945 A.D.	....	King Rat
1963 A.D.	....	Noble House